What are we doing about Zoya?

ABOUT THE AUTHOR

Born and brought up in Mumbai, India, Anisha Bhatia now lives in San Diego, California with her husband and their two children. She loves tea, biryani, books and beaches, not necessarily in that order.

What Are We Doing About Zoya? is her first novel.

What are we doing about Zoya?

ANISHA BHATIA

First published in eBook in 2021 by
HEADLINE ACCENT
An imprint of HEADLINE PUBLISHING GROUP

First published in paperback in 2021 by
HEADLINE ACCENT
An imprint of HEADLINE PUBLISHING GROUP

3

Cataloguing in Publication Data is available from the British Library

ISBN 978 1 4722 8494 5

Offset in 11.04/15.38 pt Adobe Garamond Pro by Jouve (UK), Milton Keynes

Printed and bound in Great Britain by Clays Ltd, Elcograf S.p.A.

Headline's policy is to use papers that are natural, renewable and recyclable products and made from wood grown in well-managed forests and other controlled sources. The logging and manufacturing processes are expected to conform to the environmental regulations of the country of origin.

HEADLINE PUBLISHING GROUP
An Hachette UK Company
Carmelite House
50 Victoria Embankment
London EC4Y 0DZ

www.headline.co.uk
www.hachette.co.uk

What are we doing about Zoya?

CHAPTER ONE

"So? What are we doing about Zoya?"

That's me. Zoya Sahni. The one something should be done about.

This Voice, from across the living room, is my aunt Sheila Bua. Pa's oldest sister. Yesterday, to her acute horror, I turned an ancient twenty-six. I'm still unmarried, with no sign of a husband on the horizon. Which is like wading ankle deep into the Swamp of Eternal Spinsterhood.

"Tell me, what is our plan of action?" Sheila Bua says, her hands on her hips. Her voice, on the other hand, can qualify as a whole annoying person in its own right.

As if in agreement, a lone auto rickshaw sputters reluctantly two floors below in our tiny by-lane. It's ten in the morning on a scorching Saturday, and in Bombay, nothing moves before noon on a weekend, not even the lethargic cuckoos in the mango trees. Nothing except Sheila Bua.

"What do you mean, Sheila didi?" My Mum's soft voice is like piano music after Sheila Bua's squawk.

"You know perfectly well, Geeta. It's high time Zoya was married." Sheila Bua struggles to wrench her feet out of her pearly flip-flops near the main door." That's all I can see of her, courtesy of my curly locks flowing over my face. This is far more romantic in theory than reality: gorgeous windswept hair versus coiled strands on your tongue. You might think I'm of the windswept hair variety. Nope. Coiled strands. Always.

It's the stinking gutter of seasons—sticky and hot, so no point trying to cool my sweaty posterior on the marble floor. Might as well wear pajama bottoms inside a wet sauna. Mum, up on the fancy leather couch behind me, yanks a handful of my hair and pours sticky coconut oil on my scalp. It's the usual Saturday morning hair massage, prescribed to be washed on Sunday afternoons. A centuries-old tradition no Indian female can escape. It's a ritual. A lifestyle. Or maybe a rule. Sometimes I can't tell the difference.

Sheila Bua is quite interested in getting me married. Because (a) she's the custodian of our extended family—self-appointed, of course, and (b) that's what she does. Arrange marriages. Matches grooms, brides, and families. Aiming her sights at unsuspecting bachelors and spinsters like a laser beam. For a hobby. They nestle inside her large, hideous lime-green purse—their pictures and bios, that is, as sent by hopeful parents, not the actual brides and grooms.

That I've lasted this long without being on her radar is a miracle in itself. Better to marry off the fair-slim-pretty one before beginning on a lost cause like Zoya. My fair-slim-pretty cousin Aisha is a done deal next week, Sheila Bua having arranged the rich, fat proposal herself.

Sheila Bua's naked feet come closer, slapping on the creamy floor. Her rough fingers coil around my curls. "What have you done to your hair, Zoya? So dry. Like a carpet."

"That's just how it's always been, Bua."

"Are you letting the oil settle in? For hours?"

"I've been doing that since I was born. Hasn't made a difference, has it?"

"Of course it has. Your hair is like a new carpet." Sheila Bua says to Mum. "Just pour some more oil, Geeta. That is the *only* way it works!"

The trick with our traditions is to not argue. Things don't change just because *you* want them to. We've all rebelled passively for centuries—do your thing, quietly, without anyone *knowing* you've rebelled. Two hours is all I'll give this truckload of shit. Any mention of my bad hair day—which, by the way, is every day—drives Mum batty. My bad hair day is just one of my many non-virtues in the marriage market. Mum's frustration spills onto my itchy scalp as she overturns the blue plastic bottle of oil. A sticky trail joins the coiled strands on my face.

To be honest, I love this massage. Warm oil rubbed onto your scalp is bliss. Plus, that's *our* time, Mum's and mine, to catch up, to gossip. About my boss, who is slightly annoying and totally taciturn. About Mum, like when she secretly studied criminal law after being forbidden, or when she swore violently at Pa that one time. I love those stories, especially the rule-breaking ones. The only times Mum rebelled in her life, directly.

Not that she's a doormat or anything. She's a modern, educated woman and a law college professor. But she's still my very Indian mother, who, like most of her brethren, is quite desperate to marry her daughter off by a certain age.

"Sheila didi, look how much oil she needs," Mum smacks my head. "I can't even get to the middle of this bird's nest. The one thing she inherits from her father. Rough hair."

Pa's bald. Not the time to remind Mum of that. She pulls the giant mass of curls yet again, jerking my neck up so hard I swear I've developed spondylitis. I yank my neck up, and my abundant aunt blazes into focus. Squeezed into an expensive kurti tunic and tights, fluorescent pink and bright orange, she's a migraine in waiting. Which, had the oil massage been relaxing, would have rendered it completely useless.

The doorbell rings in a sing-songy tune, first of many buzzers in a day, its suddenness making Sheila Bua jump. Sujata bai, one of our three maids, saunters in. Her pink sari hangs limp on her thin body and she brings with her a musky odor.

"Tell me, Geeta," Sheila Bua reverts her attention from the maid to the topic of the day, "have you started looking for boys yet?"

"No, we haven't started. How can we start without you? But this stupid girl wants to wait for another year before getting married. Can you imagine?" She clicks her tongue and smacks my shoulder. "That we *start* looking for boys when she is twenty-seven! What are we to do?"

What happens to modern, fairly sane mothers when it is time to get their daughters married? "Yes, I want to wait for another year," I mutter.

"Wait?" Sheila Bua staggers as if she's discovered a dead body right in the living room. She turns to Mum. "Are you out of your mind to let her wait? These girls of today! She wants to give me my first gray hair, turn me into an old woman?" Sheila Bua's silky black hair, almost blue in its darkness (regular double doses of L'Oreal hair dye) is pulled back into a low ponytail. Angry little crinkles gather on her forehead at the collective foolishness of the young.

"You talk to her father, Sheila didi. I've tried to tell him exactly how long it takes to find a good boy, but fathers have no notion of what it's like to get a daughter married." The horror of having a spinster daughter transforms my mother's sweet voice into a hoarse grumble, especially now that other girls my age are being rapidly packaged off as brides as if on an assembly line.

Pa is the only one who agrees with me. Indirectly, because (a) he does not actively breathe down my neck or (b) he changes the topic anytime Mum tries to broach marriage, then winks at me, which pisses her off greatly. Pa, the over-dedicated head surgeon, absconded this morning to his hospital at the crack of dawn. I think he knew Sheila Bua would show up—he has a sixth sense about her that could rival any psychic. How long my father or I last in the face of this strengthened alliance between Mum and my aunt is another matter, for arranging marriages and subduing dissent are Sheila Bua's special domain.

"What is this new-fangled *waiting*? Most girls will be nicely married, probably mothers by the time Zoya decides she is ready. All good boys will be snapped up!" Sheila Bua snaps her stubby, diamond-studded fingers, but they make no sound. "What will she find then? The leftovers?" It is a grand stroke of luck that

Sheila Bua has no daughters, only a twenty-eight-year-old son Yuvi, recently married, which gives her free time to meddle. Help, I mean. Help people.

"I really don't want leftovers—"

"You will end up all alone! Pitied. All because you *waited.* What kind of a family would we be if we didn't do our duty and help you?" Sheila Bua is in her element. "Waiting! I never heard of such a thing! You can afford to wait when you are twenty, not twenty-six. Like that neighbor of yours, that Kamya Sharma? She's still waiting. At thirty-three!" Her arms move in the air like the conductor of an orchestra, and the peach window curtains gently swish behind her like a hushed audience.

I am close to my expiration date in the arranged marriage supermarket. And haven't even *started* the search for a husband due to, horror of horrors, an education and a career.

To start the search at twenty-six means you're halfway to oblivion. A girl like me is moved lower and lower on the marriage shelf, replaced by younger, fresher models. And when the dreaded three-zero hits, you're taken off the shelf and stuffed onto the back aisle, the "clearance, expired goods" area. Proposals will wane and there I'll be, still unmarried at forty. Neither wife nor mother; neither divorced nor widowed nor abandoned. I'll be like those extra pieces of a puzzle that don't fit anywhere, and no one knows what to do with them so they are banished to a dusty corner till they crumble into dust.

I don't want to marry just because that's what needs to be done, like a tick mark on a checklist. But ever since Aisha's engagement six months ago, I kind of secretly wish I was more like her and other normal girls, doing the right thing at the right time. The family would look upon me with approval, too, and not as a weak link either to be borne or disposed of to the nearest bidder as quickly as possible. And I don't want to stand out more than I already do; oh, you'll know why soon enough.

Our doorbell shrieks yet again. Argh! Bombay should be renamed the City of Shrieking Doorbells because of the continuous stream of humanity in and out through our doors. Our second maid for the day, Mala the cook, glides in, permanently snooty about her high position in the hierarchy of domestic labor. She rotates her whole body toward Mum, like a large drum. "What to make today, Geeta bhabi?"

"Make potato sandwiches for breakfast and chicken curry for lunch, please. Sheila didi, you're staying for lunch, na?"

"Of course. We have a lot of work to do. And you leave Zoya's father to me. He will never disagree with what I say." The leather sofa emits a squeaky little hiss as she sits.

"Before we start," she aims a pointed stare at me, "tell me if you like some boy already? Come on, don't be shy. Either we arrange a marriage for you or, if you like a boy, I dig up some dirt about him and his family, and *then* we arrange it for you. Tell me the truth."

Technically, there was Raunak three months ago. Nothing serious, just drinks and other . . . benefits. Hooded eyes and a sneery intellectual voice. Also, he's addicted to pot. My family is modern by Indian standards, but not fling modern. Or pot modern. "No, I don't have anyone."

"Of course she doesn't." Mum continues to thwack my head as if she's decided to fight my bad hair day till the bitter end. "How would she find anyone, shut up in that office all day, staring at a computer? She doesn't even come with me to weddings of our relations."

Technically, Indian weddings are a union of two individuals and their families. But in reality, weddings are prime bride/groom hunting arenas for unmarried offspring. You walk into a wedding and a gaggle of assorted aunties descend out of nowhere to pinch your cheeks as if you were five. Followed by a sly full-body inspection to check your weight (gain, not loss) to feel infinitely better about their still-slim daughters/nieces/best-friends'-daughters. Thanks, but no thanks. "Weddings are boring, Mum."

"Sushh, child!" Sheila Bua holds up a palm to silence me, gold bangles gleaming on her wrist. "I will find someone for you. See what a nice boy I found for Aisha?" Varun Sethi, the nice boy, is the scion of a large toilet-making fortune. It is rumored, Sheila Bua tells her clients in a conspiratorial whisper, that he plops on a golden commode every morning, which sprays jets of French perfume on his, umm, nether regions. Aisha is marrying Toilet Boy in less than a week and her henna ceremony is in two days. This is an extra reason for my hair massage: to tame the devil of frizz who lives in my hair so I don't show up at the ceremony with a lion's mane in its full glory.

Toilet Boy meets all the criteria for an arranged match: same religion, same language (out of the twenty-two official ones), and same caste: Hindu-Punjabi-Khatri. This whole arranged marriage thing, it's like being in space. Multiple universes hover in darkness, distant and aloof; a separate religion reigns supreme in each. Within each universe is an abundance of galaxies, all of them speaking different languages. And within *each* galaxy, a gazillion planets of socioeconomic castes orbit around their own importance.

Plus, Toilet Boy is educated, wealthy, has good future prospects, and is from a fairly sane family. And is reasonably sane himself. All mandatory, because who wants to marry a psychotic loser?

So you see, Sheila Bua's job demands Einstein's intelligence. The Theory of Arranged Marriagivity: Keep to your own planet. The rest of space can go eff themselves.

A pungent smell sneaks into the living room from the kitchen and hovers near the open French windows. Smoky hot oil, tangy hing, and crackly mustard seeds. Food makes everything better. *And never judges.*

Sheila Bua sniffs the air and sighs in pleasure. She pats her purse as if caressing a beloved pet. "Before we start the search for a husband, let's look at the kind of photos other girls have sent. They are like portfolios of supermodels." She winces at my oily face and wild hair. She sets her jaw in a determined look, her bunny teeth gleaming from behind a coat of pink lipstick. "At least look at Zoya's competition. What is the use of being a matchmaker if we can't preempt all rivals to use it to our family's advantage, I ask?"

Mum stops all pretense of an oil massage, rests her palms on my shoulders, and stares at the 8 × 10 glossy picture of a twenty-two-year-old girl, Pooja. Sheila Bua dangles the photo in front of my face. "See?" she says. "Twenty-two. She started almost a year ago. I've shown her family six boys already!"

> Fair, slim, homely postgraduate in Finance. 5'5", proficient in cooking Indian, Thai, Chinese, and Continental food. Excellent homemaker, earning in seven figures, but not very ambitious. Very flexible when it comes to career, can leave job for family. Father has a business of copper metal; mother is a housewife. PunjabiMatrimony.com profile: pooja21. More details on contact.

Mum turns the picture over, and a fashion model stares out of it, all pouts and sucked-in cheeks. Her fair skin gleams due to Photoshop or the layers of expert concealer and foundation, I can't tell. My heart sinks, despite the feigned disinterest. How can I compete with that?

"Has Zoya been using that face cream I gave you?" Sheila Bua asks Mum.

"Yes. You know, I don't like this whole 'make your skin fairer' idea, but at this point, we have to try anything." Mum and Sheila Bua look grim, as though discussing the last weapons in their arsenal. "Anyway, it's good for her occasional pimples." Mum gives Sheila Bua a weird look. It's nothing unusual, lots of strange looks pass between them, which mean nothing to a third person. They lived in the same neighborhood and were close friends, way before Mum married into the family. So it's an old friendship, and pretty solid, much to my detriment. I bet they know all kinds of stuff about each other. Not that there would be much "stuff" to know; they don't look like they ever did anything remotely interesting in their youth. I mean, Mum, maybe, because I know those quasi-rebellious stories about her, but Sheila Bua? Apart from some dumb painting hobby, I'd say not a chance in hell. I bet she started marrying people the moment she was born.

But this cream. It masquerades as a moisturizer to turn you four shades lighter. I am a dark-skinned Punjabi girl about to enter the gladiatorial arena of arranged marriages. Or "wheatish complexion," as the women of the family explain, without using the dreaded D-word, slightly apologetic, as if they really tried for fair skin but what to do if the girl-baby had a mind of her own?

Now, I didn't exactly use the cream. Just dabbed it on once a week instead of once a day and squeezed a substantial amount in the sink. Remember the passive rebellion?

The photo-girl's highlighted face stares out of the picture, nonthreatening, but still somehow confident in her ability to land a groom in a jiffy. Her nose, her eyes, her lips, her cheeks are all angled in soft light. She looks like she's made of spun wool and sugar. Her tight salwar kameez is pasted to her slim body. Loose-fitted pants that taper at the ankles and a long pink tunic as tight as decorum allows. She sucks in every limb except her chest, which sticks out like two giant blobs.

"We need to get Zoya some new clothes. Something bright and colorful and unique. This is just—" Sheila Bua is speechless as she tugs on my loose penguin pajamas and faded gray T-shirt. *Who the hell gets dressed at ten thirty on a weekend for oiling their hair?*

To complete the professional and personal nightmare for Sheila Bua, I am what is politely called "filled out in body."

Which, in arranged marriage lingo, means fat. And brands you as almost unmarriageable unless you can make certain "compromises" in your choice of groom.

The word has lived with me as long as I can remember, like an unloved but tolerated relative. Some days, when I see other fat girls, I mentally compare our bodies, and if I perceive that I am less fat, I feel a wretched little blip of joy. Pathetic, yes, I know. After which I am so thoroughly ashamed that I gobble up a plateful of greasy hakka noodles followed by a large piece of coffee cake from Birdy's. I wish someone would start a Fataholics Anonymous someday.

Back to the marriage race, which is practically lost even before the start. There's no difference between twenty-nine and thirty, and everyone knows thirty is just a front for thirty-one, so unless I am married off in the next three years, I'll have officially kicked the bucket. For Sheila Bua, that is.

Another doorbell rings. At our neighbor's apartment this time. Several rickshaws stutter, followed by snarling vehicles and hammers knocking. And so it begins. "Achcha Geeta, is Zoya five feet two or five feet two and a half?"

"How does that matter? Half here and there?" Mum asks.

"Don't forget the half inch. It's very important. We'll take any water in the dryness of this desert!" Sheila Bua mutters, somber as a marine ready for war.

Really, what chance do I have?

CHAPTER TWO

Today is Aisha's mehendi, the henna ceremony before the wedding. I can't believe she's getting married in two days. That's such a grown-up thing to do, giving you instant "woman" status: you are now officially an adult, your opinions are actually listened to, and you get the family stamp of approval.

The banquet hall of the henna ceremony is surrounded by what looks like a small rainforest of drab buildings, tall and small. The inside of the backlit hall is air-conditioned (thank goodness), decorated with pink lilies and filled with brightly dressed women. They chat and sip Fanta on red-and-white-striped couches while the henna assistants draw intricate designs on their palms. It's kind of like being inside a massive jewelry expo: *Bright yellow gold at Aisle number 4—Meena Auntie wearing India's entire gold reserves! Check our finest twenty-one-carat diamond display on Aisle number 8—shield your eyes before you meet Sudha Auntie and her baubles!*

As soon as Mum and I enter the venue, Sheila Bua swoops upon us in a silk salwar kameez, the tunic of which looks like psychedelic rainbows tripping on acid.

"Geeta! *Where* have you been?" She heaves a sigh of relief as Mum hugs her. "Thank goodness, you've arrived before Aisha's mother-in-law! Rama is at her wits' end. Not that she has a lot of wit to begin with! Could you go help her with the preparations? I need to tell the mehendi appliers to butter up the groom's family so they feel important."

Rama Bua, my other aunt, who's the mother of the bride and Sheila Bua's sister, *and* the most loony-moony person this side of the galaxy, currently walks around in a daze with a silver plate in one hennaed hand, her sparkly sari pallu sweeping the white granite floor behind her. Sheila Bua, on the other hand, is in her element, with multitudes of diamonds sparkling on her body. "What, these little things?" She chuckles when an obscure relative, a second cousin of a third cousin, compliments her. "It's only one choker, half a dozen bangles, and three rings. Need to save the big ones for the wedding, don't we?" Oh, and not to forget her ubiquitous, precious gold necklace—the one with a golden bird pendant on it—which always leads any jewelry exhibit. *No* one is allowed to touch *that*, ever.

"Zoya, beta, go sit with Aisha, she's been asking for you for the last hour. Oh, you wore the green outfit? I thought you didn't like green?" Sheila gapes at me in surprise.

I just shrug. This outfit, chosen by Mum, is a greenish blue churidaar kameez, a long, knee-length tunic and leggings, with shiny little blue flowers all over it. Not my favorite, but at least it's not a hideous pink like my friend Amrita's. She's currently being paraded in a revolting shade of fuchsia by her mother, like a live bottle of Digene antacid, in front of a gaggle of appreciative Punjabi aunties.

If I had my way today, the kameez would've been light yellow cotton, and I'd be wearing oxidized bangles and jhumkas—my favorite long earrings. But the family thinks that is a jhola, the attire of starving artists, which is *not* what they want to project to the groom's clan—that one of us could be starving—and certainly not that one of us could be an artist. In communities like ours (and, I'm quite sure, across India), an artist = free thinking + free sex + drugs = DANGER to our values. No wonder Sheila Bua's painting never advanced beyond a forgotten hobby.

Mum, thankfully, is not a ghastly-pink person. But then again, she isn't a jhola person either. So here I am in the clothes chosen by her, only to avoid a confrontation. Only to fit in yet again. Only to save her from the pitying looks of having a fat, dowdy, unmarried daughter wearing arty-farty clothes. In the futile hope that Sheila Bua is right. That if I looked even one-fourth as thin and pretty as Aisha does today, I would be "snapped up" in no time and maybe all this would've been for me.

The deafening beat of the latest Bollywood song helps to squash these silly thoughts. "You always liked yellow, didn't you? Is it still your favorite?" Sheila Bua smiles at me absently. Something inside me flips in a surprised little somersault. She used to shop for my clothes, Sheila Bua, way back in the beyond. I still remember the dazzling fairy dress on my eighth birthday, the soft and sparkly mix of lemon and ivory. Somehow, Sheila Bua always knew what I wanted, even before I knew it myself. She was my Magic Bua. I'm not sure when my Magic Bua disappeared, and this Sheila Bua took her place.

Never mind. I need to find Aisha in this ambush of silk and perfume. Oh, there she is! On the red couch in the center of the room, under a canopy of pink lilies, her slender hands and feet covered with mehendi. She is the family favorite, having done the right thing at the right time. She wanted to be a journalist, but the family disapproved. I mean, covering crimes and scandals? That's no job for a respectable girl! Armed with a docile diploma in human resources, she quit a lucrative HR job to get engaged, with the communal approval of the matrons in our clan. There was a time during our teenage years when I was *slightly* jealous of her slim prettiness, just a wee bit. But really, how long can you be envious of a gentle creature whose reactions never go beyond an "Oh, dearie" no matter what happens? Look at her now. The belle of the ball. She's handed a bunch of her special flower jewelry—white jasmine florets and red rose petals—to a group of goggly-eyed little girls who look like they've just glimpsed all the Disney princesses rolled into one, instead of shooing them away or asking them to bring food, as I probably would've.

"Little Zoya! All grown up!"

Shit.

An assortment of silk-swathed women, busy dancing a minute ago, ambush me out of nowhere, breathless but still shaking their alarmingly large hips. Here it comes. The Attack of the Ambushing Aunties. An affliction most common to all Indian ceremonies, regardless of language or religion.

"Oh, let me look at you! I'm sure you've put on *at least* five kilos since I last saw you!"

"We thought it would be your turn first! After all, you are two years older than Aisha!"

"Why are you always eating?"

"How did the younger cousin get married before the older?"

"Well, don't make us wait anymore to dance at your wedding, okay?"

This is why I don't go to weddings.

God, why hasn't Peehu arrived yet? She's my best friend. She moved to Paris six months ago but is visiting for Aisha's wedding. If she were here right now, we'd be extra-sweet to all the Ambushing Aunties before the slaughter. Kind of like fattening the calf.

Where does your daughter live, the one who eloped with the chauffeur, who then ran off with the maid after a week? So she's single again?

What a lovely sari you're wearing! By the way, didn't your son fail his engineering exams this year? Again? What, isn't he like thirty now?

Nothing sends the aunties packing like their own scandals under the spotlight.

"Don't you remember me?" One slim AA squishes my cheeks. "I lived in your building years ago! You and my son Lalit would run around in the building compound as toddlers, holding hands, stark naked." She giggles and the collective ambushers giggle along. "He came to drop me today. I could've introduced you both, but he had to leave to make an urgent call." She points behind me.

The said Lalit is some distance away, walking toward the door in the middle of a phone conversation. "—simply loathsome—"

is all I can hear. Who talks like that? I'm sure his mother will find another time to introduce us. They always do. (He's furiously texting now. Crisp white shirt, tight over his back muscles. A bit too tight but not bad; fully clothed, what a pity.)

A sudden flurry of activity propels Loathsome Lalit's mother and all other aunties away from me (thank you, merciful God) in a rustle of fabric toward the ornate hall doors. Aisha's in-laws are here with the bridal mehendi in a small silver pot on a sterling tray decked with rose petals. Everyone rushes over: women, assorted men, the photographer, the video guy.

An imposing woman sashays in with the tray, ablaze in a flaming red-gold sari more suited to cooler evenings than a snarly Bombay afternoon. This is *her*, Aisha's mother-in-law; the original toilet woman herself. And smells like one. Well, not really, just an overpowering floral scent that makes me retch. Her minions are dressed in equally blistering shades: smoldery oranges, fiery rusts, glittery golds, and all of them smell just as sugary.

The bright lights of the videographer ignite this Sisterhood of the Traveling Inferno. Some people discreetly wear sunglasses before they rush to greet the new in-laws. "Welcome, welcome, Shobhaji!" My aunt Rama Bua, the mother of the bride, and Mum lead the Inferno toward the bride to be. The toilet woman grabs Aisha in a proprietary embrace; it's like an ethereal fairy disappearing under a flood of glitter.

"What took you so long?" Aisha hisses in mock anger at me, not the toilet woman, when I finally reach her (as if she would be stupid enough to question her mother-in-law so blatantly, that too *before* marriage). The Ambushing Aunties have dragged the Sisterhood to join their breathless butt-shaking dance.

"Aashoo, try to make a decent effort to sound pissed." I roll my eyes. "Your mom-in-law will walk all over you if this is how you fight!" Aisha's Buddhist monk of a temper, if it can be called a temper, that is, has always baffled me. But then again, she is the sorted sorts and I am the twitchy sorts.

Aisha giggles, a tinkling crystal of a sound, and my heart turns over. I squeeze her in a tight hug, like she's off to a distant land and who knows when we'll see her again.

"You okay, Zee?" she asks.

"Yes. No! I'm just . . . I'm going to miss you so much."

"But I'm right here, you silly twit. Just moving from Khar to Dadar. That's like, only fifteen minutes away."

Or two hours, depending on Bombay's eccentric mood. Plus, moving in with your in-laws, especially Indian ones, isn't exactly conducive to having a life because of FAMILY HONOR (yes, it deserves all uppercase letters), which includes all of the following: the length of your dress, the food you eat, the food you cook, your job, your career, your friends. You.

Plus, now it's her and Varun (not her and *me*), who's always hugging and touching her, wanting her close. Which is wonderful for my cousin, but it's like little needle jabs in my heart. Why can't I have that?

But I did catch him with a harem of females last week at a restaurant. One in particular, a birdlike creature, tittered around him and looked like she was about to plonk herself into his lap, before he waved to me. It means nothing, I'm sure; that's why I didn't bother Aisha with it. Still. No harm in keeping an eye out. Because if he hurts my cousin, I will break his nuts.

"Madam, please move away from the bride." The henna master puckers her brow in irritation. "You will ruin the mehendi." She uses a tiny amount of the bridal henna on Aisha's palm and then distributes the rest of it to the assistants. No henna master ever uses anything but their own homemade concoction, which likely has been brewed for hours. For who knows what instant-color-crap festers in the henna brought by the in-laws or relatives?

Sheila Bua, the leader of the dancing auntie brigade, rushes out of the hip-shaking group, gestures to the henna attendants, points to me, and rushes back in. It sends a manic blast of an espresso shot into my blood. An old myth says if an unmarried girl from the bride or groom's side uses another girl's bridal mehendi on her own hands, she gets married next. I've been marked.

A young henna assistant winks at me. "Just you wait and see. My sister's bridal mehendi was used on my hands, and bas! That was it. I got married within six months."

Tanya, my *other* girl cousin, the evil one, tries to get to the bridal henna before it gets to me, but some auntie blocks her way. Just as well, because her phone bings, she smiles and runs off into a corner to check it. Curious, because the text alert was a distinct sing-songy one, not one of her usual alert tones. Seems like a boyfriend for sure, and a special one.

And yes, you're right, I don't like her. Because according to her, she is la-di-dah and I am nothing compared with her. Plus we've always had this weird rivalry. Like who's the smartest (she thinks the search for the God particle began in a temple), who's the prettiest (just saying that I'm not exactly unpretty, you know, even with all the cellulite), and who's the slimmest. I refuse to answer that question on the grounds that it may incriminate me in the Tanya-is-flat-as-a-board name incident. I had nothing to do with it.

Fine, maybe I had a little to do with it. It was me. *I* spread the rumor that her boyfriend said she lacked in the, umm, chest department. I know, despicable, sexist, et cetera; and I'm not proud of it. But think high school; think end-of-the-year party for us final year students; me in a tight black skirt, having mustered up enough courage to go up to a boy to confess that I liked him. And think Tanya sauntering up to us in a slinky sheath dress and calling me a greedy fat-ass. In front of *everyone.* I think I let her off too easy.

Peehu, and my still-waiting-at-thirty-three friend Kamya—they're here, thank goodness!

"Congratulations, Aashoo!" Kamya tries to hug her, but Aisha is trapped by the henna masters and their pointy applicator cones.

"Zee!" Peehu screeches and throws herself on Aisha, trapped or not, and then on me, bony arms outstretched. Colorful African bracelets roll all the way down to her elbows. Kamya, always mature and restrained, somehow manages to give Aisha a gentle hug, and both females plonk themselves on either side of me.

"So good to see you girls." Kamya smiles, eyes shining. How dainty and confident she looks, in her cream-colored salwar kameez with pale yellow flowers all over it. That she dared to wear a funereal tunic, pastel to boot, to a blingy Punjabi ceremony just goes to show her nerves of steel. Like covering yourself with meat and entering the tiger's lair. Now, had *I* worn such a color at an important family function, the AA brigade would have swallowed me whole.

"Uh oh. I know you just arrived, but you might want to turn right back around," Peehu whispers, tilting her body in the general direction of Kamya. "I see an auntie coming your way. Run! Save yourself from faltu proposals!"

Kamya rolls her eyes, jumps off the couch and rushes off toward the drinks counter.

"Poor thing." Peehu's pixie face is scrunched up in a mix of irritation and pity. "The aunties have been waiting for her. Such unmentionable proposals, I tell you. One of them was a middle-aged Testo-Stallone type. An *underwear* salesman, can you believe it?" She pretends to retch.

I can totally believe it. The thing is, Kamya has voluntarily elected to not get married. She and her boyfriend—*live-in* boyfriend, mind you—have dated for the last four years, and he is perfectly okay not getting married either. Which is like speaking in Parseltongue to the Ambushing Aunties, you know, the snake-language from *Harry Potter*.

Kamya also works at ISRO, the Indian Space Research Organization, and she was on the team that sent a probe to Mars.

To *Mars*.

This woman created something that reached another *planet*. And she's being fixed up with a chaddi-selling oaf. Which just elicits communal sighs; what use is talent and education and propelling things into space without marriage and children, pray tell us?

"At the rate you keep rejecting good Gujarati boys, you're next in line for the unmentionable proposals," I tease her.

Peehu grabs a plate of tangy potatoes from a passing server instead of chicken tikka skewers. No meat, garlic, or onions for her on Tuesday, thanks to her conservative Gujarati upbringing. "Like hell I am." Her eyes have a faraway, determined look, as if daring any of the aunties to come up with a crappy boy.

Peehu's mom, kind of, faked an illness (I forget which) to stop her from dating—and eventually wanting to marry—a boy of another religion. Everyone was in on it, their entire family, even their servants. It worked, and Peehu found out six months later and all hell broke loose. Inside her head. After which she started going to the neighborhood Shiva temple twice a day in a dark fury. I tried everything to get her out of this dark funk: drinks, gossip about aunties, analyzing the crappy lives of our mutual acquaintances. To my growing alarm, nothing worked. Paris came just in time, thank God. Had she not left for Paris she would've landed in a mental ward. Or in jail for murder, because she, as Americans say, "don't take shit from nobody."

Sudden happy yelps pierce the air-conditioned air when the DJ starts a fast number—"Balam Pichkari," a popular, peppy song. The sari-clad hip-shake in the center of the hall reaches maniac fiendish levels; all the years of decorum drilled into Indian women gone to the dogs. Weddings often do that. And poor Kamya. Pulled into the feverish dancing whorl of the very aunties she was trying to escape.

A sharp buzz in my hand makes me drop my mobile phone. A single black line gleams on the bright screen:

We need to talk ASAP when you get into the office on Friday.
—A

Why does my boss send cryptic emails when he knows I'm out of the office for my cousin's wedding? And whatever he wants to talk about can't be that urgent because if it was, he'd be blasting my ear off on the phone right now, on a Tuesday. Or be at my doorstep, wherever I was. Not a chance in hell that he'd wait for two whole days till I'm in the office to "discuss." ASAP indeed. (Why on earth is he texting then?)

> We also need to go over the ad themes and marketing plan for the Maharani hair oil campaign one final time.
> —A

For God's sake, the print ads and social media plan are ready to go. I've rechecked the graphics on the ads so many times that if you woke me up from death, I could tell you the exact inches between the Maharani logo and its surrounding red space.

"Did you get any responses from Zoya's profile yet?" Meena Auntie asks Mum, as all the Sahni women—Mum, Sheila Bua, Rita Chachi—descend on the couch next to us.

"Oh yes! So many!" Mum whips out my profile proudly on her phone as if it was a picture of me receiving an award. There I am, on Punjabimatrimony.com, Shaadi.com, and a horde of other websites, in my nineteen-year-old avatar. This antique picture was deemed to be the most appropriate in getting responses.

"This is at least ten kilos less. I don't even look like this anymore!" My protest is lost in the air heavy with flowery perfumes and sharp eucalyptus. The mehendi assistant snaps in irritation, an iron grip on my half-hennaed open palm, "Zoya Madam, can't you sit still?"

"We weren't about to put a fa—err, filled-out photo of you, Zoya. And this one was taken in Dubai, which only helps to show that we are wealthy enough to afford vacations abroad." That's Rita Chachi, Ronny Chacha's wife. (Punjabi Relations 101: Chachi—the wife of your father's brother, called Chacha.) She likes everything just so, preferably imported. She also happens to be Tanya's mother. You'd guess instantly they were mother and daughter. Both of them chic and uppity and slim.

"Zoya beta, this photo will get you lot of views so you can meet the boys. That is key—the meeting. A bad photo cuts your chances in half, right there!" says Sheila Bua, helping herself to her sixth samosa in five minutes. "Hello, waiter-boy? Keep the Fantas coming, now there's a good lad!" The liveried waiter, who's at least fifty, runs off to the back kitchens at her command. She turns her attention to me. "And you are the only child your parents have. Their respect in society depends upon your behavior, na?"

One of the younger henna assistants, dressed to the gills in red and gold, squeals in sudden delight. A bit of dried mehendi has scraped off my palm, "Look! The color is such a deep brown, so fast."

It takes hours of drying and patting the henna with a mixture of sugar and lime juice to get a dark, almost reddish black hue. And here it is on my small palm, in less than ten minutes, without any special effort. The assistant means to praise their own product to please her boss, but the aunties crowd around me in excited twitters.

"Oh! Zoya's hands are really taking in the mehendi!" Aisha beams like a proud mother hen.

Tanya, stylishly cross-legged in this season's latest mermaid lehenga and a chic bob, and back after her sojourn with her text-boyfriend, averts her eyes skyward and smirks, the slightest of sniffs intended only for my ears. (I pretend to ignore as always.) "It's not *that* deep. Now, if you'd put it on *my* hand—" Her tall claims are cut off by the squeals of aunties who crowd around me with tinkling bangles and acrid makeup.

"So rich and deep!"

"It's lovely and dark!"

Hah! Take that, you designer-wearing-twenty-two-inch-waisted witch! I could smirk but my face remains Zen, like a functional adult.

Aisha's glittery mother-in-law incarnates next to us out of the blue, a glassy smile on her powdered face.

"You know what that means, don't you?" she purrs in a deceptively sweet voice.

The women all giggle, pleased with this unexpected development; Aisha winks at me, and Mum has turned into a shiny glowworm.

"Auntie, that's all rubbish." Peehu says, her mouth full of samosa, to the gasps of the collective women. One does not disagree with any in-law's opinions, and certainly not *before* the wedding.

"It's the warmth of the hand. Also the blood in your palm." Kamya, back from the drinks counter, is ready with logical facts.

"Oh shush, child! Don't get your science-shience in here! Have some paneer potlis!" Sheila Bua thrusts a large plate of fried cheese bundles into Kamya's hands right under my nose.

A legend is the basis of these nudges and winks and beams. The darker the color of dried mehendi on your hands, the deeper is your husband's love for you. That absurdly comforting thought sends a rush of blood to my face in a secret smile. Maybe, just maybe, it's my turn this time.

CHAPTER THREE

I'm hungover *and late* for work, thanks to the wedding last night. Aisha looked gorgeous as usual in a ghagra choli, a pink and blue ankle-length skirt and short blouse with crystals. And Varun, the strapping groom, wore . . . well, something beige. Really, no one from the bride's party cares about the groom's outfit as long as he shows up fully clothed and reasonably sober for the wedding.

As soon as I heard the priest's chants and saw the bride and groom start their pheras around the fire, I slipped away to follow red-faced uncles, all the way past guests chatting on gold-colored chairs, past three buffet tables outside the hall, and bam! No, not booze but Raunak, my on-and-off fling, of the drunk eyes and sneer fame, in a dark corner of the open-air wedding hall. (Apparently his parents are related to Aisha's dad's cousin. Or is it the cousin's in-laws?)

A joint and a snog in a dark corner later, we hit the jackpot. An entire tableful of lovelies: shiny bottles of whiskey, scotch, beer, vodka, you name it, behind a white curtain that separated the wedding hall and the attached medical college.

Enter my post-wedding hangover this morning. And I would've been abysmally late had Mum not arranged my clothes the evening before, and Pa not dropped me to the station in the car.

In the meantime, two more cryptic texts from the boss showed up on the train.

> Come straight to my office when you get here.
> —A
> Need to talk. Where are you?
> —A

What the hell can't wait forty frigging minutes?

After a rattling train ride, I finally arrive in South Bombay, with its pewter-stoned relics of British rule, to be met with a screech of vehicles and the deafening clang of temple bells. Hell sounds like that for sure.

My office is all cubes and steel, and my cubicle is way at the back, right next to the boss's office, thereby deprived of any peace. A couple of stray early-bird colleagues clack sluggishly on the keyboard.

Just as I pull out my laptop, a muddy white shirt appears near my nook. It appears to dangle on a clothes hangar all by itself. No, not my boss but Chotu, the thirteen-year-old canteen boy from downstairs, the youngest child of the canteen owner. His real name is Ali, but someone in his extended family nicknamed him Chotu—the little one—when he was born, and now no one within a twenty-kilometer radius remembers his real name, not even his teachers at the neighborhood night school.

"Some breakfast, Madam?" he asks. "Poori bhaji today."

Deep fried bread and spicy, oily potatoes. "Yes, please."

"So, Zoya Madam." Chotu pushes files and papers off my desk and plonks a sectional steel plate on my table. "I heard Arnav Sir was looking for you."

"Yeah, I know. Food first." If I have to face the boss hungover, I need some serious nourishment. In the bigger section of the plate are two large fried pooris; the smaller two sections overflow with a spicy, boiled potato bhaji with liberal amounts of green coriander leaves. The warmth and tang are the only saving grace of this dish. Which means Chotu is totally enjoying the new Byomkesh Bakshi mystery I got him. Because when Chotu is engrossed in a book, he forgets to supervise the canteen cook, who isn't exactly a culinary genius, to put it mildly, so the food is uneven at best. Oh well. I can always top it up with my stash of Kit Kats from the overhead cabinet, tucked under a stack of vendor invoices. Chocolate can cure most ills.

But Chotu isn't that absentminded always. He did leave an extra cup of creamy chai on my desk last week, before I took off for the start of Aisha's wedding festivities. He does that often, I think in exchange for the books. Little things actually. Extra sticky notes or felt-tipped pens from the supply closet, or Gobble tea cakes from the canteen that we both like, the ones with bits of candied orange.

A plastic yellow daisy resting happily inside its miniature blue vase on my desk almost topples over in my haste to satisfy my starving stomach. Did I ever tell you that the daisy is my favorite flower? This one is made of plastic, but still. She really is a most happy little flower. This one just showed up on my desk in its bulb-vase one day, looking a little forlorn, kind of like a fake pet, so she's stayed with me ever since.

Just as I take another bite of the wretched poori bhaji, a deep voice rumbles from above. "Good morning, Zoya."

My heart rattles in shock. There's my boss, in his usual uniform of striped gray shirt and black formal trousers, standing in his standard pose of legs slightly apart and arms crossed across his chest, rocking back and forth on his heels. Watching me intently as my cheeks swell to twice their size with pooris.

Arnav-the-Dragon-Bajaj is one of the youngest directors of our company, heading the Marketing and Client Management departments, all confidence. Supremely tall and never satisfied with your work. His motto is: You compete only with yourself, and you can always do better. He is like a slightly positive dragon. If the dragon had a five o'clock shadow on his face at ten in the morning and ringlets for hair.

"Good morning, Boss." I choke down the food. He glances up from a sheaf of papers for just an instant, satisfied that I haven't choked to death yet. It's like being hit with the blinding light of crystals and the sun combined. Liquid amber with flecks of green. Sand and straw in a ring of grass. Like beach eyes.

Everyone he meets gushes over them, especially the girls. I did too, but not out loud. He caught me staring at my job interview two years ago: a morning ray flashed through the windows straight into his eyes, and it was like a fiery explosion of two blazing stars, after which the chairs, whiteboard, table, everything in that conference room seemed to disappear into their brilliance. That dazed explosion in my head lasted for about two seconds before the irritation in his voice pulled me back to earth. I really wanted this job, so I kept my mouth shut and eyes on another sunlit window behind him. After thirty seconds of staring straight into the sun, he looked like a dark blob, so that worked out well. At the end of the interview, he gave me a strange look before leaving the conference room.

They still startle me, the beach eyes, every single time, like they could read my thoughts as if displayed on a teleprompter and know exactly what non-work trickery I was up to (posting a totally harmless picture of the poori bhaji on my Insta).

"For the umpteenth time, Zoya, it is A.r.n.a.v.—Arnav, thank you very much," he corrects with a short tilt of his head.

We are expressly forbidden to call him Boss or Arnav Sir or anything that denotes hierarchical formality—we're Mosaic Inc., a small but hip subsidiary of Bucklebee & Owens, one of the top advertising and marketing agencies in the world—but the suffix has stuck because of his draconian ways. Mostly behind his back. (Remember that award-winning tennis shoe ad with Rafael Nadal last year? That was from the B&O mother ship in New York. And I, little ol' me, am a small part of that agency. Just thinking about that sends a shiver of thrill up my spine.)

"In my office, please," he says in a cryptic low tone and walks off. He even talks like his emails, in abrupt one-liners. The pooris play havoc inside my stomach.

Arnav Sir is already near his cabin, so I waddle after him, a penguin trying to catch up to a long-limbed cheetah. "Shut the door, Zoya." He whips around and stares at me dead straight. The muscles in his face are completely static, like they weren't programmed for any movement. I don't think I've ever seen him smile. His shirt is a bit crumpled, tie is loose in an

"I've-been-at-work-since-ages" look (at ten in the morning?), which looks kind of . . . umm, nice, when you think about such things. Which I don't.

"I thought you did a great job on the pressure cooker campaign. The theme, messaging, and ads were pitch perfect," he rumbles.

"Err, yes, thank you. I was just doing my job."

Shut up, you fool; not the time to be modest now. Does he have to work inside a glacier? I'm still hungry and now I have to pee.

"You also brought in your printing vendor contacts, which saved us about five crore rupees this year. Remarkable," he adds. "And you're the only campaign manager who's consistently delivered every project before the deadline in the two years you've been here. So, all in all, you are doing really well," he nods at me.

Wow. I bet he's run out of his yearly quota of words. Maybe he'll breathe fire now instead of talk and it'll all be my fault.

This is surreal. Hangover, icy bladder, praise. Maybe I'm in an alternate universe, in which I am tall, thin, and freakishly brilliant and anything I work on turns into the Next Big Thing.

"Thank you, Arnav Si—err, Arnav." I hesitate, not sure if this means I have to compete with myself now?

"So, Zoya." He takes a deep breath, his chest expands under that crumpled white shirt. "I'm here to tell you that you're now the Associate Director of Projects. Congratulations on the promotion."

Oh my. It would be unprofessional if I started squealing and jumping. "Thank you," I say in a modest subdued voice (totally fake). Almost executive management. OMG! That totally calls for a feast—butter chicken and biryani to be eaten together.

Home delivery from Lucky's Restaurant tonight and Bastian on the weekend with family (their Malay crab is my one true love).

"There's more." He says, slicing through my imaginary food fest. No "well done," or "well deserved," or anything. "We've had an opening at the B&O office. For a small but new division working on American products targeting the South Asian market."

"Oh." Like it has anything to do with me. I can almost taste the butter chicken . . .

"They reached out to me to see if I could recommend a campaign manager from our Bombay office."

What?

"Did you mean campaign managers from . . . this office?"

"Yes, I did. As you know, ours is their only India branch," he says and starts pacing behind his chair. Which is a cue that he's winding things up. "So here's what I'm going to do: I'm opening it to the company. Whoever can get the highest engagement rate on their next campaign within the next six weeks, I'll recommend them for a job at B&O. I will inform them personally if they've been chosen."

"B&O." The disbelief must be apparent in my voice. "The actual Bucklebee & Owens. As in the one in New York City?"

"The very one." A hint of a smile hovers on his face.

"Wait, you mean a marketing campaign can get me . . . a campaign manager to . . . B&O in New York?" I add, just to make sure I'm not hallucinating because I binge-watched a whole season of *Mad Men* last weekend on my phone, in the midst of Aisha's wedding prep.

"Yes." He says the word with solidity. "But it's not like you . . . the person will get the job on my endorsement. You have to apply for it and formally interview with them. It's a long shot," he says, then looks up at me, the beach eyes like a bolt of light on my face. "But I think you have a chance.

* * *

Associate Director! Take that, Sheila Bua, and your "hard work, shard work, all comes to naught" philosophy. Just think of Pa's ecstatic face when I reach home. "Meet my daughter, the Associate Director. And at just twenty-six. I didn't reach Director level till my forties!"

I have no recollection of leaving Arnav Sir's office or reaching my desk. But apparently I did and called my parents immediately. Both Mum and Pa were so thrilled. Pa also sort of lost his head, but then immediately made up for it with several cautionary tales of what can happen if I get complacent and don't work even harder now. I didn't tell them about the other project. Not yet, anyway. All in good time.

A ripple of hysteria is stuck inside my throat. B&O in New York! As in *the* New York in the US of A. A chance at the B&O head office is like the mother ship calling me home. And it's okay that it's a long shot; at least it's a shot. I can dream, can't I? My feet don't seem to touch the ground today.

The rest of the day passes in a blur. I think I've wasted my entire time binge-watching the fourth season of *Mad Men* and *Friends* in between work breaks on my phone and beaming at the congratulatory messages about my promotion pouring in on our family WhatsApp group. Oh, come on, cut me some slack here, like I'm ever the center of family attention! Let me enjoy this feeling while it lasts. It's not going to be more than a day, so relax, it's not like I'll while away all my time now that I'm promoted. Because if Tanya ends up buying that new outfit tonight for her friend's birthday party, Rita Chachi is sure to send a gazillion pictures of her darling daughter from all angles on our WhatsApp group, and the family will be duty bound to fawn over how lovely she looks. So, yeah.

I have no sense of time or space as I step out of the tin-roofed station at Khar. Evening lights gleam and a fading blue sky gathers tired commuters in its fold. The air is the usual mix of cigarette smoke, incense, and spices. I start walking toward home with a sea of people and the heavens open up with a loud crack.

Ooh, the rains! Finally! The thick, angry droplets are greeted with yelps of joy on the street. Giant mango trees swish like drunks in the wind and stray dogs hide in muddy puddles under parked cars. I get gloriously drenched within seconds into my short walk home.

I'll be there for you, as the rain starts to pour . . . The title track from *Friends* swirls in my head in an incessant, happy loop. I mean, an Associate Director in two years!

"Geeta! Look, look. Your daughter has gone mad on the street!"

And here we are, back from the skies in a thud. Mrs. Iyer, our next-door neighbor, giggles raucously from her brightly lit second-floor balcony.

"Zoya!" Mum's shriek precedes her on the adjacent balcony. "Come upstairs at once!" She gestures for me to use the back entrance.

"What on earth are you doing?" Mum bristles as I step inside the door. "You'll catch pneumonia! Then what will everyone say?"

What kind of a reception is this for a newly promoted, almost-top-management daughter? And why is she so twitchy?

"Won't they just say I've got pneumonia? What's the big deal? It's only rain." I answer in a sing-song voice.

"Shush! That is quite enough or the Sharmas will hear it. They are HERE in the living room." She pounds me with towels.

"Who?"

"Now go get changed into the dress I've laid out on your bed."

"What? Mum, but my promo . . ."

"Yes, yes, all that will be later." She cuts me off and maneuvers me from the passage toward my room. "And please, clean your hair up so you don't look like a jungle beast in front of the Sharmas. You need to look your best."

She walks off mumbling, "If this goes well, I'll offer a thousand rupees at Siddhivinayak temple . . ."

Is she talking about the promotion? The rain has completely blunted my senses.

I'll be there for you, as I've been there before . . .

A muffled hum of voices, far too many for a normal evening, buzzes in the air like dulled music wafting from a faraway festival stall.

I'll be there for you . . .

Samosas! Someone's frying samosas. Hot, fried food in the rain is *heaven*. And special paneer samosas, not the regular potato-peas ones. I can smell the difference all the way from my room. But why has Mala the cook fried them by the pound (and grumbled for sure about the extra work at short notice)?

I'll be there for you, cause you're there for me too . . .

Sheila Bua lurks from behind the living room door and snaps me back to attention. Sheila Bua never lurks when she can explode on the scene. She points at the bed.

I'll be there for—

I follow her silent gaze and the song screeches to a halt. The Dress! It sparkles wickedly on my bed under the sharp recessed lights. Like glossy artwork on display. It's a long chiffon tunic and leggings with crystal work and is my absolute favorite. But so rich and heavy, it's only worn for weddings. Or when you want to look your absolute, glowing best.

Look your best. The Sharmas.

What the hell is going on? Who on earth are the Sharmas?

"Mum! What the efff . . . is going on?" I demand, rushing out of my room into the narrow corridor. I almost say "fuck" in front of Mum, and it is a measure of her frenzy that she doesn't even notice. She shoos me back into my bedroom with Sheila Bua almost falling over her.

"Hai, Sheila didi, easy! You don't want to squash the bride's mother before the wedding, do you?"

Oh God.

A boy to see me. *Today* of all days. In the living room, at the end of the corridor.

Okay. Relax. Breathe. This doesn't mean I'll have to give up my job. It's not as if the boy's family will make me quit. But Aisha had to quit.

Twenty-six. Young for a promotion but apparently ankle-deep in the Swamp of Eternal Spinsterhood. Something sour gurgles inside my stomach.

"Mum! You cannot be serious." My head starts to pound; zero sleep because of Aisha's wedding last night, exhaustion, and shock finally catch up with me.

"Don't you worry, the family is just here to say hello," Mum pacifies. "They all liked your profile and called me today. Go on, wear the dress."

To *say hello*? What am I, five, to believe that? No, wait, even the iPad-savvy five-year-olds of today wouldn't buy that lie. I put the outfit on grudgingly as Mum and Sheila Bua saunter out to give me five minutes of privacy and then barge right back in. I'm still kind of wet, my hair's a mess, and surely I smell like hot soaked pavement.

Sheila Bua pats my wet hair with a fluffy towel and uses what she thinks is her softest tone of voice. "This is the first time for you. That's why you are nervous. You know, it is like riding a bicycle; the more you do it, the easier it gets."

Bicycle?

But my head. My poor head. Sheila Bua's kurta—a tunic with red, yellow, and green concentric circles (all fluorescent, thank you)—blurs the entire room. Behind her I can only see patches of dark color everywhere I look, including little black splotches on the soft underside of her right arm. Is that real color or just my blinded eyes? Is that . . . paint?

I don't even know why Sheila Bua's in our house all the time. Mum doesn't mind; they've been close friends since time. And if I'm really, really honest (PLEASE don't tell my cousins), I don't mind it too much either. Our home always feels a bit empty when Sheila Bua leaves, like energy whooshing out, leaving a vacuum for a short while before it settles back into place. She and

Mum were friends since before Mum and Pa married, and I spent my summers in her house till I was almost twelve, because Mum had to be at work. She was like a proxy mother, feeding and hugging and buying.

I also know she lost a baby after Yuvi, the same time Mum was pregnant with me. It was a daughter. The family, especially Mum, were scared that it would put her right off me in bitterness, but the exact opposite happened. I am told that she and I were inseparable when I was little, until her husband Uncle Balli reminded her that she had a son and a home to take care of. I feel a strange pull toward her sometimes, like this intense pressure inside my chest. I don't know why or what to do about it. I tried to tell Peehu and Aisha once, and they burst into cackles. Telling your peers that you actually do not mind—forget like—your matchmaking auntie is like social suicide. You are an instant anomaly. I've never told anyone about it after and squashed that feeling almost completely. No problem there now.

"Bicycle? *Uff,* Sheila didi, the things you say sometimes!" Mum puts a loving arm around my shoulders, "Just meet them like you'd meet any other family. It is just the boy and his parents. And his aunt and uncle."

"What is this, a circus, that they bring every person they can find? Why are they here today? And *why* wasn't I told?" *Oh come on, Zoya, it's not like you didn't expect to be meeting a boy soon? Yes, but not so soon!*

"You don't have to give us an answer today," starts Sheila Bua.

"There is no pressure to marry, just see if you like the boy," Mum cajoles.

"You could have told them to come another day!"

"We couldn't very well turn them away, could we? How would that look?" Mum is aghast at the suggestion.

"And you were on your way back as it is, no?" chimes Sheila Bua.

It's like a tennis match in a fantasy novel, only I am the ball. There is no choice. How do you say no? After all, elders are our guiding lights, aren't they? And guiding lights don't willingly lead you into a mire. Walking out would be blasphemy and headline the world of arranged marriages for eternity.

And what's wrong with this dress? I try to scratch my back, but it feels too tight. (I haven't put on weight, I *haven't.*)

"Oh, I altered it a bit, you know. To make it figure-hugging." Mum looks a teeny bit apologetic and Sheila Bua doesn't look apologetic in the least. She beams like a tube light, mighty pleased with this figure-hugging development. There is no way I can take the dress off without a large pair of scissors.

A miracle of science, I have been alive for a full five minutes now without breathing. Sheila Bua and Mum pull and pluck and tweak and tease my look into place before going back out to entertain our guests. Wet hair soaks the back of the tunic and I bulge over from *everywhere.*

Can't get any worse, certainly?

CHAPTER FOUR

My cousin Karan, Tanya's un-evil brother, once told Aisha to go see boys like she was going to see a bad Hindi movie. You know those shitty ones from the eighties? With those icky macho heroes with bare chests, over-the-top villains, and no story? This is exactly what I will do.

Mum walks in with the props for girl-viewing: a large, freshly polished silver tray filled with our best china set from England, which was a wedding present for my grandparents, inherited by my parents at their wedding, and waiting in hope for mine. The porcelain plates are filled with hot samosas, cream biscuits, malai pedas (small heavenly blobs of sugar, cream, and flour), and six cups of fragrant, steamy chai.

Maybe I could sneak in one peda? Maybe not, in case I burst out of this dress in my underwear, much like a paunchy, gone-to-seed Superman. But I'm so hungry.

Of course, the tray *has* to be silver. We must show off our wealth in front of the Sharmas to indicate that we can manage the entire expense of the wedding. In a subtle way, of course, not to appear too vulgar or imply that we're richer than the boy's family. What's more subtle than shiny silver for mundane household items?

"Good thing your promotion came in today. How much extra money will you get now?" Sheila Bua gets straight to the point.

"I have no idea." I mean, I only just found out. How unprofessional would it have been to just flat out talk money? "All the details will be shared later. Maybe fifteen percent more, I don't know."

"A fat salary totally offsets being fat—oh, I didn't mean that!" Sheila Bua gasps, pretending to cover her mouth. "I meant, you know, fuller in body. And the dark skin. And I already called the Sharmas and told them about the raise. I have such a good feeling about today." She sighs in pleasure, as Mum tries to thrust the heavy silver tray into my hands.

"I can't carry that heavy tray. I can barely move in my dress. Why can't you have Mala carry it?"

"What if the boy ends up liking her? How will you live that down? A boy choosing a maid over you?" whispers Sheila Bua as Mum opens my bedroom door. Mala, our cook, is forty-five years old, and married with three grown children.

"It's an old tradition, beta, that's what we do. We can't just have you walk in there and say, 'Here! What do you think of her?' Can you *please* not fight me on everything?" Mum half pleads, half orders.

"It's crap! We might as well go back a hundred years and veil my face with this dupatta!" The red chiffon wrap, which is supposed to go around the front of your neck or dangle down over one shoulder, has now entangled itself near my posterior like a long tail.

"Just do it this once. You won't have to do this again," she coaxes.

"Well, come on, let's go. What are we waiting for?" Sheila Bua herds us out of the chilly room into the warm corridor lined with shut doors and random paintings of obscure landscapes.

Alright, okay, I can do this. I can *do* this. Think bad Hindi movie, imagine a room of hairy lead actors and vapid heroines. A sense of profound unease spreads through my body.

Sheila Bua and Mum twitter and flutter nervously, sandwiching me as we pass through the long passageway. My unease explodes into a full-on twitch. If I could only scratch my damp bottom a little!

The door of the living room opens with an elaborate swish and a blast of cold synthetic breeze mixes with the warm air. The muffled voices stop all of a sudden.

Bad movie time. And . . . Action!

Seven pairs of eyes turn in our direction and I want to bolt like a cat to my room and hide under the safety of my bed. Six pairs of eyes stare at me with open scrutiny.

Relax, just relax.

There's the boy, the hero of the movie. If you can call him that. Completely colorless and unmacho, his face is bland with no hint of spice. Hair deathly straight, oiled (who the hell goes out to *see* a girl with oiled hair?), and combed within an inch of its life. Something snakes down my back. A small blip of disappointment. Or sweat.

Well, what did I expect? Chris Hemsworth?

Pa's round, spectacled face is a mixture of warmth and pride, as if showing me off to these strangers thinking: *Look at my clever, successful, educated daughter.*

The senior Sharma men, the father and uncle—the hairy extras in the movie—are sunk into the brown love seat. (The uncle apparently is some big-shot cancer doctor, Sheila Bua told Mum just before we left my bedroom. I bet Sheila Bua heard cash registers ring in her ears.) The Sharma men nod and smile at me absently. The uncle looks behind me and sways in his seat as if stung. Ah, he's seen Sheila Bua and her tunic with the concentric circles.

The two Sharma women, the mother and aunt—the villain and her accomplice— look me over openly from the dark leather couch across the love seat. From the top of my hair trying to escape its clip all the way down to my unpolished nails in silver, open-toed sandals. Their eyes settle on my waist and they exchange a look of barely concealed dismay.

I feel naked, like when I was ten and my cousins Yuvi and Tanya threw open the shower door, pointed at my bulging stomach and laughed. I felt like someone had peeled away my skin, exposing my raw and bloody insides to the world's amusement. Until this moment I didn't realize it was possible to feel worse. And here I thought that being unkind was a family thing, and the cruelty of strangers couldn't hurt as much. *How wrong I was.*

Stop, stop. Think bad movie.

I slide the silver tray onto our mahogany coffee table with as much haste as my tightly squeezed body allows. Mum gestures to a beige armchair, bang in front of the Sharma women, and I manage to stick my itchy bottom to the cushy edge somehow, just enough to stop from sliding down in an ungainly hump at their feet. *If I could only scratch my bottom.*

"Beta, this is Puneet," says the accomplice aunt. She smiles at me after a loud, harrumphing burp, courtesy of the chai.

The boy's white, short-sleeved T-shirt (with zigzag stripes, good God) hangs limp on his hairy chest. My hands itch for a razor. Ick factor: ten on ten.

"Um, hi." He says it fast on low volume, a mere peep. The hero *cannot* have a squeaky voice. Can you imagine if the Terminator cheeps "I'll be baaack" like a baby chicken?

"Sorry?" I ask. Come on, our AC hums louder than him.

"Child, he said 'Hi,'" explains the accomplice auntie.

"Our Puneet is very soft-spoken. I've never heard him raise his voice," says his father, whose face mirrors Pa's indulgent pride. I guess all parents think their kids are superstars.

"Oh! Yes, hello." I keep my eyes lowered, more flustered than out of respect or decency.

"Thank goodness it rained!" Sheila Bua makes random conversation. "A good omen, especially for our families today, don't you think?"

"Yes, people are nicer when the weather is cooler," the accomplice auntie says.

As Sheila Bua and the aunt banter, the hero steals a glance at me and immediately looks down at his sneakers. His acid-wash jeans, in vogue a century ago, end in giant, blinding white Nikes, which he taps at the toes. Striped T-shirt and acid-wash jeans? What, did his mother choose his clothes? At least we have one thing in common.

"So much traffic. Took us so long to reach . . . this place from South Bombay." A syrupy voice sniffs in disapproval. The mother-villain finally speaks. Drum roll. She stares at me the whole time. Hasn't blinked or smiled or looked human. Brr.

The mother-villain adjusts her stiff, starched cotton sari, the palest of yellows and bland like her son. Its pallu is neatly pinned over her left shoulder with *exactly* four folds, like those stern female politicians on TV.

Okay, shake it off, shake it off. Think movie, think bad story line. Maybe we throw in an item song or two with dancing girls in scanty clothes to, you know, loosen up things a bit? Or loosen *her*? The thought just makes me want to giggle desperately from somewhere deep inside my stomach. Stop, this won't do. And my bottom is still itchy. Maybe if I just moved it back and forth on the seat?

As if she can sense my blasphemous thoughts, Sheila Bua—who has somehow managed to squeeze herself into a cream-colored dining chair across the room—glares at me bug-eyed. Her pupils bulge, she shakes her head a smidge and *grunts.* She actually grunts. Which just makes me giggle more. And scratch. Giggle, scratch, scratch, giggle. Just a vicious cycle.

The mother-villain's eyes, which have taken a break from me, dart from place to place, noting the richness of the wide living room: polished wood wall unit, the large Samsung flat screen, huge French windows, the sleek Panasonic AC unit overhead.

Her thin lips are pressed together with some force. Does she disapprove of the room, or me, or everything that crosses her path? Or did someone glue those lips together when we weren't looking and now they cannot be unstuck?

"Your name is Zoya, isn't it?" The accomplice aunt asks, not unkindly.

"Muslim name, isn't it?" The cold, stiff voice is the mother villain. It drips with the disapproval of her prejudiced mind. As if she'd ever have a voice as melodious as Mum's. (*No one* has a voice as sweet as my Mum's.)

They knew my name before they arrived. Basic market research principles. Know the name of the girl you are going to see, in addition to a vague idea about her family history and the precise amount of their wealth.

"Well . . ." Mum looks stumped at this turn of events. Mine is very much a Muslim name, plagiarized from a Pakistani social drama she watched at the time of my birth.

"That won't work in our house," clips the mother-villain. And what is wrong with my name? My family loves it; I love it. "We are devout Hindus, we say our prayers every morning, light incense sticks, and diya in the evening," she says. It is quite miraculous how she manages to talk without ever opening her mouth.

I wonder if they'd all jump out of their skins if I rose up to my full height of five feet one-and-a-half inches and said politely: *If you had such a problem with my name, why did you come to see me, you biased crone?*

How long would it take for my reputation and that of my family to be in tatters because a rude, obnoxious girl means she's from a rude, obnoxious family because the fruit doesn't fall far from the tree? An hour? A day? Surely not a full day.

"But, you know, names are changed after marriage, it is a ritual in all weddings," pacifies the aunt. "We can choose a nice new name for Puneet's bride."

My hands are suddenly cold and my mouth tastes sour. So it begins. Name change, life change, job change; from almost Director of Projects to director of household, cooking, cleaning, and a full-time supervisor of maids. And before you know it, you are a complete stranger to yourself.

The kurta feels snug, binding my body. My stomach tries hard to expand, but can only manage half a breath. I hear a soft *rrr* sound from somewhere. Good Lord, did one of the Sharmas pass gas? Doesn't smell like it. Still smells like samosas and chai and perfume.

"Sit up straighter. And suck in your stomach!" Sheila Bua hisses, only for my ears, as I begin to slouch. Her eyes bulge and her teeth are stretched into a pretend smile. She dangles dangerously on the arm of my couch, threatening to spill over completely onto the mousy uncle-extra next to her. Her bottom almost touches his arm and he turns a deep red, in excitement or fear, I cannot say. Well, purple actually, based on his skin.

"Beta, what are your hobbies?" asks Mr. Sharma.

What?

"Hobbies, hobbies. Sharmaji is asking you." Sheila Bua sounds breathless. "Tell, tell."

"Oh! Okay, well. I like to read, travel. Then there's music and a little bit of cooking, Uncleji." My voice is strangled. How much cellulite can you suck in without choking yourself to death?

The Sharma women perk up at the mention of cooking. Of course. That's our purpose in life, isn't it? To cook and breed? Well, these days, educated, career-oriented-for-a-limited-time breeder and cook.

"What do you like cooking, child?"

Really? You can't ask what I read? Where do I want to travel next after my trip to Bhutan? Or ask about my job? What if I ask the un-Chris Hemsworth boy if *he* knows how to cook? Would they all fall off their chairs in shock? Sheila Bua grunts at me, bug-eyed yet again. The uncle-extra blinks and twitches in his seat and turns completely violet, like a large eggplant. "I've learnt how to make a good mutton biryani," I say.

The Sharma women balk like I asked them to dance naked in the moonlight around a pagan fire. The men look like confused little bunnies. "We are vegetarians; we don't even eat eggs," says the mother-villain with a weird mixture of distaste and pride. "Puneet's wife will have to give up eating *flesh* before she marries him. And we will have to perform a puja to purify her."

What? Every atom in my being protests, jerking to its full size in fury. Everything except my mouth.

The dress seems to be slowly squeezing my breath. I wish they hadn't tightened it so. I hear another *rrr* sound, this time a wee bit louder. What—

"Oh, that's not a problem, is it, Zoya?" Sheila Bua nudges me, her sharp nails jab my skin through my clothes, willing me to nod my head. I can only manage a tight smile in return. *Remember: elders = guiding lights. Right?*

"We always talk about your example, Sheilaji," the boy's auntie says. "Such respect you have in the *entire* Punjabi community—all castes! I mean raising your three younger siblings after your mother had a stroke is no laughing matter. So selfless. And so young. We hope your niece will be just like you."

Sheila Bua's face stretches in a perfunctory, formal sort of smile, which is a bit odd. She stuffs a fourth malai pedha into her mouth, startled at its taste, as if unaware of how that evil piece of dessert climbed up from the plate and reached inside her mouth. I thought she'd be quite pleased at her "sacrifices" bought center stage. She always is. Maybe she's having an off day. Like Bua, like niece. To give her credit, she's never thrown her "selflessness" in the family's face. Not directly.

"As for Zoya's job," says the auntie, "it's wonderful that she will be at such a good post so soon." I remember, Sheila Bua told them about my promotion. The thought of it is like a little fizzy pick-me-up. "We always wanted an educated, talented daughter-in-law. But you know . . . all these long hours . . ." The auntie trails off in mid-sentence, looking at the mother.

"Yes. There will be future responsibilities. To her husband, in-laws, then kids . . . We just want to make sure that my son gets preference over a job." She looks directly at me for the first time and manages a smite of a smile. Or maybe it was gas. I can't really tell.

"Of course. We understand," says my college-professor mother.

"She could leave the job if your family wants," Sheila Bua says, hesitantly.

So, an education and a career are only valued when they fall in line with tradition?

Oxygen doesn't seem to be passing through me. I can barely move my limbs; the dress seems has turned into a vise. I can hear a wheezing sound from somewhere. Oh wait, it's coming from my lungs, desperate to expand.

Pa opens his mouth, as if to bristle at the casual dismissal of my hard work, *their* hard work: tired nights of geometry and algebra drills, endless MBA projects, waking up at four in the morning to make sure I studied, driving me to infinite exams and interviews. And then long nights working on client projects, constantly learning new skills outside of work. All for what? To give it up for "her son"? But Sheila Bua silences Pa with another grunt. Of course. We are supposed to agree; the girl's side can't seem openly defiant in front of the boy's family. A dead weight clamps on my chest.

The bad Hindi movie doesn't help anymore. I keep my eyes to the ground in confusion, away from the giant white Nikes. I try to conjure up a fury, to push the weight off my chest. But it stays pressed and stops my breath. Is this what we're expected to do in the name of marriage? Would the boy give up the fruits of his hard work for me?

The left side of my body is icy. I bet dying feels like this, cold seeping through you, freezing you bit by bit.

"Maybe Puneet and Zoya want to go talk to each other, away from us oldies," asks Sheila Bua, forcing a chuckle.

"No, that won't be necessary right now," says his mother with a finality that signals they've seen enough. The boy raises himself ever so slightly from his seat and sits down again. He hasn't said a word or looked away from his tapping shoes all this while.

Mum and Sheila Bua exchange surprised looks—how can they leave without the boy talking to the girl? It feels like sports day again when everyone is picked except me. Volleyball, soccer, badminton? We want athletes, not a tubby girl who can barely run. Volleyball made me heave, soccer hurt my feet, but I didn't want to be the only one left behind.

I can't do this. I have to breathe or I might collapse. I take a full, real breath, filling my lungs, my stomach, its energy rushing and expanding my limbs. And feel a yanking wrench on my side.

Nooo.

My kurta is ripped!

But no one seems to have noticed. Not Mum, not the mother-villain, nor the auntie-extra. I cover it with my left arm immediately, so the rip stays hidden. But I cannot hide it from Sheila Bua, who has spied the tear and seems to be in the grip of an intense spasm of horror as little tires of flesh creep out of the ripped tunic.

But I was wrong about no one noticing. "What was that sound?" One of the extras looks at her pointedly. Sheila Bua leaps out of her seat to jump onto the arm of my beige armchair, a desperate attempt to cover for me.

"Probably the AC," she says hurriedly. "These new, expensive ones, you can't trust them, can you? Oh, but you haven't eaten at all!" Sheila Bua's voice takes on a near-hysterical pitch. "Only four samosas each? How can that be?"

"I think we've had enough," the mother-villain says.

"We will consult with the elders in our house and have our family astrologer match their horoscopes. If they match, we can have them meet again," explains his aunt.

The look on Mum's face says it all. Grumble all we can, there is no choice but to accept this sudden departure. We are the girl's side, after all. We have to honor the wish of the boy's family, within the outer limits of reason.

They say their goodbyes and Mum and Sheila Bua collapse on the leather couch in confused relief. Pa switches off the air conditioner with a loud beep of the remote.

Sheila Bua clutches her chest for a moment, suddenly out of breath.

"What's wrong, Sheila didi?" Pa looks at her in concern.

"Oh, nothing. Just exhaustion. Don't you worry. Now we'll have Zoya's wedding to plan soon!" Sheila Bua has convinced herself of the success of this meeting.

I cannot, just cannot, bear to be in this room, or be a part of this conversation anymore, and before I know it, I'm back in my bedroom with a plate of samosas in my hand. For which I have no real appetite. (Now that's a first.) My brain has finally collapsed with exhaustion and dead weight and resigned fury.

The hot rain outside has trickled down to a sweaty drizzle; the sky is an inky, ominous gray. A lone voice floats up through the open French windows, bland, tetchy. An eerie yellow glow lights up the giant white Nikes.

"Mummy, I didn't want to come here in the first place and now you are showing me a girl who is so dark. And so fat. And now she'll probably earn more than me!"

The silent hero finds his voice at last.

* * *

I knew what it would be like, didn't I? Like being displayed in a bazaar? Found wanting and put back on the shelf? But how can the theory of something prepare you for the reality that you are *not* enough? That you won't be till you change your name, till you give up your favorite foods, till you are purified, by the end of which you won't know who you are. Then, only then, will you be enough. But just barely.

But is that even true or are these the rambles of an exhausted mind? Mum did it and she and Pa have mostly been happy, give or take a bunch of fights. Aisha did it, Rita Chachi did it, even Sheila Bua. It all turned out fine for them, right? Then why make a big deal out of it?

How long has it been since the Sharmas left? I don't trust myself today to tell time. But small mercies, I have finally managed to tear the blasted dress off.

The living room is silent in the absence of the AC hum. The blush curtains are pulled wide open to let in the meager, rain-soaked breeze from the French windows. The ceiling fan whirs over Pa, who seems to have disappeared inside the *Hindustan Times*. The fan would've curled his hair if he had any. Eyes fixated on the TV, Mum and Sheila Bua are busy sorting the cash gifts received at Aisha's wedding yesterday.

Aisha's wedding.

What a long time ago that seems. A different era. Which yesterday *was*. The rain starts again, a sudden onslaught of white noise. I need to get out of here.

The squelchy roads shine in the post-downpour mist. Late commuters make a wild dash for a crowded bus. They jostle, fight, scratch, to not be left behind. I walk and walk till I don't feel my legs anymore.

I find myself outside a familiar multistoried, green building. Raunak's building. Pothead Raunak of the hooded eyes, nasal voice, and permanent smirk. How did I get here?

My limbs are heavy; the walk from the elevator to his door feels like a monstrous, painful chore, like lifting weights with sore muscles. I'm moving without thinking, really. A plain brown door looks strangely bereft of the colorful festoons and religious stickers of its fellow doors.

Raunak's door.

I know, I know what you think. Yes, I shouldn't go back to a pot-smoking, unemployed ex, who my parents detest, et cetera. But we don't all make smart decisions a hundred percent of the time.

Raunak opens the door and his arms dangle at his side in his careless lazy slouch, "You knew my parents were out of the country, didn't you?" His face is unshaven, his hair tousled as if he doesn't bother to ever run a comb through it. Which is true.

The modernist clock on the wall behind him ticks loudly. It's nine at night, only an hour since the Sharmas left. And a full eleven hours since this morning in Arnav Sir's office.

"Aren't your parents always out of the country?" I can barely manage a coherent sentence before my body begins to shake violently and a tear falls down my cheek.

"You cold?" He backs off, half revolted, half curious. Any outward show of emotion and he bolts, physically and emotionally. But that's exactly what you need on some days: indifference.

"I know just what'll warm you up." He dangles a small Ziploc bag stuffed with a muddy green substance inside. "Come inside my parlor for a joint. Or something else . . ." He grins wickedly, opening the door to his smoke-filled lair.

At least *he* wants me.

CHAPTER FIVE

It's another Friday afternoon, just before lunch, and the office is buzzing. Keyboards clackity-clack, papers rustle, phones ring berserk, and the rain outside switches from a gentle drip to a whiplash, over and back in an instant. I twirl the cylindrical bottle of glue over and over in my hands, trying to think of a slogan. That's my product for this campaign—Affixer Glue. The product which could get me an endorsement for a job at B&O. I've been working on it for a couple of weeks now, scoping the target audience and creating the marketing material. Bharat is working on Kake's Chilled Turmeric Milk, Kaya on Saibal Ayurveda, and Farhan on Khao, the new restaurant rating app. Bharat is doing this wrong, using only the "hip" factor for the milk—he should be using turmeric's healing properties front and center for his Millennial audience, who are learning to embrace natural healing. Not that I care, they're all good at their jobs, but it helps to keep an eye open.

My Phase One banners are already online and are getting plenty of hits. I just need a slogan for my social media campaign, which will then be incorporated into Phase Two. I dug around for more info on the job and found that it's a three-year stint in New York. This person will not only manage the creative side but also help train the rest of the marketing and creative team, and bring an Indian perspective to their marketing campaigns. (Maybe one of my ads at B&O will win an award—I can already see my picture in *Ad Week.*) Yes, I know what you want to say, that there's no guarantee I'll reach anywhere close to New York. But if nothing else, a good job on this project might me get me another raise *here*. Or a shot at becoming an actual Director and Arnav Sir's peer. That wouldn't be so bad.

And it's not like I have a husband lined up or in-laws to consider, both of which could give one significant pause before contemplating the America project. I have now seen three boys in the last month—all rejections: the giant-white-sneaker disaster, plus another who lived with fifteen people in a single flat, and a third one who was honest right off the bat saying that he was quite happy with his boyfriend and was only participating in this charade to please his mother. We're friends now and I chat with him on WhatsApp all the time.

And that thing with Raunak? How could I have been *so* stupid? Pot and emotionally stunted sex? Peehu gave me a mighty earful on the phone from Paris for a full forty-five minutes. And after I promised myself that it would never happen again. I don't even like Raunak. Why do I do such dumb things?

There was a reason, whatever you may say. I was exhausted and ironically very upset about the giant-white-sneaker disaster.

That it happened, not that he rejected me. Fine, a little bit because he rejected me. I didn't want him to choose me, but couldn't he just have let me say no? But I do not just go around sleeping with people. Raunak is, was, the only . . . well, what is one supposed to do when these blasted feelings hijack you all at once? Afterward it felt grimy, like eating greasy food at a street stall that adds the grease to mask the staleness, but you eat there anyway because, well. You just do.

I should've just eaten instead of going to that donkey's flat. Maybe two jumbo grilled toast sandwiches (with extra cheese) from the stall under my building? That would've kept me occupied and all those feelings at bay. And topped it off with a decaf cappuccino from Barista across the street? Actually no; I might've run into Sheila Bua there. She's been trying to get the Barista franchise manager married, so she loiters in the coffee shop at all times, telling random customers that the gigantic coffee mugs are lottas: you know, mugs used for pouring bath water over you in the olden days or used in toilets for, umm, washing up.

But I have to put all that behind me because tonight is my high school reunion, and I need my wits around to tackle all the marriage questions. It starts at seven thirty in the evening, which means no one important will show up before eight. But before that, back to the Affixer Glue.

Chotu walks by right that instant, with his rack of pre-lunch chai in little glass cups the size of shot glasses. I stretch my tired limbs and take the chai from him.

"So nice, no, that Arnav Sir is at an off-site? Such freedom when he isn't around."

"Freedom? What, Madam, I've always been confused. Why are you all so afraid of him?" He puts the plastic rack on the carpeted floor and leans on my cube wall, his curious face on.

"I'm not afraid," I protest.

"Not specifically you, but all the office people."

"Because he's kind of a dragon." I take a sip of the hot, milky tea. And immediately cringe, because it's clearly overdosing on cardamom and ginger. Which means Chotu is really enjoying a book and forgot to supervise the canteen cook. Maybe I should give him crappy books more often. Oh well. At least the tea is hot.

"So, what book are you reading that you love so much?" I ask.

"*Death of a Hollow Man*. So much blood!" He positively shivers in joy.

"The one by Caroline Graham?" I certainly didn't give it to him. "Where did you get that from?"

"Oh, here and there. A friend."

"A friend." I raise my eyebrows. None of his "friends" are into anything that resembles words printed on paper, except when forced to read textbooks for school. Maybe one of these "friends" is a new book supplier because he hastily stuffed Satyajit Ray's *The Complete Adventures of Feluda* in his school satchel when I chanced upon him in the canteen this morning, which I didn't give him either.

"Yes, Zoya Madam. I have friends other than you. And also, Arnav Sir is not a dragon. He's the nicest person in this whole office."

"Nicest person? You are joking, surely?"

"Do you know," he glances around to make sure no one is eavesdropping—other colleagues are busy clacking away at their desks—and then whispers, "he once helped us pack food for our catering order when we were running late. You know, na, that we do a separate catering business in the evenings after the office closes? And when Abba was so stressed that we would not get the order delivered on time because the van driver canceled at the last moment, Arnav Sir helped us transport the order. In his own car!"

I rise up from my chair, in a sort of disbelief, spilling some chai on my desk. Chotu promptly wipes it off with a rag cloth he always has slung on the tea rack, almost overturning my plastic daisy.

"Careful! Don't hurt my pet flower. She's delicate."

The dragon? Helping someone who missed a deadline? "Arnav Sir delivered food in his car?"

At the doubt on my face, he says serenely, "It's true. I'm not supposed to tell anyone about it. But I told you because you're just as nice as him."

"Just as nice? Please. I'm way nicer." I smack his head, which is neatly combed with a liberal dollop of coconut oil. "Wait, did he really help you pack food?" It seems incredible, the man with the death stare to end all death stares.

"Yup," he says, picking up the tea rack off the floor and swinging it again. "He also has the nicest laugh. Loud and fizzy, kind of like a Pepsi bottle, just explodes. What fun that evening was, packing food, talking about books and laughing!" Chotu, lost in the memory, waves to me absently and walks off to deliver chai to others in the office.

Laugh? An alien word to associate with my boss. It's as if I've gotten a little glimpse into the dragon's world and what do you know, he doesn't blow hellfire all the time. But still, it's a bit hard to reconcile this image with his chop-chop behavior at work. And just because a person is good to someone else, doesn't mean he's good for you. To you, I mean, not *for* you.

Come on, Zoya, get back to glue. Alright, final check on the new banner ads for Phase Two of the campaign; the brand name starts hazy with the top ends of the *r* curled, and then gets stronger, almost solid-like by the end, with a small space at the bottom for the slogan. Simple and powerful. And a hashtag campaign on Insta is perfect to attract the younger audience the client wants. Everything is set and in motion. All I need is the slogan. I rack my brain—stick . . . sticky . . . something stick like . . . ack!

The shrill peal of my desk phone puts the tagline right out of my head. I abandon the glass of chai on the table gladly and take my seat to pick up the phone.

"Mosaic Agency. This is Zoya Sahni."

A hurried, melodious, and way too familiar voice answers at the other end, "Zoya beta, I forgot to tell you in the morning. Sheila Bua will stop by your office today."

"Mum? Why did you call on my office phone? Did you misplace my mobile number?"

"Oh, is that what this number is? I was in such a rush that I called on the first one I could see for you. She'll arrive in a couple of minutes to pick you up. I just called to warn . . . inform you."

Click.

What just happened? Did I hallucinate that Sheila Bua was coming to the office? It can't be, of course not. Relatives and parents have no reason to come to your office. Can't this be the one place where I am safe?

The lobby doors are yanked open that very moment with a loud squeak followed by annoyed shouts of "Excuse me, Auntie!" and "What's going on?"

I can hear Rima, the receptionist, mumbling in her soothing tone, and a shrill voice answering her. "Arre, I know she's in there somewhere . . . no, *you* wait here . . ."

"Ma'am, ma'am, please . . ." Rima's voice is so high-pitched it reaches all the way to my cube. "Ma'am . . . you can't just go in without an appointment—"

I lean my head out of my cube.

Good God. It's real. Sheila Bua is here. In my office!

Why, why? I was so close to figuring out that tagline, damn it. I feel a spike of irritation at both my mother and my auntie. And it doesn't help that I've been so tired and annoyed with everyone at work. How am I supposed to deal with this now? Even Arnav Sir raised an eyebrow the other day as I snapped at Kaya in the staff meeting because she was three hours late in sending me contact details for our new print vendors. I can't have Sheila Bua in my office on top of all else. Half of my colleagues are single, and she's going to try and lure them into her matchmaking schemes and they'll never forgive me. There she is: my auntie, in a tie-dye brown-orange-green tunic, her loud voice filling the entire lobby, arguing with the receptionist, who has one hand over her ear.

My desk phone rings again: it's Rima sounding decidedly disgruntled. "Zoya? Your auntie is here in the lobby. Can you *please* come?"

"Thank you. I'll be right out."

I gawk around my office in a panic, but calm faces stare back. What is wrong with people? Why don't they flee for their lives? I have to get her out before she marries my entire office to each other.

Oh God, Sheila Bua's trapped Rima with her matchmaking business cards—I knew it. Rima's clearly shocked that someone would hand out matchmaking cards in an office and tries to tell Sheila Bua she's already married—in vain. Sheila Bua's lips move: *no matter, child, one never knows, na?* Joe from IT gets one because religion is no bar for her—Christian, Muslim, Hindu: we are all Indians, desperate to marry off our children (safely within our own religions, mind you).

And then I see *him* getting out of the elevator, opening the glass doors of our office, walking into the lobby, toward her. Oblivious.

Now *she* sees him. Wasn't he supposed to be at an off-site?

Her eyes gleam as she hurls herself from the sofa toward Arnav Sir. Her jaw opens wide, and I can see New York and B&O vaporizing inside it . . .

God, no!

"—thirty, you don't say? Girls don't like boys with stubbles. Don't you shave when you come to work?"

She has him pinned against the lobby wall, blocking his escape into the office. He struggles to escape deeper into the wall behind him. His beach eyes are saucer-wide in alarm, which he tries desperately to mask.

I slide next to Sheila Bua in a clumsy tumble, grabbing her cold, pudgy arm to pull her back. (She was about to pat my boss on his stubbled cheek. I could die.)

"Arnav . . . S . . . sir, hello!" I try to muster a gentle, feminine greeting but gasp like a strangled toad. Goodness, she was almost upon him. I pry her limbs away from him.

His shoulders relax in immediate relief. "Oh, thank God, I mean, hello! This, err, is—" His hand hovers in the general direction of Sheila Bua, from as great a distance as he can, then toward me, then back again. As if he doesn't really know what to do with his hand. Or with her.

"This is, actually, um. My aunt." It has to be forced out.

"What? Really?" he blurts before he can stop himself.

"Of course! Zoya is my niece. Don't you think we look alike?"

Oh my. On anyone else, the tie-dye brown-orange-green tunic would've looked like a sad little toast with orange marmalade and fungus in the middle, but Sheila Bua, bountiful and all, *owns* it, as if the colors and the pattern are in love with her. *How does she do that?* I bet I was off stuffing my face with fried carbs when the gods were handing out body-positive genes. Wish I could own my clothes like she does.

"Err, no . . . umm . . . yes! . . . I . . . Err, maybe." Arnav Sir's tongue seems to have folded on itself. My normally taciturn boss is a blithering mess and squirms in extreme discomfort. Wow. I have entirely new respect for Sheila Bua.

"And how many people in your family?"

Here we go.

"Bua!" I squeak in horror. "We have to go! Do you want to go shopping? Let's hurry! The market gets really crowded at lunchtime!" I have no idea why she's really here or where we're supposed to go, but hurrying from here seems an exceptionally good option right now.

"Hein? Shopping?" She looks confused. "Well, okay, let's do that too."

That too? What other torture does she have in mind? Oh God, why is she here and why can I never shake her off? Seriously, it's so hard to peel relatives off you.

Wait a minute . . .

"I will see you later, beta." She waves to Arnav Sir as I yank her arm, desperate to drag her away from him. "Bajaj, you said, right? Arnav Bajaj? I know some Bajajs. Don't worry, I will find your mother somehow!" she threatens in a professionally pleasant voice.

I use all my might to push her toward the glass door exit, to no avail. Good God, the carnage if she *does* find his mother. We need to get the hell out of here.

"Arre, don't rush me. Let me see your fancy office!" She turns in a huff, out of breath again for some reason.

I look back into the lobby and the office beyond. Arnav Sir seems to have speedily disappeared. Thank the gods of all religions. Sheila Bua's ponytail swings from side to side, eyes wide as she drinks in every detail of the place; shiny lobby, a toran of marigolds hanging in inverted arches from the top of entrance, sari-clad maid scrubbing the glass doors. Despite myself, I can't help but hope she's impressed.

"So, this is what it is like. *Wah!* So lovely! Look at the gray walls, those big rooms—what do you call them? Ah, conferencing rooms? And all these important people with laptops and coffee."

"Why do you want to see an office? Haven't you ever seen one before?" I ask as we walk away toward the corridor. Okay, I'll admit, it's a distraction technique. Not like I'm really interested in her life.

"Why no, I've never been in such a proper office before. You know, I used to work in an art gallery in my first year of college. In Kala Ghoda, not too far from here. Dorabjee Art Gallery."

My legs stop in their tracks, mildly stunned. Kala Ghoda? The boho-chic art district next to my office?

A memory flashes in front of my eyes, a fast-moving film reel. In an instant, I'm eleven years old, transported to a little storage room at the back of her large apartment. No one ever went to that storage room except to get supplies, but somehow I found my way there, lured by the mistaken idea of a giant packet of masala chips. I opened the door and jumped in fright: Sheila Bua stood in her faded yellow nightgown, a paintbrush in her hand, red paint on her fingers, surrounded by large steel tins of rice and flour. She stood underneath a row of aluminum pans, bent over a canvas. She turned toward me in a trance, as if from another world, as if she didn't know who I was, startled at finding me there, as if I had caught her out. Frightened by that unearthly ghostly look, I'd fled as fast as my legs could run. I've never heard of, or seen her paint, since. And I never told anyone about that painting. I don't know why; it felt like betraying an intimate secret.

I often think about that canvas with a queer distress. Bleeding slashes of crimson and raging bruises of dark sapphire. An endless, despondent burning. But the Sheila Bua I know isn't muted pain. She is noise and interference and cheek. Who did I see that day?

A rush of heat hits our air-conditioned bodies as we exit into the crumbly corridor.

"But . . . but I thought you always . . ."

"Always what? Wanted to stay at home, cook and clean? Or marry people?" Her smile stretches tightly across her face.

She continues to talk, oblivious of me. "It was a small art gallery, nothing fancy-shmancy like this office; certainly nothing as big as Jehangir Art Gallery. Mr. Dorabjee, the owner, was always at some art retreat or the other, so I did all the accounting, sales, everything. What fun I had, putting those little red sale dots on paintings!" She giggles, and it's such an un-Sheila-Bua sound that I'm forced to look directly at her. It's like she's transformed. The frown on her brow melts into laugh lines and her eyes are bright bulbs of light in this dim corridor. She giggles again, hope and innocence all rolled into a buoyant little chime. "You know, I'd got accepted into the Fine Arts program at Oxford when I was twenty."

What?

She drops this little bomb conversationally, as if it were an item on a grocery list we forgot to add. The torrent of rain stops all of a sudden. The corridor is filled with a hollow silence; there's nothing except an echo of the last sound I heard. *Oxford. Oxford.*

That queer, familiar distress threatens to overtake me again. There was more to her painting than just a hobby?

Surely not *that* Oxford? The real one?

My Sheila Bua?

A light flickers in the passage. It brightens the windowless corridor for a split second and transforms her into the faint outline of . . . a person. It's like I'm seeing her for the first time. Her gold necklace gleams like a beacon. The tiny bird pendant rises and falls with her breath.

We cousins have always wondered who gave Sheila Bua that necklace. It went missing once and she was distraught. No, distraught is an understatement: she was like a drunk mad horse. Turned out her loony-moony sister, my auntie Rama Bua (Aisha's mother), borrowed it and forgot it in the freezer, dangling on a mutton bone sticking out of a white plastic bag. Sheila Bua's fury at her sister that night is now family legend. Rama Bua's become even more forgetful since that night, but she's never dared to touch that necklace since. Nor has anyone else.

Maybe it was a gift from Uncle Balli to Sheila Bua? Not likely, because they aren't, to put it mildly, affectionate. And he's not the gift-giving kind. He's the not-give-anything-to-anyone kind.

The hundred-year-old cement roof above us leaks a little. Four thick rain drops splat on my head and run down my face. I wipe them away.

Poor Sheila Bua.

To my astonishment, that thought appears with no warning inside my head. Folks my age don't feel sorry for their elders. Why, we barely think of them as real people.

"Never mind me; think about that poor lonely young man." She pauses at the door of the lift, watching its abysmally slow climb on the indicator.

"Who?"

"That Arnav boy."

My stomach clenches at his name. The urge to flee is so great, I rock back and forth on my heels simply to give my body some semblance of motion, just so my legs don't bolt or kick like a trapped donkey.

"How can you say that, Sheila Bua? You spoke to him for all of ninety seconds."

"If you were better matched physically, I'd fix you up with this Arnav boy in a jiffy." Of course. Arranged Marriage Rule No. 1: A marriage works only when the boy and girl are physically well matched. Matching personalities, or even blood groups (sacrilege!) can go to the dogs.

"It's not allowed anyway."

"What is not allowed?"

"Datin . . . I mean, marrying a colleague. I'd have to give up my job if something were to happen." I have to say "not allowed." Simply saying it's "frowned upon" won't work; she'll take it as a personal challenge to fix me up with a colleague.

She opens her mouth as if to say something, but I preempt her. "Come on, Bua, you know how hard it was to get into this company. Into this team. I had to go through three rounds of interviews before I got hired."

"Hein? What does that mean?"

"That means I'm good at what I do. And I want to keep doing it and earning my own money and being independent. So not him, okay? Please?"

She pauses in the corridor, outside the crisscross bars of the lift. She peers down the empty shaft. Thick wires go up and down silently, helping the elevator in its journey. "Achcha? I suppose . . . oh well, let it be."

What?

An empty lift comes to a jangling stop on our floor.

Let it be? I can't believe my luck. An eligible male and female within her sight, and she isn't pursuing it because I might lose my job and waste all the hard work I've put in? Is she ill?

"Hmm. Now let me think, who could be a good fit for this boy—"

Not ill at all.

She doesn't let up, does she?

The tagline blazes inside my head like a firecracker:

Affixer Glue.
Sticky Like Your Relatives.
#stickylikeyourrelatives

Yes! I can feel a tingling excitement all over me. The eighteen- to twenty-four-year-olds will so lap this up. I immediately start typing an email on my phone to Parth, our intern. He needs to fit the slogan into the new creatives and keep it ready for me to check so Phase Two can start as soon as tomorrow. I need to finish this shopping or whatever this is ASAP so I can get back to work.

"Chalo, chalo, Bua, hurry or my lunchtime will be over and then I won't be able to come with you!"

"Oh yes, yes. He's waiting for us."

"Who is waiting? What are we doing exactly?" I follow her into the small rickety lift.

"Arre, didn't your mother tell you? I told her I would pick you up on the way. We are going to Pandit Verma, the famous astrologer from Byculla!" She says this with a flourish as if revealing a much-awaited masterpiece. "We will finally know the reason why no proposals are working out for you, even with such a nice salary."

CHAPTER SIX

Here we are, in the back of beyond called Byculla, where Pandit Verma the astrologer lives. Apparently he is a specialist, you know, like those doctors with MDs? He clears faults in people's stars. And since I've seen three boys with no results so far there must be some dosh in my stars, no?

Technically, Byculla is a suburb of South Bombay, you know, the hip SoBo. Technically. But nothing is glitzy or shiny. Everything around us is small, rusted, or abandoned. It's only lunchtime and Byculla is close to my office, so plenty of time to finish up with this astrologer and go back to work, change out of these sad khakis and red blouse into something nicer before I leave for the reunion late in the evening. I have a bunch of options that I brought to work in an extra tote bag. That magenta dress with little pink butterflies? Maybe not. It's too snug. Maybe the blue one with the pink whorls. Blue and pink automatically put me in a good mood. That dress has some give, not like the magenta one, which was Mum's gift.

Sheila Bua's large chauffeured SUV navigates a sea of cars in a lane surrounded by empty petrochemical factories. The factory workers may have long since gone but the stink of decayed chemicals lingers on and sneaks into our air-conditioned vehicle. Sheila Bua, in the meantime, is on a speaker call with her husband for purely domestic reasons.

"—Yes. We are on our way to show Zoya's horoscope to the astrologer. Zoya beta, say hello to your Uncle. He's calling from Pune." Sheila Bua beams with her latest iPhone on speaker mode.

"Err . . . hello, Uncle."

"Hmm," he grunts, acknowledging my presence with sound, before directing the conversation toward Sheila Bua in short, sharp barks. "Come to Rakesh's house for lunch tomorrow. I will arrive there straight from Pune. He has invited the family for a pre-birthday celebration. And our new business partner is coming, so you need to be there to entertain his wife." If you didn't know him, you'd think Uncle Balli was a cigar-smoking, rasping mafia don on the phone. Instead, he's small-eyed and limps, with bony hands constantly tucked into the pockets of his dull brown trousers.

"But . . . when did that get decided?" she says, flustered.

"Now he needs to ask *you* before making his decisions?" He voice is scathing, like a whip.

"I didn't mean that." She gets even more flustered, swallowing rapidly. "I don't think I can . . . could you ask him to do it the day after . . ."

"No."

"But tomorrow is . . ." Her face seems to close in upon itself. ". . . February 29th . . ." she says, her voice tapering into a whisper.

"So what?"

"That's the day I lost my bab . . ." Her face is frozen, unable to utter the word. "I spend the morning at the temple and volunteer at the children's clinic . . ."

There is not even a moment's pause on the other end. "High time for this nonsense to end. Rakesh's home for lunch tomorrow." Click.

The AC turns the car into a little ice box. Other frozen boxes like ours zip past on wet roads, honking and leaving a shower of muddy water in their wake.

She turns her face to the car window. A blip of a sob slips out of her mouth and it's like déjà vu. I've heard that that pitiful morsel of a cry before, at the very end. When I was nine. I'd rushed out of the lift in the brightly lit hallway outside our apartment, swinging a wooden cricket bat twice my size after a riotous game with my building friends. I was just about to walk through the door, which was slightly open, when a wail from inside stopped me in my tracks.

"—Gone . . . all of them . . . *Gone!*" Sheila Bua's breath sounded like it struggled to find a way outside her throat.

"What happened, didi, what is gone?" Pa pleaded. I stepped closer and peered in.

"My life's work. Gone. It's all gone." She was slumped in the middle of the living room floor clutching a pile of ashen papers to her chest as if clutching a dead child. A piece of thick white paper with burnt edges slipped and landed at her feet. It was a scrap of painting: a bird swirling in gold and aqua hues, abruptly chopped from its sky by jagged black ends.

Mum and Pa tried to hold her up, to stop her from collapsing further. I couldn't tell if they recognized any of her paintings, piled there in gray.

"Destroyed . . . all of it," she sobbed.

"But who would do that?"

"Your *precious* brother-in-law and his mother!" The words slashed out of her mouth like a blade. "How could he . . . how *could* he—?"

Pa looked angrier at Sheila Bua than at the burnt art.

"Sheila didi, sambhalo. Get a hold of yourself. Why were you painting again? And after you promised not to! You know that some of those paintings were not respectable."

"—what will people say if they saw—"

"—but my work . . . my *life* . . ." Her smooth unlined face was scrunched up in pain.

I don't know how long I stood outside the door, but it was long enough, till her terrible wails subsided into wretched little yips, like the one I hear in the car. I guess today is a day for old memories. This one, of seeing Sheila Bua, my formidable Sheila Bua, broken, is so clear I can still smell the sweat and feel the scratched wood of the bat handle.

The rage I feel now takes me by surprise. It sneaks inside my body like a biker snaking through clogged streets on his motorcycle. I see myself, gripping the handle of the cricket bat, taking it from my nine-year-old self and smashing Uncle Balli's face with it again and again and again.

D'Mello, as if he can feel the heated rage emanating, turns the AC to full blast. I focus on the back of D'Mello's greasy head, the strands of gray from his crown to the nape of his dark neck and breathe. I ask, "Do you still paint, Sheila Bua? Sometimes?"

It's like I've physically hit her. She flinches and her face closes up in an instant.

"No."

She stares transfixed at the line of food stalls that zip by on the street outside and that dead little answer cracks a hole in my heart.

The car screeches to a halt near an old decrepit little mill, now a housing society. As usual, D'Mello waits silently for us to disembark so he can park the SUV in a shaded spot, recline his seat, and listen to '60s jazz on FM radio. This tiny lane bustles with what seems to be the entire population of India and China combined. Pandit Verma's fossilized building is across from what I usually call fish paradise—several miniature shacks that sell fried, spiced fish. But what is wrong with the fish today? My stomach heaves at the smell as we walk through. Maybe it's stale?

The astrologer's home office is on the first floor, up a flight of broken stairs. When we arrive, he's perched behind a wooden desk in the middle of a small room surrounded by a stack of papers and idols of various gods and goddesses. And looks rather like Cousin Itt from the Addams family, if Cousin Itt was clad in white muslin. "So, this is your niece? Hmm." He gestures to me in a squealy nasal voice as we take our seats across the table, my horoscope unfolded on his desk.

"Yes, Panditji! Please tell us what is going on. Why hasn't any boy liked her yet?" Sheila Bua looks to him in appeal.

"Hmmm. That Saturn has messed with her life." He peers into the little scrap of paper, my future in grids and circles that no sane person can decipher. "That naughty boy Saturn is very stubborn and must be *coerced* into doing what we want." Hip-hop hymns echo in the background, musically threatening you with purgatory.

"If your niece fasts for twenty-four Saturdays, I guarantee she'll find a diamond of a husband!"

"A diamond merchant husband?"

"No, no. I meant a boy as good as a real diamond. Something big is coming in her life! Hmm. I see something else." He peers intently at the little parchment. "Maybe a big announcement, a big change perhaps, I don't know, but something *big*."

Maybe it's about the glue campaign? The Phase One metrics were off the charts. Please let Arnav Sir recommend me!

"So, Sheilaji, how are things with you now? Did you get that *thing* sorted—" A loud crash thunders in the apartment next door, several steel utensils land all at once on a tiled floor.

Sheila Bua squeaks in alarm and cuts him off before he can resume. "Panditji! I have a thousand rupees I would like to donate toward your services."

"Oh! How generous!" He practically froths. "God bless you and your family. Yes, you can keep it at the feet of the gods in my little temple in the next room."

Wait though, what *thing*?

"Come on, Zoya. Let's go. Come on, child, be quick." She prods my back to spur me on. "What are your plans for the rest of the day? Do you want to come shopping with me? There's a new shop in the mall right behind Crawford Market, with lovely colored fabrics. There's so many shades of yellow to choose from." She says the last sentence with a twinkle in her eyes, and a sing-song voice as we climb into her SUV, as if yellow was a physical thing like candy to be dangled in front of me.

I used to shop with Sheila Bua when I was younger. Wait, let me rephrase that. I used to shop often with my Magic Bua when I was younger. I would tag along with her on my summer break, when Mum was at work. Sheila Bua would grab hold of my hand to make sure I didn't get lost in the crowd, and dive into a sea of tiny ordinary-looking stores and suddenly we'd come upon a little shop that no one knew existed, except for her. She would give me a secret smile, we'd walk inside, and my heart would stop. It was like entering Aladdin's cave filled with treasures: antiques, paintings, artifacts, mysterious-looking globes, giant golden clocks, armchairs with swirly handles that looked like they came straight from a palace. To me, *she* was a part of the treasures, the light of the store illuminating her into a giant aura, turning her into a magical being radiating light, my Magic Bua.

I loved going with Sheila Bua to unusual places, off the beaten path. And she'd never tell me to sit like a lady or not touch the treasures, stuff that kids are told. When I was with her, I could sit as I wanted, do what my heart desired; I was free to be.

"I'd like to, Sheila Bua, but . . ." To my surprise, I realize that I really would. She'd totally buy me an expensive dress without a second thought. She does that, for all us cousins. ". . . but I have a ton of work to do before I leave for . . ."

"Leave? To go where?" Sheila Bua asks.

Oops. Better not tell her about the reunion. If I show up with my matchmaking auntie, I'll never live it down. It's like bringing a hungry lion into a house filled with meat.

The car comes to a stop outside the bustling street of my office building. Groups of formally dressed people stroll lazily on their post-lunch walks near buildings and shops and restaurants.

"Home. Before I leave for home. My boss has given me so much work, and he's so . . . bossy."

"Oh, bossy-fossy! He's lonely, that's what he is. I'll find a nice girl for him, don't you worry."

"I'm not worried, trust me. His loneliness is the least of my worries. Okay, Bua, I really have to go."

"Well, if you say so. Since you're not coming, maybe I should go and visit the galle . . ." She shuts up as if she's said too much and starts foraging into the deep recesses of her lime-green purse. Yes, you remember correctly: the same hideous lime-green one with pictures of prospective grooms and brides. I would've totally asked her what "galle" was, but three emails bing on my phone, all from our new intern, all with the same subject in scary capitals: HELP!!!!

"Really, really got to go, Bua! Bye!" I rush into the office building, Sheila Bua forgotten in the car.

* * *

After Sheila Bua dropped me off, I spent the afternoon cleaning up a nice little mess, thanks to our newest baby-faced intern, Parth, who reports to me because, you know, Associate Director and all. He would've reported to Arnav Sir but he conveniently foisted Parth on to me. A promotion just means you get to do what your boss doesn't want to.

Anyway, back to Parth. All he had to do was add the slogan into the banner. A simple copy and paste. And what does he do, even after I spent hours training him on this exact same thing last week? He inputs it crooked. Half a frigging inch off, which messes up the space around the logo. And he saves it, replacing the original design. Why? Because he was distracted listening to Radio Mirchi—*Rain Songs* with Chai & Pakoras on his phone, while texting his girlfriend. (Yes, that's a real show and no, the tea and fried fritters are in name only.) He also has zero experience with our design software to fix this.

But little Parth begged me not to tell Arnav Sir. His parents and the boss are family friends; he almost crashed on my desk in relief when I said Arnav Sir was out at a client's. I redid the creative, which took me a full five hours with a hurriedly gobbled canteen lunch, and sent him home with a Kit Kat from my stash. (A new box. Which I didn't buy. This is the second time it's happened. I really must check with HR on why they keep stocking my Kit Kats.)

And Parth's mishap is also why I still have to get changed for the reunion, which starts in an hour. I'll be fashionably late. Good. I've never been "fashionably" anything.

I rush to the bathroom, yank my clothes off in a stall and put on the sky-blue dress with light pink whorls. Okay, hair: curls left loose—done; makeup: pressed powder—done; cherry lipstick—done; black eyeliner—damn it, one eyelid is thicker than the other, but no time to clean up, so now I have to make the other one just as thick. Hmm. The thick lines make me look sultry. Thank God the office is empty.

I zip out of the bathroom, which is outside the lobby, dangling my little beige party purse, when I collide straight into Arnav Sir in the corridor.

"I'm sorry. I didn't see—" He tears his eyes away from his phone with great reluctance, and then stops in his tracks. "Going someplace special, Zoya?" He pauses just before saying my name.

Damn the eyeliner. "Yes, a party. Kind of." I stretch my dress at the waist, suck in my stomach, and try to stem the curls springing up like wild plants behind my ears. "It's my school reunion."

"So, a proper party then. Not kind of."

"You know what school reunions are like."

"Not really. My dad was in the army, so we moved around a lot." His gaze, usually direct, is now aimed behind me, at the office lobby doors and the empty office inside. "I guess I didn't really stick around at any school long enough to go to reunions." His eyes are dull, like dim, faraway stars.

All I can manage is a pathetic little "Oh." It's so different from my childhood; the same comforting suburb, the same school friends and building friends and neighborhood friends, a life lived within a two-kilometer radius.

A gray vista of isolation opens up in front me: a thin, curly-haired teenager sits alone on a bench near the canteen eating his lunch (probably chicken cutlets; kids are shown eating cutlets with ketchup in old commercials). His beach eyes are dull as he stares at the other kids walking away from him to sit in groups of their own, laughing, talking, and sharing each other's lunches.

Yes, okay, I know, filmy and dramatic, but my heart hurts for him. The perils of discovering that your boss is human.

"Would you . . . umm . . ."

Don't say it, don't.

"Would you . . ." Oh God. Stop me, someone, stop me! ". . . like to come to my reunion? I'm planning to hang around just for an hour or so, and then head home."

His eyes are back on me in a flash. Why is he always so poker faced? I can't tell if he's pissed or just doesn't care right now. All is silent; the tube light in the corridor doesn't crackle, the lift doors don't rattle, the lobby is quiet behind us.

"No one will eat you up, I promise." I giggle, trying to fill the awkward and twitchy silence. Oh God, Zoya, just bloody put a sock in your mouth. Why are you still asking your boss to the reunion when he has shown no interest, no interest at all?

"Thank you. You're very . . . kind." He looks like he's about to cry or vomit. Good. I mean, good that his face is somewhat expressive, so I vaguely know what he feels. Do I really? Is he sad, happy, grateful to be asked? "I should be heading home right now. Splitting headache. And the rain and humidity doesn't help my sinus."

Ah. Neither sad nor happy. Just indifferent. And it's not like I was asking him on a *date*. I just felt bad for him, my feelings are certainly not injured. I have *no* feelings regarding him.

His hand is already on the shiny handle of the office door. As if he can't wait to get away from me. He squints his eyes, rubbing his temples so hard it's a wonder his brow doesn't stay wrinkled. He may have a headache, I grant him that. Someone who speaks only when necessary is bound to have a throbbing head after a whole day of client meetings. "Okay," I say, breezier than I feel.

"I have to take off." Why does this feel like a personal rejection? The urge to say "go eff yourself" to him bobs dangerously in my mouth. For God's sake, Zoya.

"Yeah, I stopped by to pick up some papers. I'll head home in a few, too. See you on Monday." He turns to go back inside the office but stops and looks back at me. "And thank you, Zoya. For asking me."

There. That pause again, as if he's amused at my name. Maybe I do amuse him, you know, in my party dress and thick eyeliner. I'm always fidgety when I wear a dress; it feels like everyone stares at my midsection. I know I'm projecting, but still. "Umm. Sure. See you Monday."

He walks away from me, back into the still-lit office. I leave in the other direction toward the crisscross doors of the lift at the end of the shadowy corridor.

In hindsight, it's a good thing he isn't coming, and I don't know what came over me to ask him. Imagine showing up with your boss at your reunion, and one who looks, well, you know. Not your average handsome, but tie loosened, sleeves rolled up, lean-mean-brooding type. More than enough to spike estrogen levels. Peehu and Aisha ask me for his pictures on our girls-only WhatsApp group all the time, especially his tired corporate look. You send them *one* picture (cropped from a team photo; as if I would take secret pictures of my boss!) and they want you to tip over the entire can of worms. Peehu even asked me if I had more pictures from different angles. What the actual fuck? Yup, totally good thing he declined to come.

* * *

One train, three weird stomach cramps, and sixty minutes later, I reach the brightly lit assembly hall hosting the Second Five-Year Reunion of Saint Theresa's High School, sandwiched between St. Theresa's Church and the Prarthna Samaj Vishnu Temple. The racket, though, could be heard a mile away. NSYNC, Beyoncé, Lady Gaga, Britney Spears. Plus all the Bollywood hit songs from the last twenty years, greasy, spicy food, strobe lights, cheap booze, and a questionable AC that switches on and off every twenty minutes to save energy and money.

And . . . 3, 2, 1 . . . "What are you up to these days, Zoya?"

The questioner is Amaya Banerjee, who installs herself next to me. Head Prefect back in the day. Stylish in her skinny jeans, sequined dress top, and movie-star hair, looking like a million bucks as always.

If taken at face value, this phrase seems utterly mild and brims with polite curiosity, a placid conversation starter in most situations. But all questions at reunions are traps. This one in particular, asked by a flourishing twenty-seven-year-old-wife-and-mother to a decaying-twenty-six-year-old, who is *none* of those things, attracts others to the conversation like maggots to a carcass.

Plus let's not forget, she married a young textile tycoon before her CPA exams and now has a six-month-old son. And by the looks of her glamorous tummy bulge, another one on the way.

"What do you do, Zoya?" Amaya Banerjee, the perfect Prefect, asks.

"I work at Mosaic Inc. The marketing and ad agency? Yes, the same one. I run marketing campaigns for a bunch of products. And I was recently promoted to Associate Director."

"That's great! I love to hear about people from our school doing so well!" Amaya rubs her large tummy in irritation. "I need to sit down somewhere. No one tells you that you'll always be fatigued when pregnant. So, what does your husband do?" She asks, sipping fresh watermelon juice from a white plastic glass.

And why wouldn't a spouse be in full existence or hovering on the horizon by this age? A large diamond mocks me like a beacon from her ring finger.

"Oh, I'm still looking."

"But . . . haven't you been looking for a while now?" she blurts, confused and horrified at her faux pas all at once. About two and a half months now, but how the hell did she know? At that very moment, my cousin Tanya, the designer-wearing witch, comes sashaying toward us. Of course. She has her twin sidekicks in tow, all of them in identical skinny jeans and sequined blouses, like some kind of *Mean Girls* parody, holding their plastic glasses as daintily as if they were champagne flutes. Never have I seen a better match between a movie title and real people.

Punjabi Relations 101: If any of your cousins happen to live nearby, the family will herd you all like cattle into the same school so "the kids can look out for each other." Translation: extra pairs of eyes on you and your shenanigans, which will be reported back to the mother ship, because one cousin is bound to be a mommy's boy/girl/snitch. Or your shenanigans reported from the mother ship back to school.

In my case, that snitch is my cousin Tanya.

"Bargain dress, of course," Tanya titters, towering over me. "Hope it's stretchy."

"It is, don't you worry." Hold on. Is she wearing black nail paint? Tanya? Whose mother never lets her wear any color darker than baby pink because "a lady's nails are always understated, not in-your-face"?

"What's this?" I grab her hand to hold it up for others to see. "How did Rita Chachi ever let you out with black nail polish?" Fine, weak retort, but I can never think straight when irritated. She looks alarmed and closes her fist, as if to hide her nails, or to punch me, then thinks better of it, unfurls her slender fingers and gazes at her nails. "This? Just experimenting with my . . . look. Something *you* wouldn't know."

"Come, Tanya, join us. We were just talking about husbands," Amaya says. Great, just great.

"Were you? Then what is Zoya doing in this conversation?" She smirks.

Have I told you just how much I'd like to smack her across those rouge-lathered cheeks?

Her phone bings with a text. That special sing-songy one. She gives it a cursory glance and shoves it back viciously inside her clutch.

Aha. Looks like the special boyfriend is special no more. Tanya's face falls like she's about to cry. What's that about? She looks more upset than any other break-up. One of the mean girl sidekicks immediately hands Tanya her own plastic glass and says, "Drink this, babe, it'll help you forget that jerk." Tanya chugs the entire contents of the plastic glass and walks off, all snoot and smugness, in the direction of Fardeen, her ex-boyfriend from an era ago. Maybe not so upset after all. The sidekicks decide to give her privacy and disperse into the dancing crowd.

Amaya, in the meantime, continues to grill me. "Tell me, Zoya, and as an old friend, you know that I have your best interest at heart . . ." Her voice drops and she leans in close, her clean manicured palm on my thankfully waxed arm, in a gesture of sympathy. "If you're still looking for grooms, is there a *problem*? We can catch it early and remedy it."

They really should hand out Valium at reunions.

A gaggle of obscure girlfriends join the conversation mid-chat, a mix of flowery perfumes and whiskey breath.

"Ooh, Amaya! Congratulations! Look at you!"

"When did you find out?"

"I was two weeks late . . . and when your period is late, what do you think of first?" Amaya giggles, rubbing her stomach.

Late?

Something stirs in my brain over the rum and Coke, over Saturn and Sheila Bua and my flip-flopping stomach aches. I break out into a cold sweat as I fumble through the calendar on my phone. The last time I got my period was—

The dim room swirls. Celine Dion croons with a desperate edge to her voice as if her life depends upon her pitch.

"I was always so exhausted in the first three months! And I couldn't eat a thing!" Amaya places a slender hand on her well-rounded bosom. "I love fish so much but the mere thought of it was enough to send me rushing to the toilet!" They giggle together like a collective pregnant consciousness.

My hands shake and my heart stops. The plastic glass slips from my sweaty fingers and lands on the floor in a puddle of rum, Coke, and footprints. Voices go back and forth; they mimic the dizzy strobe lights that flash around the dark room. "Are you okay, Zoya?" Amaya touches my arm.

A smoke-filled bedroom. An unshaved pothead. Fatigue. Fish.

Two weeks late.

No. It cannot be.

I stumble away, turn and run.

Thank God, Tanya was busy with her group of friends in a dark corner somewhere. How I got out of that blasted reunion without that gossipy gaggle of girls on my tail, I'll never know, but I escaped into the blessed smog and sweat on the street outside. Someone, *please* tell me it's all just a nightmare.

CHAPTER SEVEN

I tried to call Raunak but got his voice mail; God knows which part of Europe he's screwing around in and for God knows how long. Like he would help even if he were here. He'd just say "You figure it out" in his smoke-filled sneer as if it was my bloody fault and then hang up and light a joint. That asshole.

Breathe, just breathe. All is not lost.

Yet.

No!

No, I cannot be. I *cannot* be *preg—*. No. Don't even say the word. Do not. Nope. Not at all.

A police jeep whizzes past the cars and hawkers and crowds, its siren on full blast. Its earsplitting sound is nothing compared to the screams inside my head right now.

Okay, think, think. There can be many reasons for a missed period, can't there? Anemia? Low blood count? Something to do with hormones? There's such a thing as low hormones, isn't there? ISN'T THERE?

Pandit Verma's hairy face flashes before my eyes and I hear all over again, "Something big is coming in your life."

What the hell have I done?

I squeeze my eyes shut and will my uterus to be empty. Hell, I've never used words like uterus before. Why would I use such words? I'm not married so it hasn't taken on national importance yet. I forget to suck in my stomach and my muscles feel different, looser, which is so alien that I'm convinced I'm . . . no! Don't. Please, God, Universe, whoever you are, wherever you are, I'll do *anything*. I'll fast for forty-eight Saturdays instead of twenty-four, I'll walk barefoot to far-off temples, I'll light uterus-shaped candles in every church in Bombay, and fast even when it's not Ramzan. Just. Make me. Not. Pregnant.

"Excuse me? Are you okay? You, the girl in the blue dress." A group of excited forty-something couples gather around me under the crude yellow streetlights, presumably on their after-dinner walk.

"Err . . . yes . . . I'm . . . okay." I've stood still for so long that flies buzz around my head, some settling on it as if I were a statue. Who the hell cares about flies?

The group looks unconvinced and passes odd glances at each other. "You've been standing at this corner under the lamppost for ten minutes now," one of the men says. He reeks of deodorant, which makes me want to hurl this afternoon's hurriedly gobbled butter chicken pasta into a puddle at his feet. "Do you need help crossing the road?" Yes, far away from you.

A stern woman with a chic bob jerks him away from me. The wife. She waves a palm in front of my eyes. "Well, she doesn't seem blind."

Another one thrusts her eager saggy face into the middle of the congregation. "Check if she's hypnotized!"

"What nonsense you talk! Hypnotized, indeed."

"Arre, you never know. I read in the paper about young girls being hypnotized and kidnapped . . ." The wide-eyed woman comes close and snaps her fingers in my face.

Maybe I *am* hypnotized and someone will snap me out of this nightmare.

"Do you want us to accompany you to a hospital?" A third nudges her swarthy husband, who whistles loud for a rickshaw.

The sharp shriek of the whistle snaps me right out of the funk. "Oh no, no, I'm alright. I think I'm getting my . . . umm . . . is there a chemist nearby?"

"Oh! Yes, of course." Their bodies relax at once. That time of the month, they nod to each other, relieved I haven't said the word "period" out loud. The men are suddenly interested in the plaque of an ancient building behind them and the women speak in hushed voices as if using a normal voice could suddenly bring a horde of disapproving policemen at their door. What would happen if I told them about being two weeks late? *Unwed?* Then they'd actually have to acknowledge the existence of sex without marriage. All of society would have to officially acknowledge the existence of sex without marriage. And then where would we be? Would these fine people be so solicitous then, to a so-called slut? A woman disgraced?

They shove me into the rickshaw, the collective women, in a sort of protective distaste, as if they could catch my germs. "Bhaiyya, go to Khar Gymkhana, there's a nice chemist nearby."

Khar Gymkhana? Too bloody close to my school, my home, to Sheila Bua, to my whole life. Every shopkeeper within a two-kilometer radius in Khar knows my family.

"Bhaiyya, take it to Bandra," I whisper to the rickshaw driver, as the auto slices through the humanity that mills around late evening lights. The Bandra area is far enough away into safety. It would be the disaster of the century if even a hint of this leaks to anyone remotely connected to my family.

Pregnant and unmarried.

The epitome of slut-ness in Indian society.

Mothers will snatch their daughters from my path; they won't allow them within five feet of me lest my slut-ness rubs off. And marriage? Especially arranged marriage? Hah! Perish the thought! Because Arranged Marriage Rule No. 2: The girl *must* be chaste, no matter how wanton the boy is. Chaste, as in minimal number of boyfriends, zilch being the optimum count. And none of those distasteful "affairs" either, which is just as worse. And no affair/boyfriend = the most virginal of golden nymphs for their beloved son. Oh, what was that you asked? What about someone pregnant out of wedlock or someone who had an abortion? Goodness gracious; why on earth would we pollute our family with *such* a girl?

I won't be fired from my job, of course, discrimination laws and all that, but offices are made up of the same people who inhabit the country, and they will find a way to sideline me. If this gets out, my parents, my entire family, no one will *ever* be able to show their faces in society for a long, long, long time. Hindi swear words from 1950s movies swirl in my muddled head: *Kalmoohi! Kulta! You've tarnished our honor! Better you had died!* Okay, not those exact words, but you get the gist. I will be *that girl*, reviled for eternity. She Who Must Not Be Named.

I will be Voldemort.

Oh God.

Oh God.

The rattling auto reaches Bandra too soon, screeches to a stop at the curbside too soon. Where the *fuck* is Bombay's traffic when you need it? There it sits, the white board of Lucky Chemist and Pharmacy, Now Open 24 Hours! with the red medical cross, as if of no great importance. It sits nestled between a jewelry store that looks like the sun exploded inside and a tobacco-cigarette shack.

Lucky Chemist. Yes. Please, all the luck you can give me. And a pregnancy kit.

The inside of the shop is silent for a brief moment, protected from the beeps and blares of the street outside. The hum of the AC seems almost reverential.

"Oh, hello, hello, hello! May I help you, young lady?" A cheery old shopkeeper appears from an inner room, blasting through the silence with a face so shriveled it makes you wonder if he stood a tad too long under the shower.

"Umm . . . I need . . . umm . . ." The bitterness of chemicals almost makes me gag. Everything frigging makes me gag.

"Yes?"

". . . need a . . ."

"Yyyeess?" He stretches each syllable as if I were five and we were both part of some giant fun exercise which would result in a "well done!" and a lollipop at the end.

". . . need a . . . Benadryl!"

(Oh, come on, it's *way* tougher than you'd think!)

"Of course! And would you need some . . . err . . . ladies' products? We have all the brands. Kotex, Stayfree, Whisper, Carefree." He rattles off the names as if reading a specials menu in a restaurant. Can these chemist people *see* PMS on our faces, or do they just offer pads by default to every woman who walks into their store? He waits for my answer, adjusting the row of tablet strips, talcum powder, and medicine bottles on the open shelves behind him.

Because I'm a complete wuss, I've accumulated, let's see, six strips of Crocin paracetamol, three bottles of Benadryl, two bottles of Pond's talcum powder, and a ginormous pack of Kotex Maxi Super Pads, which will possibly last me through menopause. Oh, and zero pregnancy kits.

Come on, Zoya, come on! Time is of the essence. I rub my eyes hard—what was that kit I saw on TV, the one with coy women and gleeful men?

"You kids are so tired all the time." The chemist empties his little glass of chai in one deep swig. "These modern companies work you to the bone. Don't you worry," he says in a singsong voice. "I'll throw in a strip of vitamin C— free—just for you. Work-life balance is the key. Today is all you have!"

Good God. A caffeinated shopkeeper doling out life lessons. *No thank you, Uncle, I'm bang in the middle of a big lesson right now.*

Yes! Got it! i-Can! That's the home test kit.

"Could I also have a . . ."

"Don't be afraid to ask, child. Fear is just an illusion."

Good grief.

"Could I have . . . a, err . . . i-Can p . . . pregnancy test?"

"Oh! Oh, of course. Well, well. Congratulations, young lady!" He beams and strains his wrinkled neck to look at the empty space behind me. "No one's come with you in this condition? Mother? Mother-in-law? Husband?"

"He . . . they . . . on their way . . ."

The chatty salesman vanishes in a poof of suspicion at the absent family members. "Hmm, okay." His voice is flat, and his bushy brows are drawn in. He moves two steps away from the glass counter that separates us, as if I'm loaded with airborne slut germs that could infect the susceptible females in his family by remote association.

A sudden blast of warm air snakes into the air-conditioned shop and sends a shiver down my spine. A presence looms behind me, a ghost.

"May I have two strips of aspirin, please?" The ghost's voice, painfully familiar, booms inside the quiet little shop.

Or you know, just my doom. Or my boss, Arnav Sir. Same thing.

Come the HELL on, God!

The furred lines on the shopkeeper's brow disappear all of a sudden. The chatty uncle is back in a flash. It's frightening how he switches personalities. And how, how, how the *fuck* did I forget my boss lives in this very area?

"Of course, Sir. Two aspirins coming up," the chemist says before heading to the storeroom at the back. "Glad you showed up. You shouldn't be sending your wife here alone. In her condition."

The store is silent like a tomb, except the death rattle of the AC.

"Reunion ended early, Zoya?"

My voice is dead. My breath is dead. *I* am dead.

"Yes . . . hello," I squeak. I cannot turn and look directly at him. I can't or my eyes might smoke. I remain looking straight ahead at our caffeinated philosophical chemist.

"Are you . . . alright?" He steps up beside me.

No, I'm not, you idiot. The chemist thinks we're married and I'm pregnant. With your child.

"I've been better."

He rubs his forehead, squeezing his eyes shut. Ah, the headache still persists. "Definitely ready for the weekend."

Maybe his headache is so bad he'll take the aspirin and disappear. Maybe he has a rickshaw waiting and doesn't want to pay an additional twenty rupees. Maybe someone added an extra zero to an invoice and the client blew his top and he has to leave like right now. Maybe he didn't hear what the chemist said.

One can hope, right?

"Did . . . did that chemist think I was your . . . that we were—?" Arnav Sir tilts his head towards me, his face blank.

"Here you go, Sir." The old uncle trudges back from the storeroom. "Your aspirin strips. That will be seven hundred rupees."

"*Seven* hundred? For two strips of aspirin?" Arnav Sir's eyes widen, his voice astounded. "What's in it, cocaine?"

"Oh no, Sir. We don't sell coc . . . that stuff." The shopkeeper stiffens, affronted. "We're a respectable establishment." He thwacks the black calculator on the glass desk, his brow furrowed. "Now, let's see. There's the aspirin. And six strips of Crocin, three Benadryls, two bottles of talcum powder, a packet of Kotex Maxi Super Pads. And one preg—"

Holy Almighty, no!

"UNCLE!" I yelp. "I'll pay for all that myself." I hold the edge of the counter so hard my palms are etched with deep groves. I'd bolt like a hare if I wasn't holding on to something solid.

"You kids of today. Your money and my money, indeed! Oh well, well. Such a nice couple you both are. But why such a height and weight difference between you two, eh?" He chuckles. "Ah, I know! Must be a love marriage, not an arranged one, no?"

Arnav Sir's hands stop mid-head massage.

"Cash or card, Uncle?" My voice is so high-pitched it's a wonder the glass shelves haven't cracked yet. "I'm in a bit of a hurry!"

"Cash is so much better, thank you. Oh, I almost forgot. Here is your pregnancy test, Mrs. . . . ?"

Bajaj, I want to say, Mrs. Bajaj, whoever she may be, but the earth jerks to a halt. Or I implode upon myself and the only thing left of me is a dark nothing. A possibly pregnant nothing.

This dark nothing is devoid of sound. Except a sharp intake of breath. Behind me.

The pregnancy test sits on the glass counter, so innocent. The words i-Can gleam in bold red letters under the tube light. Before

I can grab the test and shove it into my beige purse, the chemist stuffs everything together into one plastic bag. Even the aspirin. *Damn it.* A shrill screech of brakes makes me jump. A crash averted outside. Please let that be a sign!

"Now, do you both have a good obstetrician?" The chemist beams at us, as if it were his bloody grandchild. "Have you seen Dr. Kashyap? You won't even know when the baby's born, she's wonderful. How long have you two been trying to conceive?"

The voice behind me purrs pure ice. "I didn't know we were . . . trying."

This is it, isn't it? This is the moment I die. I don't dare meet his eyes, lest I combust into flames. (I hope I *do* combust into flames.) His gaze burns the back of my neck. God, what must that chemist uncle think right now? That I can have sex with my husband but can't look at him?

My skin tingles at epic levels as Arnav Sir inches closer, places a lean arm around my shoulders and says, "Come . . . *darling.* Let's go . . . home."

I can only manage a choked gasp.

"God bless you both. Hope you have a boy!"

CHAPTER EIGHT

The city rushes by in a shock of blinding light; cars, buses, motorbikes, almost crashing in their race to overtake one another on slick, wet roads. How long have I been standing outside the chemist's shop? How long have *we*?

A passerby dribbles a red spittle of paan on the building wall. I dodge it by default, even in my dazed state.

"I'm sorry that you were caught in the middle of . . . that the chemist thought we were . . ." That's all I can manage. My body and mind have shut down.

"It . . . happens, I guess."

No, it doesn't happen. I made it happen with my stupidity.

We linger at the edge of the sidewalk, waiting for the river of honking traffic to stop for the ten seconds needed to cross the main road. It's almost nine at night but the throng of people waiting to cross the street makes it appear as if it's peak evening time. Arnav Sir is behind me, close, so close. The warmth of his chest prickles my back, like a comforting heater, while the rest of my body shivers. For just a moment I want to sink into him and weep.

How can this happen to girls from good, decent families? Awful parents—that's what they'll say. Poor upbringing. Defective family.

No. Stop. This won't do. This is my problem and I need to deal with it. (And fast.)

What am I going to do? Where do I test this bloody kit, and what if I am . . . ? No. Can't think like that. It'll be negative, I'm sure. Yes. Just repeat, like Sheila Bua advises. Just positive statements. Like "I am thin and pretty" or that "Yuvi loves his Mummy more than his wife." *Not pregnant, not pregnant.*

But I can't help it. What if I am?

I've been walking and walking God knows where, and Arnav Sir seems to be walking along, sometimes beside me, sometimes behind me. The busy sidewalk is long gone. We're in a quiet dark lane, with parked cars and tall buildings with lit balconies that blot out the night sky. Large gulmohar trees cover the lane like a cloudy tent, their green leaves and orange flowers an indeterminate ghostly color under yellow streetlights. Wait, did my boss just give money to a bunch of deep-voiced transgenders dressed in colorful saris? They usually come to bless a new marriage. Or a new baby. Oh God.

Breathe slow and steady. Just like they taught in the yoga class Mum, Pa, and I took last year. It was our New Year's resolution to spend more time together as a family. Their smiling faces flash in front of my eyes and my stomach clenches so hard I almost fold over in pain. They don't deserve this, they don't deserve the ridicule that will follow: the censure, the taunts. I, who was supposed to make them proud, will cause them to hang their heads in shame.

I hear Arnav Sir shooing one of those lime-selling boys. "I have plenty of limes in my fridge, thank you." Who the hell cares about limes? I swear to every god on this effing planet that if the test is negative I will never, EVER do anything to jeopardize my family's reputation and the good, safe life they've given me. I will be the good girl, the best daughter in the whole bloody world, the Diamond Daughter! I'll do whatever they ask me to without question—

My screwy mind screeches to a halt. A visibly exhausted woman in a pink and grey salwar kameez, carrying a cloth bag filled with vegetables in one hand and a heavy laptop bag in another, bangs into me. She gives me an annoyed look and stomps through an open gate of a four-storied building.

Wait. We just passed an auditorium. What happened to the quiet lane with the gulmohar trees? Where the hell are we? And somehow, the white plastic bag filled with stuff from the chemist landed in Arnav Sir's hands, including my little party purse. When did that happen? My boss is carrying my purse. A feverish giggle tries to escape my throat.

Groups of costumed actors sit at chai stalls near the rough, gurgling sea. Sea? The thought spears through the fog in my brain. The chemist shop was nowhere near the sea. Hold on. That auditorium, isn't that Rang Sharada, the theater for staged plays? I stop in my tracks.

"You okay?" He asks. I almost say, *Are you effing crazy? I don't know where I am and there's a time bomb ticking inside the plastic bag you swing in your hand. Can't you hear its tick-tock? Just take your aspirin and go!*

Arnav Sir stops suddenly near a large creaking gate in front of a freshly painted building. His hand on the small of my back is warm, leading me toward the dim lobby.

"Why . . . where are . . . ?" I gaze at the crisscross bars of the elevator in a rising panic.

"My flat." His voice is a soft rumble not the boss-man's steel. "You need a place to . . . test. A safe place." The voice is softer, warmer. Human. Okay, stop, Zoya, you *cannot* cry. Not now.

Before I know it, we're in the clanging lift and rushing up to his apartment. To my doom. Or was Aman's apartment my doom? I'll know soon enough; five minutes, it said on the test packet.

"Don't worry. My flat is empty. My old cook is out for a week visiting his village." Arnav Sir leads me straight inside the empty flat without ceremony. "Do you want to . . . eat something?" He asks, more to break the crackling silence than to be the genial host. "I can order a veggie sandwich from the stall downstairs. With extra cheese." He smiles.

Can I cry now?

"I . . . no . . . thank you. I just . . . need . . ." I clear my throat to stop a sob from sneaking up. I would love for this building to collapse and be dead under a rubble of bricks and concrete.

He nods and points to a sliding door at the end of a corridor, and I rush toward it as if it were a train leaving the station that I must catch because who knows when the next one will come. I step inside his bedroom.

Even in my altered state of fucked-up mind, I realize the enormity of this. I'm in my boss's *bedroom*. Oh crap, I hope no one from the office finds out. They just need one tidbit to start a full-fledged rumor. And this room is shocking because despite my hurry, I notice it looks . . . normal. And peaceful with light blue walls. Not freaky clean as I expected. There's a pair of blue checkered pajamas looking all soft and crumply on the accent chair by the window. I thought Arnav Sir would be the kind of person who ironed his pajamas and would have no idea what an accent chair was, much less have a striped one in his bedroom. Just to tell you, I've never thought about his bedroom, really haven't, except for a general platonic wonderment, but here it is, all warm wood and color and coziness.

Zoya, get it together! Not the time to think about his pajamas or his home furnishings.

His bathroom is pristine, almost sparse. The pregnancy test gleams, the whiteness of its package blinding. I lock the door behind me. The click of the lock echoes in the silence. I almost shush it but there seems to be no air in my lungs.

This is it. The moment of truth. I tear the box open.

Okay, here goes.

I did my job.

Results in five minutes.

Five minutes will make or break my life. Time to start counting. One minute.

Tick tock, tick tock—why does Arnav Sir have a clock inside a *toilet*? Why am I even surprised?

I hear a doorbell's bing-bong.

Two minutes. Is that pee stick even bloody doing anything? Is there a line? Maybe I should shake it? Oh, for fuck's sake, there's a clock on it, too! If I could just eat something, I'd feel better. Does he have candy stashed behind the mirror door like me? Nope, just a green toothbrush and toothpaste, a razor, a bottle of shaving foam, and two strips of aspirin.

Aspirin? But didn't he just walk into the chemist shop twenty minutes ago to buy—

Three minutes. *Distract yourself, Zoya, distract.* How much did I spend in that chemist shop? 300 rupees + 250 + 134 . . . screw it, I can't figure this shit out, stupid phone calculator doesn't work, my fingers are so sweaty. And now I've bitten holes near the hem of my blue dress and toppled his razor and shaving foam bottle into the sink, making such a racket. Bloody hell.

"Zoya, are you okay in there?" I jump off the toilet, his voice is so clear. Almost as if he were right next to me.

"Yes, fine. Just dropped . . . err, something."

"What did you drop? Are you hurt?" I can hear his hand on the door handle.

Does he have anything in this bathroom for me to drop? I could say "your razor" but then he'd know I opened his private mirror. Even saying "your razor" in my head seems salaciously intimate. Shit.

"Just, err, my phone. I'm alright."

"Okay. Call out if you need anything." His feet tread softly on the tiled floor, away from the bathroom.

Four minutes. *Distract, distract.* Oh help, now I can't get off this bloody toilet, my legs seem chained to the floor. My blood has stopped pumping. And now Google thinks I'm having a heart attack. Google is right.

The pee stick sits on a side table by the toilet. I can't look at it. I can't. I can't. Maybe I should call Arnav Sir in to . . . OMG, no. Have I lost my mind? I have to look. There's no choice.

Okay, here goes. Moment of truth. Make or break.

Something big coming in your life.

You are their only child.

Defective family.

She Who Must Not Be Named.

How the fuck can you see the lines in this stupid dim light? What is it? ONE BLOODY LINE OR TWO?!!

One line on the right side marked C. What the fuck does that mean? POSITIVE OR NEGATIVE? Where are the instructions? Where?? There, phew! I suppose I put them there, on a *Pilates of the Caribbean* book behind the toilet bowl.

Why the hell do these instructions drone on *so* long? I don't want to read a bloody Jane Austen novel, I just want the result! Dear God, please! *Diamond Daughter!*

If you see one pink colored line along the right side marked "C," it indicates that your pregnancy test is negative.

I turn to the toilet and throw up.

* * *

My knees buckle, limp with relief. I don't know how long I've been on the cold tiled floor. And I don't know how long I've been crying.

I will never, EVER have pot in my life again. Or sex. Ever. I'll become a nun. Yes, that's it. The safest path for me—a pot-free, sex-free nun. Sister Zoya of Bandra Reclamation—

My phone springs into life all of a sudden.

So no one told you life was gonna be this way—

The volume of my *Friends* ringtone catapults me off the bathroom floor as if springing to the command of a military general. Sheila Bua's face flashes like a gargoyle on my mobile screen. It's like she'd been testing me all along and was calling to congratulate my passing.

Am I really expected to answer her call right now? In my boss's toilet after a pregnancy test?

"Are you okay, Zoya?" Arnav Sir knocks on the bathroom door again, his clear voice makes me jump some more.

"Yes . . . all okay!"

"Do you need . . . something? Anything?" If the phone wasn't distracting me, I'd burst into tears at his voice.

"No, no, I'll be right out."

Negative. Negative. Negative.

Chant like your life depends upon it. N-E-G-A-T-I-V-E.

Your life's a joke, you're broke—

What the hell, Sheila Bua? Stop calling me! Why doesn't she text like other sane people? Why keep calling when you're obviously being ignored? I flick the little button on the side of my phone to silence it. The phone immediately starts to vibrate and then stops. Within seconds it starts to buzz again, like a deranged bee.

For God's sake.

"Hello? Zoya, is that you?" Sheila Bua's screech sounds unnatural in this blurry toilet, like an elder who shows up at a rave party. Also, who else would I be? She called my cell phone, didn't she?

"How is your party, child?"

My throat closes up. "It's good, it's great. What a fantastic party. Yeah, I'm having one hell . . . sorry, heck of a party."

And how did she know about the reunion? The family grapevine, I guess. Never fails.

"Oh good. You're still in Khar, right? You aren't . . . err . . . roaming with your friends in . . . err . . . *Bandra*? Bandra Reclamation area, to be precise?"

A loud cheer echoes from outside, across the street, as the theater audience walks out of Rang Sharada. My pee stick clatters to the floor. "No! I'm not in Bandra. Why would I be in *Bandra* of all places? Hah!"

"That's wonderf . . . good! That's all I wanted to know. Stay away from Reclamation, okay. There's been an accident. Sooo much traffic!"

". . . hurry . . ." a man's voice whispers in the background on her end.

Her voice is thick, breathless. "Bye, Zoya! Don't go to Bandra, okay?"

Click.

What on earth was that? There's been no accident in this area, there was no traffic.

"Zoya, I'm coming in!" Arnav Sir booms decisively and bangs on the door. Has he been waiting outside this whole time? And, what, will he break the bathroom door to scare the pee stick into working faster?

"No, no! It's fine! I'm coming out."

He's so close to the door that I bang into him head-on and he lands straight on the large double bed in the dark bedroom.

It's like a jolt, seeing him sprawled on the bed, the sheets rumpled.

And he's barefoot. I've never seen him barefoot before. Somehow, bare feet feel so . . . risqué, more intimate than being in his house, or him sprawled on his bed, or testing for a pregnancy inside his attached private bathroom. I feel a slow burn on my face. Maybe I should immediately resign from my job; it should be illegal to see your colleague in this state.

The dark sea rumbles outside the open French windows, next to cozy bookshelves on either side of his plush bed. It's almost as if his bed was an afterthought between all those books. But it's soft and inviting and rumpled and for a moment, I just want to forget and sink into the warmth of the sheets and close my eyes. The Bandra-Worli Sea Link shimmers like a jewel in the distance from the windows.

His bed. Too intimate. *Get out, Zoya!*

"I'm so sorry!" I cry instead. I spy a Caroline Graham novel in the bookshelf. Maybe he's the one who gave . . . never mind, I'm seeing things.

He holds up a hand. "No, no, my fault. *I'm* sorry! But is everything alright . . ."

"Yes." My body shudders. "The chemist will have to look elsewhere for a grandchild."

He almost grins but decides against it and blows a little breath of air. He gestures toward a steel dinner plate on the bedside table. The plate is piled with a large grilled sandwich in the shape of a triangle, cut into six wedges, with extra grated cheese on top. "I ordered you some food. I know you said no, but I figured you might need it, after . . ." A red Kit Kat packet sits next to the plate. "Sugar helps, too," he says, and suddenly I want to flee. Run far away from this place. From him.

But I don't move. I don't know how long I've been here. We stand next to each other in silence, the sandwich and the Kit Kat wait forlorn. A ray of light trickles into the room from the flickering streetlamp. My legs are mush. I need to sit down but the accent chair is too far. Plus, his pajamas are on it. I'm not touching his pajamas, not a chance in hell. So I sit on the edge of the bed facing the bathroom door, almost levitating, with a layer of air between me and his navy striped bedsheet.

The theater audience is gone; it's just us and the hush of the sea and the distant sound of children playing. "So." He tries to break the silence. "I guess the reunion wasn't that fun." The sheets rustle as he sits beside me on the bed and sighs. We're not touching, not even sitting that close, but somehow, that soft exhale sends warmth my way.

"No, it wasn't fun."

"I could've told you that."

I know I should appreciate his gestures, be indebted to him, but the shock and embarrassment (and eventual relief) of tonight distract me from saying something like "Yes, you're right" and comes out as "But you've never been to one." *Ah, shut up, Zoya, look how his eyes dulled again, you idiot.*

"I'm sorry . . . I don't mean . . ." I stop fidgeting with the dangling ends of his bedsheet, with the hem of my dress, and tell him the truth. "I'm so messed up right now I don't really know what I'm saying. I didn't mean to be, well, mean."

"You're not mean." His legs are so long, he has to bend at the waist to join his palms over his knees. He moves his head sideways and up to look at me. "I think you *should* be a bit mean. People won't take advantage of you."

I sit up straighter and move to the absolute rim of the bed, and almost slide off. "No one took advantage of me. I'm not that stupid. It was, well, just a tough time, and my ex and I . . . it's an on-off thing. Definitely off now. For good." I add extra force on the "good."

But why am I rambling, telling him my life story? Better not mention that it was the day I was promoted, when my life was in flux. (Hah. If that was flux, what about the events of tonight?) Despite what happened in his bathroom, I want him to see me as a tough woman and not an indecisive damsel in distress. Professionally, of course. (And recommend me for the B&O job.)

Sitting on my boss's bed in his dark bedroom and peeing on a stick in his private bathroom. Yes, very professional. I really should go.

I jump off his bed and pace up to the bathroom instead. "So. You into Pilates?"

"What?"

"I saw a *Pilates of the Caribbean* book in there." I gesture to the bathroom. "Have you been to the Caribbean?"

"No." A shutter comes over his eyes. The warm, open, Arnav is gone in a flash. "The book is a . . . friend's." His head faces the floor tiles so I can't see his eyes anymore.

It's so not a *friend's*, going by that robot tone. I should tell Sheila Bua he's not been that lonely. Why does that irritate me so? It may be a delayed sort of reaction to the trauma of tonight.

He gets off the bed swiftly and is back to his usual Arnav-Sir pose: hands crossed over his chest, rocking back and forth on his feet. "Stay as long as you like. I'll drop you home whenever you want," he says when the silence begins to boom in our ears, and starts pacing the room.

Yup. End of topic and a clear hint for me to leave.

"You don't need to drop me. I can take an auto." He's done enough favors already. I don't need another one.

"Not asking. I'm not letting you go alone."

There seems to be a little twinge in the region of my heart. So strange. I'm tired and reacting to odd things. *Leave, Zoya, before you do something idiotic again.*

* * *

As we walk out of the elevator into the bright lobby outside—I bite into the Kit Kat, as if I'd leave that—a bunch of energetic seven-year-olds appear out of nowhere and jump on Arnav Sir, brandishing sticks. "Arnav Uncle! You are now our prisoner!"

One gangly girl has climbed onto his shoulders, another boy hangs off his leg. He deftly turns them around, as if they're made of air, and growls, pretending to bite off the girl's arm. "Well, hello, pirates!" (Arnav Sir and a Jack Sparrow voice? Who *is* this man?) "And why are you all still outside? Come on, get home, it's almost ten!"

"Dinner is late today. We still have fifteen minutes." A little pigtailed girl stares at me, blatantly curious. "Is that your new girlfriend?"

Yeah, it's just not my day.

"Err . . . no . . . we work together in the office."

"I like this one because she looks funny." The damn eyeliner's smudged and I'm wearing my patented mad hedgehog look, thanks to my frizzy hair. "She seems nice. And she likes chocolates," the girl adds as an afterthought, looking at the half-eaten pack of Kit Kats in my hands.

I guess funny is better than pregnant.

"We didn't like the last one," the leg-dangling boy pretends to whisper. "She was kind of mean, wasn't she, Misha?" He looks to the gangly girl for confirmation. "And she went to the gym a hundred times a day!"

"She said bread is the food of the devil on your hips." Misha swings her hips in a dance, happy that devil hadn't got to her yet.

What kind of an alien did he date?

"Arnav Uncle and the Beanstalk!" The leg dangler says triumphantly.

"Kabir! What did we warn you about telling on people?" A couple of kids gather threateningly close, without any effect on the said Kabir.

"It's a good thing she ran away with the gym instructor!"

"That's enough," Arnav Sir booms, but his face remains blank. "Make sure you're back home in fifteen minutes."

As we head out, the kids run toward the snoozing watchman and surround him with earsplitting pirate screams. The watchman does not stir.

We are cooped into Arnav Sir's car, one of those new fancy sedans with cushy seats, cozy interiors, and a drive so smoothly silent you can barely feel the jolt of the potholes. All traces of the playful Jack Sparrow have vanished. A little vein pops near his right forehead as always when he's angry or tense. Or deeply upset. Maybe he really did love her, the bread-hating, gym-loving beanstalk. My stomach clenches sharply. It's the sandwich piece I just shoved inside my mouth, the one he packed in a plastic lunchbox for me to take. I shared a wedge with him, too, the one with a thick slice of boiled potato and no tomatoes. (He doesn't like raw tomatoes. It's quite amazing what you can learn about people when you observe them silently in conference rooms.)

"I'm sorry about your . . . friend. I guess it was her Pilates book, wasn't it?"

His knuckles are white on the brown steering wheel. The vein still throbs on his forehead.

"Yes." He looks straight ahead. "We were not . . . close . . . by the end." The lights from the shops and arcades flash on his face, turning his eyes translucent, luminous. "Too many vegetables between us."

Vegetables? I dislike her already. Wait, was that meant to be funny? Arnav Sir is back to being the no-nonsense boss with his closed-up face, rather like a horse with blinders, so it's hard to say. "Here, keep this. My personal mobile number. Just in case."

It all comes rushing back; I was so close to disaster. I tuck the note inside the zipper of my little purse. How does one even begin to thank—

Something swishes outside the car window, past the bustling stalls, past honking vehicles and swarming humanity. Brown bread going fungus green. My heart hammers in shock.

Sheila Bua! What is she doing here?

Just—*how*? In a city of millions; in a neighborhood of thousands.

So much coincidence? All in one day? I need to hide. She can't see me. Why, oh, why is this bleeping traffic signal so long?

Has she seen me? Seen Arnav Sir with me at ten in the night? Has she seen us? *Has* she?

"Zoya, what on earth . . . did you just slide down the seat?"

I could flat out lie and say no, I slipped. But how can I not tell him the truth? After tonight? We're on a new level now. There's no going back.

"I just saw . . . my aunt."

"Your *aunt*?" He shudders, the whites of his eyes popping in alarm. "Not the . . . one who came to the office at lunchtime?"

"Yes, the same one. My Sheila Bua."

"Fuck." He cusses hotly under his breath in a shaky voice. His fingers start a furious tap dance on the steering wheel. Ah, so Sheila Bua can make him nervous by her mere existence. The thought makes me weirdly protective of him. Like I could stretch my arms and shield him from the onslaught of the Soviet warship (we cousins call her that sometimes). Nothing forms a warm kinship like a common nemesis.

A disheveled Sheila Bua paces restless across the market street, outside downing shutters of jewelry stores, doctors' clinics, lingerie shops, all stacked on top of each other in a slapdash manner. Behind her is a skinny plastic dummy in lace underwear and what looks to be a squirmy shop assistant (male) peeling off her (the dummy's) racy bra without actually touching the mannequin. Sheila Bua peeks behind her repeatedly and squints at the price tags that dangle off the now removed bra.

Arnav Sir shudders again and looks away. His interest piques in FM frequencies. Radio ads blend into one another without a second's break.

"—Prestige pressure cooker! A man who loves his wife can never deny her Prestige!"

"—Physical strength, mental strength for your child with Bournvita Chocolate Malt—"

"—Seagram's Whiskey. Smooth as—"

But Sheila Bua and a racy bra? The thought is sobering. Also, ick. I mean, this is a woman who calls underthings "brazier-and-penties" and thinks "lingerie" is "laundry" in French. What is going on?

"—This year's blockbuster and the winner of four Filmfare awards—"

"—Indian Premier League Cricket begins March 19th—"

And what's on her arm? And on her light blue kurta? Splotches of purple, green. I can see them from across the street they're so prominent. Is that *paint*? But didn't she say in the car that she didn't . . . And wait a minute, she's not alone. A man walks out of the building, pot-bellied and bald. It's certainly not Uncle Balli, who'd rather hang himself in a public square than buy bras with Sheila Bua. Why does this man look so familiar? Where have I seen . . .?

No. Way.

It's *his* uncle. The giant-white-sneaker-disaster's uncle. The one who'd turned all purple making sheep-eyes at Sheila Bua.

She holds on to his arm, all her weight on that poor limb. The man totters on his feet as beads of sweat, visible even from here, slide off his head. Sheila Bua gazes earnestly at him and hoists herself into the passenger side of his purring Honda City.

I stay hunched in my seat for the rest of the ride, covering my cheeks with my hands to hide the shock. Also to hide my face in case another relative decides to show up on the street. Arnav Sir is silent too. The beams of headlights from the opposite side shine onto his face. For one moment, his eyes, looking straight ahead, are shining crystals, shafts of light passing right through them. He squints. Maybe he still has a headache; he forgot to take the aspirin because of my pregnancy fiasco. And I forgot that plastic bag with the lifelong supply of Kotex at his house. Damn it.

The radio blares dreamy Hindi film songs. The singer's drunken pitch is tailor-made for long drives and romance. The shops outside are shuttered, the vegetable carts cozily covered with faded sheets. It takes Arnav Sir less than ten minutes to drop me home from Bandra Reclamation to Khar, a thirty-minute ride in peak traffic.

We don't say goodbyes. "Take care," he says. His gaze is on me as I get out of the car and shut the door, as if there's more to say. But if there's more, it's lost in the hum of the car engine. I feel a twinge of disappointment. Really, what did I expect him to say? He drives off, but only after I'm safely inside the building.

I am halfway up to my home, when my brain pings into focus: *Lingerie? Sheila Bua? Another man?*

Holy Mother of God.

My aunt is having an affair.

CHAPTER NINE

"Zoya!"

A chubby baby slaps my cheeks with its cold hands. It smiles a dastardly grin, ringlets for hair.

It looks like Arnav Sir.

Sheila Bua spills out of a black lace teddy. One hand holds the baby and the other rests in purple-faced bald-uncle's arms (Uncle Purple!). A green vomit emoji floats by idly.

The baby has Michelin tire arms. I mean, what else would my baby look like?

My baby?

But, wasn't the test negative? My heart races in mad thuds. The emoji hurls a projectile flood of green.

"*Zoya!*"

Sheila Bua grows, the baby grows, the emoji grows . . . . MONSTERS!

My eyes pop open, my heart is racing. A wicked glint reflects off Sheila Bua's diamond nose stud, mere centimeters from my sleepy face.

"Your mother sent me to wake you up." There's an extra layer of concealer over the dark circles under her eyes. I bet all that gallivanting with Uncle Purple has caught up to her, the minx! "Hurry up! We need to leave in fifteen minutes."

I know she's speaking to me, but all I can hear is *affair, affair!* I mean, Sheila Bua's cheating on Uncle Balli, of all things. How is that possible? Because when my Pa's brother Ronny Chacha was involved with another woman, it was Sheila Bua who almost completely ostracized him (her own brother) from family events and then dragged him back from the woman's place to sit him down and threaten, I mean, drill sense into him. His wife Rita Chachi will never publicly admit it, but Sheila Bua saved their marriage. Who's going to drill sense into Sheila Bua now?

Mum waltzes into the room, dressed and ready to go in a pale blue salwar kameez. How odd. Ready to go where?

"So, did you check with them, Sheila didi? What time will they reach the temple?"

"Ten-thirty. Hai, look at the time! Get up, get moving, child. Hrrrrr!" Sheila Bua heckles me like steering a cow to pasture.

Maybe I *should* pay my respects at the temple, you know, considering what *didn't* happen last night. With five coconuts and a bunch of expensive roses instead of cheap marigolds from the vendors outside?

"Alright, I'll come to the temple."

"Damn right you will." Sheila Bua talks to herself in the slim full-length mirror and sucks her stomach in. "Do you think the boy's coming to see us?"

Good God.

You know, when your life is so bizarre that your relative ambushes your boss and then whisks you away to an astrologer, you discover you're almost pregnant at your high school reunion, the chemist thinks it's your boss's child, you test for a pregnancy in your boss's private bathroom, and your middle-aged keeper-of-the-family aunt is having an affair—all in one day—and after all that, you have to see a boy, you kind of just have to roll with it.

Despite trying to roll with it, a protest tries to rise in my throat at this boy viewing. But wait, I promised myself last night that I would the best Diamond Daughter on this goddamn planet. That's what I'll do: put on the greasepaint and deal with it.

"Okay, Mum, what do I wear?"

They stop dead in their tracks, Mum and Sheila Bua, in the midst of exchanging lipsticks, and stare at each other in what appears to be mild alarm.

"This . . . ?" Mum timidly hands me the clingy tunic and leggings. "Green makes your skin look light . . . umm, glow, I mean. Makes it glow."

"Sure."

Mum throws a side glance at Sheila Bua in puzzlement and touches my forehead with her warm hands. "No fever, so she's not hallucinating."

Sheila Bua looks equally bamboozled; she snaps her fingers in my face. "Maybe she's been hypnotized?"

Was I so bad that the slightest compliance on my part stuns them? I vow to be a good, obedient daughter from now on.

The monstrous dream-baby haunts my subconscious. Can you be possessed by something that didn't exist? Who can answer such existential questions? Certainly not Sheila Bua, who is outside my bathroom with her ear glued to the door. Listening to me pee.

"What a little trickle! Are you drinking enough water? It should be a waterfall in the mornings! Now hurry up and brush your teeth and put the water heater on."

I give up.

* * *

Pa looks back from the passenger seat at me, squished in the middle of Mum and Sheila Bua. "So, this boy is the son of our hospital's most important Board of Directors."

"Yes. That Mr. Khurana. The main trustee. Don't you remember him, Sheila didi?" Mum fans herself and Sheila Bua with a newspaper in Bua's air-conditioned beast of a car.

"*That* man? The one who made me exercise after an eye checkup?" Sheila Bua gasps, horrified at the memory.

"Drive a little faster today, will you, D'Mello?" Mum orders the driver. "Not nice to make the boy's family wait, no?" The speed-phobic D'Mello miraculously connects his foot to the accelerator.

I remember this Mr. Khurana; he'd served butter-less, potato-less pav bhaji at a hospital benefit buffet once. How do you even cook a popular entrée without the star ingredients? It was just a sad little mound of mashed cauliflower and peas in tomato puree. Like ice cream without cream or sugar. What's the point?

"So, what's this boy's name?" I ask.

"Lalit Khurana."

The car jolts in the air for two seconds and lands back on the ground with a thud. Bless the crater-sized potholes to snap us all to attention.

The name seems familiar. "Don't worry," I say, keeping chill. "I will show him the good Zoya, the real Zoya." Very best daughter.

"Now, now. There's no need to be too real," Sheila Bua butts in, highly affronted that Pa and not she facilitated this proposal. "Just show him your nicest side for now, all real-sheal can come after marriage."

Yeah, Sheila Bua is totally miffed that she didn't bring this proposal. Punjabi Relations 101: The day a girl hits twenty-two years of age, every relative, family friend, and neighbor—all females—will have a say in who she should marry. They will conjure proposals from their own social strata like an endless string of handkerchiefs from a hat. Physical location of the collective matchmakers is immaterial; they could have moved halfway across the world but will still be in touch, thanks to WhatsApp's "Good Morning," "Happy Monday/Tuesday/etc." memes. In some conservative communities, like the Marwaris, the proposal conjuring could start at the ripe old age of twenty.

So here we are, at the ISKCON Krishna temple in Juhu. I often come here when my life is screwy. I don't know what best soothes the frazzled mind here: the high-domed ceilings or the cool white marble or the hypnotic chants. The whiteness also makes Sheila Bua look aflame in her yellow-green-magenta-purple salwar kameez. Why anyone would want *four* colors scrambling for space in one garment is beyond me. Or maybe I shouldn't question someone who got into Oxford art college.

So we have to meet this Lalit person *outside* the temple because I finally got my period. And period = no baby. Which is super phenomenal. Of course, Sheila Bua banging on your bathroom door is quite enough to scare your body into behaving. You should know, too, that period = no temple; apparently we females aren't pure enough for God that time of the month. Honestly, had I just waited till this morning to take the pregnancy test I'd have saved myself so much trauma. But ugh. This means every human near the temple can guess why I'm not going inside. Great. We start off by this Lalit person knowing my most intimate details.

Not the most intimate, a voice inside my head says. *A dark bedroom. A toilet. Arnav Sir waiting outside with a sandwich.*

My body shivers at that near disaster.

"Are you cold, Zoya? Here, take this shawl." Mum whips out a woolen wrap which she finished last night. She always knits when stressed. She must've been anxious about today, then. Had she known what really happened last night, or what almost didn't, that wrap would've been a king-size blanket.

Just as well we're not going inside the temple because I can smell weed mixed in the incense smoke, courtesy of some swaying devotees. And I don't need any more weed, thank you very much. (But these boy-girl meetings would be *way* less torture if all concerned parties were stoned, no?)

Not that I'm eager to meet this butter-less offspring outside the vegetarian restaurant of the temple. Going by the rejections of the last three boys, this isn't going to turn out different for me just because it happens to be "near God," as Sheila Bua and Mum said. Why would it?

The bells of the temple clang and chants of morning prayers boom from inside the dome: *Hare Rama, Hare Krishna!*

"Why does everything to do with God have to be so loud?" Pa covers one ear as he takes his loafers off near the shoe station at the temple gate.

Mum hurries toward the restaurant, her sandals deposited, fully expecting Sheila Bua to be four spaces ahead. But Sheila Bua is slower than usual today.

"Are you feeling alright?" Mum touches Sheila Bua's arm in concern. "You've been looking peaky and tired lately."

(As would I, if I were gadding about with someone who wasn't my husband. Peaky, indeed!)

"Who, *me*?" Sheila Bua laughs, extra high-pitched. "I was just telling the watchman to pay special attention to my imported sandals. We don't want anyone to steal them. Oh look, there are the Khuranas!"

The Khuranas are just the parents and the boy, not their entire extended family like the other boys. One bonus point for being courteous. Which is instantly negated because they all look supremely fit, without an ounce of fat on them. Ugh.

The boy's back faces me, and a nice-looking back it is, with a surplus of muscles—the kinds that overeager actors have—rippling out of his tight white shirt. A bit extra tight for Punjabi modesty. Maybe all that butter-less food really works. *Shut up, Zoya. Cribbing about too many muscles? Honestly.*

Okay, okay, let's start over. Straight hair, tight jeans. Three bonus points simply for the sturdy physique. This looks promising—

Oh.

It's Loathsome Lalit. Of the "you both would run around naked" fame from Aisha's mehendi.

No giant white sneakers, only super-shiny formal shoes. And certainly not gay, by the way he's checking me out in my colorful outfit. Is it approval? I mean, he stopped right in his tracks and stared at me. He's standing a few paces behind his parents, still staring. A resolute little smile spreads on his face and he catches up to his parents, as if coming to a decision. At least he's checking me out. Aman was full of disdain even while we were—

"Hello, hello, Khuranaji!" Pa brims with fake bonhomie, arms stretched as if reaching out for a long-lost brother. Fake, because the last time he spoke about Mr. Khurana, Pa called him a penny-pinching, henpecked excuse of a clown. (Also, Sheila Bua called his wife a dried-up karela, maligning the bitter, wrinkled vegetable some more.)

"Welcome, welcome, Sahniji! What a beautiful day!" Mr. Khurana matches Pa's heartiness raised to two.

"Does he *own* this temple to welcome us here?" Sheila Bua mumbles. "And when exactly has Bombay's humidity *ever* permitted a beautiful day?"

"Sheila didi, leave it, no?" Mum whispers back. "This would be such a good match for our family. We know them, no strange surprises here. What does it matter if we like them individually? They're decent people and the boy is so educated and wealthy.

And the only son! It's like a Diwali bonanza. Let's pray this works out."

"The morning timing was wonderful today." Mr. Khurana brims with vastly more energy than should be permissible in the morning. "Just enough for us to finish our family pie-lates workout."

Family workout? Good God.

"No, Lalit-ke-Papa, not pie-lates. Plateees, plateees," his mother enunciates, completely swallowing the first syllable. She does look a bit wilted as Sheila Bua said, like she was in urgent need of an infusion of helium from the balloon sellers at the beach.

"Ah, yes, plateees! The family that exercises together, stays together." His father alters a soppy movie dialogue to suit himself. Sheila Bua winces, putting a good distance between her and the exercising family.

"It's Pilates, Papa, not pie-lates or platees," Lalit says, nodding at me. "You do know they meant Pilates, right?"

"Yes, I do." I smile at him. "My mom does that too. Show-arm-a kebabs instead of shawarma." Like it's a bicep flexing contest and the winner gets a plate of kebabs. Mum smacks me lightly on the arm in mock anger. I suppose a case of syllable-clipping parents does kind of unite us. One more bonus point. Total points—four.

As if my smile was a primal mating call, Mrs. Khurana asks Mum, "Should we let the youngsters get to know each other? Let us oldies go for a stroll in the temple?" She looks expectantly around her. "Good excuse for a walk, no?"

Sheila Bua, one of the most anti-walk people I know, says, "Why, of course. The jewelry on the Krishna and Radha idols is worth millions of rupees!"

"Ah! Jewelry and exercise. Two of my favorite things!" Mrs. Khurana cackles and inches closer to Sheila Bua.

"Well, go on, you both!" Sheila Bua glances at me and Loathsome Lalit. "Get to know each other properly!" Her parting shot, with a wink no less, cannot be any more obvious. A couple of devotees with loaded plates of fruit, incense, and marigolds glance our way with sly giggles.

Loathsome . . . er, Lalit has the same thought. "Families are like herding cats, no?" He looks a bit alarmed at Sheila Bua's retreating back.

"Herding cows is more like it," I say. We're not supposed to diss family, at least not the first time, but I don't have an atom of a chance with this fitness freak so might as well be myself, right? Show him the real Zoya.

"So. Shall we start getting to know each other right away? I am five feet one and a half, blah, blah, blah." I giggle.

"Oh!" He startles. "But your biodata said five feet four . . ." He's clearly taken aback that I started the conversation. We're supposed to be docile and say our hellos and start with inane questions like hobbies. Why are *hobbies* important in a marriage? Unless your hobby is serial killing. If psycho Norman Bates was Indian, his mother would've married him to that shower girl by now.

"Ah, I see you've checked my online profile," I say.

"Yes. Didn't you check mine?"

Oops.

"Sure, I did. It was really . . . umm . . . nice." What a promising start—lies.

"So, I take it that this isn't your first time meeting a boy?" He smiles, his fair skin gleams as if he just had a facial.

"No. But I'm not a veteran. If you are, you could give me pointers," I say, which makes him laugh, gums and nostrils on full display.

"Well, a bit about me. I am an engineer and MBA, as you may well know."

"I do." *Lies!* And nothing wrong with engineers. They're perfectly respectable people, even though the country is overflowing with them.

"I work for Larsen and Toubro as a Director of Operations. I like a simple life and hope to find the same quality in my . . . err, wife. And I cook sometimes."

"What? A Punjabi man who cooks? It's a miracle!" I blurt. Only son and cooking? What, does he not live in India? Man-cooking totally means three extra bonus points. Total points: seven.

"Yes, you've found a unicorn." He takes a little bow. Bad image because now I am picturing a sturdy man with a pink horn and a purple tail.

"Well, you like to cook, and I like to eat."

"Ah, good." His attention wanders to the large glass windows of the restaurant next door. He smiles absently and grooms his hair.

"Okay, more about me." He straightens, as if in a business meeting. "I like to read a lot, mostly nonfiction books, you know, the ones that actually teach you something."

"Oh, okay. I like to read fict—"

"And I'm completely into fitness and work out twice a day."

"That's nic—"

"It's a kind of meditation, you know, exercising."

"Oh, is—"

"How many times do you work out?"

Yikes. How much did Mum and Sheila Bua lie on my PunjabiMatrimony profile?

"Well . . . I don't really . . . err . . . believe in . . . formal . . . workouts. I do more, you know, naturalistic . . . umm . . . healing."

He jerks his head back from his reflection; his entire attention is now on me. "That's interesting. Like how?"

Shit.

"Well . . . there's this . . . and that . . ." Okay, think, think. Which exercise could be believable? Pie-lates? Weights? Better not draw attention to a double-meaning word like that. Walking? *Yes.* Totally harmless and doable.

". . . walking, you know . . . and connecting . . . with, yes, nature."

Nature? In Bombay? Is he supposed to buy that?

"Wow." His eyes widen, as if I've reappeared in an entirely new wise-hippie avatar. "What a holistic attitude to health. I'm very impressed."

Yes. Very holistic, stuffing your face with a fried potato vada pav after an imaginary walk. But I *will* begin walks. It was one of my New Year's resolutions from, well, three years ago, so I'm not technically lying. It takes a while for an exercise routine to get going.

We smile and nod at each other, look away and smile again, the conversation depleted in a rush, like a packet of chips emptied too soon. The devotees sing along inside the dome, their loud claps are like harsh slaps, which for some reason evokes Sheila Bua's advice—*say something witty, engage the boy in conversation, Zoya!*

Okay, real conversation. Ask him if he's had a girlfriend. I'm sure there were a few.

"Have you . . . had any girlfriends?" It's so important to be upfront about these things. Plus, his attention had started to drift toward his own reflection again.

He draws a sharp breath, as if I said something shocking. Maybe he doesn't want to talk about it. "Yes, but it didn't . . . work out. But enough about me. How about you? Any skeletons I should know about?"

Pot. Fatigue. Two weeks late. Not *that* important to be upfront.

"Yeah. Just the one. That's been over . . . for a while." I suck in my stomach, way in. My hands are sweaty with shame and fear. There's no way I can tell him about, you know. I mean what's to tell, right?

(And he didn't exactly spill the beans about his girlfriends.)

"I really want to simplify my life, you know?" His eyes take on a faraway look. "Fewer gadgets, less social media, less drama . . . it will be nice to settle down with someone nice and simple . . . you know, trouble-free." His eyes rest, pensive, on my fully covered chest in the green chiffon.

Was that a compliment? "Trouble-free" and a melancholy boob-stare is flattering, right? In some ways?

A young woman in all black—dark T-shirt, black lipstick (in a temple?), black leggings—brushes past him. He tenses, his body in position as if about to dash, using me as a shield with alarming speed. "So what do you say, Zoya? Do I pass?"

"I'm sorry? Do you pass in what?"

"As in, do I pass as someone you'd like to marry?"

The morning prayers end suddenly, and for an instant the temple is silent. Everything freezes like in the movies—devotees, flower vendors, priests, temple bells. The startling lack of sound thunders in a white noise that stabs my ears.

Marry after spending ten minutes with each other? Is it the 1950s? Doesn't a modern arranged marriage need at least three meetings and several weeks of online or in-person chats, if not months, before deciding?

The phone in my purse beeps loud but I ignore it.

How do I know if he passes for a lifetime in just ten minutes?

But my parents didn't talk when they met the first time; everything was decided for them and look how happy they are. It worked for my aunts and uncles. And as Sheila Bua says, the less you get to know of your spouse before you marry, the better. And she'd know, doing this marriage-arranging thing for a living.

My family and Lalit's parents are some distance away. They pretend to bow to the bejeweled idols, but really glance back at us every five seconds in hope.

A hard lump bumps against my left arm. "Oh, sorry," says a monstrous pregnant belly with a woman attached to it.

Lalit continues to talk to himself, his voice breathless behind me.

"—my parents know your family—"

"—So respectable, dress well—"

"—Marriage is a risk—"

"—Security in it—"

"—What do you say, Zoya? Let us go for it!" His face is flushed, like at the end of a torturous run.

Us. Such safety in that word. No uncertainty, no stigma. Safe and secure. Like a protective barricade around you. Us.

The pregnant woman waddles slowly to the temple dome, still in mid-apology, and the words in my mouth slip away.

He wants to marry me. I should be jumping with joy.

I should.

My stomach folds over in a cramp.

My phone beeps again, louder this time.

"Do you want to check your phone? It may be something important."

Arnav Sir's name screams bright on the black screen in two separate texts.

The Insta campaign already has a 6% engagement rate. And it's only been eight hours. You have a real shot at B&O.

—A

I didn't realize I was holding my breath. I had the second phase of the campaign go live last night when I couldn't sleep, after which I finally managed to crash. A chance at B&O. A real one. But New York seems so far away right now . . . like a faint mirage. The dome of the temple echoes with muted chants of Hare Krishna that have restarted.

Another text comes on the heels of the former and freezes my body.

Feeling better this morning? You took my aspirin with you last night.
—A

It terrifies me that he knows my secret. I'm terrified that I *have* a secret that could be known. But I know he won't rat me out. Don't ask me how I know, I just do. But another living soul *does* have the knowledge that could ruin my reputation in society. I can't forget that.

Mum and Pa drop their pretend prayer and walk back toward us. Pa scoops the prasad with a little plastic spoon, without a clue that his glasses have slid from his bald head on to his nose. He pats his head looking for them, bewildered, and Mum nudges him with an irritated sigh. My heart twists into mangled little knots looking at them.

He wants to marry you. You! An overweight, dark, almost-pregnant girl. Put the pregnancy-scare disaster behind you. But B&O, and New York? Oh come on, Zoya, it's nothing but a recommendation. Not even an official one at that. And it may remain just that; nothing may come of it. Nothing *will* come of it. *Lalit is your ticket. He's everything your family wanted for you. Do it, Zoya, it's all within reach. This was the goal all along, wasn't it? You just have to say one word.*

My phone beeps again with another text from Arnav Sir. I shove it savagely into an inner pocket at the back of my purse.

"Okay."

"What?" Lalit swings around to face me.

"As in okay, yes, you pass and okay, let's get married." I smile at him, a little too wide.

CHAPTER TEN

"I need the fiancée. Yes, Zoya Madam, could you please move front and center?"

It's our engagement party, and the photographer gestures for me to move closer to Lalit, just a wee bit in front. Lalit frowns, his brows drawn together to create two hard little lines in the middle of his forehead, and his cheeks seem like they're in the process of wilting. That's the second time I've seen that frowny face. The first one was two weeks ago, when we met at the ISKCON temple for the first time.

"Yes, you too, Lalit Sir." The astute photographer asks him to step forward.

"Sure." He steps closer, almost an inch ahead of me.

We are next to each other, standing in front of the plush cream sofa with red decorative pillows, smiling brightly for the camera. My heavy powder-pink and blue lehenga-choli (a floor-length skirt and short dressy top), and full makeup feel unreal, like a fake face painted on. The feel of Lalit's dark linen suit brushes roughly against the skin of my arm as he adjusts his position for the photographer.

Silver chairs arranged in neat rows in the open-air banquet hall are filled with family and friends literally just drinking cocktails, eating appetizers, and watching us change positions for the photos. It's like we're stage actors on display for all these people.

The photographer clicks multiple photos from all angles. With my hand on Lalit's chest, his navy shirt silky over bulging muscles, or smiling into each other's eyes, which is totally awkward since we've known each other for only five days, and his teeth almost jump out at me from his gums. Our first pictures as an official couple. My limbs sag in a little thrill of relief. It's over. I mean, the search for a groom is over.

By tradition, this roka ceremony (the official engagement so we can openly date) is a low-key celebration. Usually. But no one believed I would ever reach here, and Lalit and I are both the only children of wealthy parents, so it's Hoopla Incorporated, with bright halogen lights, at least three photographers, two video guys, and a crowd the size of which could pass for a full wedding reception in other countries.

And you're not properly engaged until both sets of extended families and their close relations witness the ring ceremony. It's not like *Friends*, where Chandler puts a ring on Monica's finger in her apartment and they yell to four of their friends, "We're engaged!" which had me confused for an entire week because how can you be Engaged, by *yourselves*? Like, either of them could wake up the next day and just get out of it without any family opposition or naming or shaming or their worlds crashing around them, and not be known for eternity as *that* person who couldn't even hold on to a fiancé? What kind of sorcery is that?

Now that I've finally landed a man, the pitying questions and the snide remarks on my weight will stop, because the Ambushing Aunties are done with their business and will move on to the next victim. Girl, I mean, next girl. Likely Tanya.

Speaking of Tanya, here she is, in her green designer mermaid skirt and short top showing off an impossibly flat stomach (damn), come to stand by my side. Of course, the outfit is from Sabyasachi, and costs more than the entire trousseau of a middle-class bride. No black nail paint today, thanks to Rita Chachi, I guess. Baby pink nails that perfectly complement her outfit. And wearing Sheila Bua's diamond choker. How the heck does she always manage to look so stylish? Does she spend her entire free time grooming?

And who the frick asked her to join me here? Standing next to thin people is a big NO in my book; it makes you look way bigger than you are. But I can hardly excuse myself from my fiancé's side, can I, leaving her next to him as if *she* were the bride, simply because I don't want to look fat next to her?

I grudgingly move and tap Lalit on his arm to get his attention away from the photographer. "I wanted to introduce you to my cousin, Tanya. She's my Ronny Chacha's daughter."

He starts, and almost takes a step back, as if shocked. I don't blame him. I'd do the same if we weren't related by blood. But he recovers quickly, smiles wide, puts an arm around my shoulders and turns to her. "Hi." The arm around my shoulders is muscled and hard, like a line of bricks, weighing my shoulders down. But I can't move it because a good fiancée wouldn't, and certainly not in front of my horrid cousin.

"Hello." Tanya's face looks like thunder. Why, she hasn't yet tried to inveigle herself into our photos, like she does at every other engagement or wedding. I know the reason—because I, her larger cousin, am getting engaged first—ha!

We stand around in an awkward silence, Lalit's arm still on my shoulder, his palm cupped around my upper arm tight. Tanya keeps staring at his arm. What, it's not like we're making out in front of her. To stop her staring, I ask, "So, how come you're wearing Sheila Bua's choker?"

"Oh, that. I wanted her gold necklace. The bird one she always wears. But . . ."

Yeah, good luck with that.

"She offered me this twenty-four-carat diamond choker instead." She chuckles, as if to pretend indifference, as if she wears diamond chokers all the time. She might as well have said Sheila Bua likes me better than you. She turns to Lalit and asks, "What do you think of it?"

Excuse me? Jutting your chest in front of my fiancé to show him jewelry that isn't even yours? Obviously, I don't say that out loud. I have to pretend to be nicer now that I'm engaged.

"It's . . . eh . . . fine." Lalit looks at Tanya and then immediately looks away. "Ah yes, I think Zoya's father and my Dad are waving to me. I think I should join them. Excuse me." He rushes off in the direction of the bar at the other end of the terrace. And was that a sigh of relief I heard as he rushed past?

Tanya watches his retreating back under the fairy lights, as long as it's visible in the midst of dark suits, glistening silks, and rustling chiffons, and then turns toward me. Her eyes are so malevolent, I step back and almost collapse on the cream couch behind me.

"What?" I ask, nerves making me equally mean. "He doesn't meet your high standards?"

"No. He does. *You* don't." Her green dupatta whirls over her shoulder as she turns, and the heavily embroidered wrap smacks me across my chest as she zooms off toward the buffet at the back.

I hate her. I wish she wasn't family so today could be Tanya-free. But, Punjabi Relations 101: No matter how much you detest any/each member of your extended family, one always presents a united front, especially at events when outsiders could judge your family.

"A little to the side, ma'am. Lovely! Keep that lovely smile!" Click, click, click.

"Zoya, you look so pretty!" The Ambushing Auntie brigade is out in full force.

"Congratulations! Oh, look at you, Zoya, you look . . . thin . . . ner, good!"

I've lost count of the number of times I've heard "You're *such* a lucky girl!" Which is a soothing balm after Tanya's nasty barb.

So this is what newbie stars feel at their first movie premiere, this rush of adrenaline, as if you could take on anyone and win.

How swiftly opinions change when you have a man by your side.

You shouldn't be here. This strange thought sneaks into my head with no warning.

Oh stop it, Zoya. Think roka, think diamond ring, think happy parents. And his parents too. Ever so nice. They didn't ask me to give up my job, like that sneaker disaster's villain mother.

The Ambushing Aunties led by Mum giggle and glide in their colorful finery, prepping for the engagement ceremony. "No, no, not this one, Sheila didi, use the other diya. The wick will last longer."

"Where is that red chunri? We need to cover the couple's heads with it!"

"What happened to that damn coconut? We need to break it before such a big life event!"

The priest in a saffron tunic and a harem pant–style dhoti, sitting across a small glass table some distance away from our couch, could not be more disinterested in the proceedings. He sits on a chair across a small glass table about three feet sideways from our couch. The glass table, which faces an empty beige couch for Lalit and me to sit on during the actual ceremony, is covered with a saffron cloth, and the assorted aunties keep bringing stuff as per the priest's instructions. The table already has a small silver bowl filled with uncooked white rice, a brass idol of the elephant-headed god, Ganpati, the Remover of Obstacles, and rose petals. The priest swipes his gold iPhone to answer a call. "Yes, six weddings to perform this week! I suppose I could do one or two over WhatsApp video—"

A trickle of sweat snakes down my thighs. I lift my heavily embroidered skirt, desperate to air my insides, as Lalit comes back.

"Are you okay?" He asks.

"Yeah, just adjusting this lehenga."

"Ah." He chuckles awkwardly and looks away. We aren't acquainted enough to be talking about sweat and skirts yet. We haven't met since that day at the temple. A sudden urge to talk to Peehu attacks me all at once. She isn't here because she had to defend her thesis in person, and it was also too expensive to fly to India so soon after Aisha's wedding. God, I wish she were here. She'd joke and laugh in her uproarious way and I wouldn't be so nervy and twitchy. The sweaty bead, in the meantime, slides down my thigh, followed by several more.

"Umm, excuse me. I need to just freshen up a bit. This heat, you know," I say to Lalit. Also, Peehu promised that she'd FaceTime me during the ring ceremony, but I can't wait that long. Maybe I could just nip off to the bathroom and call her? It's not like this is our wedding; Lalit and I don't have to stand next to each other all the time.

"Yeah, sure, whatever." He smiles at me, genuine enough, lessening the impact of that casual "whatever." It confuses me, this breezy "whatever"; isn't a new fiancé supposed to be more, well, concerned? Maybe it's nerves. Can't be easy for him either, tying your life to a stranger.

Fiancé. How strange that word feels on my tongue. Like an exotic food that needs an acquired taste. I'm sure I'll acquire it soon.

But first, I need a map to navigate my way through this crowd to the bathroom without being waylaid. Let me just wave to people and walk real fast—ack!

"Ouch!"

"Oh, sorry, Mum."

"Zoya!" Mum looks at me in relief. "Where are you off to?" Why does she look relieved? Doesn't she have a thousand things to do? Wasn't she just looking for Lalit's mom a while ago? Before I open my mouth, a very familiar face swoops in from behind Mum. "Zoya beta! Congratulations!"

Ah, Peehu's mom, Daksha Auntie. Who seems to be pouring out her life story to Mum next to the waist-length walls of the terrace, her arm around a light globule as if it were a person. Mum, in one of her vintage pink silk saris, has been nodding in sympathy, I'm sure, but waiting for someone to save her. And that someone seems to be me.

Daksha Auntie sighs, her hand on her white-gold necklace, which is totally wrong for her orange sari. "How lovely you look, Zoya!" She grabs me in a hug but continues to talk to Mum. "How lucky you are, Geetaben. Your daughter doing the right thing at the right time." Her eyes are droopy, as if in a permanent state of sorrow. "Can you please make Peehu understand, Zoya beta? If she keeps refusing to see boys, there will be nothing left for her to see. Such good proposals we got till last year; now it's all drying up . . ." Her chest heaves, she rubs her hands vigorously, and the words tumble out one after the other. "And her father hasn't spoken to her since she left for Paris. Every time she visits, I'm the middleman carrying their messages. Can you imagine?" Yup, Daksha Auntie's stress is fever pitch at my engagement.

"Don't you worry, Dakshaben." Mum pats her arm in a vain attempt to soothe. "I'm sure Zoya will make her understand. Zoya, has Peehu called?"

"No, not yet. But Daksha Auntie, come, I'll introduce you to Lalit." I mean, okay, I can call Peehu later. The least I can do for her mom is help calm her down.

"Ah, yes, yes. Sure." She looks anything but excited, almost shrinking back into the wall as if I was going to introduce her to the very devil. But Mum, who understands the pain of meeting other young women's fiancés when your own daughter is unmarried, says, "But wait, Dakshaben, come with me first. Let me get you a nice glass of our authentic Punjabi lassi. Don't you want to see how the yogurt is made frothy in a washing machine, just like they do in Punjab? Come with me." She accompanies a relieved Daksha Auntie to the back end of the terrace, near the closed kitchen.

And as if telepathy exists between mother and daughter, Peehu's name flashes on the screen, making my phone vibrate so hard I almost drop it on the tiled floor. I mute the phone, hitch up my lehenga, and rush down the dozen steps of the passage to the bathroom. Thankfully the passage is empty. The bathroom stall door is ajar, so I know no one is in there either. "Pee!" I scream into the phone, as her face pieces together slowly on WhatsApp video.

"Zee!" She screams equally loud and slurred. "Is it time yet? For the ring ceremony? Show me the ring, show me!"

"Calm down. Not yet. Are you drunk? It's just five PM your time!"

"A bit. It's Friday, so we started happy hour early. But how can you tell?" She hiccups as if on cue.

"That little shrine behind you."

So, Peehu has a small temple in her Paris flat, right next to the living room window, overlooking wintry trees and a boulangerie across the street. She lights a diya and an incense stick before the little idols in the temple every day after a shower. And, right this very moment, the temple is completely covered with a large crochet doily, because any time she drinks more than two cocktails, she covers the shrine so that "God doesn't see her drunk".

"Can you move closer to the light?" She squints her eyes trying to see me.

The little white tube light is the only source of light in this gray passage. I move closer to it, thereby closer to the open toilet.

"So. You're marrying Loathsome Lalit." She giggles. I texted her this nickname the day we met at the ISKCON temple.

"Oh, don't call him that. He's rather nice."

"I know, I know. I'm being catty, I'm sorry. He looks perfectly lovely." To her credit, she does look a bit sheepish. "I had six drinks today. Three in sorrow that I could not be with you. And three in celebration of your engagement," she says, covering her mouth, as if I can smell her alcohol breath.

The lace doily over the temple is so Peehu it makes my heart hurt. A little tear slides down my face. *What on earth do you have to cry for, Zoya?*

"Are you not happy, Zee?" Her voice is so clear she could be right next to me.

"I am. I really am. Happy that it's done. But I wish . . ."

"Wish what, babe?" Her face turns upside down as she adjusts her phone display. It rights itself in an instant and she looks up at me, her pixie face cupped in her hands.

"I don't know. I guess this is so monumental that I just wish you were here." I want to tell her that I'm nervous and afraid and full of doubt if I've made the right decision, and that I'm not so ecstatic as I thought I'd be. But I don't. Because I might be called up to the hall any moment, and this is neither the time nor the place. This engagement was scheduled so fast that I never really got a chance to sit down and discuss things with her. Or with anyone, really. Maybe the ecstatic joy comes later in a relationship. Maybe there is no such thing in this world.

"I know. I'm sorry. But I won't miss your wedding for the world."

I nod.

"Do you like Lalit? Is he nice? He looks smart in the picture you sent."

"Yes, he is . . ." I shake off the memory of that casual "whatever." I'm giving needless thoughts too much importance.

"Okay, now that you'll be engaged, Aisha and Kamya and I will plan something special for you." She says the last bit in a sing-song voice.

"Like what? Tell me?"

"You'll just have to wait for it." She smiles like a sly fox.

"I really should convey your mom's message like an obedient friend: she asked me to tell you that you also need to get married."

"Yeah, yeah, blah, blah. Speaking of marriage, how's that cute boss of yours? Still single? Why haven't you sent me another picture of him?"

Hello? I sent her *one* measly group photo with Arnav Sir in it, months ago. Because she had broken up with that Indo-German boyfriend of hers and needed cheering up.

"He's not that cute. And you're drunk."

"Yes, I am drunk. Tell you what, let me grab a coffee, freshen up and call you again in ten minutes? I really want to see you both in the ceremony. Bye!" She's gone before I can stop her, leaving me alone with a sour stench in the narrow passage under the bleached glare of the tube light. And now I actually have to pee.

I lift my lehenga yet again and enter the little bathroom gingerly. It's just one room with a toilet and a sink, but at least it's a bit cleaner (and drier) than the passage outside. But tinny. Oh God, how is one supposed to squeeze oneself into a rusty little toilet wearing eight kilos of zari and crystal work? I lock the door behind me, and as I turn, I knock over a small nozzle on the side of the wall, which whooshes a spray of water on the floor—eek! The hem of my lehenga is wet now. Ugh.

"—I told you not to come after me—!"

What?

That voice, that hiss outside the toilet door, why is it so familiar—

"—Sheilaji, I had to—"

Sheila Bua's outside? But wasn't she in the middle of a spat with Uncle Balli when I left? (He was berating her for something simple, as usual, I forget what. Yeah, he's not nice.) And who belongs to the other ratty voice? I peep through seams between the door and the wall.

Light shines on a bald head outside the door and my fingers freeze halfway through the knot on my lehenga.

Holy fuck.

My skirt drops to the wet floor.

Uncle Purple! What the hell is he doing here?

CHAPTER ELEVEN

The giant-white-sneaker-disaster's uncle? Suited and booted? At my engagement party? But he wasn't invited.

"—Sheilaji, please! Its urgent that you—"

"—Nobody knows—"

"—You have to tell them—"

"—Nothing to tell—"

Oh, there are things to tell, for sure. I should leave, I really should. It's the polite thing to do, but it's like an accident site; you can't *not* look.

"How dare you show up here?" Sheila Bua's voice drips ice. She adjusts her lace sari (nine yards of bottle-green fabric instead of the standard six), twirls her diamond bangles, her diamond earrings, anything to avoid looking at him. She peeks anxiously over his bald head, everywhere except the toilet right next to her.

"You weren't taking my calls—"

"—*Not* about me—"

"—Sheilaji, my office . . . tomorrow . . . please—"

"Yes, yes, okay! Are you happy? Now, go!"

In his office? They're . . . doing it in his *office*? I have to make a heroic effort to control myself and douse my grudging admiration. To make a rendezvous in the middle of family festivities? I'd give her a full salute if I were actually facing her!

But I can't tell anyone about this rendezvous. Somehow, that car ride to the astrologer brought up more buried memories of when she was my Magic Bua. The one who would drive me around in her new Maruti Esteem, back when cars were a luxury, no matter what time of the day I asked, no matter how much it delayed her. And the only person who didn't laugh when I wanted to go as Superman instead of a princess for a fancy dress party at age five, and said if anyone made fun of me to send them straight to her. I mean, how can I betray her secret? And anyone married to Uncle Balli deserves to have a nice little affair simply for putting up with him. Maybe I should walk out of the toilet with my skirt hitched up to my waist, almost half-naked so Sheila Bua's lover can slip away unnoticed. Sheila Bua has a lover—dear God.

Shake it off, shake it off, think engagement rituals, think lovely buffet, think Lalit. Lehenga adjusted and heart back to a normal speed, I return from the hushed toilet into a circus. My parents are like VIPs, greeting and being greeted, congratulated, beamed at more than Lalit and I.

I'm back on the plush cream couch, perching my behind as daintily as my heavily embroidered outfit allows. Let me just shove this little red pillow behind me for support—ah, much better. Now I can slump without looking like I'm slumping.

There's my Pa, across three rows of chairs with Lalit, all smiles, showing my fiancé off to his back-thumping friends, all of them eye surgeons. And Mum, my usually rational mother, has completely lost her mind. She's everywhere all at once, swishing in her cream and red silks, surrounded by frothing Ambushing Aunties, and so gleeful that she might spasm into hives.

"Congratulations, Geeta! What a lovely family you've found for your daughter!"

"What a fabulous engagement!"

"Zoya is *such* a lucky girl!"

"Lalit is such a catch!"

"Oh, you must bring Zoya and Lalit to our house for lunch before the wedding!"

"Don't you worry about wedding shopping! I know the most exclusive places. We'll go together!"

I may have to put Mum to bed tonight with a stiff dose of Pa's strongest whiskey. Maybe two.

Lalit saunters back and finally plops on the couch next to me with a grunt. "Phew! So hot!" He blows a puff of air and takes a swig of his chilled white wine, while I sip my Coke from a crystal glass. I've lost two kilos just *sitting* here in a puddle of sweat. I'd give anything to throw off these heavy, itchy clothes and squeeze my naked body inside an air conditioner. So I tell him the truth, as a new docile fiancée should.

"Yeah, it's a bit warm."

Arranged Marriage Rule No. 3: Do *not* be the complaining wife or fiancée; at least not until you are safely married. Better still, safely married for at least a year.

Also, my cousin Karan spiked the Coke with liberal amounts of rum, which helps a little with the marriage rules. But no one knows I'm drinking rum, especially not Loathsome Lalit. *Would you stop with that name, Zoya!*

"Zee! Lalit jeeju! Many congratulations to you both!" Aisha's here, thank goodness.

"Aashoo, I've been waiting for you!" What took her so long? At her wedding, our entire family had reached the venue an hour before the groom's family side. And I was by her side right from zero hour at her engagement party.

"I know, I'm sorry! Varun had a thing . . ." She trails off.

"Why are your eyes so red? Have you been crying?"

"Are you mad? What reason would I have to cry?" She twirls the ends of her orange sari, drops it, and twirls it again. "Just some mascara in my eye." She spots Varun in the crowd. "Lalit jeeju, come, come, I will introduce you to my husband Varun." She grabs Lalit by the arm and yanks him off to meet her husband, who, I can see, has already started slugging drinks at the bar. And I'm alone again on the stupid bride-groom sofa. Something's off with Aisha. Majorly.

Oh, but there's Kamya! She's gliding toward me with a large bouquet of gerbera daisies.

Mum appears besides me all of a sudden before Kamya, bends toward my ear, and whispers, "Zoya, be kind to Kamya, okay?"

What? Mum's never asked me to be kind to *any* of my friends. Ever. According to her, they are the source of all my troubles and rebellions (which is partly true).

"Kind?" I ask, bewildered.

"Arre, she must be feeling so sad, na? Because *she's* not married—at thirty-three, good God—and now *you* will be. So don't throw your happiness in her face. Be subdued, okay?"

Kamya saunters toward me, all ease with the giant bouquet, bobbing with joy; she has pretty much hugged, kissed, and laughed the whole way over to our part of the room.

"Little Zee getting engaged!" Kamya finally reaches me, arms outstretched in a warm hug. "You look radiant!" She plants a big fat kiss on my made-up cheek.

She looks at me with a lightning beam of a smile, like a mother hen proud of her chick who's just learnt to walk. She perches next to me on the empty sofa as Lalit is still away, chatting to Aisha and her husband Varun near the bar, and Mrs. Iyer, our neighbor, immediately pounces on Kamya with questions.

Also, why hasn't Peehu called yet? She said she'd call back in ten minutes. I want her by my side at the ceremony, even if only virtually. I clench my phone tight, as if it were a lifeline, willing that dead piece of circuitry to come alive.

And then, as if it knows my innermost desires, my phone beeps. Must be Peehu! I swipe the text open before seeing who it's from.

Congratulations.

What's *wrong* with her? Oh my God, did she hurt herself trying to freshen up? I mean, Peehu was drunk. Should I yell for her mother, who is in the middle row of chairs looking lost and eating spring rolls?

> You have the highest metrics on your campaign in the agency. It's official. I'm recommending you for the B&O job. Wanted to let you know personally before I email their HR manager. Will copy you on it. Well done.

O.M.Friggin.G.

It's not Peehu. It's Arnav Sir.

I want to get off the couch and jump in the air and squeal in joy. But I am unable to move, the lehenga sits heavy on my body. My hands are frozen on the phone screen, as if trying to decide between shock and thrill.

I can see myself at the airport, waving to my family with a JFK tag on my suitcase. *Don't be silly, Zoya. This is not a job offer, just an endorsement. Look at Lalit, smart in his suit, look at Mum and Pa, shining in happiness.*

I'm sorely tempted to type in www.bucklebeeagency.com on my phone browser.

No. Be Zen, Zoya. I feel a thrill passing through my body and take a deep breath. I'm going to enjoy this day. An endorsement from the boss *and* a fiancé. Getting engaged is like almost reaching the finish line. Well done, indeed.

But there are times when I seriously wonder if Arnav Sir is a little, you know, el loco? Today is one such day. Who sends messages like these on a girl's engagement? He could've sent an email tomorrow. Or the day after. And it would've been fine. And it's not like he doesn't know about my engagement, since I formally invited him. I didn't want to, but Kaya, Abhi, Joe, Chotu, and a bunch of others were coming, and you can't invite other colleagues and *not* invite your boss; that's like career suicide. We were in the conference room last week, revising some slides, when I told him about the engagement. The zooming mouse stopped abruptly on the screen.

"I guess congratulations are in order," he said with a tight blip of a smile and ended the PowerPoint. When I gave him the gilt-edged party invite, he took it without a glance and said he would be in China on the day of.

Thank you!! Are you texting from China?

Yes.

He's *so* not in China right now. Kaya told me he was totally in town, at a client conference. Why did he feel the need to lie to me? Did his nose get Pinocchio-long as he typed that "yes"? His nose with that dashing pirate-like scar by it, to the right, courtesy of a fight he tried to stop in college? *Zoya, you idiot. Think ring, think cute fiancé, Diamond Boy with diamond ring.*

We're waiting for the ring ceremony to begin.

He pulled me into all sorts of projects last week after I told him of my engagement. With all that work, there was barely time for my lehenga fitting before the engagement. No wonder the blouse feels a bit too snug.

Mrs. Iyer is gone, replaced by Aisha, who hugs Kamya and props herself next to me on the other side of the sofa. Look at us, three dressed-up chicks, gleaming in our finery. Me in my powder-pink and blue outfit, Aisha looking fresh and peachy in her orange designer sari, and Kamya, radiant as ever in her pastels, a light-green tunic, and leggings, with crystal work to add the necessary bling.

"Zee, would you stop fiddling with your phone?" Aisha tries to smack my hand.

"I was just texting."

It's not like I'm texting *while* Lalit slips the diamond ring on my finger.

"Who the hell is important enough to text *today*?" Aisha is distinctly unmeditative with her eyes aflame and her hands alert on her tiny waist, kind of like a combative Shaolin monk. *Aisha and combative? How much rum did Karan pour into my Coke?*

"My boss," I tell her. I still can't believe that my name will go to B&O's HR in New York. *My* name. The jazzy title song from *Mad Men* starts playing in my head, which I squash immediately. I need to be fully present at my engagement.

"Let him text as much as he likes, you are under no obligation to text him back, especially today."

"Aashoo." I look her in the eye. "Have you not heard my stories about him? Do you not *know* this boss at all? He needs immediate answers. Or better, he expects you to know his demands *before* he's made them."

"Tell him to buzz off. It's the most important day of your *life*, right? It's supposed to be." She spits the words out in a whisper, almost to herself; her jaw moves as if chewing pointy shards of glass. "I mean, what else is there?" Her eyes shift around as her words drift off.

What's going on with her? She's never been so . . . questioning. And what's the deal with switching from frantic to a funk within minutes? Dr. Jekyll and Hyde or whatever. Once this engagement hoopla is over, I'll take her out for a nice cocktail. That Varun better be treating her right. No reason he isn't—I mean, it's *Aisha*, the sweetest, prettiest girl in the world—but it's always nice to periodically remind him that I could chop his balls and place them in a jar of formaldehyde by his bedside. No biggie. That's what BFFs are for. To drink and frighten spouses.

Kamya interjects her body between Aisha and me, just like she'd do as a prefect in school. "Ladies. Lalit is on his way back . . ." Thank goodness. Yes, I'm nervous about this big life decision, but having a good-looking fiancé physically by my side will help ease some nerves for sure. Kamya continues, "The ring ceremony will start anytime now. Aisha, why don't you get a Coke for me with a large amount of scotch—don't tell anyone it's scotch!—and I'll make sure Zoya isn't texting her boss."

Aisha walks off in the direction of the bar.

I can see Lalit coming back toward me. He walks past Tanya but is waylaid by a bunch of Ambushing Aunties, who practically molest him with tittering hugs and kisses. Wait, what's going on? Did I see Tanya's mom, Rita Chachi, yank a spring roll out of Tanya's mouth after Lalit walked by? No, that can't be right because Tanya doesn't eat carbs. And certainly not fried carbs. No, my eyes are deceiving me—why, just a moment ago, I thought I saw Tanya shoving a forkful of Hakka noodles into her mouth. Nope. Can't have happened.

My fiancé is finally here, plopped next to me on the couch, looking dapper and handsome. A little frisson of joy at a job well done spreads through my body. I wonder if the thrill of associating the word "fiancé" with yourself ever gets old? I look over at him, just to make sure I'm not in a dream. He glowers at something on his phone screen and shoves his phone savagely inside the pocket of his blazer.

"All okay?" I ask, concerned, a hesitant hand on his arm.

"None of y . . . I mean, yes, all okay. Nothing for you to bother yourself with." The two little frown lines and sagging cheeks are back, the ones I saw earlier in the evening. Is he sulking? At his own engagement? Why would he? The feeling of doubt, of being where I do not belong, smashes the well-being with such force that for a moment a blustering panic races through me.

An assortment of women relatives charge toward Lalit and me in a throng, chanting "come, come, let's start" like a mantra. Mum holds a silver plate in both hands, with a small lit diya next to some broken brown-and-white coconut pieces, a little round stand holding two smoking incense sticks and red powdered vermillion.

"The pooja table is ready. Please get the couple," the priest says in the general direction of the crowd, even though Lalit and I are sitting three feet away from him. (New additions to the table: two little velvet boxes with the diamond engagement rings, a crystal bowl filled with water; a large red box of kaju katli—the diamond-shaped sweet made of cashews and milk; small silver bowls with turmeric in one, red vermillion in another, and water in the third. The water bowl has a little baby spoon sticking out.)

Lalit and I walk to the glass table toward the priest, led by an entourage of swishing fabrics and tinkling bangles, and sit on the beige sofa with a red-gold silk cloth over its back.

"Arre, leave your phones now. Concentrate on each other!" says a matronly woman I do not recognize as I give my phone to Aisha for safekeeping. Aisha has moved two silver chairs behind the beige couch so that she and Kamya can be around me during the ceremony. She fiddles with my phone and flashes it to me: Peehu's here on video! My throat closes up and Aisha and Kamya squeeze my hand and whisper, "We got you, Zee."

A woman from the back of the crowd, probably another in-law, her nasal voice gleeful with pleasure or spite, I cannot tell, says, "Your whole life is going to change now, only husband and in-laws, and soon babies!"

"Yes, no working late nights, no more flinging clothes on the bed and chilling with Netflix in the evenings! Your Mum won't be around to make tea for you now! You'll have to make tea for everyone!" Rita Chachi says with malicious pleasure.

I have a sudden flashback of my parents and me, late one Friday evening after work, sprawled on the living room couch with delicious fried pakoras and steamy mugs of chai made by Mum, relaxing to Kishore Kumar songs on Old Is Gold FM.

"And forget your party-sharty now! Go curtain-shopping and buy groceries instead!"

"First year joy, second year boy!"

The hysteria rises and rises, almost lifts me off my feet. I wiggle my toes inside the tight strappy sandals, dig into the four-inch heels, tap my feet furiously, whatever it takes to stay grounded inside this banquet hall. And wish I had a samosa to stuff in my mouth.

"The wedding date is fixed for June twenty-second!" The priest looks up from his phone, after checking the Hindu calendar for dates.

As hearty cries of "Vadhaiyaan! Congratulations!!" rend the brightly lit terrace, Sheila Bua squeezes her way to the front of the crowd. But for just a moment, her round face is shorn of everything but an odd despair. *She can't be still thinking about Uncle Purple, can she? Or her own bad marriage? Why would Sheila Bua remember that today of all days?* But it's gone in a flash, that despair; her diamond earrings glint under the lights, her face is wreathed in smiles as usual and all is normal.

What's wrong with me today? Why do I see weird things, think stupid thoughts? Maybe it's too much all at once. I should be enjoying my engagement day . . . *our* engagement day. Everything my family wanted is happening, so why do I feel off kilter —

"Hello, hello, everyone! I need to announce something today!" Lalit's father, red-faced courtesy a glass of whiskey, raises one palm to shush the crowd. "Sahniji, please come up here!"

Pa strides across the terrace to much applause, also with a glass of whiskey in his hand. (His third. Mum already grunted at Pa on his way to the stage, indicating The End of his booze quota. He pretended to ignore it as usual.)

"Today is such an auspicious day!" Lalit's father pauses to ensure everyone's attention is on him. "Our families are becoming one! On this wonderful occasion, I want to officially invite

Sahniji, one of our hospital's best eye surgeons—one of *Bombay's* best—to join our professional family as a Director on our Board!" The crowd of relatives and eye surgeons explodes into delight followed by much hugging between the two fathers.

My uncle, Ronny Chacha, thumps me on the back. "Your father's waited for this Board position for decades. This is all because of you. Well done, beta!"

My knees are shaky. I need to sit down.

"You're so lucky, Zoya!" Ronny Chacha says.

A sudden rush of people surrounds Lalit and me. It is time. The priest adjusts his thin dhoti and chants in Sanskrit in a loud, austere voice. Lalit's mother winds the silver prayer plate around both of us in broad circles. The priest asks us to hold hands; my fleshy hand rests in Lalit's boyish one. For all his muscles, his hands are so bony and cold. A steel vise tightens around my chest. Incense smoke swirls around us, marking the beginning of the pooja and binds us together in a new life.

CHAPTER TWELVE

One week since engagement to darling son-in-law and less than four months to D-Day!

Followed by a GIF of Severus Snape, that mean-professor-turned-savior from *Harry Potter*, greasy hair and all, dancing in a black party dress.

Yes, okay, I decided to teach Sheila Bua how to text. I know, I know, egg on my face because I volunteered and now she's texting me at 6:01 AM. It sounds more wretched when you say it out loud.

The day after my engagement party, at a family lunch at her place, Sheila Bua claimed that she wanted to be the most tech-savvy woman in her social circle, and could either Yuvi or Karan or Tanya or I please teach her to be proficient with GIFs or FIFs or those hashing tags or memes-sheems, whatever they were? Yuvi said he didn't have time, and my other cousin Karan, in an obviously pathetic attempt to escape, said that he had accidentally smacked his head against a wall yesterday and has since experienced a temporary loss of texting and social media memory. (Sheila Bua immediately called her maid for a glass of hot sugared milk with turmeric for him.) And then I saw myself, in an out-of-body experience, raising my hand to say, "Of course, Sheila Bua, I'll teach you, don't worry." Karan's eyes widened as he mouthed silently behind Sheila Bua's back, "Are you mad?" followed by a discreet hangman's noose sign. At another time, I would've run in the opposite direction at her request, and fast. But after that car incident . . . well, I couldn't turn away when she needed help, could I?

Oh, I'm fully aware now why Karan made that excuse and what he meant by that hangman's noose. Because after I taught Sheila Bua where to find GIFs and how to download more, she has started bombarding me with them every morning, and when I don't respond, she calls. At six in the bloody morning. To ask if everything is okay, and if it is, why haven't I responded? Ever heard of Pandora's Box? Yup, that's what's happened here.

I've learnt to just send smileys in reply to her messages instead of actual words. As in, I open one eye in the morning, fumble for my phone by the bedside, open her text, send two smileys without seeing what she sent, and go right back to sleep. She seems fine with it, as long as the smileys convince her that I'm alive and responding to her. And it's not just GIFs. She also texts me a countdown to my wedding date, which she thinks makes me happy. It does, sure, but it also stresses me out—there's so much to do!

I wasn't able to go right back to sleep today, which is why I'm almost at work at seven thirty AM right now instead of the usual nine AM. And because of general grogginess, wearing a dull gray blouse over black skinny pants, a recipe for drab, especially with my brown skin. The death rattle of the ascending lift is like an explosion in the silent corridor outside my office. Two dusty sun rays trickle through a side window into the peeling passage, all of it a bit creepy, like walking out of a rusted elevator into an abandoned building. The lobby of the office is unnaturally quiet. No ringing phones, or clacking feet, or squeaking doors opening and shutting all day, no human voices.

I tiptoe to my desk, not wanting to wake any residing ghosts. Wait, what's this?

A gift. It's a gift!

A box of Kit Kats with a blue bow, and a giant bouquet of yellow daisies. Oh my. Maybe it's from HR for my engagement? No, that can't be, because they gave me a bouquet of roses last week, the day after. Actually presented it to me, in front of the entire office (Arnav Sir was out at a meeting) as if I was some kind of chief guest at an event.

Let's see if there's a name. The plastic wrap around the daisies crinkles as I hunt for a card. And it's crisp, elegant plastic, mind you—which means the flowers are from a bona fide florist—not the flimsy cling-wrap from the vendor across the street, who is rumored to steal flowers off graves to sell them. I can see his little shop outside the French windows if I stand on my tippy toes; the aluminum shutter is still down, and a man sleeps in front on a long wooden handcart. Yup, the daisies are not from there for sure.

Maybe they're from a happy client. But how would they know my favorite flowers? Yes, I do talk a lot, I know, so I may have told them unintentionally. Ah, here's a little white card stuck in between the daises that says "For Zoya" in printed letters. I turn the card upside down, inside out. What, that's it? No "congratulations" or "good job" or something to indicate what it's for? Very cryptic.

"Hello, Zoya."

I jump at the deep voice, almost dropping the card. What is he doing at work so early? This is also the first time we're seeing each other since my engagement. Well, not "seeing" each other, obviously. Also, the China thing he had texted wasn't technically wrong. He did go to China for a week right after my engagement.

"Good morning." I turn around, somehow reluctant to face him. He looks a bit sheepish, not meeting my eyes, as if I caught him at something naughty. And okay, this is a totally different Arnav Sir. He still has his usual blue and red coffee mug with the logo of Arsenal Football Club, but he hasn't shaved. His stubble—which looks rough to the touch—is dark and ominous, his light pink shirt is crumpled and his tie loosened, as if he slept in these clothes. And the beach eyes are fenced by dark circles. The overhead tube lights, which are always on, cast shadows on the dark circles, making them appear melancholy. Like he's battling great sadness. Maybe he's jet-lagged. No, he actually looks ill. Without thinking, I reach out to check his temperature—goodness! Phew, stopped my hand from touching his forehead just in time, and maneuvered it into tucking my hair behind my ear. Honestly, Zoya.

"I see you're already celebrating the recommendation to B&O." He grins. "Kit Kat in the morning?" He points to the big red box with the blue bow that rests on my table.

He did send a recommendation email to B&O's HR three days ago. To which the HR replied the day after. With a job link. I've opened that email every half hour since then and stared at it moony-eyed like it was a love letter. I haven't applied for it yet; I just finished cleaning up my résumé last night.

And I did celebrate. The day after my engagement, I cabbed it up to Persian Durbar and ordered their large plate of raan mutton biryani, all for myself. "I found this on my desk right now," I say, pointing to the Kit Kat box. "It's a present, I think."

"Chocolates. Flowers." He comes around to my cube in lounge mode, his arm lazily over my cubicle wall. "Quite predictably cheesy, in my opinion."

And why would I care what his opinion is? Cheesy, indeed. (A little bit cheesy, but still, I won't tell him that.)

"So, who's sending you cheesy presents?"

"Doesn't say. Just a mysterious little note." I wave the white note at him.

"May I?" he asks as he takes the note from me to read, and raises his eyebrows at the basic message.

I rack my brain to think of who might've sent this. Who would forget to say more on the card? No, it can't be for the B&O job. It's very un-corporate. Maybe the card-maker accidentally left the rest of the message out. So then: Mum? Pa? No, why would my parents send me stuff to the office? Wait! I know! It's the newest person in my life—Lalit! It has to be. Who else could send me my favorite flowers and chocolates, the very essence of romance? I'm so happy today I could twirl around in circles.

"I know who it is! It's my fiancé!" I thrust my left hand in his face to show him the big diamond rock on my ring finger, as if the sparkling solitaire was personally responsible for the chocolates and flowers on my desk. Also, the more I say "fiancé," the easier it rolls off my tongue. I'm acquiring the acquired taste.

He chokes on his coffee and his face collapses into racking coughs. I take the mug from him, put it on my desk, and pat his back gently (like Mum does when I cough). His back is warm, a bit too warm. Uh oh. The muscles contract and expand under my hand as he's beset by cough after cough. It takes him a full thirty seconds with his hand on his chest to come back to normal. See? I'm telling you he's unwell.

"Thank you." He somehow manages to say.

"You don't look good right now. You really should rest at home."

"So, you thought I looked good before?" he says in a hoarse voice, his chin sinking into his thick neck to adjust his vocal cords. "Thank you for that back-handed compliment."

"Umm . . . no, I meant . . . yes . . . well." Oh God, babbling moron. I sigh and look up at him. "Truly, you look ill. You need to go home."

"Why? You don't want me around in the office?"

What is wrong with him? And what is wrong with *me*? Because as soon as my brain starts to say "No, I don't want you around," another voice jumps up and cries "Yes, I do, please don't go." What the eff, Zoya? You're an engaged woman now. Leave your boss for Peehu, who keeps asking for his picture. *Not Peehu!* A second voice in my head screams so loud that it blasts the thought of Peehu and him away. I say nothing to him, and just smile. I'm getting married soon, why complicate things?

He starts to cough again and I feel instantly ashamed that I'm in my own world, not paying attention to his condition. "Okay, that's it. Come. Sit." I point toward my chair, and when he doesn't follow orders, I pull him by his arm, which is also too warm, and gently guide him to my seat. We face each other in my tiny cube for a moment. A delicious musky hint of old cologne wafts into my senses along with a radiating warmth. The chair screeches as he flops on it, while I remain standing. Distract yourself with paracetamol, Zoya—where is that damn Crocin strip I always carry? I dig into my purse to find the tablet. "Are your parents around to look after you?" I ask.

"No, they travel a lot. Wanderlust left over from my Dad's army days. They're up north right now, in Shimla."

I think about my Mum and Pa and their nurturing when I am sick (chicken soup, a savory and gooey khichdi with a spoonful of ghee on top, hot water bottles, books), and I want to scoop him up in a hug. Thank goodness for that sharp poke of the tablet strip on my finger. Ah, there's that Crocin, in a side zipper. I hand him a circular white pill and my steel water bottle. "Down in one gulp. Come now, hurry up." He looks amused but does as he's told. He makes a good patient, no?

"Do you have anyone else here to . . ." Put you to bed, I was about to say, but stopped just in time, yet again. Thank God. That thought is even more intimate than seeing him barefoot inside his house. Today is my day of saying and thinking abysmally dumb things.

"No, I don't. Well, I have you now. Sort of." He points to the torn silver cover and the water bottle and smiles a quiet, honest smile, full beamed, that reaches beyond the dark fences into his beach eyes and hits me like dazzling sunlight.

"Err, um, yes. I think. Have you eaten anything?"

"No." He's still looking up at me with that quiet smile, as if I was a cross between Florence Nightingale and Wonder Woman. Very unsettling since I'm neither; mostly just a pill hauler.

"Here." I tear open the red box of chocolates and hand him one pack of Kit Kat. "Eat this. Never take medicine on an empty stomach."

He hesitates, gazing at me in his unnerving direct stare, before taking the Kit Kat. The dark circles make his gaze even more intense, like looking into glistening crystals. He opens the pack, breaks one rectangular piece off and hands it to me. "Only if you share."

For a moment, we both hold each end of the chocolate-covered wafer, he handing it to me and I taking it, as if it was an enchanted conduit binding us forever in this lifetime.

My phone chimes and he lets the Kit Kat piece go, and the conduit goes back to being a chocolate-covered wafer. It's Sheila Bua.

> Hellooooo and good morning again. Don't forget to give my regards to Lalit's mother at dinner today.

I'll be visiting my in-laws' house after work today. I have a bright blue and pink kurta and leggings in my bag for that occasion. Can't show up wearing gray and black for my first visit to my future home. Talk about inauspicious and dullness rolled into one. It's a whole lot of nerves because I've heard from Pa that their home is totally posh. Pa, Mum, and Sheila Bua visited Lalit's place before the engagement ceremony to finalize the relationship and formally invite him and his parents to the party and to "check out their house before entrusting them with our darling child," as Sheila Bua said. Of course, I can't wait to see their home, but if it's so fancy, how will I—a distinctly un-fancy person—fit into their lives?

I send Sheila Bua a smiley—there's no need to send her an actual reply and start a full-blown conversation just because I'm fully awake. I stuff the half piece of Kit Kat in my mouth, and so does Arnav Sir before he reaches for another one. Sheila Bua is on fire today. She sends another GIF, this time a mule raising a brass mug with the words "Cheers" splashed across a backdrop of Moscow, and a text underneath:

> This is what donkeys look like in Russia.
> #geography #knowledge

I snort into feverish giggles and can't seem to stop. "Oh God, Sheila Bua thinks the Moscow Mule is an animal!"

"What?" He clutches the arms of my chair and jumps up. "Your Sheila Bua's here? Maybe I should go home." I bet being pinned between Sheila Bua and the wall is still fresh in his memory, which just makes me giggle more. I better cover my mouth before I spit all over him.

"No, no, she's not here," I hiccup. "I'm teaching her to use GIFs and it's a . . . you don't even want to know." I show him the Russian donkey, the dancing Snape from this morning, and another one from yesterday: a fluffy white cat with a decidedly sensual expression and the words "Purr" written in all caps. I hold my stomach, oh, it hurts. "She has no idea of context."

His eyes widen in horror before he collapses again, this time in a full-throated laugh.

Chotu was right; his laugh is a like an explosion of fizz.

His entire body shakes and his head is thrown back, as if the mirth seeps into every cell in his being. Why does his normal behavior get me in the gut? Why? His stubble runs down to his neck, all the way to his Adam's apple, and my heart flips. I'm not laughing now. The weak haze outside the French windows begins to lift as clear sunlight beams in; a flock of pigeons flutter between the short buildings as the city slowly awakens.

"Not a dull day with you around." He wipes the tears from his eyes, and yawns. "But I think you're right. I am unwell. Will head home and leave you to enjoy your . . . gift." He rises from the chair to leave. He starts to walk toward his office but then turns back toward me and points to the last piece of Kit Kat in his hand. "Are you sure the flowers and this . . . are from your . . . fiancé?"

"Yes. And his name's Lalit." Didn't he read it on the engagement invite that I gave him?

"Yup. Sure is."

What does that even mean? He takes another pack of Kit Kat and walks off into his office. Two minutes later, he walks out with his laptop bag on his shoulder. He looks my way, touches the new packet of Kit Kat to his forehead in a salute, and is gone in a flash before I can wave back.

I open my inbox the moment I hear the lobby doors closing behind him, and immediately scroll down to a date three days ago. There it is, the email from Selena.Jones@bucklebee-agency.com. I can feel my heart expanding, a mixture of thrill and joy.

Dear Ms. Sahni,

As per Arnav Bajaj's recommendation, we are inviting you to apply for the position of Sr. Campaign Manager—

—please attach your latest resume and cover letter, along with your responses to the three questions listed below the job description—

I find myself blowing wisps of air slowly, as if practicing to breathe. It's a good thing the office is empty, or someone would've come over asking if I was alright. I click on the link. The red and black B&O colors unfurl and I'm swept off my feet again. The website banner shows a moving photo reel of their best creatives (the Steffi Graf one is there, too!).

1. Why do you want to work for us?

Its B-effing-O, only one of the top agencies in the world, which I've dreamed of working for even before I went to college for an MBA. The Steffi Graf Pepsi ad that's on their website right now was the one that made them world famous. It was everywhere, played before and in the middle of every TV show that I can remember. My Pa would stop whatever he was doing and gaze like a lovestruck teenager at Steffi Graf slowly guzzling Pepsi. Mum would be so pissed. Their new ads with Christiano Ronaldo are just as good. I never knew that a soccer player selling car oil could make you want to run out that instant and buy a car to put that oil in. Maybe I could rise up B&O's ranks like little Peggy Olson in *Mad Men*, minus the affairs and pregnancy (holy hell, don't go there).

I start typing, each click of the keyboard rings sweet and clear: B&O is one of the most renowned agencies in the world, with a history of creating unique campaigns. I have followed the agency's trajectory since before I began my career in marketing. It would be an honor to work for you, and a privilege to bring an Indian perspective to the agency's creatives.

2. Would you be open to relocating to New York?

I have never lived alone. Not even for a day. We are expected to live with our parents and then with our husband's parents, and not go gadding about to far-off lands. It's also eight thousand miles from anything familiar. I don't even know which way the door opens in America.

I'm not sure I can live alone. There was that one overnight picnic disaster in tenth grade, when I realized that I was alone in a new city without my parents, without any family who could look after me, the realization of which sent me into violent fits of crying, so I had to be sent back home on the next train. Yeah, living alone didn't work out that well. And since then, I've come home every day to hot meals, folded laundry, and paid bills (with my money, but paid for me). I have never looked after myself and wouldn't know where to start.

But it doesn't matter, does it? I'm not ten anymore. They're not asking if I'd be able to live alone. They're asking if I would be open to relocating to New York. THE New York. One of the most famous cities on this planet. If I wanted to show New York in an ad, all I'd need is a picture of a green hand holding aloft a green flame. Even a blurred silhouette would be instantly recognizable.

Hell yeah, I'd be open to relocating. I type a sedate Yes.

3. Where do you see yourself five years down the line?

I know what you are thinking: Zoya, you're engaged. But it's only a job application. It's not like I'm going to get it; advertising jobs in New York are notoriously hard to get. Even if I did, I wouldn't take it because, like you said, I'm engaged. I have a life here; parents, relatives, friends, now a fiancé and in-laws. But I can't *not* apply to something I've looked up to for years. Plus, Arnav Sir recommended only me from the entire company. It would be such poor etiquette to not even apply for the job.

Wouldn't it make a fine anecdote to tell my kids that their mom almost made it to America once? Hah. The very thought makes me melt into a puddle of joy. Or tell my parents and family, years later, when all danger of actually going to America has passed, simply to enjoy the shock on their faces?

I type: In the next five years, I see myself heading a team of creatives and helping brands in their marketing and advertising across a global platform.

I don't add, once I'm done looking after a home, and if my in-laws and husband are fine with it, or if they don't insist on having kids immediately.

Shake it off, Zoya. Lalit sent you flowers and you're applying for a bona fide job at B&O with a recommendation from your boss in tow. How much more can life look up?

I attach my cover letter, the most current project metrics, my résumé (which I scrubbed and shined, and then some), and check my answers to the application questions one final time. The little arrow on the monitor hovers on SEND. My palm tingles, as if all nerve ends are standing to attention. The office is silent, but I can hear loud thuds. Maybe it's the construction that's going on upstairs. No, it's too early for that. What . . . it's coming from me, loud thuds of my heart as the arrow on the monitor clicks SEND.

CHAPTER THIRTEEN

Njoy ur 1st visit to in-laws! Bless, bless.

Sheila Bua's eight PM pre-dinner text is followed by a meme of Pope Francis, his white cape flying behind him like Superman, and the letters "Like A Boss."

God give me strength.

Also, Sheila Bua has started GIFfing at all times of the day now. Okay, then. I keep my response short and sweet.

Thank you. Just sitting down for dinner.

It's so quiet in Lalit's house that I almost shushed my keyboard while typing that. The sleeve of my blue and pink tunic rustles as I keep the phone aside on the table. Why hasn't Arnav Sir responded to my texts checking on him? If he doesn't text at the end of dinner, I'll just call him.

Even my thoughts seem to echo in this spacious, hushed dining room with high ceilings. Would you look at that glittery mini-chandelier hanging over our heads? Whoever heard of a chandelier in a Bombay flat? Wow. But why are they all talking so softly, Lalit and his parents? As if using regular voices could crack the chandelier.

"Why are we so quiet?" I whisper to Lalit beside me. His parents sit across the table, his father checking his own phone and his mother carefully arranging the serving bowls and spoons so that they're easily accessible from both sides. Even the serving spoons don't clatter, made of silicon instead of the usual steel ones.

"We're a soft-spoken family. That's how we speak." He smiles, all nostrils. His mom arranges the bowls around the table as if her life depends on the precise distance between the crockery and the humans around it, and Lalit even smiles at me. Look at him, buffed up and cute in white T-shirt and gray trousers. His hair is combed all the way back. (Lots of hair gel. A bit eww.) He'd be way cuter with floppy hair, but I'll tell him that once we have gotten to know each other a bit better. And he's wearing white and blue house slippers on his feet; hmm, not barefoot like . . . hush, Zoya! Why did that pop into your head? Because I'm worried about Arnav Sir, that's why. He hasn't texted me back. I do hope his fever is gone now.

"Soft-spoken. Ah, okay," I say, lowering my voice even more. And no, it's not okay. No one in our extended family has ever considered the need for silence. I don't think they know the concept exists. Why, Sheila Bua can have three ongoing conversations with different people, in person, at the same time.

I can work around the quiet-family disorder. But the food? We are at the dinner table, and there are exactly three serving bowls with the simplest of fare. Lalit's mother opens the lids and my heart sinks as each one reveals its un-treasures. Or tortures. Same thing. There's no meat, no parathas or pooris, and zero potato or paneer dishes; all of which are supposed to be standard fare for guests, not to mention a future daughter of the house.

I do see some meat on the other end of the table, but it's just some boiled chicken pieces, which don't seem to have any other spice except salt and pepper.

A cabbage and carrot stir fry sits in a bowl, happily getting soggier by the second. Holy Mother of God, what self-respecting Punjabi serves cabbage subzi to a guest? And on their first visit? The other bowl is filled with sprouts in a tomato masala (sprouts? Did I walk into a health clinic by mistake?), not to forget the watery rajma bean curry (nonbuttery, noncreamy) to be eaten with what looks like dehydrated brown rice and a container stacked with round wheat rotis, without a patch of oil, ghee, or butter on the miserable little flatbreads.

My heart sinks to my empty stomach at the serving sizes. Each large bowl is only half full. Is this all there is for four grown adults? This is usually the size of our leftovers at home every night. His mom looks at me from across the unusually shiny glass table, waiting for my approval at this measly spread, anticipation writ large on her small face.

"It looks . . . delicious!" Okay, what, I'm supposed to be completely honest on my first visit to the in-laws? Such sweet parents, and I'm supposed to ruin it all with truth?

"So, how do you like our home?" Lalit turns to me with a mechanical smile, trying to attempt a conversation.

"It's lovely." And it is. I'm not lying this time. Lalit and his parents gave me a tour of the four-bedroom apartment as soon as I arrived. The flat is posh, even for Pali Hill. All minimalist steel furniture and sleek cream couches not meant for sitting, and expensive-looking giant abstract paintings. Like obscenely bright splotches of colors on the whiter-than-white walls. I need oversize sunglasses, you know, the ones used while skiing, to shield my eyes from all this snowy white glare.

Maybe I should send a picture of one of these paintings to Sheila Bua; she'll probably know who the artist is. I wonder, did Sheila Bua paint abstracts or portraits or something else? I have no idea. Oh well. I guess being on the Board of Directors of a Bombay eye hospital is a lucrative proposition for Lalit's father. Good for Pa, the newest member. A little rush of pride floods my heart—I made that possible for my father!

I snap a picture of what looks like several mismatched colors randomly splashed on a large canvas and send it to Sheila Bua with a caption: From my future living room.

It's all a bit scary and intimidating, to be honest, you know, like peeking into a five-star hotel dressed in your non-five-star clothes. I walked on my tippy toes as soon as I entered the apartment, leaving my simple, two-hundred-rupee sandals from Linking Road outside the front door. Seated at the well-laid-out dinner table, with all forks and spoons in the right *Downton Abbey* position, a strange thought pops into my head: should I just run for it? All this steel and shine, this is not me. Run off, indeed, Zoya. What a stupid thought. Yeah, you'd look like an ideal daughter-in-law running away from the dinner table of your perfectly nice future home. Well, I'm halfway to running already because I'm levitating like a horse jockey on this dining chair; my butt barely touches the white seat.

My phone chimes with a text from Sheila Bua:

> What garbage painting is this? Like someone's maid didn't show up so they got frustrated and sat on the poor canvas before it dried.

Another text follows immediately after.

> But don't tell the Khuranas, ok? Can't insult your in-laws like that, no? Tell them namaste from me!

Followed by several smileys.

Goodness. Sheila Bua is savage when it comes to art. No wonder she was accepted into Oxford. But in Bombay, maids are more valued than priceless artwork, so she's not entirely wrong in the frustrated reaction to an absconding maid. I quickly turn my phone over on the table so no one can see the family art critic in action.

"Come, Zoya beta, do start. You're the guest of honor." My future father-in-law, sitting next to my future mother-in-law, beams at me and a feeling of quiet well-being edges out the nerves. A woman is considered very lucky if she strikes gold with nice in-laws. Leaving aside the wretched food. Not to worry, I'll slowly bring some fat into this home, including the culinary kinds. (Must text Mum and remind her to save me some dinner: yogurt kadhi and her special long-grained jeera rice.)

Lalit's father and mother start to serve themselves, but I stop them. "Let me, please." I smile. Arranged Marriage Rule No. 4: When visiting future in-laws, always help around the house. In fact, act as if it's your birthright to do their chores. For all else, demurely ask permission. Mum and Sheila Bua have taught me well.

I serve Lalit some soggy cabbage subzi. A little trail of yellowed water drains from the cabbage and settles around the groove of his white dinner plate. "Thank you, that's enough." He blocks the serving spoon with his thick hairy hand.

"That's it?" Isn't cabbage supposed to be made primarily of water? What's the harm in eating double then?

"Yup. I have to count my macros."

"Macros?" What the hell is a macro? "Is that short for macaroni?"

They all burst out laughing, the health-conscious family chuckling indulgently at a fitness rookie. "Glad to know you still have the same sense of humor as that first time at the temple," Lalit says.

So, that went well. Note to self: must Google macros.

Plates filled with miniscule portions, we all get to the business of eating. In silence. I eat slowly and carefully, trying to not make a sound, either with the spoon clattering on the plate, or my mouth. God, I can even hear my teeth gnashing against each other, trying to make sense of the sprouts wrapped in the piece of roti. No one takes a second helping, so neither do I, not wanting to appear a glutton. Also, why would I voluntarily want more of the bland, spice-less food? It's like ill-people fare served in hospitals. Am I supposed to live on a diet like this for the rest of my life? Nope. Not happening. So I'm going to check out the restaurants and the food stall options around this area on my way back home, if I am to survive in this family.

"Zoya, beta, you're not eating anything at all!" Lalit's mother cries, looking at my plate which is still half full. "Do you not like our food? I made it myself for you."

Arranged Marriage Rule No. 5: Always, always praise your mother-in-law's cooking, no matter how toxic to your system, especially in front of her family.

"Oh, no, nothing like that. I love it. I'm just . . . slow." I smile sweetly and mix the rajma with brown rice, scoop it with a spoon and shove it into my mouth like medicine. The chewy rice grains are positively evil, each attacking a different group of teeth in my mouth.

"Lalli, beta, why are you mixing rajma with cabbage? Save some for the brown rice, too." His mother picks up the bowl of rice to serve him. "Lalli?"

Lalit, his attention deeply focused not on his plate but on his phone screen, looks up at his mother, almost in a snarl. "Can you just—"

He stops abruptly, realizing my presence, pushes his chair back, and says, "Excuse me." He crosses the long passage behind the dining room in short, thumping strides, enters the middle room, and slams the door shut.

What just happened? His mother looks as surprised as I am. His parents glance at each other, puzzled, and then at me. "Sorry, beta. He's so stressed at work, you know."

That didn't sound like work at all. I want to ask them, but can't. It's too new, this relationship.

"Maybe I could go . . . and see how he is? If that would help," I ask Lalit's mother.

"Yes, yes, do, please."

I pick up my plate in a bid to clear up but his mother waves it away. "Don't you worry about cleaning up. Just, well . . ." She tilts her head in the direction of the passage. I scrape my chair back, as quietly as I can, almost lifting it off the ground. The chair is surprisingly light for all that steel. I walk quietly through the passage to the door that was just slammed, a thick wooden door with a round brass handle, wondering whether I should go in, whether I will be welcomed. But I'm his future wife and it's my job to support him in times of need.

I knock on the door, with more confidence than I feel. "May I come in?"

There is no answer for almost thirty seconds, and I feel a little trickle of anxiety. Oh gosh, no one taught me what to do when your fiancé fights with his parents on your first visit to their house, and now you're standing outside his shut door wondering if you should even be here. And why is it that just when everything is nicely falling into place, something happens to shake the entire picture?

After what seems like a full era, in which I've berated myself for not anticipating my fiancé's problems like a good wife-to-be, and not being qualified enough to handle familial disputes, the round handle turns and there he is, still in his white T-shirt and gray trousers and home slippers, but his hair is scrunched, as if he tried to run his fingers through it but forgot halfway. And the now familiar hard little frown lines. Also, cheek-sag alert.

"May I?" I repeat.

"Of course." He waves me in. "I'm sorry about . . ." He points toward the dining room.

"It's alright. Are you okay?" I want to ask him more. But I'm not sure I want to know the answer.

"Yeah, I am okay." He holds the door open for me to enter the room and leaves it open behind me.

This room—my room too, one day—is all white just like the rest of his house. White sheets, cream walls, small open window with white edges and beige curtains. Dark gray pillow covers and a striped beige duvet tucked tightly into the mattress corners. Gray and beige are all from the same dull family of shades, so in my opinion, do not qualify as "colors." Maybe that's why I feel so bleak right now, such wintry hues. Note to self: start introducing bits of brightness into your future bedroom, beginning with a cheerful yellow.

I keep my phone on the bedside glass table as if it belongs there. It looks stark against the transparent surface, like a vulgar red blot distended in the air. How many times does their maid clean this table? Do they have maids simply for scrubbing glass in their house all day? It's so sparkly and clean that if it weren't for the steel edges, it would be totally invisible. For a moment, I'm so struck by a yearning to be back home, next to all our cozy wooden furniture and squishy couches, that my throat blocks up. Our square coffee table at home always has stuff on it: old newspapers, books, multicolored mugs filled with steaming tea, and my Pa's feet resting against its edge as he reads the newspaper.

In this room, it's just me and Lalit. He walks away from me, toward the white chair by the window across the room, sits down, and swipes at his black phone up, down, left, right. I know what he's doing. Using his phone as a crutch to avoid conversation. I do that too. I remain standing by the white bed, and for some strange reason, feel like I'm letting my parents down due to my inability to improve this situation.

Come on, Zoya, say something to make him feel better. He's your future husband, for God's sake. But what do I say? I don't know him well enough yet. Let's see: I could talk about health stuff. A grain of brown rice niggles inside a tooth in the back of my mouth. Ugh, no.

Just as I agonize over a common topic, my phone rings, like a loud gong in this silent room, shaking the see-through table. It's a text from Arnav Sir.

> Sorry for the late response to your messages. Was asleep. Feeling loads better, thanks to your caretaking and Crocin.

> Me: Good to know. Take care.

Lalit looks up at me from his phone, and I shake my head casually to indicate that the text is of no importance. It really isn't, not right this minute, no matter how much I waited for a response and wondered about Arnav Sir's health. But this text has given me a way to make Lalit feel better. The presents, of course! Which he sent to my office earlier today. How could I have forgotten to thank him as soon as I entered?

"Thank you for the flowers and chocolates." I sidle closer to him. Closer, as in, stand near his chair next to the open window.

He keeps looking at his phone, as if expecting it to come to life any second. "Chocolates?"

"Yes. The ones you sent to me this morning?"

"Err . . . yes, yes, of course." He is distracted, quickly typing a text and then thrusting his phone inside his trouser pocket. Okay, I tried to eavesdrop on that text (can you eavesdrop on a non-conversation?) but he typed so fast I couldn't see what it was, and only saw the first two letters of the contact name of the person. "Tee" something. Is he still in touch with his ex-girlfriend? What was her name? Maybe I should ask him about it. Stupid Zoya, it's not the right time. Privacy, you say? Oh come on, I'm going to marry him, don't I have a right to peek at a text?

"It was very thoughtful of you. How did you know daisies were my favorite flower?"

"Eh? Oh, that, yeah, I figured that out." He shrugs, not meeting my glance. Ah, isn't that sweet? He's shy about the good things he does. He jolts out of the chair, thrusts his hands in his pockets, and says "So, shall we go outside?"

"Yes," I say, and my heart is light, masking the gnawing doubt about making the right decision, for my family, and for myself, and that ex-girlfriend blip. It's just been a week since our engagement, and he took the time to find out my favorite things and surprised me with them. Totally a Diamond Boy fiancé, no? And if that is not a sign of a good relationship, then what is?

I walk to the open window, breathing in the air from the sixteenth floor, which somehow seems cleaner and cooler. A distant plane glides by, a small blip of light in a dark sky, and a thought sneaks into my head: maybe it's headed to New York.

I keep the beige curtains open, watching the plane glide by till it disappears into the dark clouds, before I follow Lalit out of the room like a good little fiancé.

CHAPTER FOURTEEN

1 month since engagement to darling son-in-law and 3 months to D-Day! Happy Holi!

Thank my stars that Sheila Bua waited all the way until six thirty *PM* today. Her text is followed by a GIF of a woman, her long hair parted in the middle, the face and hair covered in so much powdered color that all you can see are creepy dark dings for eyes and large hideous teeth. More Halloween than Holi.

So B&O replied to my email and I have a brief interview tomorrow night. Probably just with the HR person, so no need to be nervous, but I prepped just the same, studied their most recent marketing campaigns and dug up some of their metrics. A feeling of quiet peace passes through me right now. Because I'm sitting beside Lalit in the passenger seat of his luxury Audi, not because I was thinking of New York. Honestly. Lalit's just dropping me to my office this evening for our annual Holi (the festival of colors) party.

Speaking of the office, Lalit sent me another gift. It was a crooked Harry Potter mug with a single blue gerbera daisy in it. Oh, and it's a magic mug. Well, as close to magic as we poor Muggles will get. As soon as I poured hot chai into it, the words "I Solemnly Swear I'm Up to No Good" slowly appeared, transforming the plain black mug into a beige and red colored map of Hogwarts. Isn't my fiancé the best?

The feeling of peace evolves into total Zen mode.

But why is it so cold in the car? What is with men and death zone temperatures? I stretch my hand from the passenger seat and adjust the air-conditioning, turning it up to a comfortable heat.

"Uff, Zoya, why are you making the car so warm?" Lalit looks over from the driver's seat, irritated.

"Because I don't want to sit inside an igloo. And it makes me want to go to the bathroom."

He reaches for the air-conditioning and turns the heat down as soon I sit back in my seat. Look at us, like an old married couple already, bickering over the AC after just four weeks of knowing each other. The well-being lodges itself firmly inside.

Lalit had come over for tea earlier this evening, which was lovely. Both that he came, which made Mum and Pa so happy, and the food: samosas (baked, because I warned Mum about their dietary restrictions), paneer sandwiches (on wheat bread), and milky ginger tea (minimal sugar). Pa kept saying "my son-in-law" to no one in general, as if trying to taste that phrase and finding it delicious. And Lalit was supposed to meet with his colleagues for drinks in the same area as my office, so I asked him to drop me after tea.

We're slowly snaking through evening traffic. It's a government bank holiday today, which means all schools and colleges are shut—not the shops, though—and traffic is supposed to be low. But, Bombay. And car-logged traffic, with motorbikes and bicycles thrown in.

The festival of colors is evident everywhere; on the gray streets with residual powdered colors and dyed water, the remnants of a day of playing Holi, and people with half-colored faces trying to cross the road. It's kind of symbiotic, the city and this mind-bending chaos. But the outside bedlam is muted inside the cold car.

"What is this color you're wearing?" Lalit glances at my pale-yellow tunic, baby-pink dupatta, and pajama-type pants that are all the rage these days. I quite understand the attraction—so soft and loose, I mean talk about comfort. Added to that are oxidized bangles and my favorite dangly earrings. And the yellow is also in keeping with the color theme for the Holi party: pastels.

"Yellow." I smile at him, fully expecting him to smile back at me. "You know it's my favorite."

"Yellow doesn't suit you. Makes your complexion darker." He doesn't look at me. His eyes are focused on the red back lights of the traffic in front.

"No, it doesn't." How can he tell? The car is dark inside, so maybe the reflection of all those headlights make me look dark? No one else has ever told me that yellow darkens my complexion. And "looking dark" in our fairness-obsessed world falls squarely in the realm of disapproval. "Wait, does it really make me darker? It's not as if I'm wearing something in black . . . ," I say hesitantly, and he jerks his head toward me, as if I've said something shocking.

Should I start using concealer or something? What exactly is a concealer used for? Or that fairness cream that Mum used to insist upon? I grab my purse from the floor of the car and dig for my phone to check my face, and see a text from Arnav Sir:

Thank you for catching the error on our client invoice today.

I smile and forget about the yellow dress comment for the moment. Lalit's eyes are on the road.

Me: That was nothing. Just doing my job.

Hold on, why is my bag so empty . . . "Oh shit! My wallet! Shit shit shit. I left it at the mithai store!"

"What?" Lalit jerks his head toward me for an instant, before recalling the traffic in front of the car.

"At the mithai store! We were just there, getting sweets for your parents?" Mum and Pa insisted that I buy four packs of low-cal mithai for my future in-laws for the festival. Also, Arranged Marriage Rule No. 6: Large packets of mithai have to make their way over to the in-laws' house at every festival. Whether they eat sweets or not is immaterial. Zero mithai from the daughter's maternal home means you've made a bad deal for your son.

"Are you sure you left it there?"

"Yes. Right on the glass countertop."

"How can you lose your wallet, Zoya?" He takes his hands off the steering wheel for just a second to put them up in the air, acknowledging an event of great frustration.

"I didn't lose it. I know exactly where it is." I squint at him in surprise. Why is he so irritated? "It's not a big deal. It happens.

I know the store people; they're honest. I'll call and ask them to keep the wallet aside. Could you pick it up on the way back, please?"

"I don't know when I'll reach that store. I have to meet my colleagues for a drink. It won't even be open when I'm done."

I could go there myself, but that will mean a train change on the way back. Thank god, I have extra cash in a side pocket of my purse, along with the train pass. So much for my fiancé helping me. (And he didn't seem very keen on dropping me to the party in the first place, so I didn't insist that he drop me back home.) "It's okay, I can manage. I'll call them and tell them to keep it so I can pick it up tomorrow."

"Manage? How can you *manage* when you can't even keep ahold of your wallet?" He shakes his head in exasperation. "Women!"

What the hell was that? "It's just a wallet, and it's never happened before," I say, my jaw tightening. There's no need to give me the third degree, berate the entire female race, and make me feel like a failure simply because I left my wallet in a store. An honest mistake as I was distracted by the jostling crowd in the shop, all of them wanting those stupid low-cal desserts.

"Do you know what's in a wallet? Your whole life. Your credit cards can cause identity theft, someone could use them to buy illegal things, someone could take your ID and commit a crime. And the cash will be gone, of course. So many things could go wrong. It's not just a wallet." He mimics my tone, and continues shaking his head, while bending forward to the shiny dashboard to put the radio on.

I am totally disgruntled now. Just imagine, if this New York job works out and I actually live in America, how could I survive if all this identity theft and criminal stuff happened to me there? It's just better to be married and safe.

"Keto is the new Atkins! New research has shown that Keto can reverse diabetes, liver disease, and many others . . ."

Of course, a health show. I debate whether to change it to some music, but let it be. All those big health words will calm him down and put him in a better mood. And crime? Identity theft? Such big scary words. Am I really such a loser? I mean, a good looking, successful man thinks that, so it must be true?

I look out the window at the brightly lit shops outside. The car seems even colder and bleaker.

Stop, Zoya. Think happy parents, think wedding shopping, think reds and blues for the trousseau, colors that *do* suit you, and forget the yellow that you wanted for the reception outfit.

But am I not good enough for him? Maybe he'd have been better off with someone smarter. I'm overweight and dark skinned, but I'm clever and street smart, which the family has always told me is my redeeming factor. If my intellect is in question, what do I bring to the table in this marriage; and in life? A pleasant personality? Gah! We're supposed to inject pleasantness and deference into our very DNA post-marriage, so that's dime-a-dozen.

All this self-doubt is making me twitchy. Let me see if there are more texts from Arnav Sir. I scroll absently through my phone. Nothing. Damn it. Maybe I should look at the engagement photos, saved in a special album on my iPhone. They might put me in a better mood.

My WhatsApp bings with a text. From Tanya, of all people. She's sent me a picture of Lalit and me and her. She's sucking in her flat stomach next to my abundant one. The text says:

You really should stop eating. Period.

She is the last person to put me in a better mood. If I didn't know better, I'd say she's being extra mean to me these days. Not that she wasn't before, but these days it's more blatantly vicious since the engagement. At dinner at our place last week, she kept narrowing her eyes, staring at me, as if trying to decipher something, and then turning away with smirks every time I caught her eye. It's not my fault I got engaged before her.

Suddenly, before I can stop myself, I ask, "Do you know Tanya from before?"

He grabs steering wheel tight. "Not really." The plain gold engagement ring on his left hand looks tight as if it's squeezing the life out of his finger.

"What does that mean? Do you know her or do you not?"

"What is this, an interrogation?"

I don't say anything, but shift in my seat to turn toward him, and continue to stare till he answers.

"I can't . . . recall. She seemed . . . familiar." He looks away from me, blinking rapidly. "Why? Are you jealous of her? Don't worry, you're nicer, simpler—"

Simpler? That should make me happy, it should, but strangely the only thing it makes me feel is a spike of wrath.

". . . you are more moldable . . . ," he says.

Moldable? A whistling pressure rises in my head. Is there smoke coming out of my ears? It sure feels like it. I should have sounds coming from my mouth but it's all silent inside the car. A large truck honks like a ghoul and drives past us.

"Moldable? What the fuck, Lalit?" I finally find my voice. I know I shouldn't, but I can't stop the words, they tumble all out of my mouth in anger. "I suppose you couldn't mold that ex-girlfriend of yours and that's why you broke up with her?" Totally uncalled for since I don't know why they broke up, but I can't control myself.

The car brakes with a screech, and narrowly avoids hitting the motorcycle in front.

"What?" His face takes on an ugly hue, his eyes and nostrils so large that they could swallow me whole. The back light of the motorbike reflects on Lalit's face, a dark glowering stain of red.

"Your ex-girlfriend. The one you mentioned at the temple, when we first met."

He is silent for a whole minute. Cars start zipping by. One honks loudly from behind, urging him to drive on. Oh, Zoya, you don't learn, do you? Why add the ex-girlfriend on top of the Tanya question? I should've saved this question for another time, when we weren't arguing already. Lalit grips the side gears hard, upping the stick shift savagely. Dark green veins pop on the skin of his arms, from his wrist to the short sleeves folded over bloated biceps.

"She was not . . ."

"She was not . . . what? Not moldable?" Also, no point in telling my mouth to take a break.

"That's not what I meant."

"Then what exactly did you mean?" As if moldable could have any other meaning.

"It just didn't work out with her, okay? Now can we please drop the topic?"

Drop the topic? We barely just started. Just as I'm about to ask him another question, he says, "Don't ask me about her ever again, if you want our relationship to work." He breathes hard. The car stops again in traffic and he curses.

"But do you still . . ."

"Zoya, I'm warning you." A ragged teenage vendor knocks on the car window, selling a stack of pirated books at the traffic light. Lalit waves him away brusquely, but I smile at the boy in apology for Lalit's terseness and buy a book for Chotu quickly, without bargaining, and stuff it into my purse.

I am beyond irritated by the conversation. He thinks yellow makes me look dark, and that I can't manage my wallet or life, and doesn't want to talk about his ex-girlfriend. Is this what a real relationship is supposed to be like? Bubbling anger mixed with twisting anguish? And copious amounts of self-doubt?

"I just want to know what happened with you and that girl . . ."

"That's enough!" he yells. His black eyes are hard little rocks in the split second he looks away from the road at me.

"Fine!" I spit out the word and turn away from him in a dejected funk, hands crossed over my chest. I am suddenly glad that I applied for that job in New York.

The traffic opens up a bit and the car picks up speed on the busy evening street.

How does night fall in the Big Apple?

He's just like any other guy, I realize with a stab of disappointment. I was expecting . . . I don't know, not this.

Does night in New York tease you into a warm lilac dusk like Bombay?

Yes, okay, I know I agreed to marry him after a fifteen-minute meeting and have known him just a short while. But that's arranged marriage for you.

Or does night fall on the Empire City all at once, like a swift, dark blanket?

And marriage is advertised as the Ultimate Solution in our society: Daughter depressed? Get her married and she'll be fine! Son has no aim in life? Get him married and he'll get right back on track! Girl wants a different life? Get her married; once she has a home to take care of, there won't be time for such wayward thoughts! How can any relationship survive such lofty, life-altering expectations?

Wonder what else you will be disappointed by, says the little voice inside my head. This despairing little thought makes me feel colder in the car than before.

We drive the rest of the way in complete silence. No words, no glances, but there's enough noise around us. The hum of people and vendors and stray animals, vehicles honking one after the other. Streetlamps, headlights, glowing over large outdoor advertisements, lights in shops and shrines. It slowly trickles into the car, the sounds, the lights, mixing into the silence. I want to shut my ears and shout to make it all go away. I scroll through my phone again, and sure enough, there's a text from Arnav Sir:

I should make all invoices go through you now.

Why does that make me want to bawl my eyes out?

Me: You can't do that. You'll piss off the accounting team.

A: Why aren't you at the party yet?

Me: Be there soon. Do you not have any patience?

A: Not in the least.

Even Arnav Sir's texts don't help with this wrangling discontent that I feel. Within five minutes, the car screeches to a stop outside my office building. The vehicles behind honk loudly and pedestrians cuss, vexed at the sudden stop. I get out and slam the car door, and Lalit drives off without a backward glance. I really should've slammed the door harder.

I call the mithai shop immediately after he drives away: they found my wallet and it'll be in safekeeping till I can pick it up. There! Only then do I let myself say it loud (inside my head): *Jerk!*

I'm outside the office building, facing the busy street with cars and buses zipping by, still cussing under my breath, when I see Sheila Bua across the road.

What?

All thoughts of Lalit and Tanya and lost wallets go flying out of my mind.

What is she doing here? Shopping? She's on the sidewalk standing like a zombie, immobile outside the decrepit entrance of a tiny art deco building, her ponytailed black hair in disarray. A rusted sign over the door says something-Art Gallery. I know it starts with a D and ends with two ees. The rest of the letters are practically erased. And she has a stack of rolled-up papers under her arms.

Hold on. If she was coming anywhere near my office to shop, she'd have called or texted for sure, to offer to pick me up or drop me or just generally pry into my life.

Why didn't she?

And what's with the blobs on her white tunic? That seems like color but I can't make out from across the road. But Sheila Bua hates playing Holi and will fake her own death rather than step out on the day when people throw color at everyone on the street. She seems out of breath. What's that all about? She steadies herself with a hand on her chest and gulps great big globs of air. I almost cross the street to check on her, but she gets into a waiting taxi and zips off.

I text her in the lift on my way up to the office. (Old lifts win over snazzy new ones: no break in cell phone signals.)

Where are you, Sheila Bua?

Her message comes right back within seconds.

At home. Where else would I be on Holi?

Maybe I was mistaken. Maybe it was someone else. No, it was her, with her lime-green bag. But why is she lying?

CHAPTER FIFTEEN

Would you look at our office? Transformed from a black-and-white movie into a blast of technicolor tonight. Color, color, everywhere: orange marigold garlands on walls and desks, yellow fairy lights strewn over cubes. Multicolored pinwheels, ribbons, and balloons dangle from the ceilings. Little earthen bowls of powdered color sit on every desk. HR's really outdone themselves with decorations this time. Holi isn't called the Festival of Colors for nothing. It's like Eastman Color on magic mushrooms. That could totally be a tagline for Hindustan Paints. But it won't work for a family audience. (It's not my product, so I really don't have to worry about it, but I can't turn my brain off sometimes.)

"Zoya! There you are." My colleague Kaya throws herself upon me in a bear hug and a giggle outside the door of the conference room. A large puff of dry colors—reds, blues, greens, pinks—sprinkle from her face on my pastel yellow kurta. Wild laughter and Holi songs sound totally unnatural in the office. All of that mixed with sports commentary on full blast coming from the conference room.

"What took you so long? We've all been waiting for you to lead the mad dancing." Kaya drags me toward the crowded conference room without waiting for my response.

"And what number drink are you on, Ms. Kaya?" I ask. The sounds of "Rang Barse," the pervasive Holi song about raining colors, wafts over the conversation and cricket commentary.

"Ah, this is thandai. Made of milk. Doesn't really count as a drink," Kaya says, a silly distracted smile on her face. She sways to the music.

Joe from IT and Ayan from Finance, with identical pink hair and green faces, DJ under a strobe light in a corner of our largest conference room. Joe notches up the volume, which is greeted by loud whoops of colleagues dancing around the table piled with food.

"Thandai laced with bhaang. Pot. So, very much a drink," I say.

Faroukh and Abhi from Sales dance by themselves inside their cubicles, amid marigolds and fairy lights. I bet there's actual booze at this party. I hope so, at least.

Technically, we can't drink alcohol on office premises. But the nutty thandai is a Holi custom and adding pot is a centuries-old tradition. Tradition trumps rules. And Kaya never leaves a chance to add alcohol or weed to anything if she can help it. It's a blessing HR isn't present at this party. (HR is all of Pinali and Hetal, who both leave at five PM on the dot, party or no party, even if they did put it all together. They also live at the other end of the city: a two-hour commute one way.)

"You caught me." Kaya giggles again, and she's not a giggly girl. In her drunk state, Kaya's completely forgotten to smear color on my cheeks—the first thing people do at Holi on seeing their friends. "Come on, Zoya, let's dance!" Kaya rushes headlong into the grooving batch of colleagues in the conference room, all of them gently dabbing dry color on each other's cheeks.

Office etiquette stops us from playing real Holi, which entails grabbing your friend in a stranglehold from the back and smearing globs of colors on their face, neck, and hair, which then sprinkles onto every object within sight. Last year, Aiden Bauer, visiting from the Boston office, reeled in shock as if witnessing a real live crime. In the end, no one would've guessed he was white under all that color, at least until he spoke. And a few beers later, all accents sounded similarly slurred, so random drunk colleagues discussed philosophy with him in Hinglish (Hindi + English) and he nodded along, giving appropriately dubious answers in English.

And as for off-key dancing, I wouldn't dare, not with my boss looming somewhere in the office. My phone lights up with a text from Arnav Sir—ah—and the text opens by itself. (My phone auto-lock stopped working and I keep forgetting to fix it.)

You're late.

Yup, he's looming, alright. As if he was waiting for me. The pressure in my head seems to ease a little.

Nope. Only you think so.

Not late, but pissed, because of usual fiancé stuff. But all the lights and flowers and colors help with my mood. Okay, so Lalit didn't like what I was wearing and seems to not want to talk about his ex-girlfriend.

Oh God. I've been such a fool.

He's hung up on her and hurting. Maybe that's why he was so mean. I should've been more considerate. And not stormed off in a huff. Why can't I just be a good fiancé? Like other normal girls? Why am I being so angsty? Oh, Zoya, just call him, will you? I mean, he's a good guy. And everyone has faults, don't they? At least he's not the jealous type and doesn't stop me from going to parties like other crazy possessive ones. It's progressive, really, if you think about it.

I walk to my cube to put my purse down and debate over calling Lalit. He's hurting, fine, but there was no need to make me feel as if I was incompetent. I pull out my phone and keep it on my desk, still debating, still irritated, when a shirt on a hangar magically appears next to me. "Happy Holi, Madam."

The only way to know it's Chotu under all that color is his gummy smile, which he flashes regularly.

"Here's something for you." He plonks a paper plate filled with fresh, warm vada pav and what looks to be a book; it's rectangular and covered in a yellow daisies wrapping paper, so it's got to be a book.

"What is it?"

He sighs in a theatrical frustration. "Zoya Madam, you really have to tell your fiancé to call me and I'll arrange the gifts for you. What is the need for all this secrecy and leaving things in the canteen with a note? Look at this." He points to another little white card, which says:

Hope you liked the Kit Kats and flowers and mug. This is the best vada pav this side of town. Bon Appetit.

Lalit's sorry, he's really sorry. A sharp little thread of cheer snakes its way through the pique at Lalit. It burrows through but is unable to completely make it go away. Come on, Zoya, that's a really thoughtful way of apologizing. And look at this vada pav—the batter-fried potato balls are warm, and the two buns are still joined at the hip, stuffed with potato and accompanied by a single fried green chili on the side. Exactly the way I like it.

I'm *such* a lucky girl.

But I don't feel lucky. I feel all twisted and knotty inside. You can't just call me things and send food and make it all better. Wait a minute. Food? And Lalit? But that health podcast . . . ?

Doubt stirs in my brain. Surely . . . no, no, Lalit sent those gifts. I'm just overreacting to everything because of the wallet and molding incident in the car. I know, I should call Aisha and ask her if she and Varun had teething troubles like us. Yes, that's a good idea.

"Thank you," I say to Chotu, keeping the wrapped book aside to open later. Because if it's a book, Chotu might want to borrow it and I don't feel like lending this one just yet, whatever it is.

"And here's something for you." I whip out the paperback that I bought for him from that teenage street vendor. "*Agatha Raisin and the Quiche of Death* by M. C. Beaton. Fun crime series."

"Oh," he says, his face disappointed. "I've read everything in this series already. But thank you."

"Read it already? From where?"

He doesn't answer my question but rambles on. "But you see, Zoya Madam, the Beaton series are nice British mysteries, but they are such mild murders. What is this bonking someone on the head and then that's it—they're dead? Where is the twisting knife and the spray of blood and chopped-up limbs?"

Note to self: no more mysteries for him. Next time I'll get him *A Man Called Ove* or something equally charming.

"Speaking of chopping limbs, how much did you score on your Math test this week?"

He stares sheepishly at his flip-flopped feet. "Fifteen out of twenty-five," he says, tucking the Beaton paperback into his back pocket. He does like collecting books so, even multiple copies.

"No! Fifteen is horrible!" I whack him on the head with a folded yellow file. A sprinkle of orange powdered color falls on his head. "What happened?"

"But Zoya Madam, see, I got you this gift! It was left in the canteen and I brought it all the way to your desk!" He tries to pacify me by dangling the paper plate of vada pav in front of my face.

"Yes, thank you. But what does my gift have to do with your Math score? Do you want to serve vada pav in an office your whole life? Why did you score so bad?"

He doesn't meet my eyes. "Umm . . . well . . . I was reading *The Killings at Badger's Drift* the night before and couldn't put it down. You know, one character gets his throat slit and the blood fills the entire room . . . ," he says, immediately animated, his forefinger slicing across his throat in a gurgling gag.

For God's sake. "Just you wait. I'll call your father right now and tell him you were reading a novel instead of studying!" I grab my desk phone to make good on my threat. The bad test score is my fault, really. With all this engagement and in-laws hoopla, I've been totally lax with Chotu. No one in his family bothers about his schoolwork and if I don't either, he'll end up running a canteen like his father. Which isn't a bad thing, but this kid has so much potential.

"No, Zoya Madam! Not my Abba, please!" He squeaks, dashing into the wall of my cube to stop me from calling. "I have another test next week. I promise I'll do better."

"Oh, yes you will. Or I won't buy you any more books." Maybe I should cut his supply of novels to one a month instead of three. "And speaking of books, who got you textbooks for the next school year already? And the other mysteries? I've been watching you with that bag of yours, filled with stuff that you certainly didn't get from me. Who's taken my place, tell me or I'm calling your Abba!" The bangles on my wrists tinkle like wind chimes as my hand hovers over the phone.

"I've taken your place."

The voice booms from above, deep and rich, like the entry of the star in a movie, and I feel sort of . . . faint. I really should've eaten that vada pav.

There he is, in a short white kurta over blue jeans. A tunic and Arnav Sir? My heart bangs. I've never seen him in casuals, forget anything ethnic. The white tunic makes his shoulders look broader and he towers over both Chotu and me. It rattles me, this . . . this . . . kurta, already splashed with multiple colors, which, for some reason, seems like a state of undress. And those lean jeans? Why can't he be dressed in his business-casual uniform? I don't like change.

"I've been giving him books," he says. "I told you to keep your mouth shut, didn't I?" Arnav Sir growls at Chotu, hands crossed, rocking on his heels. Is that a twinkle in his eye or am I seeing things?

Chotu doesn't look the least bit scared. "But I didn't tell her. I promise, I didn't! I never told her that you've been paying—"

"Chotu." He glowers, beach eyes shoot lightning darts, but the Chotu-train is unable to stop.

"— paying my school fees for years—"

The hammering in my heart is very loud. I bet the whole office can hear it. The music, the cricket, the laughter, all suspends in a split second of silence. My hand hovers over my stomach, making the bangles tinkle. As if a mere hand can stop the stomach from a deep dive.

"And since you're so fond of talking, mind telling me your test score from Monday?" Arnav Sir talks to Chotu but his gaze is glued to my bangles.

"Oh God, not my Math score again!" Chotu clamps a hand to his forehead in exaggerated melodrama. Didn't I tell you he had potential? "Why are you after my life? I think you both should marry and trouble each other, not me."

A loud cheer bursts from the audience watching the cricket match in the conference room; a Mumbai Indian batsman hits the ball into the crowd for six runs.

"Shut up!" I screech at Chotu, louder than I mean. I didn't even intend to yell at him, it just burst out of me. What an absurd thing for him to say. Why didn't Kaya smear color on my face?

All that color could've hidden how red it is right now. "Now GO before I really call your father." Chotu, not the least bit perturbed, rushes off in the direction of the conference room in a puff of colors.

Arnav Sir pays for him to go to school? And he's the one giving him novels to read?

"Arnav! Zoya! What are you both doing, talking amongst yourselves over there?" Sohail Borekar, one of our other Directors, short and stumpy, calls out from near the lobby. We walk up to him. "Come on. It's time for hand-painting!" A horde of colleagues follow him like a clomping herd to the big white canvas set up near the reception desk, all of them shouting several versions of "Holi hai! It's Holi!" at the top of their drunk lungs.

"Okay, people." Sohail holds his hands up, always eager to address a throng. "Here's what you do—dip your hands in these lovely brass bowls filled with colored paste, and plant one hand or even both on this pristine white canvas. There are sponges and rags to clean up after if you so wish. Or just wipe it on each other!" he harr-harrs.

And because it's a Bombay crowd and the concept of a queue is absent from our DNA, everyone rushes at once to dip their hands in the four bowls, overturning the red one on the gray carpet. "Now that's the true essence of Holi!"

"—Oh, hurry up, people—"

"—The green, I said green—"

"—Mine's pink—"

"—How many hands do you bloody have—"

"—Don't you dare cover my handprint—"

A stoned Kaya staggers over to Arnav Sir and me. "Arnav, you should put your handprints next to Zoya's. She's is the only one who understands your instructions!" Hearty laughter explodes from assorted colleagues, especially Samir Iyer, our Senior Manager of Creatives, who often comes reeling out of Arnav Sir's office, disheveled, clutching a sheaf of red-inked papers. Well, if they just listened to his explicit directions instead of fiddling on their phones in meetings, they wouldn't need to redo their work multiple times. Arnav Sir shrugs it off with a laugh and dips his hands into the bowl of yellow color. I choose blue.

Colored handprints start to appear on walls and people's backs. Arnav Sir and I finally manage to make our mark on the swarming canvas in the midst of pungent breaths and puffs of powdered colors.

His handprint looks gigantic; the soft part of his palm overlaps mine on the canvas. Yellow blends into blue in a seamless lush green, as if it belongs. His hands surround me on both sides without touching as his palms are still colored, to shield me from the throng of colleagues. His soft kurta brushes against my cheeks and I turn around. The white of his tunic is all I can see, musky sweat and fresh perfume all I can smell.

We might as well be alone.

A spike of hot coals rushes up my spine. My voice seems lodged behind a boulder inside my throat. I duck under his hands, wiggling out of the crowd, and hurry off to my desk in a mad dash. I'm in my cubicle, vigorously rubbing the color off my palms with a rag cloth when he walks up.

"You okay?" An empty plastic glass dangles from his hand. Kaya's pot thandai. Is he a bit tipsy?

"I'm sorry . . . it's just . . . I don't know . . . ," I blabber, as usual, in his presence. It's too much. First the white kurta, then Chotu's books, now that stupid hand-over-handprint. "I'm just having a hard time . . . I mean the school fees . . . books . . . that was you?" For some reason I can't meet his eyes. "I wouldn't have ever . . . you?" I'm stuck on the "you," which whooshes out of my mouth as an undertone, an intimate whisper. Fairy lights twinkle in my dim cube. The hum of riotous colleagues rumbles in the distance, as if far away.

"Yes, Zoya, me. Is it so hard to believe? Am I such a monster?" He tilts his head, a sad little smile hovers near his eyes.

No, it isn't hard to believe at all. "You're not a monster. That's not what I'd call you."

"Then what would you call me?"

A vortex of colors explodes inside my head but my mouth can't translate them into sensible words. I finally look up at him and smile. His hand rises to my face and in excruciating slow motion smears a trail of wet yellow on my cheek. "Happy Holi, Zoya."

It's as if I've been electrocuted.

His fingers fall by his side, but we face each other, his drunk, blazing eyes and my singed self. The fairy lights set his beach eyes aflame. The space between us is a split second long, infinite.

The loud ring of my phone spears the moment into shards. I tear my eyes away from him—why is it so difficult to look away?—to see a face on my mobile screen, all nostrils and teeth.

Lalit.

I had forgotten him.

A collective groan rises from the conference room, followed by cusses and desk thuds. Mumbai Indians have lost a key player.

My hand hovers over the phone, hesitating for a second. I really don't want to talk to Lalit right now, at this moment, even though he sent me a gesture of apology. My cheek still tingles with Arnav Sir's touch. And his deep eyes: even though mine are turned away, they burn into my soul. But the phone keeps ringing. Arnav Sir looks at the screen, his face blank, and he walks away.

I let out a shaky breath. Just as well. The little black phone rings and vibrates so hard it could jump off the desk straight into my hands. I have to take this call. How can I ignore my fiancé for my . . . boss?

"Hi." I speak softly into the phone, not because I'm trying to be kind, but I don't want to broadcast this conversation.

"Hi." Lalit's voice is faint, as if he's on one of those trunk calls from a destination far away, like they show in movies from the '70s, with two actors straining to hear each other on the phone. "You forgot yet another thing. The mithai packets in the car."

"That's what you think." Whatever happened to being warm and appropriately contrite when calling your fiancé after an argument? Not fun to piss her off more. And I'm not as stupid as he believes. "I didn't forget them. They're for your parents."

"My parents don't need four packets of desserts. I thought two of them were for your colleagues."

"No. They're all for your parents. I just did what Mum and Pa asked me to do." Are we still talking about desserts? "And if you didn't want me to buy that many, why didn't you tell me at the store?" I bark into the phone. Be kind, Zoya, be kind, remember he sent you a present to apologize.

It's the thought of the present that makes me do it. And the health podcast in the car, the low-cal sweets, that he thinks my favorite color darkens my complexion, that he may be still hung up on his ex-girlfriend. "Forget the packets. I just wanted to say, well, thank you for the presents. The . . . biryani was delicious." I lie.

Please be confused and say it was not biryani. Say you sent vada pav. Say it, please.

The silence on the other end of the line crackles, persisting for the longest time, but it's only a second or two in reality. "I'm glad you enjoyed it."

No, no. Is this what a heart attack feels like? A heavy weight pressing on your gut, spreading up, engulfing everything under its load?

The voice inside me says I knew it all along.

Hurt and anger at my own credulity bubble dangerously to the surface, crashing into a torrent of dejection. I'm powerless to stop it. "You're lying! Why did you say you sent me those presents when you clearly didn't?"

He doesn't even try to deny it. "You seemed happy so I went along with it. I don't have time for such juvenile things, but if you *thought* I did, hey."

"No time? You have no time for your future wife? Then what the hell do you have time for?" What have I done? Have I made a giant mistake, simply to please my parents, to please society? Then again, I wanted this marriage thing for myself too. But is this how all arranged marriage relationships start? Lies, arguments, disappointment?

"Look, this is going nowhere." I can hear the car door slam and the beep of the car lock. He's reached the venue where his colleagues are waiting. "Let's talk tomorrow when we're both a bit calmer."

"Yeah, whatever," I say to Lalit, but he's gone before I've finished speaking. I'm still holding the phone to my ear, as if my body has no energy for mundane tasks like hanging up.

Finally, I thwack the End button. I really want to smack the phone hard on the table, but I set it down it ever so gently. My hands are stained with color—blue and some of Arnav Sir's yellow, from our handprints. I try to rub my tired eyes before I can stop myself. Blue-yellow-green eyelid. Mental groan.

Also, Arnav Sir didn't really walk away. I see he's hovering three cubes away, trying to give me privacy with his face turned away. I pick up the rectangular gift that came with the vada pav. I slowly tear the wrapping paper off. I was right; it's a book. The latest psychological thriller, one that I've been itching to read, with the heroine in a coma who can hear everyone. I wish I was in a coma. I guess I'd be more *moldable* then.

Arnav Sir turns toward me at the sound of ripping paper, his forehead filled with worry lines.

I give him a self-conscious smile, and he immediately reaches my cube, as if that is a signal of sorts. I guess it is. "It was not Lalit who sent me the chocolates, the mug, this food." I point to the bread stuffed with potato and almost crumple.

He gazes at me with worry lines still intact on his forehead, apologetic, and something else in his face. Oh God, I hope it's not pity.

"And he also thinks yellow is not my color." I point to my pale-yellow kurta and shrug. God, Zoya, stop. Yes, you're pissed, but that's no excuse to diss your Diamond Boy fiancé in front of other people. No one says you can't diss him, just do it like in the movie *Inception*: deep in your subconscious, three layers down.

The two vada pavs lie forlorn on the paper plate. "I've been stupid, haven't I? Lalit wouldn't give me fried potato even on my deathbed." I laugh, a harsh little bark. "Maybe some dried-up brown rice. But never bread and potato."

"You mean something with actual carbs?"

That's rich coming from him. Did he forget his bread-hating ex-girlfriend? "You should know. Bread is the food of the devil, no?" I need to tape my mouth shut.

He presses his lips and his fiery beach eyes are back. "I see your brown rice—real carbs—and raise you low-sodium-no-butter-flour-less bread." He lifts the empty white plastic glass, which is now colored yellow (and some blue-green) in his hands. "What food group that is, only the devil knows. And if you eat it, you'd beg the same devil to take you straight to hell." His eyes crinkle and a hiccup-like sound escapes his mouth. Oh yeah, he's tipsy.

I giggle, too, the little shards of the phone call gently dissipating. Some people just have a knack for untwisting things. I wish Lalit and I had that together, that easy comfort. "Maybe we should open a club. Martyr spouses of health fiends."

"Or introduce my ex-girlfriend to your . . . fiancé?"

"Do you want me divorced before my wedding?" I feign shock, a hand over my heart. My chest is now smeared with color. For God's sake.

"So. Who sent you this stuff then? Your Sheila Bua maybe? Who would know you so well?"

"Can we not talk about presents? It's a bit depressing." I really thought it was Lalit. How could I have been so wrong? Why is this arranged marriage thing so hard, why can't it be easy and flowing as . . . well, other things?

"Speaking of non-depressing things, have you heard from B&O?"

"Yes. I have a brief phone interview tomorrow." My voice is flat. All of this drama has put a pall over it. "The word brief doesn't seem like they're too interested," I say, feeling a little deflated. "Maybe they're just doing it for a formality since the recommendation came from you, one of their regional executives."

"I'm quite sure it's nothing of the sort. If it was someone else, I'd remind them to be well prepped for even an initial interview, but with you, I *know* you will." He smiles, and his confidence in me restores some of this evening's imbalance.

"And we can't have you depressed now, can we? Not on Holi. With your permission?" He separates the two bread rolls stuffed with the fried potato. He hands one to me, takes the other, and touches the tips of both vada pavs together as if they were cocktails. "Go on. Cheers." And takes a gigantic bite out of his share. I do the same. We eat the fried starch and gluten (so yumm!) in an agreeable carb-reverent silence, while random colleagues applaud the end of the cricket match inside the conference room.

"Look over there. Our adopted teenager." Arnav Sir points to the reception desk. Kaya has restocked the reception table with more plastic glasses of her pot thandai and Chotu is in the process of sneaking one. Chotu feels our gaze—everyone can feel Arnav Sir's laser stare, not just me—and raises the white plastic glass at us with a cheeky grin. We raise our index fingers toward him and mouth, "Just one!" at the same time.

"You have a good heart, Zoya Sahni." Arnav Sir smiles.

"So, do you, Arnav Bajaj."

"And Zoya." He pauses in mid-stride on his way back to the conference room, "Yellow is your color. Don't let anyone tell you otherwise."

And he's off with that parting shot, sprinkling rainbow hues behind him.

CHAPTER SIXTEEN

5:45 AM.

> 1.5 months since engagement to darling son-in-law and 2.5 months to D-Day! Enjoy morning exercise at beach.

Sheila Bua's text is followed by a meme of Rocky Balboa and the Terminator, strung up with tubes and bandages in a hospital bed, thumbs-upping each other with the words "That was a great workout!" My family is supportive, in their own ways.

A thing happened. Nothing major, but Arnav and I have taken to texting, a lot. The "Sir" sort of dropped away after the Holi party two weeks ago. We're not supposed to call him Sir at work anyway; it was just how I addressed him in my mind. It didn't take getting used to at all. Arnav, Arnav; very easy on the tongue. Not at all an acquired taste, unlike some other words.

So we text. At odd times of the day. Well, depends on what you'd call odd. Six in the morning is not odd. Not for him, anyway, considering the daily email tomes he sends to the team before any of us are even conscious.

What is one supposed to do when your Diamond Boy fiancé and future mother-in-law invite (order) you for a six AM Pilates workout on the beach with their fitness group? You have to find ways to stay awake on your way to the workout. Texting helps.

Arranged Marriage Rule No. 7: When your in-laws ask you to accompany them, before marriage, you drop everything and go. Even if the God of Death is at your door, you bypass him and go.

The rattle of the rickshaw and the cool breeze of dawn lulls me into a wobbly drowsiness this morning. I think Lalit was suspicious over the phone last evening and sort of ended the discussion in a booming finality; the dominant tone in our conversations these days, as if I were a child to be indulged but then Daddy had the final say. "You are coming, Zoya, that's it. Our group has waited a long time to meet my fiancé. And don't lose your wallet this time." He hung up with that farewell.

So I texted him back that no, I won't forget and if he wanted, I'd get two wallets, just in case. My phone was silent afterward, so I ate a butterscotch pastry for an evening snack (fine, two), all the while telling myself that he was just looking out for me. We've had our share of arguments, but which couple doesn't? That's no reason to worry, not at all. We speak on the phone twice a week, Lalit and I, at seven in the evening like clockwork, and they're always short phone calls or texts, no nice long conversations. I always feel a twinge of unease at 6:45 PM as if I'm about to sit for an exam that I forgot to study for.

* * *

My phone bings with a text from Arnav.

So, what's the plan this morning?

Me: Plateees on the beeech, according to his mother. On my way now. Ugh.

Arnav: Aah, plateeees, yoga, strength training, HIIT. I'm very up to date with my fitness terms without doing a single one of the above, thanks to the Beanstalk.

Me: Lucky you.

My boss talks about his ex-girlfriend with me now. It started after the Incident of the Phone Call at the office party, when we compared notes about health fiend partners. *Shouldn't you call it the Incident of the Lingering Fingers on Your Cheek?* Ah, that sneaky voice inside my head is back. I'm trying extremely hard to not think about it, but you, stupid voice, aren't helping one bit. I found out that Arnav was the one who nicknamed her the Beanstalk, not that Kabir kid in his building. Pretty wicked considering what she looks like, tall and springy, and rather pretty. I stalked her on Instagram and her profile page is bursting with pictures of kale. (More than ten thousand followers—hello, influencer, for my next Turbo Blender social media plan. Maybe I should pitch the idea of influencer swag bags to the Blender clients.) There are also cats on the page. And cats eating kale. No wonder they broke up.

Arnav: So, was the "Ugh" for the mother-in-law or Pilates?

Me: Both. (Forget I said that!) Aaxxercise—again, her words—to be followed by minestrone soup at their place. Low salt and whole grain toast, extra grains, zero butter. Ugh raised to infinity.

A: Wonderful. Enjoy it while I eat my fresh paratha stuffed with potatoes. Lathered with a dollop of butter. I might send you a picture.

Me: Go to hell.

A: Speaking of hell, will The Fiancé be there?

Me: In hell?

A: On the beach. Really, Zoya, your words, not mine.

Me: He better be. I'm doing this for him.

That was the last text. It's been five minutes and nothing. Probably busy shoveling the paratha in his mouth. Of course, he would be eating a fresh paratha so early in the morning, courtesy of his ancient cook, who was also his father's retainer from his army days. The man was retiring and didn't have a home or a family, and Arnav's parents wanted to globe-trot, so my boss hired him as a cook and now the old gentleman lives with him. Not many people would do that, which just shows you the kind of person he is. And the parathas! His cook makes the most delectable stuffed bread, because we share food sometimes now. I don't really know how it happened but we're a lot more casual now. I guess a layer sort of strips off between people who eat together. Or grab food from each other's plates while passing by. Same thing.

The rickshaw is still about five minutes from the beach, so out of habit I check the Sahni-Arora family WhatsApp group, which is usually filled with crappy "Good Morning" messages and time-wasting forwards. Oh, for God's sake. Didn't need to see a picture of Tanya looking impossibly thin first thing in the morning. Of course, Rita Chachi sent Tanya's picture for everyone to admire:

At the Sabyasachi designer store, trying on lehengas for Tanya's friend's wedding. #aboutlastnight

Tanya also sent a similar picture separately to me with a text:

You'll never fit into this.

And I texted back:

Why would I want to? I don't need clothes to define my happiness.

And felt a bolt of pure pleasure at having a witty answer ready for once. Her parents really need to find her a fiancé so she stops her jealous text tirade.

But witty replies don't mask her slim beauty. Ugh. Can her stomach be any flatter? Or hair any straighter? I bet she finds clothes her size in every store she goes to, unlike me. Yesterday, I was searching for plus-sized sweatpants online and it showed me tummy-control corset panties under the "Items You May Like" section.

Never mind that now. Think fiancé, think exercise, think good health.

And I'm not sure why Arnav calls Lalit The Fiancé and never uses his real name. I asked him a couple of times (on text of course) but he didn't answer and the next time it was "THE FIANCÉ!!!" from him in all caps with a thousand exclamation marks. As if the said fiancé would burst from both our phones and catch us at I don't know what.

Some days when Arnav is in a particularly chipper mood, The Fiancé becomes Loathsome Lalit. I know, I know, I shouldn't have. Shouldn't have told him about this old nickname that I stopped using ages ago, even to myself. In my defense, it happened in a fit of depression after a particularly nasty conversation with Lalit over the number of cake slices I ate at work last week for Joe's birthday. I really shouldn't tell him anything about my food intake. (Three. It was German Black Forest and the slices were tiny.) And I told Arnav about the nickname over text, not in person. As if I would rat out my fiancé in person!

Ever since we started texting, I always wonder who I'd meet in person—Arnav-the-Dragon or Arnav-of-My-Phone. Will he be Arnav-of-My-Phone today—the anti-emoji man who I once badgered with a thousand smileys in a day, after which he sent me a green vomit emoji early next morning? Or the goofy Arnav who sends me food pictures from his dhaba visits all over the country, and when I send him drooling emoticons, back comes a picture of his empty plate and an evil laugh? Or will it be Arnav-the-Dragon—the unsmiling whiplash of the office, all cryptic barks and death stares?

Speaking of Arnav, he was right about the B&O interview. Turned out it wasn't a brief interview at all, but the real thing. Not just with their HR, but four other people, including the hiring manager. I had gotten increasingly nervous all day, even at what I believed was an initial interview with HR, so that I ate double my usual amount, by the end of which I had a terrible stomachache. I hung around at work till late, and then shut myself in the conference room to take the Zoom call at eight PM, which was 10:30 AM

EST. (I totally know what EST is now. Eastern Standard Time. American Life 101: The U.S. has *six* time zones. We Indians are barely on time in one. Maybe I should've told them about IST—Indian Standard Time, which runs two hours behind the actual schedule. And it's "skae-jule" in American English, not "shae-dule" like us.) But the moment we started talking—the hiring manager, Madeline Astley, and I—the stomachache completely disappeared. We talked for over an hour. I told them about all of their ad campaigns that I've followed over the years. We talked about the Affixer Glue project, which she loved, and we created mock taglines and hashtags for products for different target audiences. It was the funnest interview. Exhausting, but so fun.

"Madam, where to drop you?" The gray-haired rickshaw brings me back from the squires of New York City to the morning streets of Bombay. He squints at the wide stretch of brown sand in the dim light of dawn. The ocean seems miles away, as if prepping for a tsunami.

"A little further away from Silver Beach, thank you."

"Good choice, Madam, that side of the beach doesn't get the bad crowd. It's much safer for you young girls." I hide an extra ten rupees in the wad of cash I hand over, even though he's way too chatty so early in the morning.

"Zoya! You are here! Finally!" A tidal wave of middle-aged women, followed by an equal gush of springy daughters-in-law, and a few scattered sons, all rush toward me in a frenzied surge of Nikes, Reeboks, and general svelteness. They screech to a halt midway in shock at the vastness of my waist and my faded sweats with two stains from last night's mutton curry. (I had no time to change, having woken up at 5:45 AM, thanks to Sheila Bua's text, for a 6:00 AM workout. And I wonder if I could take a picture of all this fitness gear in a "real" setting and help Samir Iyer pitch to Bruno Athletics? Forget it, the lighting's bad.)

And, oh my God, Lalit, The Fiancé. In tight, black stretchy pants, which no self-respecting Punjabi man would be caught wearing in public.

Must not text Arnav, must not.

"Zoya beta, come, come, I'm just dying for you to meet everyone!" Lalit's mother rushes toward me. "Here's my son's future wife!" She leads me to the slaughter with her arm tight around my shoulders as if I might escape at any moment.

Lalit's auntie is here too—his mother's sister, just as skinny, in hot-pink capris. She's the one who's fond of the macabre and says "This won't end well" every chance she gets, I've learned. I touch her feet for a blessing as a docile fiancé should; she tries to hug me but gives up when her bony little hands don't fit around my body.

Arranged Marriage Rule No. 8: Siblings of the mother-in-law should be given equal importance by a new bride-to-be. Occupational Hazard: Show extreme tact in giving your father-in-law's sibling the same prominence or you risk pissing off your mother-in-law forever.

"Mrs. Khurana, it is such a pleasure to meet your future bahu!" says a middle-aged lady in the Pilates group.

"You have to join us for shopping next weekend!"

"You must bring Zoya home for dinner! I'm sure she loves to eat!"

The exercise group surrounds me like a mini-mob. It's as if I'm a celebrity. I wish Mum and Sheila Bua were here, they'd get such a kick out of this result of their planning and plotting over the years. Not plotted exactly, that just seems evil, but you know what I mean. I can just imagine their faces beaming with satisfaction at me, in the midst of my new family and their group of exercising friends. I've also been using a lot of health words at home, you know, being Under the Influence of the Khuranas. Especially with Sheila Bua and her wheezing these days. Like wellness and quinoa and squats. Last night, I asked Sheila Bua about her metabolism and she questioned if I needed those metaballs for the beach today, and that the grocery store under our building sold medium-sized ones but only in a muddy orange. (I've also been trying to uncover why Sheila Bua was at that gallery near my office two weeks ago. When I asked her, she pretended to not know what I was talking about and grabbed her phone and started speaking on it, though I'm fairly certain no one called.)

Lalit, after being by my side on the beach for a hot minute, has retreated to a corner of the group now, texting on his phone, with the familiar hard little frown lines on his forehead and cheeks on Sag Highway, which I've come to diagnose as The Sulk. I would go to him, but the crowd surrounds me again.

A svelte woman lingers on after the others disperse to arrange their yoga mats. She's a walking Nike advertisement: sneakers, capris, T-shirt. Even the ponytail has a thick Nike hair tie around it. "So, Lalit chose you," she says, in a deep-throated voice, which could be the result of cigarettes or a sore throat. I'm saying cigarettes, considering the stale acrid smell as soon as she opens her mouth. "I told my husband—we live in the same building as the Khuranas—that I was so glad Lalit chose a . . ." She pauses to look pointedly at the mutton curry stains and my thick thighs in sweatpants. ". . . nice girl. The other one used to wear such strange clothes, all black with creepy things on it. Such quarrels, that's why they broke . . . oh! I'm sorry, I didn't mean to tell you about his ex." She fake covers her mouth with her hand, not the least bit sorry.

What does she mean, creepy things? What the hell is wrong with people? No one thinks I'm good enough for Lalit? No, people don't think that, Zoya, you do. But I'm good enough to have a person from another continent wanting my opinion. That feeling of being an imposter, as if I am somehow less than all the Tanyas of this world, comes back with a vengeance.

"Oh, I know all about her, don't worry," I lie. I knew he was still smarting over the break-up. I resolve to be kinder to him. "Did you know Lalit bought me such a lovely present the other day at the mall?"

"Did he? Wow," she says, clearly not wowed or even interested.

"It was something related to Harry Potter." I smile. She looks completely blank, so I add, "They're a series of books."

"Oh, books. You must be the scholarly type." She moves away an inch, as if brains and books were airborne diseases. "I only read magazines. Film magazines," she says absently, her attention diverted by a group of sturdy joggers, at which she sticks out her chest in a strange warm-up exercise. I leave her to her joggers and settle on the outskirts of the group arranging their mats.

Lalit finally did buy me a present. After that fracas on Holi, he apologized the next day and said that both of us needed to work on this relationship and that he was willing to do his part. I was still pissed off, but then I heard my Pa and Mum in the other room, excitedly talking about an upcoming dinner for the hospital Board members. Pa had finally bought a suit for the event, and my Pa is someone who never buys clothes unless his current ones are in tatters. I pushed my irritation at Lalit and the presents fiasco under an imaginary carpet. What kind of a life partner would I make if I didn't even try to give him another chance? I can't let an ex-girlfriend and a few arguments get to a relationship as important as marriage. The path to marriage is littered with fights and old loves, right?

And it's not that I don't like his gift. I do, because it's the thought that counts, isn't it? What's not to love in a broom? Not a Harry Potter one, but a typical Indian jhadu, the one made of brown grass used by maidservants, and on occasion moms, to smack stubborn little butts. This one had a gigantic pink bow on it. Rather sweet, that bow. Lalit said the actual HP broom would've taken a long time to ship, and he really wanted to gift me something because that's what fiancés do, and wasn't this broom more convenient? After which we walked the entire length of the mall, with a bow-tied broom, and lots of pointing and laughing.

In return, I gifted him a mirror. Full length. Which thrilled him to no end.

We're getting to understand other. Sort of.

Or will do in the next two and a half months, by the time we get married, I'm sure of it.

Speaking of gifts, my secret admirer is still at it. A plate of steaming mutton biryani showed up on my desk yesterday, each rice grain gleaming white and saffron. And with it was a DVD of *Hum Saath Saath Hain*. Of all things. The gifts have gotten progressively better over the weeks and I think the girls are up to this. Peehu told me at the engagement party, didn't she, that she would plan something special with Aisha and Kamya? And they know I love this movie. With a title that translates "We Are All Together" it screams cheesy, crappy, and sappy. But it's happy. And it was a giant success, which just proves that we all need more happy. Just as I tore the plastic cover off the DVD, Arnav passed by and pretended to retch violently at the sight.

So it can't be him.

That stupid thought appeared out of nowhere. I didn't think it, of course I didn't, stupid thoughts just pass by like thousands of useless ones per hour, and how many of them were actually constructive? Phew. So there. I didn't think it at all, not really, consciously think it.

Within seconds after that, my phone lit up with a text. Arnav.

I wouldn't have believed this of you, Zoya. You watch revolting stuff. Tch. Tch.

Me: It's not revolting, thank you.
A: It's not a movie. It's a wedding video. And a toothpaste ad. Save some biryani for me?
Me: Can't promise if you don't show up in the next 5 min. But it's nice to watch happy weddings, no?
A: Why? Is yours not happy enough?

That's him: sharing food and always in a rush to announce the death knell of my relationship. Which makes my heart flip in a somersault of hope, despite . . . well, everything. Not good, Zoya, not good. You do not need any more snags right now; no New York, no feelings for your boss. Just focus on your fiancé and family.

* * *

"Come, come, let's get started." Lalit's mother jolts me back to the beach, to the center of the exercise group, yoga mats arranged in two horizontal lines, one behind the other.

Lalit turns toward me. "Zoya, where's your mat?"

Mat? Oh. Oops.

"Err . . . I . . ."

"I reminded you yesterday."

"I know, sorry, sorry, forgot. I was actually in the middle of wedding shopping." I give Lalit my best I'm-so-cute-please-forgive-me smile. He did remind me about the mat. But then I googled "Food in New York City" and that was the end of my brain. It's like the city was made up entirely of food. Sandwiches—I had no idea so many varieties existed—kebabs, hot dogs, lobsters, cupcakes, dumplings. And pizza. So. Much. Pizza. And something called Southern food. Southern New York food? South of New Jersey food? I clicked on the picture and my phone screen transformed into a gigantic white plate filled with a river of meat stew, a bread-like thing called biscuit (totally different from our sweet, crispy biscuits made for dipping in tea), impossibly crisp fried chicken, and a heap of cheesy macaroni. All on a single plate the size of a small car tire. I must have passed out shortly after.

"I'll remember next time. Could you lend me yours?"

Lalit sighs as if calling on the last reserves of his patience. "Zoya, you're an adult. You have to take responsibility for your actions. Plus, I don't want to get my new stretch pants dirty."

It's not a bloody crime for which I must "take responsibility." It's a fucking mat. Anything can be a mat, even those old newspapers behind us. That's what I'll use.

". . . let's start with slow deep breaths . . ."

I spread the newspapers in a huff. One of the pages has a dried red pav bhaji stain. The morbid auntie and her svelte daughter-in-law look horrified, dusting imagined grime off their yoga capris.

"Oh alright, here!" Lalit thrusts his black mat toward me with an irritated head shake. Honestly. Any other fiancé would've flirted and laid out the shirt off his back in these early romantic days of courtship. Okay then. I just handed him another thing to call me out on, in addition to the wallet. Maybe we'll keep adding things I lose/forget to this list, like that whispering game kids play. And then, at the end, the first item (the wallet) will be forgotten but it won't matter because a whole list will exist to choose from. So strange because I've never forgotten or lost things before. Does Lalit bring that out in me? Zoya, really, what a thing to say about your future husband. But I'm also learning to tune him out, which Sheila Bua says is good practice for a long-lasting marriage. Well then.

* * *

Plateees bloody sucks. Leg up, leg down, core in, what the heck? I imagined a light workout—why, I can't say—but this? Acrobatic contortions would be easier. I've thrown sand in one woman's face, twice, with leg lifts and also fallen flat on my stomach in the middle of each plank. Plank, my foot. Call it what it is: plonk.

There's more. I also lost my balance, rammed straight into my future mother-in-law's scrawny bottom, which made her fly smack into the instructor's face just as the sun rose for all to see. So people moved their mats a wee bit further, and now I'm pretty much the center point of annoyed attention.

". . . go on your fours. Straight back, core in." Where the hell is this core?

"Now raise your bottom to the sky! Lift your left leg, yes, higher, HIGHER, raise it to the sky! Oh, this feels sooo good!" Wait, isn't this a yoga pose? The female instructor breathes deeply, as if the air is fresh and crisp like on a hillside in the midst of nature, and not a buffet of smog and garbage.

How the hell are you supposed to balance your entire bulk on one leg, that too, while bent? That's it, I'm done! I shift to the child's pose so both knees are on the ground (thank God) and my hands and back are stretched in front of me.

My phone vibrates inside the zipped side pocket of my sweatpants and I grab it with one hand like a lifeline. Arnav! He's always around when you need him. I slide my phone under my face, still in child's pose, to read his text, which I don't have to swipe open, thanks to the messed-up auto-lock. (I really need to get it fixed!)

Arnav: How's it going? Hate it yet?

Me: Ugh. I forgot my mat. Lalit was not happy.

A: Is he ever?

Does he not have one good thing to say about my fiancé? Yes, Lalit's a bit testy, and we're still figuring out our groove as a couple, but he's not that bad.

A: By the way, good work on Chotu's algebra test.

Me: Thank you. It's a revelation what that kid can do if he stops talking long enough to pay attention. You're on for chemistry next week. Good luck.

A: Better chemistry than mathematics. Brrr.

Ah, a chink in the dragon's armor. Algebra. I'm learning so much about my boss these days. Like, he's the one who feeds the straggly little kitten near the tea stall outside our office. With rusk biscuits dipped in chai, of all things. After which that poor caffeinated creature—Fluff, I call it, a delusional shot at positive thinking—bounces like a lunatic for the next thirty minutes, only to crash near the office gate for a nap. And it's not like I go out of my way to spy on my boss. What can I do if I draw open the dusty curtain of the break room window, and there he is chatting with the gray-haired chaiwaala every day at eleven with the cat loitering around him?

". . . now RAISE that leg, but only an inch! HOLD IT! Hold it right there for ten seconds! YOU CAN DO IT! Ten . . . nine . . . eight . . ."

"Now, lay flat on your back." The instructor sighs in pleasure. "Raaaise your head and shoulders. Lift your legs so you look like a cup. A wonderful cup of life, full of possibilities. Now hold your toes with your fingers without lifting yourself off the mat. What a great stretch!"

It would be one if I didn't have a real, squishy stomach blocking my reach!

Bing!

What's Arnav sent this time?

You have to see this.

I can't watch a video bent in the cup of life, so I officially give up plateees. My legs thud on the ground and fling sand in other cups, which are now filled with irritation instead of possibilities. I slink out of the center of the group to perch my tired backside on a nice, firm rock behind the exercising group. Ah, blessed relief.

A loud rip of a sound, like air whooshing out of a tire, halts the instructor mid-pose. She glares at me. What on earth? My boss sent me a video of someone passing gas during Pilates. (What is he, an eight-year-old boy?)

I have to make a superhuman effort to stop the giggles stuck in my throat. And as if the bumping and sand flinging wasn't enough, now the group thinks I am the offender. God.

"I'm so sorry." Lalit says to the instructor, to the whole group, and scowls at me so hard he might pop a vein. Wallet, mat, fart. The list is growing. Uh-oh.

The exercise group scatters away; some stretch on their mats, others rush toward coconut vendors, who are well prepared for this hungry assault; straws ready in large coconuts and the creamy white flesh of the fruit arranged neatly on paper plates. Maybe I should apologize to Lalit and his mom for the Pilates fiasco and promise to really try harder the next time? Try what harder, exercise or fitting in?

Arnav: So, how was your new morning routine? Feel energetic yet?

Me: Fab. I rammed myself into MIL's bottom.

A: Holy crap. It's not even 7am and you're kicking ass.

Me: Shut up. I wanted to talk to you about something important.

A: I like the sound of that.

Me: We need to stop fanning Chotu's bloodlust. Don't get any more Twilight books for him, thank you.

A: Oh that. Nothing wrong in a bit of good ol' vampire-blood saga.

Me: He needs some variety in his reading. Can you please pick up The Fault in Our Stars and Malgudi Days from the bookshop downstairs when you get to the office?

A: Will do. He won't like it.

Me: He doesn't have to like them, he just has to read them.

A: Savage, Ms. Sahni.

My phone rings in the middle of replying to Arnav. It's Aisha on a video call! Finally! I've been texting and leaving voice mails but she's been so busy being a newlywed that we haven't gotten a chance to talk since my engagement day a month and a half ago.

"Aashoo! Where have you been?" I settle comfortably upon the rock in anticipation of a nice long phone session with my cousin and BFF, even if it's seven in the morning. Well, as long a session I can manage before paying obeisance to my future mother-in-law, who is busy some distance away with her sister on the beach, both sipping juice from their respective large coconuts with straws. And Lalit is busy on his phone, too, pacing up and down at the edge of the sea and thrashing the water. (Pacing? After an entire workout? Fiend! Fit, I mean, how fit.)

"How are you, darling?" Aisha says, somewhat subdued, even for her. He skin looks sallow and her eyes have dark circles underneath.

"I'm fine. But are you? You don't look well."

"Nothing of the sort. Just woke up a while ago and thought of calling you before the day got crazy. Wait. Peehu's calling. Let me add her to this call. And let me call Kamya too!"

Peehu appears on the screen with a slice of bread in her mouth and Kamya appears fully dressed with a frown.

"Kamya, why are you dressed at seven in the morning?" I ask.

She shakes her head and sighs. "It's nothing . . . just a flat I'm trying to rent. I have to go look at it, like right now, or I won't have anyplace to live."

"Why? Does Bangalore have a shortage of flats?" Peehu asks, having moved on to a cheesy omelet in between loud slurps of chai. (It's chai because she has a rule: sip your morning coffee and slurp your mid-morning chai. Don't ask.)

"No." Kamya looks at Peehu, but thanks to WhatsApp video, all three of us get the stern teacher stare. "Bangalore has a shortage of landlords who trust single women."

"You're kidding," Aisha gasps.

"People don't rent out their flats to unmarried women because they're suspicious that we're up to 'all sorts of immoral things' and they don't want the likes of us in their orderly, family-filled buildings."

"Even in a city like Bangalore?" I ask, my mouth in a dumbfounded O. "I can understand if this happens in smaller, more traditional cities, but an international hub like Bangalore?"

"Yes, even here. It's just like Sheila Bua all over again, isn't it, only thirty years later."

My brain cuts through all the words and background noise to halt on a name. "What do you mean, Sheila Bua?"

"Oh crap. I thought you all knew."

"No, no. What is this about Sheila Bua?" Peehu has stopped eating, but her mouth is still full. Kamya looks distressed and shakes her head, and then as if coming to a decision, she says, "Okay. Sheila Bua had left home to try and live alone, but it didn't work out. My mother had warned me that the same thing would happen to me when I left home to go work in Bangalore. Look, I really don't know more than this, okay? I have to go now!" Her video's gone in a flash, and then it's just the three of us on the screen.

The beach seems to have stopped in time and I'm the only thing that breathes. The people are frozen in whatever they're in the middle of doing: sipping coconut water, walking near the water, or in the midst of doing planks.

Sheila Bua had left home? When? As in, she did the very thing that aunties like her exist to prevent other young girls from doing? Oxford and stuff aside, but actually leaving home?

My Sheila Bua?

The quintessential auntie in multicolored clothes and diamond jewels?

The two images of Sheila Bua jar so sharply that I don't know which one to believe. How do I not know this? And what did Kamya mean by "didn't work out"? My heart breaks a little for the botched revolt. I could ask Mum. I bet she knows Sheila Bua's secrets.

"Zee, are you ill?" Peehu mumbles in between bites of omelet on buttered toast. "Why are you up so early? Is that a beach I see?"

"Yeah, don't ask. Exercising with the fam."

Peehu chokes in laughter. "Lalit's influence? There you go, becoming the typical wife and daughter-in-law."

"Shut up, Pee," Aisha says before I can ask her about Sheila Bua. Chances are, if I didn't know, she wouldn't either. Because the elders don't discuss rebellions with "children," that's why. Far more likely one would hear of something like this from neighbors or friends than one's own family. "How are you and Lalit doing? Isn't it fun being newly engaged?" Aisha asks in all seriousness, no chuckles or good-natured teasing.

Peehu interrupts as I am about to speak. "Sorry, gotta leave for class. Zee, hold that thought on how it feels. Talk to you later. Bye!" She's gone before we can say goodbye.

And how is it being newly engaged? Apart from the fact that I can't do Pilates, and the lost wallet, which was found, the forgotten yoga mat, passing gas during Pilates, and a general wonderment about relationships being twitchy and angry, we're doing just fine. The fiancé might also be a wee bit hung up on his ex-girlfriend. And he guards his phone like a vault. I really, really want to be suspicious about whether he's texting and calling her, like a proper jealous fiancé would, but then there's my boss somewhere in the middle of all this, making me feel, well, stupid feelings that have no business existing in an engaged woman's life.

So I put on my extra-loud happy voice and say to Aisha, "Fine, just fine. Lalit and I are doing great. It's lovely being engaged." If you try hard enough, you can easily fool your loved ones.

The exercise group seems to be done with their post-workout snack and disperse in different directions on the beach. Lalit's mother gestures to me as if to come my way. I wave to her and point to my phone, and hurriedly ask, "Aashoo, I was wondering, did you ever, well, doubt stuff? Sometimes?"

"What do you mean?"

"As in wonder about your relationship with Varun once you were engaged? You know, like if you did the right thing? Or that you should've chosen a different person. Or path?"

She's quiet again for a moment, and then sighs. "No, I didn't." Her voice is thick, her cheeks swell up as if she's about to cry. "I didn't at all. More's the pity."

A spear of dread shoots up my back; I hope there's nothing wrong. I have no idea of what "wrong" could mean, surely nothing to do with Varun because he loves her and they get along so well, but please God, don't let anything be wrong. "Aisha." I use her full name only when I'm trying to be stern. "What are you not telling me?"

"Nothing, nothing at all. Forget all that. Tell me, did you pick up the sari Sheila Bua wanted from the market behind your office?"

"Yeah, I did last evening. Actually, I'm a bit worried about Sheila Bua," I say, hesitantly, not wanting her to laugh like she did the one time I told her about the strange pull I feel toward Sheila Bua. "Does she, like, have asthma or something? These days she pants even while doing basic chores."

"I haven't noticed. Anyway, she doesn't have asthma for sure. If she did, we'd all know it by now."

"Good. Mum keeps telling me I'm imagining things, so I thought maybe you might know something."

"You and your Sheila Bua." The old spunk in Aisha's voice comes back for a moment of teasing. Uh oh.

I laugh nervously. "Oh, just . . . well . . . did you know about Sheila Bua leaving home?" I ask, in a macabre curiosity. And instantly feel ashamed at my ghoulishness. Why do we feel a lurid sort of boost at another person's failure to do what we were denied? Is this a girl thing?

"Oh, that. Yeah, I know." She sounds utterly disinterested in Sheila Bua.

"Why didn't you tell me?" Family gossip has a way of trickling down the food chain, so how the hell did Aisha know and I didn't, considering we're on the same level of need-to-know hierarchy?

"There was nothing to tell. It was ages ago. I heard Mummy mumbling about it once. You know how she is."

"When did she leave home? Before she was married? Do you know any details?"

"I don't know. Maybe it was before marriage. No wait, it was after. I can't recall. Mum said her paintings were unsuitable or something. Who cares? Oh, screw all this. Can we just take a break? Let's go somewhere, just us girls. I know! Let's go for a spa weekend to celebrate your birthday."

"Okay, sure." But I'm not letting up on asking the family about Sheila Bua. If anyone knows more, it's Mum.

"Let's just leave everything behind and forget for a few days?" She shuts her eyes, pressing them hard as if trying to squeeze out the last bit of tears and mumbles to herself, "I really should've continued my journalism degree."

"Forget what? And journalism? Are you okay, Aashoo?" She hasn't talked about the journalism course in years, the one her family made her leave for an HR degree for better marriage prospects.

"Yes, for the hundredth time, Zee, I am." She clearly does not look okay, and doesn't want to tell me. I can bide my time till she's ready.

"Listen, I got to go. Varun just woke up. Oh, by the way, I have to tell you: I saw that fool ex-boyfriend Raunak of yours, loitering near the international airport terminal, must've been on his way somewhere." The screen goes black and all is silent.

It takes a while for that name to find its space in my life among all the clutter. Raunak? As in the guy who almost got me pregnant? I slide off the rock straight into the sand but my body has no idea what just happened because OMG, I know who's sending me the presents. Its him! My on-again, off-again ex-boyfriend!

Of course.

CHAPTER SEVENTEEN

7:00 PM.

> 2 months since engagement and 2 months to wedding! Enjoy the dhaba with darling son-in-law. (But tell him that I make a much better misal than this dhaba place!)

Sheila Bua's text is followed by a GIF of Gordon Ramsay with a fire erupting behind him, and the words "Hell's Kitchen." I just . . . never mind. Do community colleges offer night classes on the use of context? Maybe Sheila Bua could benefit from one such class.

Focus on the date, Zoya. Lalit and I are at this wonderful little shack for dinner. He winced when I suggested the roadside dhaba yesterday (which Arnav had recommended in a random conversation). And now that we're here he detests all of it: that it's a little shack with plastic chairs and not the new French restaurant C'est

Délicieux that he wanted to go to; that it's under a railway bridge near a crumbling little Sufi shrine, the Chaabi Peer dargah and singing dervishes in tattered clothes and not at the top of the tallest building in Bombay with a fancy live jazz band; and that it only serves giant portions of one dish, misal pav—black-eyed beans in a spicy curry sprinkled with crisp salties, onions, and lime juice, to be scooped with two buttered bread rolls—and not miniscule servings of unpronounceable French food like teurgoule, which is just kheer, plain old rice pudding with a fancy upper-crust accent. (I could totally run a free marketing campaign for them. The tagline could be "Chaabi Peer Misal: Music for your soul & stomach." All they'd need is a social media plan; their food would do the rest.)

Lalit hates all of it, and I'm just not sure I care enough to convince him otherwise. Not that we make great conversation anyway; it's only been two months since our engagement and we've already run out of things to say. I tried to broach this with Mum last night that Lalit and I don't seem to have a whole lot in common, and she pretty much shooed me off.

"All these are modern talks," Mum said. "You have to *create* things in common. And once you begin to live in the same home, common things will appear." Should I have asked her a different question instead? Should I have asked her if there was a way to be happy without following rules and traditions; if there was a way to be happy living a different life? No point in that now, I guess, when my wedding invitations are almost ready.

When the topic of Lalit fizzled out, I turned the conversation to Sheila Bua. I asked Mum about Sheila Bua's leaving home. She'd know because she and Sheila Bua were friends before being related by marriage. My asking—rather my knowing—about

Sheila Bua flustered her so much she just blurted, "It happened only once, alright?" and rushed off to call the jeweler. I'll just have to pester her until she tells me more.

Meanwhile, the invites are being printed, and the two main characters in this Big Fat Indian drama, Lalit and I, are both scrolling through our phones in silence under the blurry lights of this quaint dhaba, while local trains thunder above us.

I doubt it.

The text comes in from Arnav, who doesn't believe the gifts I'm receiving are from Raunak. In fact, he's vetoed all my options: Lalit, Aman, the girls. But I know I'm right this time; Raunak must've actually paid attention to my likes and dislikes back in the day, whatever I and my friends may have thought about him. Clearly he knows I'm engaged and is trying to woo me back. It's just like him: wanting things that are forbidden. No way in hell am I going back. Not to him. It's a wee bit disappointing actually. I mean, Raunak? But still. I called and called his mobile (unreachable) and in the end sent him a text asking him to stop all this gift-sending farce because I was engaged and done with him.

I also texted a detailed little tome to Arnav about all of the above reasons and emailed him a picture of Raunak. The photo was a bit hazy, and his straggly hair looked like it needed a thorough wash, to which Arnav finally replied:

What exactly did a smart, talented woman like you see in a sad little sloth like him?

Lalit, on the other hand, doesn't seem very interested in who is sending me food and movies and books. Is this normal behavior in a fiancé? Maybe he's the progressive kind, who isn't worried or jealous, and believes that I can deal with this kind of stuff without needing a man to step in.

I fidget with my diamond engagement ring, sitting here under the dank bridge on a plastic chair. The ring is platinum with a large gleaming solitaire flanked by two small diamonds. The band is loose, even though it was custom made for my finger, so I keep taking it off and forgetting to put it back on. Mum was horrified to find it on the bathroom sill last night, next to a greasy blue bottle of coconut oil with strands of black hair around it. And the glass blinds of the window weren't entirely closed, so thank God a crow didn't fly off with the bauble.

I put my phone on the plastic table and tap the counter with my finger to get Lalit's attention. "We're planning a trip next month."

"Hmm?" he asks, his eyes still glued to his phone.

"A trip. A bachelorette combined with a birthday party."

"Yes, sure. Can you send me a text?"

"What?" Did he hear a thing I said?

"A text. Send me a test text. I'm not getting any replies to my messages so just want to make sure there's nothing wrong with my phone or network. Can you, please?" He points his large black Samsung phone toward me.

"Okay." I send him a measly Hello.

"Great. I got it." The light from his phone screen illuminates the disappointed relief on his face. "Wonder why . . . umm, people are not responding?"

"Who's not responding?" I squint my eyes at the back of his phone, as if squinting will reveal all its secrets to me. His phone-vault with state secrets.

"Oh, just colleagues." He clears his throat. "So, trip, huh?"

He *was* listening. "Yes. At an Alibaug resort. The Taj. All us girls, my friends, cousins."

His head jerks up from the phone as if the name of the hotel has a rope attached to it.

"It's not too far." I try to pacify him. "Alibaug is just an hour's boat ride from Gateway of India." Maybe he's alarmed at the thought of a bachelorette?

"Err . . . yes. I know. Good." He clears his throat with great force and puts away his phone carefully into his front pocket. A dark, thin server boy slams a Styrofoam plate filled with toasted buttered buns on my side of the table before doing the same at others. "Should you be eating a third helping of pav? Isn't that enough bread for the day?"

"I'm still hungry."

Lalit's face changes into a scowl and he looks away. His eyes wander around the dhaba, disinterested.

Does he even want to marry me? A little whiff of something, which dangerously resembles hope, floats by. No, Zoya, don't go there. *Think cream and red wedding invites, think Mum and Pa's happy faces. Think of all that scrumptious wedding food. Do not think about the New York job interview results.*

Hold on, I know what you're thinking. It's not like I'm not serious about my marriage, even with the arguments, lies, and all. But it would be churlish, wouldn't it, to not follow up and just see the results of your efforts, even if you wouldn't be profiting from those results?

What would Lalit say if I told him that I wanted to go away for three years after we got married? Would he be hurt that I didn't ask him before applying? Would he let me go? Or would he rejoice that his fiancé is skilled enough to get a job in America on her own merit? No question: not a chance in hell. (How would he mold me from eight thousand miles away?)

Better to take Sheila Bua's advice and tune Lalit out.

But I can't. He really should've chosen Tanya, because she'd totally prefer the French place instead of this dhaba. Tanya, who's—

Right here, on the other side of the dhaba.

What?

Tanya? On a dirty blue plastic chair, under the dank railway bridge?

Am I in a nightmare? Or have we all judged her wrong?

My plastic spoon plunges savagely into the misal and squirts bean curry on Lalit's pink formal shirt.

He glowers and dabs his shirt viciously with a paper napkin while one hand covers his ear over the loud singing from the shrine.

"Sorry, sorry!" I say to Lalit, not the least bit apologetic. He can wash it, can't he? What's the big deal with a little stain? I'm not sure what pisses off Lalit more; the bits of crumpled napkin on his shirt or the dervishes who sing in rustic voices of the heart and its wounds, surrounding this divine food for the soul.

Wait, is that *Arnav* and Tanya? *As in my Arn . . . ?*

What the hell?

How dare she steal all my men? Yes, I know, only Lalit is my man, but Arnav is my boss, therefore technically in the sphere considered "mine."

There she is, all hip as usual, in a short metallic dress (in a roadside dhaba?) with puffed sleeves that are all the rage. Damn.

I really shouldn't have canceled my blow-dry appointment today, just because my regular hairdresser called in sick. The blood rushes up to my head in a supersonic boil.

Wait a minute. Black lipstick? Even from this distance, I can see her dark lips under the fluorescent streetlamp. She puts her hands to her face, feigning shock at something Arnav said, and uh-oh, I see black nail paint. Again.

What, is she ill?

How on earth did Rita Chachi let her leave home with black lipstick and nails, and not collapse with one of her many fake strokes? And why on earth does she sit so *effing* close to my boss?

My thumbs shake in fury on my phone keypad.

I didn't know you hung out with my cousin.

He grabs his phone immediately to check it as Tanya continues talking. Ah, sweet revenge. Satisfaction, I mean, sweet satisfaction.

Arnav: Who's your cousin?
Me: The girl with you.

Arnav shifts in his seat across from Tanya as if caught doing something naughty. His startled eyes dart over the crowded tables in the dim light to search for me.

A: Tanya's your cousin? Where are you?
Me: Why? Is it that unbelievable?

Lalit spreads out on his plastic seat, his legs stretched, an arm over the back of the chair and surveys the dhaba as if he owns the place, which leaves me free to text. Arnav and Tanya are some distance behind Lalit. God, even saying their names together is just ugh and makes me want to gag.

A: No. I didn't mean it like that. Are you near the singing fakirs? I can't see you.

Lalit and I are in one of the corners of the dhaba, partially hidden by a stone pillar, thank goodness. You couldn't see us unless you were specifically looking. (And Lalit is busy texting, so I'm free to look around.) Tanya continues to talk—I can see her black pouty mouth move nonstop. She picks up her phone in the middle of the conversation, flicks the screen, and puts it back again. Arnav keeps nodding, pretending to stretch his neck. His eyes dart around the dhaba like the searching beam of a flashlight, which finally falls on me. His shoulders visibly relax but he sits up straighter on his plastic chair and picks up his phone.

A: Found you. I see you're with The Fiancé. He looks better in photos than real life. Wouldn't have thought this was his kind of place.

Me: It's mine.

Tanya crosses her shapely legs trying to draw Arnav's attention, but he's glued to his phone. As is Lalit, slouched on his chair in front of me. Maybe he's engrossed in whatever covert information he's hiding in that vault. Maybe I should've worn that green ethnic blouse with jeans? Jeans make me look slimmer and Mum thinks green makes my skin glow.

A: I like that dress you're wearing. It's bright and lively. Like you. When you aren't flinging sand in your mother-in-law's face.

I feel a little burst of tingly pleasure. I purposely wore yellow today. A yellow dress with light-blue daisies. These days I try to add a little yellow when I go out with Lalit. You know, passive rebellion and all. He's never repeated that it makes me look dark, but somehow I know he thinks it.

Me: Ha. Ha. Very funny. I love wearing it, no matter what others think.

A: I know you do. You mentioned it to the receptionist once. Are the others The Fiancé?

Me: Never you mind.

A train thunders overhead and Tanya clutches Arnav Sir's arm in fright. Really? This from a girl who watches *The Conjuring* alone in the dark for thrills? I hate her. Lalit, meanwhile, picks up the simple paper menu, shakes his head, and smirks as a rushed server drops all three bowls of steaming misal on the tarred black floor.

Me: So, how do you know my cousin?

A: I don't technically know her. My parents and your Sheila Bua hope I get to know her *really* well.

I have a flashback of Sheila Bua in my office: *Bajaj, you say? Don't worry, I'll find your mother!*

I have an intensely powerful desire to stab Sheila Bua in the butt with Lalit's plastic fork. No matter that I'm worried about her health, or that lately I've been harassing Mum about her "unsuitable" past. Mum shakes me off on the pretext of fake problems, like one time calling the maid who hadn't turned up (but was right outside our door). I sense I'm close to breaking her, though. I can see the paranoia in her eyes when I broach the subject. Maybe I'll make a deal with her: the truth about Sheila Bua in exchange for three fat-free dinners at Lalit's house.

"So, Zoya, what do you, err, think about Greenland for our honeymoon?" Lalit puts the paper menu back on the table and rubs his fingers together as if cleaning dirt off them.

Who the hell cares about Greenland when Tanya lightly pats my boss's arm, lingering on his shirt sleeve a tad longer than is proper? And by the way, where did Greenland come from? Did he see it in some Top Unexpected Honeymoon Destinations article?

"Why can't we go someplace warmer?" I ask, smiling at Lalit, but totally checking out the boss–cousin situation from the corner of my eye. Now she's scraped her chair even closer and flips her phone out of her tiny clutch to shove it in his face. Probably showing him her portfolio pictures. *Back off!*

"Think of the northern lights, Zoya. It's the next big thing!"

Okay, now she's cut up his kebab into little pieces and dangles a fork in front of his face. But he's not looking at her or the fork. His eyes are staring down at his phone.

Me: Are you getting to know my cousin well?

A: We are talking about fjords—not entirely sure how we reached that topic because I wasn't paying attention—and she thinks it's another word for feuds. I'm not exactly *trying* to get to know her.

Suddenly everything to do with Greenland looks wonderfully rosy. "Okay, Lalit, you win. Let's go!"

Lalit gawps, taken aback by my sudden eagerness for Greenland. "Are you sure?"

"Of course! What's not to love about a cold, remote place? Let's do this!" I could dance in the snowcapped plains of Greenland in a thin chiffon sari like in the movies and not think of food or warmth even once.

The dervishes of Chaabi Peer sing in a rising frenzy. They circle the flowery tomb of Baba Hazrat Nazir and the chaabis that dangle around it: keys for prayers answered. Maybe I should offer a key, too? I mean, I *am* getting married. The fakirs sing of secret desires in such a trance that I can feel the prickle of each hair on my arm.

My phone bings. Not a text from Arnav. The rosiness deflates in a thorny little poof. I don't want to care so much. *But you do, don't you, Zoya?* Shut up, shut up.

Dear Ms. Sahni,

Congratulations! We are pleased to offer you the position of Sr. Campaign Manager with Bucklebee & Owens. We are delighted to make you the following . . .

Wait. Bucklebee & Owens? Not *my* B&O, surely?

My stomach drops.

> —job offer of Sr. Campaign Manager, contingency of acceptance by May 2nd.

A million miles away, Lalit's voice and thoughts are firmly entrenched in Greenland. I nod and smile but keep scrolling through the email.

> The start date is flexible, but you are expected in the Manhattan office no later than May 22nd . . . Bonus of 5%. . . All benefits . . . furnished company apartment in New York City for eight weeks.

MotherOfGodForkingShit.

The world seems to have stopped. Like in those movies, where everything around you is still and dreamlike and you are the only one that is real.

I got the job! YES! I got it!

Breathe. Oh my God. Just breathe. Play it cool.

I'm going to New York!! To B&O in NEW YORK!

OMG, I'm going to be one of the Mad Men.

I feel like I could slide off this plastic chair and collapse on the muddy floor in a limp heap, or shoot up into the sky and explode into a million stars.

"Zoya? Hey!" Lalit snaps his fingers in front of my face. "Come on, be honest, what do you really think of dog-sledding near the Viking ruins in Greenland?"

I crash back to earth and remember where I am. Take a bite of misal to ground me.

Okay, okay, let's make sense of this. In a functional-mature-adult kind of way. Lay the facts on the table and figure out what needs to be done. Right?

Functional adult. Yes. Maturity. Low-key cool.

"Greenland? Zoya?" Lalit snaps his fingers in my face again. I hate it when he does that.

But all I can think is who cares, sure *I love Greenland! I love this whole planet!* "Yes? Sorry, who's going to Greenland?"

He gawks at me, horrified—what kind of a girl forgets her honeymoon moments after discussing it?

"Us?" He says the word slowly, stressing the lonely syllable. "Now, I know you wanted Kerala—"

"How about New York?" I blurt before I can stop myself. Is this the bloody way to be a functional adult? Shoot your mouth off?

"Really? I had no idea you were even interested in seeing America." Lalit sits up straighter in his plastic chair.

Autos rattle past the crowded stall, their fumes mesh with the sizzle of the grill. Some diners clap along with the new song of the fakirs, something about the mad lover at your doorstep.

I feel a sudden tingle of warmth on my back. If I didn't know it better, I'd think it was—

"Hello, Zoya."

A booming voice.

It's him, of course.

"Er . . . yes, hello." *Don't look.* Focus on Greenland. *New York.* No, Greenland.

There he is, being Arnav-the-Dragon now, in his usual pose of hands crossed over his chest, rocking back and forth on his heels, blank face firmly in place. *Is this his date face too?* And next to him is Tanya, in her metallic blue dress and black lips. Up close, the black lipstick looks totally surreal on her. Like a familiar but unknown face. She doesn't look the least bit disconcerted at running into us. In fact, she looks rather triumphant. She gives me a quick, short nod to acknowledge our unfortunate bloodline, and oh-so-casually slips her palm in the crook of Arnav's elbow. What the hell? Both men dart a glance at her, but Arnav doesn't move her hand away; he's too much of a nice guy. Lalit shifts in his seat, his face puffs as his neck sinks into his shoulders. Did he sense my pissed-off vibes? I readjust my face into a manageable Zen.

Arnav extends a large hand toward Lalit. "We haven't been introduced. Arnav Bajaj, Zoya's colleague at Mosaic."

Actually boss, but you know, call-me-Arnav.

"Lalit Khurana, Zoya's fiancé." Lalit jumps off his plastic chair, shakes Arnav's hand, and puts his other puffy muscled arm around my shoulders. He's almost a head shorter than Arnav, I notice.

"Ah, yes. The Fiancé." Arnav gives me what looks like one of his blank stares, but his eyes crinkle at the edges. I feel faint, like caught in an illicit act.

Tanya sidles even closer to Arnav. Is she planning to merge into him? "I heard you both talking about Greenland for your honeymoon." Technically she says this to me. Or her flat butt does, because her entire body is turned toward the men, especially Lalit.

"Tanya, do you know where Greenland is? Or what a fjord is?" How can I resist?

My boss is racked with sudden, savage coughs.

"I'm not *that* stupid." Tanya smirks, but immediately switches to her somber face. "Fjords, especially family fjords, are upsetting for everyone; they ruin relationships." She gazes at Arnav with a saintly smile to show him what a good, wholesome, family-oriented wife she'd make. Wholesome and family-oriented, my ass.

Lalit's face is so puffed up, I'm beginning to worry. He says, tightly, "We *were* actually talking about our honeymoon." He glances at Arnav and mimics his pose, arms crossed across his chest. "Zoya expressed an interest in New York. But now I—" He rocks back and forth to match Arnav, but almost falls back onto the bread-laden table of a family with four kids. My hand covers my phone tight, as if the deep pressure of my palm can shield the email from the world.

"New York?" Arnav Sir stretches the syllables. "Interesting."

Uh oh. None of the men know about my job offer.

"Yes, isn't it? I didn't even know Zee was interested in that place."

Zee?

My hand slips on the plastic chair, its loud scrape grating on my nerves. Tanya gives a ladylike sneeze, which I suspect was a smirk in disguise.

Zee? Lalit never calls me Zee. He doesn't even *like* that name. He says it sounds like the TV channel with tacky shows. As if he can hear my doubts, Lalit's arm tightens around my shoulders, his fingers dig painfully deep.

Am I going mad?

"Oh, I'd say she was quite interested in New York," Arnav drawls, poker-faced. "Wouldn't you say, Zoya?"

Fuck.

Please don't say anything, please don't tell Lalit anything about the B&O job. Please have forgotten that it was you who showed me a glimpse of a different life. It's not like I've decided I'm taking this job. It'd cause far too much totally avoidable melodrama. And then Lalit would never trust me again either. Not worth it. I could lose everything I've worked so hard for.

A teenage waiter thumps a handwritten paper bill on our table, which Lalit promptly picks up and studies.

"What the hell! They've charged us extra!" He thumps the paper back on the tin table hard. He's clearly reluctant to leave but being cheated out of a few rupees—by a hole-in-the-wall, no less—clearly wins over any male instinct to mark his territory. "I'll be right back." He slides carefully past Tanya, as if she was laden with germs.

Tanya's phone convulses in a cacophony of screams and bangs. Is that . . . heavy metal? Surely not. That's almost as impossible as her eating carbs.

"Hello, Mummy?" She walks some distance away, hovering mere inches over a table at the edge of the dhaba which is bustling with six old ladies licking their fingers.

Which just leaves us.

Arnav and me.

Alone.

The song of the mad lover trails off behind us, the hum of the busy stall seems frozen in the silence.

No conference room, no presentation, no phones. Just us, very close. In a casual setting.

Must not look at him. Must. Not. But his man-smell . . . sweat and aftershave mixed with spice.

"So, it's Zee now, hmm?" Arnav bends close, so close the musky man-scent burns a black hole in my brain. "I didn't know you were called Zee." They're merging again: Arnav-the-Dragon and Arnav-in-My-Phone, and it's . . . oh God, my brain has fogged.

It really is raining men. Fiancé. Secret admirer. Ex. Arnav. Admirer. Something clicks in my brain, a tiny key turning inside a lock—his rough stubble grazes my cheek as he bends down to whisper in my ear and my brain shuts down, probably forever. His lips linger dangerously close to my earlobe, his breath warm, so warm, like gooey molten chocolate. "Zee." He growls right inside my ear. "It's very . . . you." A shiver explodes in my body like a firecracker. How can my ear be so *alive*? This is twenty on a scale of ten. Lalit is five at best; even the pothead Raunak was just a seven.

Oh God, man-fog. *Stop!* Thoughts like these are cheating, aren't they? This Arnav needs to go back into my phone! In person is not good, not good for my system.

An overhead train departs in a rambunctious rattle, followed by a second of hollow peace. Sounds start to register slowly in my brain; a twang of spatulas, chewing voices, solitary notes of the harmonium, the fakirs testing their instruments. My ear remains in a microclimate as Arnav takes his own sweet time to straighten up. One would think he *wanted* to be seen doing . . . and wanted Lalit to see . . . My mind refuses to function; I don't care who saw us. New York, marriage, that email; all far, far away.

"Zoya!" Tanya jumps back into my foggy life like a sharp sliver of unwanted light. Her mouth hangs open, as if she's seen a ghost, her perfectly straight white teeth thanks to regular cosmetic dental sessions on full display. "We need to leave. Now!"

"Oh?" Despite my confusion I almost collapse on the empty paper plates in a rush of relief. Thank God. I can't do this, I can't have feelings for my boss and ruin everything.

She shakes her head ever so slightly and darts her eyes in Lalit's direction, who's on his way back, obviously smug in his victory over the working class and their so-called cheating ways.

"Is everything okay?" Lalit and Arnav ask together. Lalit stares absently around him and Arnav sends a blank death stare my way. So, we're back to Arnav-the-Dragon. Okay, then.

"All is okay," Tanya chips in blithely. "Mummy just wanted to show us some jewelry she's chosen for Zoya's wedding. At our auntie Rama Bua's house. Everyone's there. And the jeweler just has two hours for us before he flies to Belgium to scout for diamonds."

Jewelry? Belgium? My auntie Rama Bua's house? Hold on. Is her head as empty as her stomach? Why would my jewelry be at my auntie's house? If anywhere, it'll be at my house.

We walk to Lalit's Audi parked in the dark, by the roadside between the stone railway bridge and an abandoned factory. Lalit walks in front of everyone, followed by Tanya texting furiously. Arnav walks in step beside me, our hands almost brushing against each other. *How would it feel to just slip my hand into his warm one?*

"I don't buy that jewelry crap for a minute. Text me what's going on when you reach home," Arnav whispers, tilting his head, and my heart completely melts. I see Lalit rambling up ahead in short, heavy strides, and another little disloyal thought fights its way in: *Why don't we have that? Lalit and I?* What is that *that*? A connection? A level of comfort? A special understanding? All of it, I guess. And more, but I dare not name it or even think it.

Tanya opens the passenger door, as if on autopilot. "What are you doing?" I ask.

"Oh, sorry, I'm used to . . . not used to seeing you sit in the passenger seat next to a man." She tosses her hair over her shoulders, gets into the back seat, and slams the door shut. I get into the passenger seat of Lalit's gray car. Arnav stands outside the car, gazing at me with a strange expression as Lalit hands me his wallet while he buckles himself in. Arnav remains there, half-shadowed, standing on the pavement, his reflection in the side mirror getting smaller and smaller as we drive away.

Thankfully, it's a short drive to Rama Bua's house from the dhaba. Tanya sits ramrod straight at the back of the car (I can see her in that same side mirror). All is quiet in the car, no one bothers making conversation. Lalit drives silently, except for clearing his throat repeatedly and blinking into the rearview mirror, his jaw tight. Lalit and I have depleted all that we had to say to each other, which wasn't much to begin with. And why would Tanya have anything to say to Lalit at all? The three of us sit freezing in the tomb of a car, after which Tanya discretely takes a wipe from her clutch as if to sneeze into it, but quickly rubs her lipstick off with it. So. Rita Chachi does not know. Interesting.

The roads are empty; there's only a handful of cars under amber lights, packs of stray dogs rummage through garbage on the side of the street. It's as if the city senses our urgency and rushes us to whatever it was that made Tanya want to sit with me in an enclosed space for any amount of time. The last time we sat next to each other in a car was when we were five years old, getting ice cream in Pa's car. We spent the entire ten minutes hitting and slapping each other, after which, needless to say, there was no ice cream for anyone. We don't slap and hit now, but the sentiment remains the same.

"Lalit, come up and have some tea?" I turn to him as we get out of the car near Rama Bua's ancient, elevator-less building.

Arranged Marriage Rule No. EleventyThousandFive: Do not shoo away the in-laws, especially the son-in-law, at any time without feeding them till they implode upon themselves. Mum would be mortified if I didn't ask him up.

Tanya stiffens behind Lalit, frantically waving her arms as if to shoo him away. What is going on?

Wait. Do they know I got the job? Is that what this hoopla's about?

No, of course not, how could they? Even I barely read that email fifteen minutes ago. Surely they can't spy on my phone remotely? Can they?

"It's okay, Zoya, it's late anyway. You girls go ahead." Lalit doesn't hug or kiss me in front of Tanya, or even glance at me in silent question as most fiancés would. Not that I mind, because Tanya's bony finger digs into my back in an attempt to heckle me up two flights of stairs at breakneck speed.

Before my finger reaches the white doorbell of Rama Bua's flat, Tanya's mother Rita Chachi yanks the heavy wooden door open, as if she'd been listening for our footsteps.

The entire family is gathered in the living room: Ronny Chacha, Sheila Bua, my cousins Karan and Yuvi, Mum, Pa, Rama Bua. A profound sense of dread spreads through my body. All of them pace or wince or both. Even Uncle Balli sighs and shakes his head. Something's happened. Something big. I clutch the door handle tight; my other hand grabs my purse, right over the phone pocket.

I can see a disheveled Aisha from the threshold of the front door, sobbing silently on the living room couch. Her mother-in-law sits beside her, awkwardly patting her back. "Beta, these things happen . . . let it go and come home now. That's a good girl."

Aisha continues to sob. "No. Please don't. I've had enough of his philandering." Oh God no. Not my sweet Aisha! How can this be?

Varun leans against our cream-colored wall, looking more bored than apologetic, and I want to take my purse and smack it across his smug-bastard face with all the force in my body.

The mother-in-law arises from the couch to leave, and turns to Rama Bua, who stands next to Aisha's side of the couch utterly gobsmacked and says, "I think we should give Aisha some time to think it over."

"It's all over!" Rita Chachi whispers to Tanya and me standing outside the door. Her eyes are wide in a morbid excitement. "Aisha wants a divorce!"

"And, Zoya," Mum sneaks up behind Rita Chachi to say in an equally breathless whisper "we moved your wedding up. You're getting married on May twenty-second instead of June twenty-second now."

My knees buckle under me as if I've been starving for days.

May twenty-second. The very day I need to be in New York. Of course.

My phone bings and it's Arnav. I rush into the kitchen, the room closest to the front door, pretending that I need a drink of water, but it's really to check his text in private. I should rush to Aisha's side, I know; I'm a horrid friend and cousin, but my head is whirling with my own trinity of crap—marriage-New York-boss—and not my BFF's overturned life.

Tell me.

My heart collapses upon itself at Arnav's simple words. I can't do this, any of it. I can't take the B&O job, I can't go to New York, I can't have these feelings for Arnav. Not now. I owe it to my family to go through with my wedding, *especially* now that Aisha's marriage is in ruins, and give it the fullest, most heartfelt shot that I can. It's as if someone sits on my chest; I feel crushed. It's a strange suffocation, as if I am trapped in a dark tunnel, unable to raise my head or move my limbs.

Me: Do you really want to know?

A: I don't have a good feeling about this. Please. Tell me.

I push away that heavy weight on my chest. I'm going to do this right.

Me: My wedding is preponed. I'm getting married in a month, not two. I have to go. I'm sorry.

What am I sorry for? So many things; for our texts, the food we share, Chotu and his books, a quiet friendship over the anonymous gift giver. For what could've been.

My phone rings and rings. It's him. I do not answer.

Five minutes later, when my phone is silent, I open his texts again, and then shut them immediately. No point now. And then before I can stop myself, my fingers click open the email from B&O. *One last time*, I promise myself, and something inside my heart breaks.

"Zoya, can you sit with Aisha for a bit?" Mum peeps into the kitchen to ask.

"Of course." I'm instantly flooded with guilt at putting my screwy life ahead of my cousin's shattered one. I leave my phone on the kitchen counter (no need to tempt myself) and rush out to sit next to a shaking Aisha, my arms holding her tight. The family is in different corners of the flat strategizing, relieved that I'm with her, when Sheila Bua walks up to me and hands me my phone. She just keeps looking at me dazedly with her beady little eyes. And I know in an instant, because the auto-lock on my phone hasn't worked in weeks: she read the email. The one with the job offer. I can feel it inside my shaking bones.

"You should be careful." She clears her throat. "About what you . . . let into your life." Then as if she decides on something internally, she walks away slowly.

She knows about New York.

No, no, no.

CHAPTER EIGHTEEN

It's a real catastrophe. My dainty, pretty Aisha, brought up to find a nice man and settle down, wants a divorce because Varun cheated on her. Multiple times. He even screwed around the day of Aisha's mehendi, two days before their wedding.

It's been a week and Aisha still hasn't stopped crying. I should've seen the signs. The harsh edge to her voice at my engagement party, questioning the very reason for marriage, red eyes. I mean, what kind of a best-friend-cousin am I? I feel a deep pang of shameful despair.

Both families have tried many times to patch things up because no one wants to be associated with the *other* D-word—Divorce—forget broken hearts or trust. But Varun's back to drinking and cheating now after his empty promises. How do I know? Because I saw him today. I saw him making out with a bird-like woman on my way back from work—the same rum-glugging "friend" from their wedding. They were frolicking in his electric-blue Jaguar (can't miss it), which shook like an earthquake, parked in the alley behind the pasta stall (the one that Lalit thinks I stopped going to every evening before dinner). I want to tell Aisha, I really do, but I can't bring myself to break her heart even more.

Aisha alternates between scorned fury and utter grief. I don't know what to say to her, or how to "be"—I, the future bride with the world (by some perspectives at least) at my feet, and she, a soon-to-be-divorced woman in a world that still makes no allowances for an outlier.

But actually, even more than Aisha, I'm worried about Sheila Bua. Not because she's having an affair, but that she walks around in a dazed self-imposed silence now. Today is the first day in two months that she hasn't texted me with a GIF or a meme or my wedding day countdown. Sheila Bua thinks it's *her* fault that Varun cheated on Aisha, that she didn't know what kind of a person he was. It's ridiculous, but the blame is lodged firmly inside her head. Or maybe she's just pissed at me and the, you know, email? No, that can't be, because if she were, the whole family would've known by now. Sheila Bua hasn't said anything to anyone about New York. Since Mum and Pa didn't wake me up in the middle of the night to interrogate me about why I applied to an American job when I'm getting married, the logical conclusion is that she hasn't told them. Which is strange.

Meanwhile, insanity prevails all around. My gentle Mum has turned into a typhoon worthy of international mention—all because of my new wedding date. *If a man cheats on a girl like Aisha, what hope do the rest of us have?* Especially ones whose fiancés may still be hung up on ex-girlfriends. Could I somehow, possibly, you know, think about, kind of, in a way, calling it off . . . *no, just stop.*

There she is, my mother, her navy-blue kurta flying in the air behind her like a cape, going from the kitchen to the living room, giving the cook dinner instructions and talking on the phone at the same time.

"Mum!" She all but runs into the bedroom, then back into the living room, to dig into her purse for a receipt.

"Mum." I pull her by the hand and deposit her on the sofa in an ungraceful plop. "Would you stop for a minute?"

"No time, no time. I have to call the tailor—he's still waiting on the design on my blouse for the reception—and the jeweler won't start making the gold choker for the wedding ceremony till I go and pay him in person, and the—"

"Do you really want to land in the hospital before my wedding? Just, please, here." I hand her a half-filled plastic water bottle.

She takes several big gulps and sighs. "Thank God for all these things to do. If it wasn't for your wedding, Zoya, we'd all be so depressed. Its distracting us from Aisha's . . ." She can't even say the word "divorce." Her gray hair gleams under the white tube light—has it become grayer in the last week? Or did she forget to color it? She only forgets to color her hair under extreme stress or excitement. A few strands escape and swirl around her head like a halo.

I can't believe I actually thought about calling it off . . . I mean, I thought about people, *other* people, who call off their wedding . . . *distract yourself, Zoya, it always works.* I'm going to ask her again about Sheila Bua. Yes! Maybe I'll find out why she didn't rat me out to my parents.

Mala, our petite cook, rolls in from the kitchen with two mugs of our early evening tea, hands one to each of us and saunters back like the mistress of the house. Which she is, in a way. All domestic helpers in Bombay are. (She also got a big fat load of cash as a bonus to celebrate my engagement and will expect an even bigger one for the wedding.)

"So. Mum." I take a sip of the ginger chai and feel the warm liquid travel leisurely down my throat to settle comfortably into my stomach. Let me enjoy this treasure of dairy as long as I can, because Lalit and his parents recently switched to almond milk. Which tastes like nutty expired yogurt. "Since you are here, and so am I, do you think you could come clean about Sheila Bua?"

"Come clean? What do you mean? Does Sheila didi have some jewelry that needs cleaning and polishing?" Mum puts the mug of tea on the table and grabs her phone, typing the word "jeweler" in the search bar.

"God, can you stop thinking about jewelry for a minute? I meant, tell me about Sheila Bua leaving home when she was younger. Is that true? Was she a serious painter? And why were her paintings unsuitable?"

"I just really have to go—" She shifts as if to get off the couch.

"Mum, please." I'm surprised to hear a real pleading in my voice. "Aisha's divorce has changed everything. Tell me what happened to Sheila Bua, so that it doesn't happen to me."

She gasps, as if stung. But the thought of her own daughter with a crumbling marriage like Aisha or leaving home like Sheila Bua, is more than she can take.

"Yes, Sheila didi did leave home once. It was a long time ago." She sighs deeply, her whole body gives in and sinks back into the couch. "Your Uncle Balli is . . . well, he has very particular ideas about what wives can and cannot do. She had moved out, bag and baggage, a year after her marriage, and went to live with one of her artist friends. This was before Yuvi was born, of course. Please don't think her callous enough to walk out on her child."

"No. That's the last thing I would call her. What happened then?"

"One of her artist friends put her up temporarily. She tried for three months to find a place for herself. But in those days, it was difficult for single women, or divorced women, or women artists, to rent a place," Mum says.

"So, she returned home?"

"Yes. Her paintings didn't sell that fast, so money was tight. And Uncle Balli threatened her with divorce and took her back only when she swore she would never paint again."

Divorce? Poor Sheila Bua. "But why? It's only painting. Surely there's nothing wrong with painting?"

Mum scrunches her nose as if smelling something unsavory. Of course, you know what our community thinks of artists in general. "But Sheila didi used to paint those nu . . ." Mum chokes on the word, as if it was lodged inside her throat, her face turning a shade of alarming purple-red.

"Paint those what?"

She whispers, as if a hushed voice could erase the paintings off the earth. "*Those* kind of paintings," she says, her voice almost a puff between her teeth. "Totally unsuitable for a respectable married woman. She painted only two or three of them but there was *such* a furor when a neighbor saw one at an exhibition."

"Mum! What kind of paintings?"

"Those . . ." She glances around to make sure Pa or the maid aren't lurking, and whispers, "Naked paintings."

I splutter into my cup of chai and cough till my lungs turn inside out. "You mean nudes?" I yell. Mum shushes me something fierce, as if a naked woman could suddenly appear right in the middle of our living room at the sound of my voice.

Sheila Bua and naked paintings? How . . . when . . . I mean, what? "Sheila Bua" and "nudes" are not words I ever thought I'd say in the same sentence. It sounds more illicit than her affair. Naked paintings and extramarital affair. Holy smokes. Sheila Bua is something savage.

As if she's said too much, Mum thumps the empty tea mug on the wooden table (no coaster: she *is* stressed) and pulls herself off the sofa with great effort. "What's done is done. I hope you take their example and . . . ah, look at me, sitting here sipping tea, when there are so many things to be done. You have to go to the gym, don't you? Well, hurry up." She walks straight out of the front door. "I *must* go to the tailor. Bye!"

Why the gym, you ask? Because my future home is completely fat-free, and I need to prep to be low-fat for life, so I, in a fit of extreme candor (and utter madness), signed up for the six-month membership at Baby's Gym that Lalit gifted me as engagement present. Because I have to give this relationship a real, honest shot. And being healthy is how I can bond with Lalit and my in-laws. I owe it to my family.

My phone on the side table vibrates, and despite myself my heart stops, expecting Arnav, then burns and crashes to the ground in disappointment. It's just a reminder notification to email the HR rep from B&O in New York with my final decision. Today.

Yup, that New York job offer ticks like a bomb in my Inbox. As if I need a reminder.

Would you leave home after a year of marriage, Zoya?

A little pang of despair, of heartache, spears through my chest. At what? At the thought of marriage or the job, or the chance at a different life, or Sheila Bua's forlorn story, I can't say. Maybe all of them. I sent the HR rep a thank you email last week as soon as I received the offer, but I need time. I know I can't accept, but I can't let go of the dream job in New York, I can't let go of the hope of a different life.

As for Arnav, we stopped texting last week after Aisha's news. I knew I couldn't carry on. I just stopped replying to his texts.

He stops by my desk some days, looking a bit wild and unkempt, unlike his usual self, his arm causally strung on my cube wall, his gaze boring holes in me, hoping to talk or work in the empty cube next to mine. (He had started working next to me after the Holi party. He happened to walk by with his laptop one day, saw the empty cube next to mine, grinned at me, and plonked himself in the chair. He would do that sometimes, just work next to me in a pleasing, companionable silence.) But these days I only ever talk to him about campaign metrics and clients (the glue project is still getting good numbers) and Chotu's textbooks, and then paste my eyes to my monitor. I don't dare make or maintain eye contact. But he knows why it has to be this way. He knows my wedding's preponed—that was my last text to him. Because whatever *this* is can't go on any longer. So why do I reel every time I see him; why does it feel like someone, something, died?

Also, my secret admirer has gone quiet. After weeks of food, books, desserts (the ice cream falooda from Noorani's was top-notch), a calendar with quotes from *The Lord of the Rings*, and another book, this time about magical realism and food, set in rustic Mexico, it all stopped. Just like that. Nothing showed on my desk all week. The hollow pit in my stomach on Friday evening completely bewildered me. Like being stood up. I guess Raunak finally got the message . . .

Or maybe it was actually my girls all along. Didn't Peehu say there was something special in the works? And now that we have our spa weekend booked, they've stopped with these gifts. How blind was I? No one else knows me so well apart from the girls. It has to be them. Good. Mystery solved. And I'll let them go on believing that I don't know they sent me those gifts. I'll just spring it on them when we meet at the spa, that I cracked this mystery, because right now, I've got other things to worry about. Like, tonight is the last, final, ultimate evening to decide on the job offer. Just saying.

Mum's bought herself a sari worth thirty thousand rupees, which almost gave Pa a stroke, and my great grandmother's wedding sari from 1920 is being made into a wedding lehenga for me (19-effing-20; it's *vintage*!) and Pa's invited every blasted eye surgeon in Bombay to the wedding and they all know he's now one of the Board of Directors at the biggest ophthalmology hospital in the city, and my wedding is the only good thing to be happening after Aisha's divorce, and the family looks to me like I'm their queen and savior with a Diamond Boy, Holy Grail, non-fat, perfect fiancé that every girl dreams of.

Who has no idea about the impending divorce in my family or my dream job offer in New York.

I know, I know, I'm supposed to be worried about Aisha, and I really am, but this preponed wedding has turned my life upside down. I had a nightmare the other night in which I made the guests at my wedding reception wait to greet me while I frantically searched for my passport. I jerked out of bed as if struck by lightning and typed a full text with ten emojis to Arnav before I remembered *why* I stopped texting him in the first place, after which I was so disturbed that I gobbled up half a packet of chocolate bonbons that I keep in my bedside drawer for emergencies.

No point in all these thoughts, Zoya. Get your butt off the sofa and into the gym. Exercise can be used to distract yourself from the immediate matter at hand just as much as food can. Okay, then.

* * *

Here I am at six thirty PM under a dusky sky, waiting outside the gym for Sheila Bua of all people because Mum thought chaperoning me to the gym would get Sheila Bua out of Aisha's divorce funk. How, I couldn't say. But since Mum told me about her leaving home fiasco, I feel a sort of, I don't know, an invisible silent bond with Sheila Bua. So I don't really mind her coming.

Sheila Bua's big white Lexus screeches to a halt right next to me on the gym steps and out she heaves and huffs, cursing the small size of the rather large car.

She pauses on the shiny stairway of the gym and stares at the polished glass doors in reverence as if they were the steps of a historic citadel. She's in black leggings and a green T-shirt but there they are again: those strange patches of color. Today they're on her T-shirt, even her arms. If I didn't know any better, I'd say that was paint. But no, of course it isn't. Uncle Balli wouldn't stand for it. He'd divorce her in an instant if she broke her promise to stop painting. There's no way Sheila Bua will let another divorce stain the family. And as one of the stalwarts of the Punjabi community, the concept of a nude-painting Sheila Bua who matchmakes boys and girls is just borderline blasphemous.

Does she still think about her botched rebellion? When is a good time to bury your dreams; before or after marriage? I can't dare ask her. You think you know someone, don't you, but one little fact can turn that perception on its head.

Sheila Bua walks in ahead of me in a daze, heading toward the cardio space and bumping into an occupied treadmill. The gym is as large and sleek inside as the shiny outer doors indicate; the slick equipment reeks of Lysol and burnt rubber, and alarmingly healthy trainers seem in constant motion.

"Hello! You there, Auntie, watch where you're going!" A middle-aged woman shrieks at Sheila Bua's zombie face between her breathless pants.

"Going? Where am I going? I don't know . . ." If it is possible, Sheila Bua looks even more dazed.

"Well, don't ruin my workout by banging into my treadmill!" The woman says, her long braid swinging like a tail.

"What's the point, child? You'll either get divorced or life will beat you down."

Good grief! I was right to worry about Sheila Bua. I must *do* something.

"I'm sorry, my aunt is unwell," I say to the annoyed woman and turn to Sheila Bua. "Bua! Mum said a boy's mother was coming to your house today?" If anything, her favorite pastime—matchmaking, if that is indeed her favorite hobby—should snap her out of it.

"How does it matter? They can come whenever they want. It's all in God's hands anyway."

Oh lordie. Even the mention of a boy's mother didn't break through her fog. A pellet of intense dread shoots up my skull. A sort of premonition. But of what? Please, please, go back to being my annoying matchmaking auntie and all will be well.

"Who is it, Bua? Who's coming? Tell me, no?"

I steer her toward an empty treadmill. She grabs the hands of the black machine and heaves herself on it with a grunt.

"Your Arnav's mother, I guess . . ."

My Arnav?

The thought is alien, but it slips off my tongue easily like it belongs. My Arnav? *Stop, Zoya. Remember why you stopped texting him.*

"Why. . . . um, why is his mother coming to your house?"

"She thinks I can find him someone. What does she know . . ."

"So, he didn't like . . . Tanya?" Please, please.

For a moment, the wily old Sheila Bua gleams back from her eyes. "How did you know about him and Tanya?"

"Err . . . I saw them . . ." My knees are jelly at the memory of that molten chocolate ear episode.

"Now what to say? God knows what all you boys and girls want. And that Tanya? No meat on her! Who wants to marry a skeleton?" She sighs on the treadmill and plods reluctantly at a blazing speed of 1.1 miles.

Thud. Thud. Thud.

I take a machine next to her. Okay, think heart rate, think energy, think marriage, think vintage lehenga.

Thud. Thud. Thud

Sheila Bua stares straight ahead, out of the large glossy windows onto a bustling Bombay evening. Shops and offices and flats stacked haphazardly next to each other, low-hanging cable wires, petrol fumes, and packs of people, all jostling for space in a rush to get somewhere. "Do you ever wonder . . . what is the point of it all?"

"What is the point of what?"

"Marriage. Dreams . . . Life."

I almost trip on my treadmill, which also blazes at 2.0 miles. In my twenty-six years on this planet (soon to be twenty-seven), I've *never* heard anything remotely resembling philosophy from my aunt. I don't know what's worse in a relative, philandering or philosophy.

THUD!

Sheila Bua's rotund face swells bright red like the inside of a watermelon as she keeps thudding on the treadmill. She gasps, tortured wheezes, one of her hands flails in the air and I almost vomit in fright.

Oh my GOD! Stroke, stroke! She's having a STROKE!

"Help! HELP!" I thwack the red STOP button on her treadmill, rushing to grab her. "My auntie! Over here! HELP!!"

Within seconds, a fiendishly vigorous female trainer appears out of nowhere as Sheila Bua wheezes, "Paani!"

"Please, please! Someone get water for my auntie! She's having a stroke! HURRY!"

A bunch of trainers dash up with ice cold water bottles and then stop in their tracks to throw exasperated glances at each other. "No madam, it is not a stroke." They cannot seem to stand still. I bet they live on protein shakes and would explode into dust at the first bite of bread. "We've seen it before. You are just gasping hard and all your fa—weight is putting pressure on your lungs." The lead trainer shakes her head in relief, holding the lip of the bottle to Sheila Bua's mouth.

Oh thank God! I collapse on the treadmill next to Sheila Bua, knocking her hideous lime-green purse and all its junk on the carpeted floor. Sheila Bua freezes mid-wheeze as if I just spilled state secrets of the CIA on the dirty gray carpet. My dread-o-meter goes bananas. What on earth is in that bag?

The trainers disperse, grumbling under their breath about fat people, and go back to their kickboxing and cycling and Zumba. We sit side by side on the narrow edge of the treadmill, Sheila Bua and I, under bright lights amid panting voices and purring machines. Her breath slowly comes back to normal.

I gather the spilled contents of her bag off the floor and start to stuff them into her purse. Why does she need so much crap? Look at this—thousands of horoscopes, take-out menus, a large brown wallet fat with at least ten thousand rupees (hello, burglars!), two smartphones, a stack of small rolled-up parchments with color stains on the outside, three sets of keys, and some folded, yellowed official-looking papers—

"So you want to live in New York, don't you?"

The papers fall to the floor with a soft thump. Bollywood music blasts from a room behind us, with the sharp screech of the trainer: "One-two-three-KICK!"

A hammer bangs inside my head, cracking its carefully built barrier. I forget to push the thought of New York away, as I've done since I saw that email. For just a moment, it's out in the open, the hope, the dream of a different life.

"How did you know that I think about . . . ?" I whisper, unable to say it out loud, like the name of an old, star-crossed love.

Her eyes are warm, her sad little smile softens her face. She places her open palm on my head as if in a blessing. Which shocks me more than the wheezy scare.

"How can you forget something that consumes you? That thin cover you call life can't hide what lives underneath."

She would know how it feels, wouldn't she?

Our bodies are frozen, as if in a floating bubble of stillness, far removed from the bustle of the gym around us.

She knows about killing dreams.

She reaches to the floor, to the faded papers. And as if she's done it a million times, she opens a tattered paper and places it in my hands, gently, as if trusting me with a delicate and exquisite treasure.

A pungent scent of mothballs spreads into our bubble. The paper is thick and yellowed with a crest at the top, U-shaped and royal. It's her Oxford acceptance letter.

I stare at her round face, the yellowed acceptance letter cradled in my hands as if it was a precious newborn.

"Ah, yes." She answers my silent question. "Young women were expected to settle down, marry, have children, not go off to distant lands," she says simply, as if that was explanation enough. It was then.

It is now.

She whispers, as if speaking to me, but she's oblivious to everything, to everyone. "How do you fight your own mind, your own heart?" The faded paper is torn in several places, that poor sheet, as if folded and refolded more than it could bear. The parchments choose that instant to unroll. A lush carpet of abstract colors spills onto the gray carpet, all over each other, like children restrained for too long. Reds, purples, blacks, teary eyes, wondrous faces, all kinds of things look out of this iridescent rainbow. *The paint splotches on her body.* For just a moment, a luminous, radiant light appears in a dull gray sky.

But . . . does she not care about what Uncle Balli and the family and community will think of her? Why has she started painting now?

"Life doesn't give you many chances to correct." Her face is despondent with a hopeless burning. Like that time I saw her painting in that back room when I was eleven.

It hits me with all the force of a bottled-up past that explodes into a certain future—her dream, her *life*, is entombed inside the red bruises of her art.

"But how did you . . . pay for . . . the . . . admission forms?" I whisper, asking the first stupid thing that pops in my muddled head.

"I sold a few of my paintings." She tries to smile but gives up, her eyes far away in another land. "I bought this necklace with the money left after." She fingers her ever-present gold bird necklace absently, which I thought was a present from my grandmother.

A commonsense decision for a young woman then. And now.

But what is the common sense in it?

My throat is in knots. I want to scream, but my voice is stuck deep inside. And to what purpose? It would echo off a void and the darkness would close around us again, tighter and blacker for the lost echo.

But why tell me today? And why start painting again? Why now, after all this time?

The frenetic trainers gather around us again and insist on taking Sheila Bua to their health office, just in case. A rush of cold air sneaks into her vacated warmth.

I am alone on the treadmill with her papers.

I don't know what makes me do it. Her dazed look or her silent gasp at its spilled contents, but my hand reaches not for the Oxford letter, but an official white sheet that was folded inside it. Which she shoved under the treadmill when she thought I wasn't looking.

Sharma Oncology.

Sharma? That's Uncle Purple! The one she's having an affair with! Why is he sending her official papers? Holy crap, is she finally divorcing Uncle Balli? I suppose that explains the painting now. The dread is back with an entire army of unease. I never thought she'd ever do that, *now* after all these years. But another divorce in the family? We are officially ruined.

Dr. Pradeep Sharma, Oncologist, MBBS, MD, DM

Doctor? Ah, I do remember Mum vaguely telling me he was a doctor. But an oncologist?

Name: Mrs. Sheila Arora 17 January 2019
Age: 61 years
Female
Diagnosis
Cervical Cancer—Positive.
Stage 2

"One-two-three-PEDAL!" It's loud, too loud, the sound of energetic gymmers thundering on their machines. The ground has vanished beneath my feet and I sit inside a black nothing. My mind whirls—

"*—peaky and tired—*"

"*—nobody knows—*"

"*—my office . . . tomorrow . . . please—*"

She wasn't buying lingerie that night of my un-pregnancy, when Arnav and I saw her with Uncle Purple. She was at a clinic. A cancer clinic.

Sheila Bua isn't having an affair. Sheila Bua is dying.

The papers drop from my clammy fingers. I don't know where I am; it could be a street or a treadmill or a forest or in a river, I couldn't tell you.

This is why she's painting again. Because insignificant things vanish at death's door and maybe all that remains is an unfinished life. No second chances.

The commotion near the health office recedes as Sheila Bua walks back. Her green T-shirt clings to her body. Her steps are slow, measured, like the very act of walking sucks every ounce of energy out of her.

She freezes at the sight of the white paper on the floor. As if a supernatural force magically sends her energy shots, she grabs the yellowed Oxford paper, the paintings, and the white medical sheet all at once, avoiding my gaze. She folds the Oxford scroll tight around the white cancerous one and stashes it all into the deepest corners of her bag as if the tatters of a lost past can wipe out a cruel present.

We are perched on the edge of the treadmill again. We don't dare look at each other. I don't ask her about Oxford. I don't ask her about her illness. I don't ask her about *her*. Not here, not now. A claw pulls at my voice, down, down, and traps it inside my throat.

She couldn't do what she loved.

And now she may not get another chance.

But she *tried*, didn't she, no matter what life handed her? She left home to make it on her own. She failed, but she tried. *Which is more than what you did, Zoya. What a coward you are.* I don't have half her courage. She put everything on the line. What have I done?

"I know about you, Sheila Bua. I know that you had left home to become an artist."

She turns toward me, adjusting her position slightly on the edge of the treadmill. To another person looking at us, she would appear to have hardly changed positions, but she has turned front and center to face me.

She clutches the folded papers close to her chest, as if they are filled with the very oxygen she needs to live. "Yes," she says quietly. "It was . . . difficult . . ."

"Why did you come back?"

She draws a ragged breath. "It was not easy for a single woman."

I know it wouldn't be, not all those years ago. But I wait silently for her to continue. "There were rumors . . . insinuations, of loose morals, simply because I had left my husband, simply because I was an artist. And then I found out I was pregnant." She smiles a sad, knowing smile, at the sudden change of direction that women are often forced to make, at the onset of motherhood. "I left before people questioned whose child it was. There really was no choice."

I open my mouth to say that I can't imagine how hard it must have been for her, but she mistakes it for the modern person's disdain for choices made a generation ago. "It's difficult for people today to understand the censure back then. And a divorced sibling would've affected the marriage chances of my sister and brothers. I couldn't do that to them."

We are surrounded by noise: exercising people, shining lights, whirring ski machines, humming treadmills, the music beats from Zumba. It's not difficult to understand, I want to tell her. The modern woman is celebrated in the media, but then someone like Kamya can't rent a flat with her boyfriend in a big city like Bangalore simply because they aren't married.

She continues, "I took up matchmaking because, well, after Yuvi married, what did I have left? But . . . things have . . . changed." She unfolds the tightly rolled papers. "I went back to the art gallery, the one I used to work at all those years ago . . . to ask them if I could come back. But that's all over now."

"It's being turned into a shopping mall," I say in a hushed voice at the memory of Sheila Bua speeding off into a taxi outside my office, the night of the Holi party. The D and the ee that I could barely decipher that night and never paid any attention to in all my years working there; I know now what it was. Dorabjee Art Gallery. The one she told me about when she visited my office. Blast those bloody builders; as if the city needs yet another useless mall.

She doesn't ask me to cancel my wedding, despite everything that hangs in the air between us sitting on that treadmill. Doesn't tell me to take the job. Doesn't tell me *not* to take it. She won't say it out loud. Maybe because in the end, the roots of our traditions are anchored deeper than our dreams.

She clutches her lime-green bag tightly under her arms and calls her driver. Her nose stud catches the reflection of an overhead lamp and a bright shaft of starburst hits my eyes. I don't close my eyes and look away. Not this time.

I help hoist her off the edge of the treadmill (how long has it been, us sitting on this rubber monster machine?). She slings the purse on her shoulder and stops me from accompanying her to the door across the gym.

"I have to leave now. Time is . . . short. There are things to be done." She glances away from me. "Maybe there's still time to live my life." She walks toward the gym door, her tread heavy but her eyes sharp, and then disappears into the brightness of the city before I can think of a reply.

She was never a real person to me, was she? Always a placeholder in the family. They all are. The aunties and uncles, the buas, the chachas, the maasis. All of them name tags, clubbed under generic groups: Annoying, Interfering, Won't Understand, Born Old, What Do They Know.

How many stories hide inside these name tags? How many of these name tags were once something else?

For a split, bizarre second a sepia-tinted picture flashes in front of my eyes. It's from an old eighties leather-bound photo album forgotten in a dusty corner in the storeroom of her house. I went through it once and found a young Sheila Bua, tall and willowy in a pink shirt with red poppies and bootcut pants. Long black hair flying in the breeze, the gold necklace at her nape; carefree, wide-eyed, *shining*.

It hits me later, much later, long after she's gone from the gym. The pendant on that necklace, which she bought for herself. I never knew what it meant.

It was a bird spreading its wings.

Flying to freedom.

* * *

The night has transformed swiftly from a faint gray to an inky blue. The cool granite steps outside the gym send a shiver up my body as I sit down. It's time. I type on my phone in a blaze of streetlights and Bombay rush.

To: Selena.Jones@bucklebee.com
Subject: Re: Congratulations!

There is only one reply. There always was.

Dear Ms. Jones,

Thank you for considering me for the position of Sr. Campaign Manager. I am pleased to accept . . .

And I weep. There's no stopping the flood.
Who do I weep for? I cannot say.
For her.
For me.
For all of us.

CHAPTER NINETEEN

I am on the three o'clock ferry right now, bobbing over to Alibaug. It was a relief that Arnav left the office a couple of hours before me—we don't talk much these days except to discuss office stuff, so I have no idea where he went. Plus, there's always a sense of dread when you leave in the middle of the day with your boss watching. So, all good here, so far.

The boat—which carries double the passengers allowed—is being steered across the gray Arabian Sea like a dying motorcycle by a tobacco-chewing man in a green Avengers T-shirt.

My phone bings with a text from Sheila Bua:

Only three weeks to go! Enjoy your girlfriend trip to Alibaug. Do take care of Aisha. She is feeling decompressed.

Me: You mean depressed.
Sheila Bua: Same thing.

Followed by a GIF of drunk, middle-aged women in straw skirts doing the hula dance with cocktails in their hands and an Aloha sign over their heads.

I mean, true, right? For what I'm expecting on this trip? Except for the straw skirts and middle age. And Alibaug is hardly Hawaii.

The hem of my yellow skirt swirls in the breeze. I gaze away from the humanity, sitting bunched up against each other on the deck and gaze into the gray water at the collective plastic floating just beneath.

Sheila Bua's texts are back. As is the countdown. Maybe the gym incident of last week did get her out of Aisha's divorce funk. But is she counting down to the wedding or to New York? I don't know. I know she won't tell me to call off my wedding, even after all that passed between us, because that's who she is. She's still my conventional auntie. That is what time and regret have turned her into. Despite that, though, I know I have a modicum of her silent support—she still hasn't told Mum and Pa about my job offer—for which she has a permanent spot in my heart.

Exactly how I *reach* New York would make an excellent sitcom, the ones with a laugh track in the background. Yes, a laugh track would fit perfectly with my life. Because I still shop for my wedding. And also speak to my future American boss on the phone *while* wedding shopping. Madeline's quiet American drawl—which I'm told is a Yankee boroughs accent, no idea what that means—is utterly bizarre, enmeshed in my surroundings of haggling shopkeepers, swirling fabric, and sizzling fried kulchas in the crowded Lajpath Market.

I'm like a spy who leads a double life, except it makes me want to vomit most of the time. It also doesn't involve guns or fancy cars. Or naked Bond girls. Does James Bond ever want to throw up? And as if all this wasn't enough, I have to be *in* New York the day of my wedding.

I also meet Lalit for dates more frequently. (Yes, once a week is frequent.) And we converse for exactly five minutes before whipping out our phones. (How are you? You look nice. You seem to have lost weight. Thank you. How are wedding preparations? Brilliant. Okay then.) And we still plan our honeymoon to Iceland in those five minutes. Greenland is now not hip enough, according to Lalit and his parents. The Blue Lagoon in Grindavik? Sure. Maelifell volcano? But of course. Why? Because I'm a horrid person and a selfish daughter and the wimpiest of wimps on this effing planet.

And a little volcanic matter of my own almost erupted four nights ago.

We were at Baadshahi, this hip restaurant in Bandra that has waiters dressed as seventeenth-century Mughal soldiers with iPads instead of swords. It was a family dinner with the entire Sahni and Khurana clans to celebrate, well, nothing (Punjabis really don't need a reason to celebrate). Lalit, who sat next to me on the dark curvy couch, dropped his fork with a loud clatter when I mentioned my upcoming Alibaug trip with Peehu, Aisha, Kamya, and Tanya (who Sheila Bua forcibly made me invite by totally milking her illness).

"Is *everyone* going?" He blurted before he could stop himself, and then changed the topic so swiftly without waiting for my answer that if I were a loving, jealous fiancé, a *real* fiancé, I'd care, and stop him right there to demand what made him jump as if his bottom was on fire. But then he said, "Zoya, please, can you *finally* get your passport tomorrow when we meet for Pilates on the beach? You've put it off too long. My travel agent will get the Iceland visas and tickets done for us." And all thoughts of Alibaug rushed straight out of my head and toppled on the floor along with my spoon.

I should've told him then, at dinner. Grabbed him by the arm, yanked him to the stinky restaurant toilet, let people think what they wanted, and told him the truth. That I couldn't marry him and that it didn't seem like he wanted to marry me either and that I was going to America. That my passport was already at the U.S. embassy being stamped with a work visa right now. But instead I sat mute, surrounded by our boisterous families who squabbled over the wedding menu while feasting on vinegar baby onions, hot naans, and creamy curries. (Burmese food? Or Italian? Or Mughlai? How about all three *and* a separate fat-free aisle for feeding five hundred people? Wonderful!)

So I skirt around everyone. My family at home, on the phone with my fiancé, and at the office around my boss since I ceased all texting, which saddens me to no end. This is why I lost four kilos without the torture of a diet or a gym, and made Lalit and his parents delirious without doing a thing.

Fuck you, Universe.

A huge thank you to Peehu and Kamya for this escape—I mean, this girl's trip—at just the right time; a beach paradise an hour from my office. Paradise is stretching it a bit, but clean beaches and no crowds are paradise to a city dweller. No skirting anyone, no pretense, just chill by the beach, eat fried seafood, and drink beer. And brownies. "Special" brownies.

It's my twenty-seventh birthday and bachelorette rolled into one. I don't technically need a bachelorette party, more like a goodbye party, but they don't know that, do they?

After this trip, when I am peaceful and Zenned out, I will speak with Lalit in a refined first-world-problem-solving manner, and then sit the family down to break it to them that I simply can't marry him. One by one, like civilized human beings. That is key.

The ferry finally bobs up to the shaky jetty at Mandwa. The visions of sunsets, food, and friends, currently on their way to pick me up, lightens the load on my heart. So much that it takes me a moment too long, once I've transferred my skirted body from the boat to the shaded metal bench on the jetty (having successfully shut up the voice inside my head warning me about belly fat bulging out of my tank top), to recognize the booming voice next to me.

"Hello, Zoya."

Oh, my heart.

Arnav.

How screwed up can my world get?

"Err, hello." Here he is, all bones and muscle in his crisp white shirt with faint blue stripes, gray khakis, and formal black loafers. Was he *born* wearing office clothes? Ever heard of shorts? Flip-flops? I bet he goes on vacations dressed like he's about to make a presentation to top management.

We stare at each other on that metal bench, with the sea swirling in all directions around us while the sun blazes, nothing to say, loads to say.

"How are you?" Arnav asks with a little smile that does not reach his eyes.

"I'm good. And you?" I'm so rattled to see him here that I forget to ask him his reason for being in Alibaug.

"I've been better." He stops abruptly, as if about to say more. "How's Lalit?"

And because he never calls Lalit by name, it's like a punch to my stomach, and I didn't expect to be punched in this lovely beach town. I could move away but the thin strip of land from the jetty to the main road is filled with people waiting for their rides. And there's zero shade or seating. "Lalit's fine."

The jetty, which looks far sturdier than it is, bobs under the wake of an oncoming boat. I hold the steel bar of the bench to steady myself. Two hungry-looking teenage boys plonk themselves on the bench, one on either side of us, and spread out as if on a king-sized bed. Arnav moves closer, his arm reaches behind me and my heart smashes in my chest. He's so close, his Rolex pulls a strand of my hair. "Ouch!"

"Oh, sorry," he says, but doesn't look the least bit apologetic. He bends closer to untangle it from my hair. Ummm. Fresh Polo Sport and musky sweat. Man-smell.

The whole of his warm body shields me from the heat of the sun. His skin is rugged, an even dark brown. Would it feel rough under my fingers? Or smooth like the light brown gash by his nose probably is? And his eyes, his beach eyes, stare at my face in a sort of . . .

"It's your birthday this weekend, isn't it? How come you aren't with Lalit?" Tempting little dimples dent his cheeks.

How come I'm not with Lalit? Because I don't want to be. I can hardly say it to myself. How do I say it to someone else, three weeks before our wedding, without sounding utterly callous? "Well. It's my last birthday as a single woman so my friends wanted to combine it with a bachelorette party and make a weekend of it." The jetty gives an almighty jerk as a rakish sailor who, mistaking his decrepit boat for a Ferrari jet ski, slides into the port in a large, whooshy wave.

"Well, happy birthday in advance." He tilts his head and bends as if to move closer. I move away swiftly and pretend to check my Minion carry-on bag. No need to repeat the tempting-what-am-I-saying episode at the dhaba.

"What are you doing here?" I finally think to ask.

"I'm here for the off-site brainstorming with Purity Jewelers. You helped me on a pitch for them, remember?" This explains his formal uniform in a beach town. But which meeting? We do a lot of off-sites with clients at Alibaug, but I don't know of any scheduled this month. Did something come up at the last moment?

"I don't remember hearing about any meeting."

"Ah, well, yes . . . kind of urgent . . . I checked your calendar to see if you could join and saw that you were on vacation right here, in Alibaug. What a coincidence that the, err, meeting is here." He chuckles, thrusts his hands in his pocket, jerks them out immediately as if scalded, and taps his fingers furiously on the bench arm.

"Well, good luck with the deal. Bye!" I spy Peehu, Aisha, Kamya, and Tanya spilling out of a taxi. I spurt off the scorching bench to free myself just as a swarm of happy vacationers disembark from yet another ferry with picnic bags and beach balls and gaggles of kids.

"So, you're at Taj Alibaug?" He calls out to me, voice loud and clear over the whirring of boat engines and people. I can still smell his musky scent over the fumes of the purring ferry. Or maybe it's just burnt into my mind forever. Pheromones or whatever. God help me.

"Yes. How did you know? That was certainly not on my calendar," I say, walking back toward him a little. Should I have lied? No. No more lies. Alibaug is filled with many resorts, so there's no need for us to run into each other. Absolutely no need.

"I figured you would. It's near Kolaba Fort, and I know how much you like those old relics. I guess I just . . . know you well." *Don't look at him, Zoya, don't. Especially not when his voice is low and intimate like this.*

"I'm at the Taj, too." And as if I hadn't heard him clearly enough, he adds, "I mean I'm staying at Taj Alibaug, too. They put us up, so. Catch you in a bit."

Okay, my heart cannot take this anymore. I just give up. Universe, do what you want, I'm done here.

"Zeeeeee!" That loud screech, like a car brake, or several cars braking at once, can only be one person. Peehu! Arnav winces and escapes to the taxis by the side of the road. Peehu rushes up, right past him, to the top of the strip near the jetty, all arms and legs and jangly bracelets and bright-eyed glee. Tanya walks behind her, scowling.

Alright, Tanya is most definitely Goth. Yup. There's black nail paint and lipstick, then black tights, black ankle-length boots, a crisscross black choker, and, oh my word, a dark-as-a-moonless-night T-shirt with a creepy white skull and the words "Fuck Off, Humans" written underneath. I should take a picture of this right now and send it on our family WhatsApp chat group. Rita Chachi would be on the next ferry to Alibaug. But Tanya looks so, well, at ease, that I find myself extremely reluctant to throw her to the wolves. How odd.

Kamya strolls in behind Tanya in an orange tank top and white shorts, waving a cold bottle of water at me. Aisha, happier and more relaxed than I have seen in long time, smiles and twirls around. (Which could be a result of the journalism course the family is now allowing her to pursue, finally. Apparently, broken hearts are necessary for our desires to be approved, as some kind of prerequisite.) Her blue-poppies skirt floats around her like a body halo, and just like that Arnav and the mess that is my life is put aside.

"Was that your . . . boss?" Peehu strains her neck to look back at Arnav getting into a taxi. "What's he doing here? He's so much cuter in person."

"Nope. Not my boss," I lie. (Is it a lie, if technically I have an American boss who I now report to?) "It's just someone who looks like him. Now shut it and walk."

"What's got your goat? Nervous jitters before the wedding?"

"Yes. No. Nothing's got my goat." I sigh and link my arm through hers.

She stops, yanking my arm back with her. "Zee. What's up?"

"I don't know." I look up at her. "I just don't know."

"Is it Lalit? You never talk to me about him, the way you did about Raunak the dickhead. I *know* it's about Lalit."

"It is and it's not." I haven't told her I'm going to New York, I haven't told her I'm not marrying Lalit, I haven't told her Lalit and I aren't exactly what you'd call compatible. I haven't told anyone. Why, you ask? Because I feel like a failure. One who couldn't get along with her Diamond Boy fiancé and live a nice little Indian-wife life. Oh, I know, Peehu would've told me to call the wedding off instead of marrying a man I didn't want to and all that jazz, but that would somehow make it worse. Like I need assistance to make life decisions.

"You're talking in circles. Fine. Take your time."

I just smile at her, a smile secretly filled with hope and sorrow and eagerness and anguish. I didn't know one could fit so many emotions in one facial expression. *Be Zen, Zoya, be Zen.* You can tell them all once we reach the resort.

Peehu links her arm through mine a bit tighter, as if to never let go, and I feel a pang of shame at my reticence.

We shade our eyes (even with sunglasses on) and walk toward the taxi stand, with Aisha, Kamya, and a surly Tanya behind us. We stuff ourselves into a prepaid taxi; Peehu turns her attention to the sleepy driver in front of her. "Taj Alibaug, please."

The old driver stretches and yawns, his vinegar breath filling the taxi. He pretends not to notice five noisy passengers in his cab and tries to close his eyes again.

"Excuse me!" Peehu taps him hard on his sweaty shoulder. "TAJ ALIBAUG. Please!"

"Arre, ho baba." He says in Marathi. "Have some patience, you kids. I just woke up from my afternoon nap." He touches the silver cross around his neck in prayer and starts the ignition.

"So, where are you going on your honeymoon? Are you really going to Iceland?" Kamya asks, followed by Aisha's "Are your tickets booked yet?" Aisha, although still a bit subdued, is happier than I've seen her in the last few weeks. Only Tanya sulks, not asking me any questions and sitting silently ahead in the passenger seat of the taxi. Well, obviously, she's not going to talk about my honeymoon, considering she hasn't snagged a fiancé to show off at what she thinks will be my wedding day.

"Only three weeks left for your wedding. Are you excited?" Kamya asks as we exit the ferry terminal, and assuming that I am, she turns her head away to gaze at the gleaming sea outside with a contented smile on her face. Peehu arches her perfectly curved eyebrow to give me a knowing look.

The bile rises up, up my throat. I need a beer. Desperately.

CHAPTER TWENTY

"Welcome to Taj Alibaug, Ma'am. Are you here for the Contemporary and Postmodernist Art Retreat?" The young sari-clad receptionist glances at us with her impressively made-up eyes.

"No, we aren't," Kamya says, her hands on the reception desk.

"Oh, I'm sorry." The receptionist is a bit flustered but recovers herself almost immediately. "I see that you're booked into a beach-facing, nonsmoking villa for two nights with a private pool."

Art retreat? How interesting. I strain my neck behind Kamya to read the multicolored pamphlet on the reception desk with information about the retreat.

". . . maybe there's still time to live my life."

On an impulse, I whip out my phone from my purse, snap a picture of the pamphlet and send it to Sheila Bua with a text:

You said you wanted to live your life.

"One moment, let me just check your other amenities," the receptionist says, and disappears behind her computer. Everything is curved arches and wood lattice here, like a boho-chic wannabe-Goan resort.

"We are a bit crowded at the moment, Ma'am, because of this art thing, but no worries." She's back, talking and typing furiously on her desk computer at the same time. "We're offering complimentary beers to all our weekend guests." She gestures to a liveried bellboy behind us, who directs us to a side table by a pillar in the lobby, on which sits a big red cooler crammed with small bottles of Kingfisher beer floating in a pool of what was formerly ice. Peehu and Aisha, who were loitering around the quaint foyer, rush up to the table and grab a bottle each, as do Tanya and I. All of us except Kamya, who is still at the reception desk, congregate near the beer cooler like a flock around their leader.

My phone bings and I force my heart to settle. I can't have a heart attack expecting Arnav's text every time my phone comes to life. It's Sheila Bua anyway.

Sheila Bua: Are you at the Taj Alibaug? I didn't know you were at that resort.

Me: You should be here too, at this art retreat.

Sheila Bua: :-):-);-);-)

Two smiles and two winks? Why winks? Is she going to come here? No, she would've said something, for sure. Then again, why am I analyzing emoticons from my contextless auntie? Just shows you how stressed I am.

Tanya takes a swig of her free beer and leans against the column. She stares at the receptionist's enormous chest in a mixture of awe and envy and whispers in the general direction of Peehu and me. "So tacky, no?"

"She looks okay to me," I say.

"Oh please. What do *you* know about makeup? Look at her base foundation! *Two* shades lighter than her skin, like someone just slapped rice paper on her face." Tanya almost spits in disgust and pulls on her black choker as if she were suffocating. "Why wear two layers of foundation—and that *powder*—in this dull light? And don't even get me started on that repellent pink lipstick!"

Yeah, right, Goth calling the kettle black. But Goth is also right—what would I know about makeup, having used one compact powder, one eyeliner, and three shades of brown-cherry lipstick in my entire adult life?

"Here are your keys, Ma'am." The receptionist hands the key cards to Kamya. All of us follow the bellboy pushing our luggage.

"Did you know that she poses for nude paintings?" Peehu gestures behind her as we glide through the slick hotel passage

"What?" I spit into my beer. "Who? The woman at the front desk? How did you know that?"

"I overheard a hotel staff member by the door at check-in. She's posing for one in twenty minutes after her shift ends. Part of the art retreat, apparently."

Oh my . . . Is this why Sheila Bua sent me those winks? Naked paintings? She only did a couple of those, way back in the day. Please tell me she hasn't started painting naked people again.

do support her art, but wow, talk about blowing up life. Part of me can't help but be impressed. If she's here. But I have no desire to *see* one being painted live.

Tanya's phone bings in that special sing-song text. She glances at the phone and her lips tighten into an ugly black line.

A waiter passes by with a tray of appetizers, saffron-marinated fish chunks on little toothpicks. "Would you like some, Ma'am?" He stops deferentially near Tanya. "It's complimentary. The chef is trying out a new recipe."

Tanya looks up from her phone and points to me. "Give it to her. She's never full." And walks off ahead.

I would love to poke her eye with that toothpick.

Peehu sings in Disney mode. "*Let it go, let it go.* Chill, Zee. She's just jealous that you're getting married."

I have a flashback of the designer M-sized blouse Lalit gifted me a month ago. He even texted a picture of it first to "inspire" me (as if to say, *Are you there yet? Are you a size M yet?*). And I still don't fit into those clothes, even with the weight I've lost. Every time I open my closet, I'm reminded that I'm not thin enough, and not good enough till I fit into them, to gain some worth in Lalit's eyes. *In my own eyes.* So I keep my cupboard closed unless it's an underwear emergency; my regular clothes are lumped on a chair near my bed, much to Mum's dismay. I'd rather face her ire than tell her that I feel worthless when I open the closet; it would utterly destroy her heart, and then she'd fry me some paneer for dinner, which, though yum, would help nothing.

And you, Zoya—an overweight, dark girl—are you even allowed to dump a model-dater? Can a charity case reject the charity?

Brownies. I need brownies.

"I know. You need my brownies." Peehu reads my mind. "Remember, the ring is on your finger, not hers!"

"Brownies please!"

"Yes, okay, okay!" She rummages through her large rucksack, which carries every kind of crap that mankind doesn't need: a Ziploc filled with plastic knives, a four-year-old pack of chips, a truckload of African beads, sachets of Chinese hot sauce; everything except brownies. "Shit. I might've left the dabba near the beer cooler. Let me go back and—"

"You know what? It's okay, I'll get them." Or so I tell her. I need to not be around thin people right now. Or any kind of humans. I need to be away from Tanya and Lalit and his bloody molding and my whole screwy world. I need the one thing Alibaug does best. I need the beach.

I wave to Kamya and Aisha, who wave back before continuing on to our villa. I cut across the lattice screens, past the amoeba-shaped pool with the cabanas and laughing children, past the dark grassy woods filled with casuarina oaks, past the streaks of sunlight hinting at the shimmering open sea beyond. I could've taken a shorter way, cutting across the private villas on the other side of the trees, but somehow, walking past the tall, slender barks lined up close like a bamboo garden stretching into the sky gives me a sense of peace; a sense of being shielded that I have not known in months.

Ah, and then the dazzling water and the soft brown sand. The Arabian Sea is calm, a mix of turquoise and gray, at peace with itself under the evening sky. No diesel fumes or sweaty bodies or honks; just sand, seaweed, and salty air. Even the tourists are far away, out on the circular Kolaba Fort, and from my position on the almost empty beach, they look like dark little fruit pips in the evening sun. The breeze is mellow and warm; nothing can shatter this quiet peace.

But then, bing!

A text. From Arnav.

After only seventeen days, six hours, and seventeen minutes.

Earth to Zoya.

Zoya under the earth should be more like it. Fifty feet under so no one can find her. I slide the phone in a side pocket of my yellow skirt. What would be the point of texting back?

Waves swirl around my ankles, just missing the hem of my skirt, and the sand is lush and wet beneath my bare feet. The pink-orange sky is so tranquil that I don't even flinch when he falls into step beside me. Not the one who hides behind the mobile either, but the real one, flesh and blood right next to me on this beach.

"Earth to Zoya."

I don't answer. What would I say, anyway? No, go back into my phone? Or yes, please, could you whisper in my ear again so I feel like molten chocolate? Or that I'm a fugitive on the run from the mess I've made of my life?

Arnav walks with me, step in step in a comfortable silence, his backpack slung on one shoulder. Did he not check into his room yet? The beach curves around us in a soft concave arch and the walls of Kolaba Fort darken as the remains of the afternoon fade completely into evening. I steal a glance at him. He hasn't changed out of his uniform of formal shirt and khakis, only the black loafers are missing. In bare feet and unruly curls, he looks wild, untamed. And how can I look away from his warm, sparkling eyes?

He swishes the water with his feet like a little boy, light-stepped without a care.

He looks so free.

The weight of my world, my *deeds*, comes crashing back. My face crumbles into jagged sobs.

"Hey, hey, hey," he whispers in his deep, quiet voice as we stop walking. He turns and puts his arms around me. This is my undoing.

"I quit," I sniffle, looking up at him with a red nose and redder eyes.

He blows a little whistle, more breath than sound. "Ah! Of all the things that ran through my mind in the last two seconds *that* was the last one I would've picked." His thumb caresses a tiny sliver of my arm and my entire world has shrunk to that touch.

"Is . . . The Fiancé . . . Lalit making you quit?" he asks, a hard edge to his voice.

The pink evening fades instantly into a purple twilight; the world is quiet for a moment, as if it waits with him for an answer.

"No. I quit because I am going to New York."

It's the first time I've said it out loud. He is the first person I've said it to. My chest is light, as if a twenty-pound dumbbell has weighed on me for days and, finally, it just fell off. I look up at him.

"Going to New York with Lalit?" he asks, the steel in his voice reminiscent of Arnav-the-Office-Dragon. Can he please stop talking about Lalit? "Before you decide, I need to say something. Please, just hear me out—"

"No." I cut him off. "Not with Lalit. I'm not marrying him. I . . . won't. I got that job. At B&O. In New York. And I'm taking it. I'm calling off the wedding to live in New York. I don't want this wedding. I want a different life." I articulate each word. "And Lalit doesn't know it yet. No one does. Well, except you. Now."

"You got the job?!" He stops, a grin on his face, which instantly freezes as another thought grows on him. "You're . . . not marrying . . ." He says each word as if solidifying them in his mind before they disappear like the wisps of smoke that words are. Before he can help it, before he can stop himself, an even wider, more wondrous grin spreads across his face. "So, you're free."

Oh my. The mad thuds in my heart.

"What I wanted to say was: Hello from your secret admirer." He reaches into his backpack and produces a bunch of yellow daisies like a magician, and the world comes to a standstill.

It was him.

An explosion of an earthquake jolts my heart.

The flowers, the food. *It was him.*

"Of all the things that ran through my mind right now, *that* was the last one I would've picked," I say, unable to stop the smile that's made its way onto my face, into my life; a blast of plus-sized pleasure flashing from head to toe.

How daft was I to not see the signs? But then again, when you are supposed to be someone else all your life, taller or thinner or nicer or prettier, how do you believe it when someone likes you for yourself? I don't know whether to laugh or cry, so I do a bit of both.

Tiny lights appear as if by magic over the dark sea; little fishing boats making their way home.

"But why didn't you tell me?"

"Because we were starting to become friends and I didn't want to screw that up. I also want to admit that I used to keep your stash of Kit Kats stocked."

"That was you? I stupidly assumed HR was replenishing them after every client project, as an incentive."

He laughs, amused at my ideas. "Nope. And the plastic daisy that sits on your desk? All me. I was racking my head to figure out how to ask you out, if that's even 'allowed,' but then your engagement came out of nowhere. I didn't know what else to do, so I began sending you these gifts, the food, the books, in the hope that maybe . . . but then I started losing faith ever since we stopped texting. But Chotu told me that I was the most colossal fool if I didn't at least tell you, so I checked your calendar—Chotu found out that you were at this resort. I raced to Alibaug on the ferry before you, just to tell you, to ask . . ." He stops abruptly, and takes a breath to steady himself. "Since you just quit—which means I'm not your boss anymore—care for a coffee sometime? With a Kit Kat? Or a biryani?"

Every part of me reaches out for that shot of pleasure. I didn't know I could feel like this, like a giant ball of pure white light in my chest.

But the ball of light flickers, and my body tenses. I want to reach for this, but not at the cost of what I really want. Joy and confusion collide with each other inside my head.

"Maybe. Maybe in New York someday?" I wait, looking up at him, watching his eyes, hoping.

Sometimes life doesn't give you a second chance.

Sheila Bua's shaken voice, her worn-down acceptance letter and stark medical paper are lodged inside my mind. I can't lose sight of what I want—what I *need* to do. Not now. Even . . . now.

Will he wait for me if I choose a dream instead of him?

After a pause, "Why not?" He grins. "I might have some business there. Or relatives, whom I suddenly have an urge to visit."

Every part of my body unwinds into softness. My head feels lighter than it has in months, and I want to zip around the beach, flying, with stardust on my wings.

It is enough. Enough for now.

He pulls me close, his warm touch gentle on my arm. His face is inches from mine, dangerously, deliciously close. "Happy birthday." The deep voice surrounds my ear, a microclimate of man air. We are rooted ankle-deep in supple sand and warm water as a husk of breeze swirls around us.

Our hands are entwined. His mouth, his warm peppermint and coffee mouth, skims my lips and my skin explodes into life; a live, breathless, trembling being.

Here. Now.

Skin to skin, heart to heart. His heart beating through his soft shirt, racing like mine.

The purple twilight paints the earth into an aching midnight blue; the sky, the water, the sand.

"Zoya? What the . . . ?" Peehu's squeak shatters the moment. We jump apart. His hands, thick and warm, a man's hands, brush my fingers to prolong our touch.

Soon, I promise myself silently. Not before I tell Lalit. Or my family. Or the in-laws.

If I make it to New York in one piece. And by the look on Peehu's shocked face behind Arnav at the edge of the grassy forest, that does not seem likely.

Arnav retreats, ever so slowly, his shirt blowing in the breeze. Back, back, back he steps, his gaze never faltering from my face; and then he winks, and I can never be the same again. A fleeting wink and the smallest of smiles and he's gone in a flash around the tall casuarina trees, and beyond the private villas. But the smile, the wink, find a permanent place inside my heart.

"What on earth was that?" Peehu's kohl-rimmed eyes bulge out of her skull in shock.

"I don't know." I'm still in that moment of ago.

"Umm, Zee?" Peehu stumbles in the sand as she runs up to me. "What's . . . going on here?" She looks a whole lot of stunned and a wee bit jealous at the same time. Definitely no more pictures of Arnav for her now. "You do remember that you're getting married in three weeks?"

"I remember," I say and start walking away, bumbling in the sand, in the direction of the green lawn beyond the casuarina trees. I want to extend that moment, that memory of the kiss, the wink, and not spoil it by another's presence, even if that person is my closest friend. She catches up to me and we reach the green lawns of the beach-facing private villas faster than I realize, their antique porch lamps twinkling under the dark evening sky.

"Is this what you didn't want to tell me earlier? What's going on, Zee? Talk to me." The toads and crickets answer instead with their trills and croaks in the tranquil air. She stops to face me at the entrance to our lit verandah, her hands on my arms, as if to shield me from disaster. That's what we've been doing all our lives, saving the other from making disastrous choices. *Supposedly* disastrous choices. I always knew Paris was right for her. Hopefully she'll understand why I need to go now too.

"No. This is not what I was talking about. This just happened, but it has no bearing on my decision." We face each other for a few seconds, she confused, and I almost defiant. We aren't shouting, but Kamya and Tanya trickle out of the living room to the porch upon hearing our voices, cocktails in their hands. (I hope they ordered one for me and Peehu.) Aisha rocks gently on a brown hammock, her cocktail glass on the red tiled floor next to her.

"What decision?" Peehu is surrounded by the other girls now. Aisha glances at us from the hammock, Kamya emerges bewildered from her tequila haze, and Tanya's sour breath wafts a mile over the salty sea breeze and pungent booze. All of them look equally confused. The palm trees and bushes sway gently in the breeze around us.

"I'm not doing it, Pee."

"Wait a minute. What exactly are you not doing? Cheating or marrying?"

"Cheating? Who the hell is cheating?" Aisha gasps from the hammock. Oops. We shouldn't have used that word; Aisha's wounds are too raw.

"Marrying. I'm not marrying Lalit."

"Wait, was your wedding canceled?" Kamya asks, looking more confused by the second.

A strange buzz rings in my ears. "No. The wedding is not canceled. But it will be. I'm not marrying Lalit. I'm going to

New York. To work. In three weeks. For three years, maybe longer," I say, guilty and giddy all at once.

Peehu opens her mouth to say something but cannot manage any sound. Kamya spits into her drink, coughing violently. Aisha tumbles off her hammock with a gasp and lands on the ground with a thud. Tanya stares at me in abject horror.

"It's okay, it's okay." Obviously it's not okay since I'm supposed to be getting married soon, but I try to pacify them anyway. They may be my friends, but our society is what it is: they're freaking out on my behalf. "This is what I've wanted for a long time. I just didn't see it until Sheila Bua showed it to me."

"Sheila Bua?" Aisha hoists herself up from the red-tiled floor of the porch. "You mean Sheila Bua told you to go to New York? You can't be serious."

"No. Not in actual words." I tell them, then. It comes out, all of it, a teetering stack of rocks crashing to the floor: Oxford, Lalit's molding, New York jobs, the gym, the red bruised painting, Uncle Balli's divorce threat, her failed rebellion, the necklace. The little flying bird she bought all on her own. Nothing flashy—no diamonds—but it's the most prized thing she has.

I don't tell them about the biggest rock of all, the one that crashed the entire stack: the white medical report folded tightly in the torn parchment. Because I promised her I wouldn't. It was her secret to tell when she wanted, and I'd rather starve than break that promise. But I know the dream that still lives inside her, as regret. She didn't tell me to go, but then again, she didn't need to.

A bird in flight.

The pain is physical, as if a steel rope clamps tighter and tighter around my chest.

How can I tell them what it all really means? A lost dream, a lost love, a lost self. We are silent, all of us, as if the air deflates from around us in a poof. The beach, the bushes, the palm trees, are all silent, too. For us, you see, the world has spun on its head and it's like nothing we've ever seen.

What would Sheila Bua have been like, in a parallel universe, had she not given up what she loved? Would she have been a wise, bohemian auntie, the outcast in the family? Or one who was barely tolerated, simply for appearances' sake? One who wore heaps of bracelets and long flowing kaftans and antique necklaces, the one all us cousins rushed to with our young troubles? Or would she still have been the quintessential Punjabi auntie with her colorful clothes and random funny phrases, but with her liberal and traditional sides coexisting, but sadly, in secret? Can one be traditional and an artist at the same time? Or would she have been a famous, sought-after painter, with all her naysayers desperate to be in her social sphere? My heart is heavy at what could have been and all that is lost.

"I can't do it, not now. Not after I learned . . . all that. I cannot marry Lalit. Don't worry, his heart won't break." I sound callous, but was his heart ever invested in us? *Was mine?* I laugh, a humorless blip of sound.

Kamya takes it all in, hushed, motionless. "I didn't know Uncle Balli threatened to divorce her and that's why she had to abandon her art." She's stumped, like at the end of a movie when the villain is the good guy and now you have to mentally rearrange all the facts and plot and people in order to figure out the plot twist.

"How harsh of him," Aisha says, her bitter scorn evident on her face. "Husbands are cruel." She hesitates, as if making a decision, and says, "I'm with you Zoya. You don't need a husband to lead your life."

"Have you told Lalit? Or your parents?" Kamya, asks, her usual common sense and logic rising to the fore.

"No. I was going to do that when I got home."

Peehu sinks on a white lounge chair by the pool in a resigned sigh. "So. What do we do now? Haven't the wedding invites been sent already?" She takes off her pink beaded bracelet and absently counts each glob between two fingers, as if they were prayer beads. Peehu with her conservative Gujarati upbringing knows exactly the kind of scandal that will erupt (I guess all of us do) if I cancel my wedding so close to the date, for no acceptable reason. Love (*don't worry, there's enough love after marriage*), minimal compatibility (*once you have kids you will be automatically compatible*), the fiancé molding you (*that's what future husbands do, silly girl!*), and that you want a different life (*you watch too many American shows*) don't count as real reasons. Not many girls can live this down. Nor can their families.

"Goodness. I had quite forgotten about the invites. And the rest of the family." Aisha pours two shots of tequila into a double shot glass, gulps it all, lets out a burp with her palm on her chest, and muses ironically, "This should be fun."

"It's a good thing you Punjabis are a bit more liberal than my Gujju community. Now each time I visit home, I'll be taunted as *that* girl whose *friend's* marriage was broken." Peehu shakes her head, laughing a little to herself as she takes the tequila bottle from Aisha and gulps straight from it. How much booze did they order? I thought it was just cocktails, but now I can see several shot glasses, a humongous bottle of Grey Goose vodka, and multiple bottles of beer on a small patio table near the porch door. Plus the tequila they're all gulping by the gallon. What, are we supposed to bathe in alcohol?

Tanya is still rooted to her spot in silence between the hammock and the lounge chair. Is the look on her face still abject horror? Or is that hope in her eyes? Maybe she wants to ensnare Lalit. Her phone sing-songs in a text, and she stares at it, and then me, then back at the phone again. Her black clothes, black nail paint . . . wait—

The shriek of our suite doorbell is almost cruel in its shrillness. The soft silence had seeped into our bones and we jump, collectively. An impeccably dressed bellboy delivers two plates of steaming prawn balchao dry. Thank goodness there's food. I thought these girls only ordered alcohol. Tanya sniffs the spiced air, emerging from her coma.

"You." She glowers at me. The poor bellboy staggers out without another look back, stuffing Peehu's hundred-rupee tip in his pocket.

"*You!*" She paces the room, forlorn, baffled as if I spoke in another language all this time, and how was she supposed to understand? Yes, I know I'm doing a horrible thing by calling my wedding off and breaking people's hearts, but *she* is not included in *people* and I'll eat bloody kale for the rest of my life before I apologize to her. Something, an idea, a truth, tries to claw out of my messed-up head, to land in front of me, but—

"You're dumping a man like *him*? Who the hell do you think you are?" Tanya is apoplectic in disbelief, like discovering that lettuce is fattening after all, and savagely pushes me in a mad dash toward the prawns.

"Shit!" Peehu cries, as Tanya advances on us with her hands outstretched and we jump out of the way just in time. The prawns are oblivious to the chaos, calmly stewing in a fiery pickle. They would be. They're dead, the lucky bastards.

Tanya throws herself on the large rectangular plate before any of us can reach it. She grabs a fistful of peppery prawns and shoves the whole lot into her mouth like a raving lunatic.

I freeze, as do Peehu, Aisha, and Kamya. Aisha giggles nervously at me sideways, her eyes humongous in her petite face.

Tanya looks at our dumbstruck faces. "What are you little shits staring at? What use is living like this, tell me?" Her voice is a mixture of muffled yelps and rapid chomps. Red prawn juice dribbles out of her mouth and trickles down her chin. "What use is eating quinoa when you really crave a bowl of hot rice and daal with ghee?" she cries and eats in equal measure. "What use is hiding your black lipstick in the back of your closet? What use is wearing push-up bras that suffocate the breath out of you trying to create boobs out of nothing? What use is doing all of that and *still* losing to your fat cousin?"

"Be who you *are*, no matter what your mother or boyfriend or the world tells you. And for God's sake, let's *live*!" Tanya gulps an entire pint of beer in one shot, belches louder than a donkey's bray and wipes her masala-laden fingers on her black jacket.

Who *is* this woman?

A revelation explodes inside my brain in fluorescent neon: Being Thin Is No Guarantee of Happiness.

Which is so profound it's like being Enlightened. Or Awakened. Or maybe just aware, for the first time, of the most obvious thing right in front of you: plain common sense.

"Oh boy. I need to process all this info with brownies," Peehu says. "Where the hell *are* those pot brownies?"

"I have absolutely no idea. Didn't find them," I say. I found Arnav instead, which I don't say.

Aisha jumps up, dusting imaginary cobwebs off her skirt. "Since Peehu has lost her brownies, I'll be divorced, and Zoya will soon be a pariah, and Tanya . . . well, eats . . . ladies, in celebration of our collective ruin, I suggest we have another drink? And some music? Because it's still Zee's birthday!" Ah, yes. I'd forgotten that tiny detail.

We pile inside the living room, and Peehu, who never has much patience, looks pointedly at me. "Yes, now that I've wasted all those euros for nothing—eighty-four rupees to a bloody euro by the way—we'd better have something to show for it, right? MUSIC!" Peehu thwacks her phone to put it on speaker mode.

Munni badnaam hui —

Now *this* is a bachelorette song—Bollywood, totally trashy and so good, the rubbing posterior and all. Yes, things are still a mess, but I will sort them the first thing on reaching home, but for now, it's friends and booze and music, and everything and everyone can wait.

My phone, abandoned on one of the patio chairs, bings and rings like a furious, malfunctioning kiddie toy. Who wants to talk to me *this bad*? Don't care. Whoever it is can wait.

Zandu balm hui, darrrrling tere liye —

Three voices rise in unison from the grassy open area outside our villa, followed by a hurried patter of feet, as if people were going round the cottage to the front door. "Here! Sheila didi *must* be here!"

THUD!

The heavy double doors of the villa open with a thunderous crash, slamming against the white walls. Our hands stop in mid-rub on our rears, aghast.

No. No. NOOOO!

The end of my life is upon me, sooner than planned.

There they are. Everyone.

CHAPTER TWENTY-ONE

Do you remember those horrid nightmares in which you are completely naked for all the world to see? And then you wake up with a profound sense of relief that none of it was real? This is just like that, except it *is* real. Not the naked part, but the rest of it.

In this waking nightmare, double doors open with a grandiose swish and somehow, due to your past sins, bad karma, or an excess intake of carbs in this lifetime, bits of your family—Mum, Uncle Balli, and Pa—pour into the villa one by one. And behind them all is your cousin's-potential-fiancée-and-your-more-than-potential-maybe-one-day-boyfriend, Arnav, frantically pointing to his phone and you at the same time.

And there you are. Smack in the middle of it all, one of your hands rubbing your butt suggestively. The other holds a shot glass filled with whiskey.

Oh God. Cheap dancing and whiskey. In front of family elders. The strains of "Munni badnaam" suddenly vanish in mid-chorus. Bless Peehu, who's turned it off. My body doesn't seem to understand the concept of motion. Uncle Balli takes a deep drag of his cigar, his ratty cough booms in the deathly quiet.

Why the hell are they here? I mean, okay, it is Alibaug—Bombay's backyard haven—so why wouldn't they? But why the fuck, why right now, *why*? Can't I have just one moment of space?

Mum finds her voice. "Ah yes, hello Zoya beta. Sorry to burst in on you like this." She looks at Uncle Balli and says to him, "Let's rest here for a bit and then keep looking for Sheila didi."

Looking for Sheila Bua? The girls and I exchange flummoxed glances.

"Umm, sorry, what is going on?"

Pa steps out from behind Mum and Uncle Balli and clears his throat. "Well, the thing is: Sheila didi has disappeared."

"Disappeared?" The dancing fun of a moment ago turns into a giant ball of fear. And something else. Hope, I think.

"She left home last evening and hasn't been seen since," Pa says, suddenly looking tired.

"Was she in an accident? Is she alright?"

Wait. Weren't the winks sent this afternoon? My arms relax in instant relief. She's alive, thank God.

But did she disappear because of the gym conversation? Or the cancer diagnosis? Or the smileys and winks? Please tell me I had nothing to do with it.

Pa holds up a hand as if to calm me down. "We thought about that naturally, but Yuvi found a pamphlet about some art retreat under the mattress in her bedroom. Pretty sure she's here. We called the resort and they couldn't give out private information about their guests, so we came here."

She's here. Yup. My text; my fault.

Or is it? If she left home last night, she'd have known about the retreat before my text.

Pa settles Uncle Balli in an armchair right next to the mini bar, and Mum walks up to me to whisper. "I'm so sorry, beta, we crashed your party. But you see, Uncle Balli was creating such a big ruckus outside, in the lobby—you know how he is . . ." Her face is a mixture of distaste and forced acceptance. ". . . so we thought it was best if we sorted this issue in private, in your room. You don't mind, do you?" She is so distracted and worried that I don't have the heart to say that yes, I do mind this domestic invasion.

Peehu and Kamya, who are convinced that our trip is truly over, walk out to the patio, Arnav with them. They plonk themselves on the lounge chairs and scroll through their phones, listless, while Arnav keeps me in sight from his vantage point, standing on the porch, as near the door as he can manage without intruding. Aisha, Tanya, and I are right in the living room, just existing awkwardly, as if *we* crashed the family's party. Pa starts to make calls and Uncle Balli vegetates on the chair, smoking like a mafia don.

As I take in the debris of our spa weekend, the main double door, which had shut itself on impact when my family had barged in ten minutes ago, swings open—again—and in walks my Diamond Boy fiancé, utterly agitated.

What the actual fuck?

He yells at the threshold, "Tee! I know you're in here!" and promptly freezes on seeing the family.

Tanya gasps.

In an instant of utmost clarity, I know the Tee that he speaks of is Tanya. My cousin. His ex-girlfriend. That's why he's here, and that's why he was startled when I mentioned my girls trip to this resort at the family dinner.

"Tee!" Lalit finds his voice, but it's nothing like the obnoxious one he used with me. It's something I haven't been privy to, soft and acquiescing.

"Why . . . you here . . . what . . . how?" Tanya babbles.

Her outrage, her mean texts were not because she was jealous that I got engaged first. They were because I took her place in his life. She's the one he hasn't gotten over. She's the one he keeps texting. And Tanya's sing-songy text alert? Pretty sure that special person is Lalit.

He rushes up to her. "Why the fuck haven't you answered my calls and texts?" I knew it! That is why he's been guarding his phone like a vault.

The hope in Tanya's eyes wasn't because she wanted to ensnare Lalit. The hope in her eyes was because Lalit was now free. I guess she won after all.

"You jerk! You should've thought of that before you got engaged to my cousin." She cries, the kohl in her eyes draining like black tears.

Aisha, Peehu, and Kamya, have the exact same expressions, their mouths open in an outraged O.

"I didn't know, I swear!" he gurgles desperately. "I didn't know she was your cousin till it was too late!"

"Please! That's just an excuse! You did it to spite me!"

"No, please, I swear on you, I had no idea . . ."

"I can't be with someone like my mother!" Tanya screeches. "Don't wear this, don't eat that! I just can't!" she cries, a wretched look on her face.

Lalit looks at me in desperation, as if expecting me to reason with her. But the strangest thing happens. I feel a funny sort of affection for Tanya. I have no urge to throw things at her or poke her eyes out with toothpicks. A deep relief washes through me. Which lightens my body, like I'm gliding through the air. All my doubts about calling off my wedding, about going to New York, vanish for good, and a peace replaces all the stress. What use is it, trying to create a marriage, a foundation of a relationship, on the embers of a previous one, just to please your parents or for the approval of a faceless society? And on embers that, clearly, are still aflame.

I should be worried, or at least feel guilty, facing my family and fiancé. But a deathly calm overtakes my body, like the effect of a fast-acting painkiller—agony one moment, nothing the next—a little blip of time before the body begins to feel.

I could just step back and wait for Lalit and Tanya to take the blame for calling the wedding off. But I won't. Because this is not who I am. I've had enough of the lies and deceit, especially with Mum and Pa. I want them to know what I want, and I don't want to taint my journey with more deception.

Do it, Zoya, do it now.

As if the other girls can hear my silent voice, they rise up in a collective motion, from the living room and patio, to come together behind me, like pieces of a protective wall. Peehu starts counting the beads on her bracelet again.

"Lalit, I need to say something—" I block his agitated vision so he's forced to look at me for the first time. "Look at me. I have something to say to you."

They've all stopped looking for the people they came to find and turn their gazes toward me.

"I'm sorry, Lalit, but I cannot marry you." It's amazing how Zen my voice sounds after my babbles, mere minutes ago. But, alas, ironically, I'm the only one who's calm after this. The rest of the room erupts in a fallout of complete bedlam.

"WHAT? Zoya!" Mum, Pa, and even Uncle Balli shriek together in shock.

"There is no need to talk like this, Zoya beta—"

"Girls are just like boys these days—"

"Don't drink whiskey—"

I take a painful, brave breath. "Lalit." I look him straight in the eyes, my legs steady on my feet. "I can't marry you because I am going to New York. To work. To *live*."

A ghastly silence descends in the cozily lit living room. No one in the family dares to look at another human.

I turn to Mum and Pa in a voice racked with guilt. "I'm so, so sorry. We are just not suited to each other." They look completely flabbergasted, at New York, at the Lalit–Tanya liaison, like they've landed on another planet and everyone speaks in gibberish. They deserve better than this humiliation. They deserve a better daughter.

Diamond Daughter. How quickly that went down the drain.

"I want to leave because I want a different life." Had I said this out loud even a month ago, my voice would've been shaken apart. But not now. It is steady and calm. How do I explain? To him? To them? What words do I use to shine a light and dispel this fog of tradition? A life not better or worse, but just different? A life that is mine, that is ours, to live, and not others' to steer?

I look at their confused, angry faces, detached, as an entity outside of myself. The only person who would understand is nowhere in sight.

Where is Sheila Bua?

"But Zoya, *New York*?!" Mum finally finds her voice. "What is this new drama? You're throwing away your marriage for what?"

"I am not married."

"You were as good as! With only three weeks left? Relatives are responding to the wedding invites already!"

"To hell with the relatives." I turn to Lalit and Tanya. "Look at you fools. Still bickering when you're clearly not over each other. What the hell are you waiting for—"

A commotion gathers near the door, loud and boisterous.

Munni badnaam hui, darling tere liye —

Music explodes from the Bluetooth speakers, flooding the room with the horny voice of the Bollywood singer. Uncle Balli, sitting next to the speakers, starts in fright.

Who the hell started that song again?

A sumptuous blue sways into the door. Not just blue but pink and orange with greenish-yellow streaks running through it. The psychedelic tent turns ominously in my direction, smothering everything and everyone else in sight.

Sheila Bua!

Uncle Balli jumps from the armchair and cries victoriously to no one in particular. "I was right—she *is* here!"

"Zoyaaaaaa! My darrrling child!" Sheila Bua squeals with delight, ignoring everyone else. Her hands are outstretched, but she stops midway, confused at the sight of the family members.

"Helloooo, Lalit beta," she greets Lalit but saunters right past him to reach for me in a large bear hug. It's like the cool shade of large tree in merciless heat.

But what's that *smell*? And those brown crumbs on her face?

Uh oh.

CHAPTER TWENTY-TWO

It dawns on Peehu the same time as me. "My brownies!"

And whiskey.

My Sheila Bua, who never drinks publicly if she can help it, is completely sloshed. And stoned. With our pot brownies.

"What wonderful brownies!" Sheila Bua grabs one out of a dabba and eats the entire thing in one bite. "I haven't had you-know-what like this since I was twenty!"

Alcohol plus weed plus cancer.

This is not just going downhill but underground at the speed of a bullet train.

A vague sense of unease slithers up my skull. Is there anything else left to be uneasy about? Sheila Bua gestures to a steward outside to bring in the harbinger of that unease. "Careful. It still needs to dry."

She stares defiantly at Uncle Balli as the middle-aged waiter drags an entire A-shaped easel covered with a dark blue cloth, deposits it in the middle of the room, and leaves.

But who did she paint in Alibaug—

"What do you think, Zoya?" She deposits the now-empty dabba of brownies on a side table, and rips the blue sheet off the painting. A real person instantly comes into being.

The winks in her text, oh yes, I get it now. A panicky little giggle slips out of my mouth, but no one pays the slightest attention to me. It's the receptionist, a light muslin cloth covering her naked body, showing everything but not showing anything. Is this what "Postmodernist" means? Naked paintings? And the family, holy shit. Because going by the apoplexy on the other faces, the mental ward at Nanavati Hospital will be chock full with them tomorrow morning.

Pot-smoker, nude-painter Sheila Bua.

But the painting, oh, the painting. The cloth, the colors, the woman, all look like they've jumped out of the canvas and landed right in the middle of the room. Like a Raja Ravi Verma canvas, of clothed women looking utterly sensuous; this is the exact opposite. A naked woman covered with a milky sheer cloth, who looks like the epitome of nobility and honor. *How did Sheila Bua manage that effect?* I feel as if I'm at the very edge of a cliff, staring at a breathtaking view that fills my soul, yet acutely aware of the dangerous ledge.

"God damn it! I told you all we would be too late to prevent this . . . this . . . *rubbish* starting all over again!" Uncle Balli looks like he's swallowed a toad. "Sheila!" He booms like a cannon.

"Stop this at once!" He grabs her arm to pull her away, to no success.

"Stop what? Stop pretending to be who you want, or stop being who I am?"

Yikes.

"I don't care for your 'who I am' nonsense. You will *not* paint anymore. I won't allow it." He says "paint" as if swallowing vomit. "That's it, I've decided."

He races to the painting in three short strides with an ugly sneer on his face. He seizes the painting with his bony fingers, shakes it savagely, trying to yank it off the easel. But a hand stops him in his antics, a thumb making red welts on Uncle Balli's thin, hairy forearm.

Sheila Bua.

She wrenches Uncle Balli's hand off the canvas, finger by finger, and hurls it away from the painting. His hand swings back and forth for two seconds before coming to a shocked standstill by his side.

Sheila Bua sets the crooked canvas right, picks up the blue sheet cover off the floor, and flings it into some far corner of the room. "*You've* decided, have you?" She turns to him, slowly, as if making sure every part of her body faces her husband. "What will you do, *burn* my paintings again?" She spits fire from her mouth and daggers from her eyes. Her blazing eyes are frozen on Uncle Balli, as if daring him to move, to breathe. He does neither, his small eyes widen, his lips shut tight. She says through a jaw wound tight with years of silent regrets, "Balli Arora, go the *fuck* to hell."

The beach, the room, the people, the night, everything is still in a moment of distended silence. Holy mother of all religions. This evening will end in someone's death. Or divorce. For sure.

"Sheila didi, please listen." Mum tries to shake her out of this mania by the one thing that might bring her back from wherever she is right now, besides painting: matchmaking. "Zoya doesn't want to marry! Save us from this disaster!"

"Save you?" Sheila Bua mumbles. "How can I save anyone? I couldn't even save myself . . ."

"Zoya is going to New York! *New York!*" Mum wails. "How on earth can we face anyone if her wedding is called off now?" Mum finally explodes into tears.

Sheila Bua swivels toward me and I nod, just the barest of nods, and her face lights up in a surge of joy. "You are really doing it. You're taking the job in New York," she whispers to herself in hushed awe, and my heart shatters into pieces for my Magic Bua, for the wide-eyed twenty-year-old Shining Girl in that photo. "What a giant, wonderful screw-up!" she cackles in hysteric mirth and claps her hand in unrestrained glee. I will remember her face tonight, drunk and flushed with happiness, as long as I live.

Mum's mouth moves, but it's soundless. Whatever reaction they expected from Sheila Bua, drunk or not, this is certainly not it. Pa finally flops, thunderstruck, on the yellow couch near the wooden double doors. Everyone knows this is the end.

"Don't stop her today. Please. If you do . . ." Sheila Bua chokes, as if the consequence of stopping was too heavy for mere words. "All I hope is that some of you understand this yearning for a different life . . . once you think it's gone . . . but it lurks . . .

just underneath." That is all she says. And what remains is a silence drunk with heartache.

Burning her paintings, crushing her heart wasn't enough. They're still doing it after all these years. Until today.

And who are *they*? No one but us. *They* are us. We are they. We restrain and restrict and control in the name of traditions and values. But what is the price?

Sheila Bua trudges toward the doors as if each step is leaden. Shiny strands of ebony hair escape her ponytail; her face sinks in an elusive grief. For it *is* grief.

This is the price.

I can't bear to see her this way, my proud, fierce aunt, who begs, pleads, for what should be her right, *our* right, to live as we choose.

I can't let her mourn alone. I can't.

"Sheila Bua!" I call out, "Wait!"

She turns her head, surprised at a loyal voice in the abyss behind her. I rush up to her, wild-haired. The music stops and so do the voices.

I hold her hand in mine and she clutches it tightly like a lifeline; her warm skin covers my cold one. We look at each other but once, she and I, before we glance behind at the gathered assembly. They are all silent yellowed creatures like actors frozen on stage waiting for the curtain to drop on a god-awful drama.

We walk away slowly, hand in hand, toward the wide double doors. I feel strangely empty, weightless, like at the end of a long battle, but also filled with hope, with a promise of something to come. A sea of curious strangers parts silently to let us go.

We step out into the bright corridor toward twinkling lights. Their brilliance surrounds her like a glowing aura, as if she radiates a dazzling fountain of starlight, and my heart hurts in wonder yet again at my Magic Bua.

We do not look back again.

EPILOGUE

The crash of the toilet flush can be heard from as far down as 50C. People stretch and knock fellow passengers next to them into reluctant consciousness. The sharp scent of coffee bubbles in the air and the pretty Lufthansa stewardess deftly maneuvers a rolling breakfast cart as the plane teeters in turbulent American skies. It's been twenty-two hours since I left India and I am terrified.

The little Chinese grandma in the seat next to me grins and points upward with her gnarled fingers. "Don't worry, the plane won't crash. And even if it does, you'll go straight up!"

I had noticed her wispy presence in the tiny economy seat when we boarded the connecting flight at Frankfurt and felt an immediate warm connection. Asian = my people. Well, sort of. Yes, India and China share a volatile border, but it's less dangerous than the one we share with Pakistan. Regardless, had I seen someone from Pakistan on the flight I'd have thrown myself on them in a massively relieved hug—someone who looks brown enough and speaks Hindi. That only happens in strange lands. You'd dare no such thing in your own country. Go, USA—uniting enemy countries in the skies!

We make an odd pair, she and I, the petite Chinese senior and the not-so-petite Indian woman. She also hasn't spoken a single word to the white woman in the window seat next to her, reserving all her third-degree for me. I guess we are united in our shared non-whiteness.

"Why have you not married yet?" she quips, finally asking the question that I know she's itched to ask since we took off nine hours ago. (*The Art of Patience: A Book by a Grandma.*)

There's no escape from this question, is there? Not even eight thousand miles away from India. But after my wedding debacle, my stomach doesn't churn at this inquiry anymore and I don't stuff my face with Kit Kats to ease the pain. I bet this marriage question doesn't even exist in America.

"Err, job. I have work," I reply, more out of politeness than any desire to continue this particular conversation.

"Aah, job." She waves her hand in the air as if shooing a fly. "Don't wait long, okay? Here, my card." The Chinese version of my family is alive and well. And goes by the perfectly fitting ID of barbiedoll1942@foxmail.com.

Speaking of marriage, Arnav-of-My-Phone strolled by the airport earlier this evening, all dimples and smolders, and pretended to run into us outside the massive dome of the glitzy terminal 2A, as if seeing someone else off. Which he so wasn't. No daisies or goodbye hugs, just a wink and those beach eyes.

Weak-Kneed Zoya. That should be my nickname whenever he shows up.

"See you in three weeks," he whispered. "I know just the coffee place on West 38th." Was I really supposed to care about this West 38th or whatever planet it was on, when his lean arm muscled next to mine as my large family squished us together on a warm Bombay night?

So. The wedding that is no more. Yes. Sheila Bua saved me like she couldn't save herself. Not from death, for the God of Death is just as wary of my auntie as the rest of the world. She saved me from the collective wrath of the family by collapsing near the Grecian fountain in the lobby of the Alibaug resort.

We rushed back to Bombay that night and the family took turns at the hospital to stay with Sheila Bua after her emergency hysterectomy, kind of like passing the baton in a marathon—Pa, Ronny Chacha, Uncle Balli, Yuvi, me, Mum, Rita Chachi, Aisha, even Tanya, who shudders at the mention of hospitals.

The shock and reality forced my parents and the family to use the C-word, for one of us at least. Cancer. They neatly avoided the other C-word. Canceled. For we never cancel a wedding if we can "postpone" it because of "her mother-like-auntie's illness."

I also tried to postpone my job start date by two weeks so that I could be with my family for Sheila Bua's recovery from surgery, but she would have none of it. She threatened to stop her medications if I so much as delayed it by a day. "Don't ever look back," she whispered when I was with her at the hospital. Sheila Bua is now elevated to a pedestal. She can do and command anything she likes; the might of the C-word combined with family guilt is deadly. The C-word also conveniently erased Sheila Bua's pot-laced, nude-painting, F-bomb from the family cloud server, where all grievances are stored for eternity, to be retrieved as needed along the years. Except Sheila Bua's memory (and mine), who, under the influence of heavy painkillers, asked if we had any more brownies left and if the nurses could please mix some weed into the IV drip? I swear to God, Ronny Chacha got her a joint in the hospital for "pain management." In my opinion, Uncle Balli sorely needed that fuck-bomb, like ten years ago, but, you know, better late and all that jazz.

Sheila Bua's signed up for another art retreat in Panchgani at the end of the chemo (not nudes this time—abstract art only, I checked), and no one dared to even peep about it. They'll peep alright, once this cancer thing settles down or becomes the norm, but for now, hooray! Why do we need a near-fatal illness or a life-altering event that shuts people up enough to let others follow their dreams? How would life be if we didn't have to fight loved ones, cultures, traditions, entire societies, simply to live as we choose?

My family returned to some sort of forced normality after Sheila Bua's successful operation and my failed marriage—that's what they call it, I'm not kidding you—because of the City of Shrieking Doorbells. Who can dwell on pain or sorrow if your door bing-bongs every five minutes with maids, neighbors, couriers, and relatives, demanding conversation? Also, to discuss the "postponed" wedding—which no one is buying because news has spread in our community that Lalit is engaged to Tanya. But Mum and Pa present a very proud front about my New York job, at least in front of the humanity that passes through our doors, as a "look at our clever daughter, she got a job all on her own—at such a big agency, that too, in New York!"

I still got the deep freeze from Mum for calling off the wedding a mere three weeks before—as if I could escape that—even knowing that both Lalit and I didn't want to marry each other. And a hesitant one from Pa that lasted for about a day. Mum managed to hold on to hers for an entire week, the longest freeze in our mother–daughter history. (Mum also had a temporary deep freeze with Rita Chachi because of the Tanya–Lalit connection. Rita Chachi pretended to be upset about my broken engagement, but is beyond thrilled at Lalit for a son-in-law.)

Pa had enough on his plate canceling the caterers, calling the priest, emailing the wedding guests; all of which for some reason he wasn't very loath to do. I think he may be secretly proud, though he wouldn't dare say that out loud in front of anyone, especially Mum.

Pa walked into my room two nights ago, in the middle of my frantic packing, last minute of course, of clothes, spices, books, utensils, all strewn around my room. He patted me on the head and mumbled, "If only we'd known just how much you . . . and Sheila didi . . . oh, never mind now. I think you'll do just fine in America."

I really don't deserve my parents.

And Pa's still on the Board of Directors at his hospital because Lalit's father—who made him a Director in the first place—has not yet recovered from the shock of an openly Goth Tanya as his future daughter-in-law.

Tanya, apparently, swapped Lalit's beige room curtains (as a good daughter-in-law should) to black drapes with red bats and vampire teeth (as a good daughter-in-law should not). Lalit's mother has restarted her hypertension medication, which she hasn't needed in years apparently. His father keeps sending pleading glances Pa's way when they run into each other at the hospital and finally, yesterday, both sets of parents met for tea at a non-fancy restaurant. Lalit's parents polished off two plates of pav bhaji—each—loaded with butter and potatoes and begged Mum and Pa to get me to change my mind about New York. I was officially speechless.

My leaving in two weeks gave Mum something to do instead of gurgling lava. Till the next scandal in the locality, that is. Mum was mutely thrashing my head in the customary oil massage with mumbled threats—"Don't think you can get away from this oil ritual when you reach America! I'll hound you every Saturday on FaceTime to see if you've oiled your hair!"—when All-India-Radio Mrs. Iyer rushed up to our flat in an incoherent frenzy. Turned out Mr. Banerjee's twenty-four-year-old son, who lived with his parents up the street, had eloped. With a boy.

My volcanic mother completely forgot to spew fiery ash, and instead looked me in the eye for the first time since Alibaug, in utter stupefaction, and asked, "Did you hear? Good God!" (This incident, however, was not salacious enough to get Mum and Rita Chachi talking.)

So. The rest of the family gathered at CST International Airport twenty-four hours ago to bid me bon voyage. A peculiar pain pierced my chest at the smell of toxic fumes and pungent spices, at the buildings and little shops stacked haphazardly on the street, a wedding party noisily on their way to the venue, at the honking and the rush of people and the

Hindi-English-Marathi dialect, at this vibrant, living being outside the terminal.

Even Sheila Bua came to say goodbye, a weak, pale shadow in a wheelchair, against the advice of pretty much every doctor on the planet. (She has about five of the top oncologists in the best cancer hospitals in Bombay, in addition to Uncle Purple, on her consulting payroll, "for a second opinion. You never know with these doctors!")

Rita Chachi sashayed up to me at the airport gate with a plastic Ziploc filled with her taste-free ladoos to be shared with "friends in America." The ladoos, she said, were not completely fat-and-sugar-free but semi-free of those offending ingredients. Yes, it does give one pause for thought. Since Tanya is now openly grunge and Goth, Rita Chachi has taken to eating carbs, which only means digestive Marie biscuits. Goth Tanya without Lalit would've set off Operation Starchy Rice.

Sheila Bua isn't exactly matchmaking anymore, but the age-old Indian auntie urge, of seeing each eligible boy as a potential something-in-law, isn't going anywhere just yet, "cancer-shmancer be damned," as she says. She and Mum acted suspiciously chummy toward Arnav at the airport. They even invited him to dinner at our place next week, wrangled an acquaintance with his mother, and dropped blatant hints about his parents coming along (who are back from their North India trip). Mum finally thawed toward Rita Chachi after meeting Arnav; I told you it would be temporary. I'm leaving India, but is it a realistic assumption that I can escape auntie-tentacles in the age of FaceTime and WhatsApp? Especially when both my mother and auntie seem to like Arnav?

My girls came to the airport, too. Peehu, Kamya, Aisha, even Tanya showed up in all black. How could they not? I offered to pay them for the Alibaug trip considering the bachelorette fiasco, but they burst into hyena-like snickers and offered to pay me for the entertainment. Aisha snorted like a pig (loud and very un-monk-like) that she hadn't had this much fun in years, and maybe she should've said "fuck you" her soon-to-be ex Varun with as much vitriol as Sheila Bua did?

Everyone at the airport cried except for me and Arnav, who speedily escaped from Sheila Bua's clutches—she attempted to wheel herself after him, for God's sake—after several smoldery glances at me. Sheila Bua didn't cry either, not at first. She patted Mum on the back and winked at me throughout the forty minutes we spent outside the terminal. As I waited in line to enter the automatic glass doors, boarding pass and passport tight in my hands, Sheila Bua wheeled up to me for a last fierce hug, tripping a khaki-clad police constable over annoyed travelers. She shoved a small packet into my hands, a white envelope filled with a wad of crisp green dollars.

I gasped at the money. How much was it in rupees? (I need to stop converting dollars to rupees if I am to save myself from an eventual stroke.)

"This is just pocket money," she said. "What do they call it in America? Ah, yes, allowance! Now keep it safe, don't loiter around with all that cash."

"Why? I have enough with me."

"And here." She squeezed my hands as she slipped me another package, a small rectangular box prettily wrapped in a paper of pink and white daisies, a white satin bow around it.

"What's this?"

"No, no. Not here. Open it as soon as you are in New York. Promise me!"

That was my last glimpse of my family as they squinted outside the large glass windows to catch sight of me inside the terminal. For a moment, just a moment, I froze in doubt, before I saw her.

The Shining Girl of the leather album. Her radiant smile, as if all the glowing colors of her paintings lit up her face; it was all I needed.

Sheila Bua's sunken face beamed with joy in her wheelchair. Her fleshy, diamond-studded hand held tightly over her mouth, barely held back her tears. The other hand was frozen in a wave. Or was it a blessing, I cannot say now.

The metallic click of seat belts jerks me back from the airport to the plane. The garbled voice of the German pilot is lost in the roar of the engine. My stomach matches our descent. The blonde stewardess walks by one last time, checks belts, turns tray tables back up: almost there, almost. I can hardly believe it.

I peek through the small window of the descending plane, excited, terrified, desperate for my first glimpse of a city that has taken over my mind. But all I can see are dark gray clouds and little blips of light.

Wait, aren't we technically in New York?

I grab my beige purse from under the front seat and rummage through to Sheila Bua's gift, careful not to mess my dark blue passport and the boarding slip between its pages. My hand brushes over Sheila Bua's photo, the Shining Girl. She's here, tucked inside a pocket of my purse, out of her plastic jail. I couldn't leave her trapped inside the album, could I?

The satin ribbon slides easily off the pink and white wrapping paper. The tiny box is rough against my fingers. The plane swoops lower and a shiver runs down my body. The gold rope falls softly on the sepia-toned picture of the Shining Girl; the plane forgotten, New York forgotten.

She didn't.

A lone tear rolls down my cheek. And for an instant I am back at the terminal, helpless inside the huge glass windows as she breaks into gentle sobs.

There is no note. Just the necklace and the pendant.

A bird in flight.

ACKNOWLEDGMENTS

My agent, Sarah Bedingfield, who was just as excited about Zoya's story as me. This book would be nowhere without her.

My editor, Jenny Chen, for making the story richer and deeper. Matt Martz, for taking up the mantle. The team at Alcove: Madeline Rathle, Melissa Rechter, Rema Badwan. Thank you all for patiently answering my questions and supporting this book.

Courtney Paganelli, for stepping in and holding the line.

Marni Freedman. This story was born in her UCSD course. Actually, Sheila Bua was born. The reason I wrote *The Rules of Arrangement,* and very lazily, was because it was my turn to read every other week in her Read & Critique class.

Tammy Greenwood for her support and story suggestions in her R&C class.

All of my R&C friends, for their wonderful reactions to the story whenever I read. Your encouragement meant more than I can say.

The query and synopsis wizards, Traci Foust and Peggy Loftus Finck. Their work helped me understand Zoya and Sheila Bua's story better.

The Writers Studio. The teachers who were convinced I'd publish one day when I didn't have even the germ of an idea of doing so.

WFWA - Women's Fiction Writers Association. What a fantastic, supportive group of writers! They always have answers for every writing and publishing conundrum.

My writing buddies, Heidi Rauscher-Troutman and Esha Chatterjee, who've been on this journey since the beginning. They read the first draft and gently divested me of the idea that it was the final one. Little did I know.

Panera Bread in 4S Ranch, for their comfy chairs and my little corner table. The lovely staff who always stopped to chat no matter how busy and plied me with free coffees to keep me awake.

The Rancho Bernardo Public Library, for their large and airy campus, which, believe it or not, looks even more beautiful on cloudy days; for the serenity that can only be found inside a library, and for their *stellar* WiFi connection.

Friends and family who helped with ideas, let me pick their brains, and promised to help market the book. Yes, I'm looking at *you*.

My grandparents, where it all began. I started writing because I didn't want to forget their Partition stories or the Sindh they left behind, a land they could never go back to, which remained in their hearts until the end.

My mom and dad and brother, for letting me leave India without getting married. It changed my life.

My mom, who continues to be relieved that I eventually did marry and have children. Special mention to my dad, who, to my shock, said that this book was a nice birthday gift (I told him on his birthday), instead of telling me I could've used that time to get a promotion and a salary raise. I wish we lived closer.

My in-laws, especially my mother-in-law, who is one of the strongest women I know. My brother-in-law, for his conviction that this book will be a movie/TV show, and who is just waiting to say, "I told you so".

My daughter R.J. She is creative and smart and kind, and in her eyes I'm J.K Rowling. I told her she can read my book only after two years because it has cuss words, but she said not to worry, that she already knows all of them. #BigParentingFail.

My son A.D. He is clever and happy and curious and thinks that I'm working on my book every time he sees me with a laptop, and who writes proudly in school essays that his mom is an AUTHOR!

My husband Akhil, who is my safe space. He held the fort while I was out writing most weekend mornings for the longest time. He managed to stay sane in the midst of two constantly bickering children and still continues to like me; if that's not a keeper I don't know what is.

My big fat family, for always supplying raw material for my imagination. Don't worry, none of you are in the book.

KEEP IN TOUCH WITH

ANISHA BHATIA

Author photograph © Akhil Oltikar

@anisha.bhatia.author

https://www.anishabhatia.com/